Pra

SUZANNE FORSTER

"No one combines steamy suspense and breathless thrills like Suzanne Forster!"
—Susan Elizabeth Phillips

"Crackling sexual tension, a twisty mystery and some genuinely dastardly villains make this a fast, fun read."
—*BookPage* on *The Arrangement*

"Hatreds and agendas converge with very wily plot twists as Forster brings her story to an unforeseen ending... a very original and clever story."
—*The Romance Reader* on *The Arrangement*

"Only a writer of Forster's skill could take the reader to the dark places in this story."
—*Romantic Times BOOKreviews* on *The Lonely Girls Club*

"An electrifying romantic suspense thriller that grips the audience...and never lets up."
—*The Best Reviews* on *The Lonely Girls Club*

"Forster blends nail-biting suspense and steamy sexual tension into a seamless romantic thriller."
—*Publishers Weekly* on *The Morning After*

"[Forster is] a stylist who translates sexual tension into sizzle."
—*Los Angeles Daily News*

SUZANNE FORSTER

THE
PRIVATE
CONCIERGE

MIRA®

ISBN-13: 978-0-7783-2545-1
ISBN-10: 0-7783-2545-8

THE PRIVATE CONCIERGE

www.MIRABooks.com

Printed in U.S.A.

ACKNOWLEDGMENTS

Thanks must go to Sergeant Podeska of the West Los Angeles Police Station for sharing his insights about crime and punishment in the west L.A. area. Surely our one conversation set records for producing usable information. It was a pleasure—and if there's an award for demonstrating grace with rapid-fire questions and patience with a few obtuse ones, the sergeant richly deserves it.

Also, my deep gratitude to the ace concierge team at the Hyatt Regency Century Plaza, who will forever remain anonymous to ensure their continued employment. With great good humor they endured my quest for information about the concierge field and everything else relating to Century City and its environs. Plus, they answered questions no concierge should ever have to. Their restaurant recommendations and directions were great, too.

Finally, to reference librarians everywhere, and in particular to the Amazing William of the Los Angeles Public Library, for help above and beyond. And while I'm at it, I can't forget the entire reference staff at the Newport Beach Public Library, my hometown branch and personal hangout.

Thank you all!

Prologue

Cox, Lucy: juvenile unit, prostitution
Case File: COX022378 15 lapd.juv.dtb
Closed: March 3, 1993
Sealed by Court Order: April 10, 1993

He removed the legal-size folder from the file cabinet and gave the label a moment of reflection before opening it. Fifteen years ago, he'd stashed copies of the contents of the original case file in this locked cabinet in his home office. It was enough security for his purposes, although he would bring serious suspicion on himself if the file was ever discovered. The case was closed and had been sealed at the request of the juvenile offender, and the L.A. County Courthouse had the only official copy.

But he didn't work for the law anymore. He worked for himself.

He sat down at his desk, opened the folder and looked at the last entry he'd made in the file: *February 23, 1993: She walks free today, her eighteenth birthday. God help the weak of will and the feeble of mind, especially if they're male.*

He almost smiled, remembering his supervisor's reaction. He'd taken some flack for this case, enough to end his law enforcement career. But he could also remember a time when he'd been more concerned about her, Lucy Cox, than about any unwary man who might cross her path.

Not anymore. He reached for a black-ink ballpoint, the kind he'd preferred for making case notes when he'd been a vice cop in the downtown L.A. bureau. He considered assigning the case a new number, but decided to stay with the original, based in part on his theory that people, like lab rats, didn't change, they just learned new strategies for getting what they needed. Cynical, maybe, but he had more reason than most men to be that way.

He clicked the push-button pen and began writing the first new entry in fifteen years. It was about her, who she was today and why she hadn't changed, either. And it was in his own words, his own unfiltered thoughts, because he had every intention of destroying these notes when he'd done what he had to do. No one would ever read this file but him.

Case Notes: Wednesday, October 9, 11:00 p.m.

Her real name is Lucia Cox. She changed it to avoid any association with her criminal past. But she hasn't left her past behind. She's still selling what everybody wants. She's just found a way to make it legal.

He paused, aware of his quickening pulse. This was getting to him, getting too personal. And that was the problem. It *was* personal. He set down the pen, unable to write as fast as his thoughts were coming. She'd had the power at fifteen when he put her in jail. She was thirty now. She'd been free and on her own since eighteen, and it wasn't hard to imagine that she'd planned her steps carefully, including choosing the perfect profession. She had some of the country's highest-profile people in her care.

It should have been a match made in heaven for all concerned, except that Lucy's clients were dropping like flies, being brought down by scandal, innuendo, and now, death. And no one seemed to get the connection but him. Her clients moved in the special spheres of power and privilege, isolated from the real world and its rules, and from anyone who would dare to tell them the truth. When you were *that* isolated, who really knew you better than your hairstylist, your personal trainer…or your private concierge?

1

Ned Talbert hit the brakes so hard his Alfa Romeo Spider snorted and its wheels dug into the gravel like a pawing bull. The back end lifted as if the sports car was about to do a somersault, and Ned's knees knocked against the dash.

Geysering pebbles splattered the windshield.

He heaved himself back, grunting as the steering wheel disengaged from his ribs. Amazing the air bags hadn't inflated. He'd barely missed colliding head-on with the entrance gate to Rick Bayless's cabin in the San Gabriel Mountains.

The gate wasn't just closed, it was padlocked. Even in the falling light, Ned spotted the shiny new lock as he struggled to get out of the Spider. His legs were jelly. Padlocked? Rick never padlocked the gate—and it wasn't even 5:00 p.m., too early to close up the place for the night.

Ned broke into a run and didn't stop. He could see he wasn't going to get the gate open so he coiled and vaulted the chain-link mesh, leaving a strip of his pant leg on the scrollwork, leaving the door hanging open to his obscenely expensive new car, leaving it all behind, and running like a madman up the road to the darkened mountain cabin a thousand feet away.

Bayless had to be in there.

Ned could have been running the bases at Dodger Stadium. He could have been in the heat of a playoff game, that's how adrenalized he was. But he wasn't going to make it to home plate this time. Not without his friend's help.

It was getting dark, but no light glowed in the cabin windows. Rick's Jeep Commander sat in the driveway. Maybe he was taking a nap. Ned took all three porch steps in one leap and pounded on the creaky wooden door. No answer. He kept hammering, using his fist and making the door buckle with each blow. How could anyone sleep through this noise? He wondered about the odds of Rick having a girl in there. Ned had never known him to do that, but the way Ned's luck was going, this would be the time. He hated the thought of interrupting them, but he had no choice. His life was in crisis.

"Rick, you in there?" he bellowed.

Ned hit the door with his shoulder and realized it was bolted. He was going to have to kick it in. Two blows shattered the wood enough that he could reach inside and open the bolt. The interior was dark, but light from the doorway revealed the lower torso of a man sitting in a straight-back chair by the far wall. Ned could see his denim jeans and his bare feet, but little else. His face and shoulders were masked by shadows. It looked like an interrogation scene, except that no one else was in the room.

Ned didn't notice the gun until he saw Rick's hands. They were in his lap, cradling a Colt .357 Python. Rick was a former vice cop. He'd carried a gun as long as Ned could remember.

Ned's legs were jelly again. His whole body was limp.

"Rick, what the hell." It wasn't a question. It was a howl of despair. Ned *knew* what the hell was going on. He knew why Rick had a gun in his hands, and what he intended to do with it—and he couldn't, by any stretch of good conscience, try to stop his friend, or even change his mind.

Ned knew the whole wretched story. It made no sense that Rick Bayless should be dealing with this. *He was young, forty-two years old and in his physical prime.* Ned had been jealous of Rick all his life, even though Ned was the star athlete. Hell, women swooned, or whatever it was women did around men who made their eyes lose focus and their minds swim with thoughts of drowning sex. They loved the dude, but only from a distance. No one really got close to Rick Bayless, not even Ned, and they had been friends since…forever.

"Buddy, are you sure? This is it? There aren't any do overs."

Ned's voice broke, and Rick looked up. Ned couldn't see his friend's face, but he could see the movement of his head in the shadows. Rick's gaze could burn paper, and those incinerating rays were now fixed on him. But his voice was tuned low, almost surprised.

"Ned, what are you doing here?"

Ned thought about whether he should tell him the truth, but then blurted it out. "I've got a problem, man. It's bad. I've been looking for you everywhere, down at your place in Manhattan Beach, at Duke's on the pier. I even checked out the old orange grove where you go to walk and think."

Rick said nothing, which was significant because nothing wasn't "Get out of here." It wasn't "Take care of your own damn problems for a change."

Ned felt hope slam through him. It nearly knocked him over. Maybe he could talk his friend out of it? Rick was a sucker for a hard-luck story, and this one was the God's truth.

"I'm being blackmailed. I'm getting anonymous calls from some crazy dude who thinks I'm into hard-core sexual sadism—whips and chains and leaving burn marks on my girlfriend's genitals. It's sick, man. He faxed me a picture that I swear isn't me and Holly, but it looks like us. He's threatening to fax the tabloids unless I throw the next game."

Ned's throat was so dry he couldn't swallow. It sounded like he was strangling, and the pain was peppery hot. It radiated up his jaw.

He waited for his friend, and finally, Rick shook his head.

"I'm sorry, man," he said.

"Sorry?"

"I wish I could help."

Another blow to Ned's solar plexus. It felt as if his car had hit the gate and flipped this time. Ned wanted to cry. He fucking did. This should not be happening. God shouldn't do things like this.

"Rick," he implored, "we go back a long way, all the way. Don't shut me out now. What can I do to help you?"

"You can leave, Ned. It's all right. Really, it is."

Rick's voice echoed as if it were coming from somewhere else, heaven or another dimension. Ned gaped at the gun. He couldn't seem to look anywhere else. He was waiting for Rick to say something else, but it didn't happen.

Rick's fingers curled possessively around the weapon he held. It was the only thing that mattered to him now, Ned realized, the instrument of his deliverance. He was going to do it.

"You can't put this off long enough to help a friend who's in deep trouble?" Ned croaked. "Are you really that determined? Are you really that selfish?"

"Goodbye, buddy."

Ned nodded, but he couldn't say anything, not even goodbye. "Yeah" was all he could manage before his throat sealed off.

Somehow he got his shaky legs to the shattered door and closed it behind him, praying that his friend would at least let him get out of earshot. Ned would collapse if he heard that gun go off. If it had been anyone other than Rick, any situation other than this, he would have wrestled the gun away. But there was no way to save Rick. The kindest thing was to let him be. But it was a damn tragedy.

Ned picked his way down the rutted road, knowing he could easily sprain an ankle in one of the deep holes. He had a home game coming up this weekend, and another practice tomorrow.

He almost laughed, but it was the kind of laughter that scorched everything it touched. How crazy was it that he was worried about twisting his ankle when his life was crashing down around him? Everything was on the line, his career, his reputation—

And his best friend was back in that cabin with a gun to his head.

At that moment what Ned recalled most clearly about Rick was the hellishly hard time he'd had teaching the big lug how to swim when they were overgrown sixteen-year-olds. Rick had a morbid fear of water. He'd never told Ned why, but it was crucial that Rick learn to swim, because the two of them had a plan. As soon as they turned seventeen, they were going to quit school, join the army, try out for Delta Force and become bona fide heroes. What better way to escape their drug-infested cesspool of a neighborhood than by fighting the enemies of freedom and democracy? Christ, those were innocent days.

Ned had been a magnet for trouble, and Rick was always bailing him out, but in that one small area, Ned had held the upper hand—Rick's fear of water. Too bad their plan didn't work. Even if Rick had learned to swim well enough to make Delta Force, it wouldn't have mattered. A stomach ailment had kept Ned out, and Rick wouldn't join without him.

Tears burned his eyes, but what came out of his mouth was helpless laughter. Rick was still scared shitless of water. But no one could deny his courage in cleaning up the streets of downtown L.A. when he'd worked in vice. He'd focused on runaway kids, drugs and street prostitution. The man was a legend. He'd actually busted a city-sponsored youth hostel that was exploiting the kids, and got local businesses to fund a new one, with a rehab staff and vocational classes. Not that he'd ever been officially recognized for it.

He and the brass had butted heads repeatedly, and Rick had finally left the force in a storm of controversy after Rick exposed a sex scandal involving several prominent businessmen. But that was years ago. Now he did private consulting work that couldn't be discussed, for clients who couldn't be named.

Ned came to the gate and stopped, wondering how he was going to vault it. He hoped to God his friend was making the right decision. And he hoped he'd just made the right one by leaving. There was nothing left now but to go home and deal with the puke the sky had vomited on his life. It was a filthy, stinking mess, and unless he could find some way to clean it up, baseball stardom as he knew it was over.

"Lead, follow or get the hell out of the way," Ned said under his breath. It was a Pattonism that he and Rick had barked at each other repeatedly, ad nauseam, when they were kids, sometimes just for fun, but it could be a call to arms, as well. They had grown to adulthood in downtown Los Angeles, an urban jungle, and too often those three options were their only clear choices. Tonight, Ned was getting the hell out of the way.

Sunday, October 6
Three days earlier

Ginger Sue Harvey started every morning at the Midlands' Gourmet Grocery by straightening the stock on the shelves and cleaning up after customers who moved things around and left them hither and yon. She'd clerked at the store for years, but now, as the newly appointed manager, she took special pride in restoring order and preserving the folksy charm of the converted mountain chalet. And she'd long ago divided her customers into two categories—destroyers and preservers.

No way around it, the ones who messed up her magnificent produce displays or moved merchandise from aisle to aisle were, without a doubt, destroyers. Some even left open boxes of cookies and chomped-on apples lying around. They made her want to call the police. There should be a special cell for people who filched produce and abandoned it, half-eaten and usually already rotting before Ginger Sue found it. The arrogance, the unmitigated arrogance. *Really.*

But since she couldn't be calling the cops every day, she punished the destroyers by withholding new product samples. They would have none of the rich black olive butter and Seminole flour crackers she would lay out later today. Now, the preservers, they would be heaped with her gratitude and generosity. She might even make up little gift baskets for them to take home. It was Ginger Sue's own special brand of behavior modification.

As she straightened the candy bars, gum and other impulse items on her countertop, she saw him through the window. He was putting change in the newspaper box. Her heart kicked into a higher gear, embarrassing her. Apparently she'd been hoping Rick Bayless would show up, even though he was one of the destroyers. He'd been especially bad yesterday when he stopped in for some things on the way up to his cabin.

He'd bought a padlock and two bolt locks and a stack of bath towels, but even more odd was what he didn't buy. No food or drinks, nothing at all like the overflowing cart he usually brought to her checkout stand. You wouldn't think a man buying locks could do much damage, but he'd knocked over her magazine stand like he was in a trance. She'd forgiven him that because she could see something was wrong. His expression was bleak, a man under siege. His clenched jaw was the dam against whatever emotion threatened.

She'd asked if he was all right. Of course, he'd said yes. He never talked much, but when you had this man's unmistakable military bearing, close-cropped sandy hair and pale green eyes, you didn't need to. Women were happy to fill in the blanks.

Ginger Sue hadn't stopped filling in blanks since she'd met him, maybe two years ago when he'd bought his mountain cabin for cash on the barrelhead, or so the rumor went. She wouldn't have thought twice about calling him handsome, despite the scar on his cheek and the notch on his upper lip, maybe even the kind of guy who broke hearts. But she figured it might be just the opposite. Woman trouble could explain his quiet manner and his way of looking at you from an angle, like he was guarding something.

Ginger Sue liked Rick Bayless, although she wasn't sure why. She was also rather fond of his friend, the baseball player, who sometimes came up to the cabin with a girl in tow. He was polite and respectful, and he struck her as a kind soul, but Ginger Sue couldn't say she approved of his taste in women. The one he'd had with him lately was a little on the flashy side, with her brightly painted nails and her ankle bracelet. She even wore a ring with a tiny precious gem on her second toe. Ginger Sue called that tacky—and she'd pegged the woman right away as the gold-digger type.

She gave her countertop another swipe with the disinfectant rag as the bell over the door jingled. In Bayless came, paper tucked under his arm. It wasn't even nine, so he'd probably come down the mountain for some coffee, as he often did when he was in residence. Her store was in the village about twenty minutes' walk from his place.

As he came closer, she saw that he was unshaven and bleary-eyed, as if he'd been on an all-night toot. It struck her that he might be grieving some loss, although that was probably a silly romantic notion. *Keep it simple, sweetie. It's just a hangover.*

"Morning, Mr. Bayless. Anything I can help you with?" she asked.

"Just getting some coffee from the bar, thanks."

Ginger Sue watched to see if his hand was unsteady as he held his plastic cup under the spigot. "You want a cinnamon bun?" she asked. "That'd go good with your coffee." She'd heard cinnamon was some kind of sexual turn-on for men. Who knew? It might make him feel better.

When he came over to pay he set down the coffee and dug a money clip from the pocket of his jeans. He let the paper slip from under his arm and it fell open on the counter. As he laid down a five, Ginger Sue turned the paper around and skimmed the headline: Star Outfielder Dies in Murder-Suicide. The color picture of a crime investigation and the insert of a familiar male face caught her eye next.

Ned Talbert? Was that his friend, the baseball star? "Mr. Bayless, did you see this?"

She turned the paper around so he could view it. He'd just taken a sip of his coffee, and he let out a strange, strangled sound. Clearly he hadn't seen the headline until that moment. Black coffee exploded from his cup as it hit the counter.

"Oh!" Ginger Sue ducked behind the counter, shielding her face with her arms. By the time she came back up, he was gone, flying out the door like a crazy man. The bell rang madly as the door crashed shut behind him.

She grabbed her rag and mopped quickly, but there was no way to stem the steaming morass. He'd scared her half to death, and look at the mess he'd made of her countertop. The coffee had already soaked a stack of *TV Guide* magazines and some credit-card receipts she hadn't yet filed. That kind of behavior was enough to get a customer banned from her store, but right now, she just wanted to know what was going on.

2

Rick felt dread bloom in the pit of his stomach, cold and wet, like clammy flesh. He was only a few minutes from Ned's place in Pacific Palisades, and Rick knew what he would find there, a crime scene in progress. He'd seen a million of them, but this wouldn't look like anything he recognized. The corpse would not be a lifeless shell to be pitied, lamented and then analyzed down to the last gruesome detail. This was his friend, someone Rick knew only as warm, vital and human. Ned was a living, breathing part of him. And, worse, instead of wearing a badge that would give Rick jurisdiction over the nightmare, instead of taking charge and righting wrongs, he would be helpless to do anything.

His knuckles were blood-white against the steering wheel. He'd made the drive from the mountains to the beach in record time, despite having to ditch a cop in the foothills. The dread had been living inside him since he read the newspaper, but it hadn't had a chance against his abject disbelief. Not Ned. No way. He couldn't be dead. He was all that was left of their goofy boyhood dreams. He was supposed to carry the torch, be the man.

Rick had spaced out, driving without a thought to the consequences. But at some point, he'd noticed the vibration in his hands that had nothing to do with his grip on the steering wheel—and the explicable had dawned on him. His friend was dead, and Rick was probably to blame. If he'd listened last night instead of swimming in his own private pool of despair, he might have prevented this. He was guilty *and* friendless. He had nothing left and nowhere to go, yet his hands were vibrating, and he felt more alive than he had in weeks.

That wasn't right. It was totally twisted. But there was no time to analyze it now. He'd been mired in self-analysis for days, weeks, and that wasn't his style at all. Maybe anything that could drag him out of that muck would have sparked some life. But, God, why did it have to be this?

Ned Talbert's turreted Moorish-style home was on a street that sloped toward the sea. It sat like a crown jewel in a neighborhood where selling prices ran into the millions, and the terraced bluffs below the house featured one palatial property after another.

Rick pulled in down the street from the house, giving himself time to scope things out. Yellow crime scene tape roped off the area, but other than that there was no sign of a CSI team or an active investigation. The deaths had occurred last night, according to the newspaper, some time before 11:00 p.m. Apparently Ned's housekeeper had stopped by to drop off something she'd forgotten, found the bodies and called the police.

The way it looked now, the forensic guys must have done their work last night, packed up and gone. And so had the media, it seemed. Even a sports star's lurid death couldn't command attention for more than a few hours in celebrity-soaked L.A. There was money to be made on the living.

A lone police officer, young enough to be a rookie, sat

in his car, clicking away on his cell, probably texting or playing games when he should have been standing guard at the door. Sloppy security, but not unusual with murder-suicides, where in theory the case was already solved before the cops got there. The victim and killer were all wrapped up in one neat bundle, a real timesaver. It was more than some overworked and underappreciated homicide investigators could resist, especially if all the evidence was there, including a suicide note.

But Ned would not have left a suicide note. Writing wasn't his thing. He couldn't even sign a birthday card without it sounding lame.

Rick could tell when a crime scene had been body-bagged and zipped up right along with the dead, and this one had, even before the lab results came in. Were the investigators already that certain about what had gone down, or were they more interested in getting rid of this case?

A cover-up? That was jumping the gun, but Rick's mind was going there anyway. On the way down from the mountain, he had realized what the police could have found in Ned's house. He was fairly certain the brass would want to keep it under wraps because of the scandal potential, even though the information was old news—very old—which was also why they wouldn't connect it with the murder-suicide. But Rick could not get his mind around the idea that this was a murder-suicide, which only left one other possibility. Someone wanted Ned and his girlfriend dead.

Rick's original plan had been to talk his way in. He'd worked with most of the guys at the West Side station at one point or another during his time at LAPD, and knew them well. Some of them had even gone to Ned's games with him. Cops were a fraternity, as tightly bonded as the military, and they bent the rules for each other. All he wanted was to be escorted inside long enough to have a look around. Shouldn't be a problem, except that he didn't recognize the officer in the car, and his gut was telling him this *wasn't* like every other crime scene.

Sweat dampened the close-cropped hair on Rick's scalp. He needed to make his move now, while junior was still otherwise engaged. He slipped on his mirrored aviators, let himself out of the car and started for the house at a lope. With Ned's front-door key clutched in his hand, he ducked down and swept past the black and white from behind and made it all the way to the porch before he heard the guy shout.

"Police! Stop where you are!"

Rick halted, but made no attempt to turn until he was told.

"Drop what you're holding. Drop it!"

The house key clinked on the slate walk, dancing end over end until it hit the rise of the porch step.

"Put your hands up and turn around," the officer barked. *"Slowly."*

Rick turned, aware of the officer's hand hovering over his hip holster. "The guy who lives here is my closest friend," Rick said. "I just heard what happened. Please, I need to see him."

The officer blinked, his sole expression of regret, if that's what it was. "He's not here. The bodies have been taken to the coroner's office on Mission Boulevard. If a member of his family can't be located, you may have to ID him."

Rick wanted to slam the unfeeling words right down the guy's throat. He would love to have decked him, but he understood that for some of these guys, lack of empathy was protection—if they bled over every victim, or even one, they wouldn't be able to do their jobs—so Rick was going to give this SOB the benefit of the doubt.

Rick had never managed that kind of detachment on his watch. He'd been involved up to his neck, and look where that had landed him—on the sidewalk and looking for a job. He'd quit under fire, and probably just before they could fire him. He'd had the audacity to question policy decisions, but he didn't regret any of it. Nor did he miss the politics and the red tape.

The officer peered at Rick, his brow furrowing. "You look familiar."

Rick wondered if he'd made a mistake. He was pretty good when it came to names and faces, but he couldn't place this guy. He just shrugged and left his glasses on. "I doubt it."

The rookie should have asked to see ID and Rick's car registration, but he let it go, maybe out of respect for the situation.

"Look, go over to the West L.A. station and tell them who you are. Maybe they'll give you some information," he suggested. "If you want, you can drop back tomorrow. The tape should be down by then."

Rick pretended to be surprised. "They've already determined it was murder-suicide, like the newspaper said? What about burglary, a home invasion or some other kind of foul play? What if someone wanted it to *look* like murder-suicide? A jealous boyfriend? Or another ballplayer, trying to eliminate the competition? A rival team owner?"

The officer's expression said Ned Talbert wasn't *that* good an outfielder. "It was murder-suicide. Trust me, you don't want to know what happened in there."

The dread turned soft and queasy in Rick's stomach. Something fetid coated the back of his throat. He would have said it was the tide, but the onshores rarely carried the sea smells this far. Most of the time, this area existed in a velvet-draped moneyed hush.

Rick didn't want to know what had happened inside, but he had to find out. Ned wasn't violent. He was a big chicken—not a coward, just a good-hearted, easygoing guy, who could leap like a ballet dancer to snag a fly and slam a ball into the next county. He would have made a terrible member of Delta Force. He didn't like guns, and Rick had often kidded him about that, just the way Ned had dissed him about his fear of water. But even if Ned had that kind of violence in him, why kill himself and his girlfriend instead of the blackmailer?

Rick should have listened. He had nothing to go on, not even the most rudimentary details of the blackmail attempts. He didn't know when, how often or why. But there was another reason Rick needed access to Ned's house. Years ago, he'd given Ned a package for safekeeping. The police may have found the eight-by-eleven bubble pack in Ned's safe, and Rick had to get it back, if it was still there. A part of him hoped this investigation was as cut-and-dried as the officer had suggested. It was why Rick hadn't mentioned Ned's concerns about blackmail, and wouldn't.

3

Lane Chandler was doing four things at once, which was about two less than she normally did. She'd pulled up Gotcha.com, a tabloid Web site, on her computer screen, praying not to see any of her clients featured there. She was also mentally updating her to-do list, a never-ending task, *and* she was undressing…all while chatting with her favorite client on her cell-phone headset.

"She wants gangsta rappers for her sweet-sixteen party?" Lane draped her suit jacket over the back of her office chair and then perched on the edge of her desk, easing the pain of her obscenely overpriced new high heels. She turned enough to continue searching the Gotcha home page, but so far no clients in jail or rehab—and no mention of the one she was specifically looking for.

"Thank you, God," she said, mouthing the words. She felt lighter, but it was too soon to relax. She had yet to check Jack the Giant Killer's column.

"Jerry," she implored her headset, "say no! Someday your daughter will thank you for refusing to book the Gutter Punk Bone Dawgs for her special day."

"Say no to my Felicity? I'd stand a better chance against the Bone Dawgs."

Jerry's loud snort of laughter made Lane wince. She turned away from the computer screen to give her shoes a dark look. The way her day had gone, if her high-profile clients didn't kill her the Manolo Blahniks would. Fortunately, she had Jerry on the phone rather than in her office, so he couldn't see her torturing the side slit of her skirt as she bent over and pulled off the exotic footwear that was cutting her insteps to ribbons.

She sighed with relief as she sank her feet into the plush office carpet. Who invented these stilts, the Marquis de Sade? A woman in high heels was supposed to be a sexual thing, creating an inviting tilt to the pelvis and a sensual swivel when she walked. But only a guy into serious S&M could love the pain on this woman's face.

"Lane, is that heavy breathing?"

"That's me, in ecstasy. I took off my shoes, and I'm warning you, the Spanx are next."

Silence. She couldn't have shocked him. Not Jerry. He wasn't shockable, and they often bantered. It was all in good fun. He was a big sweet bear of a man with a thick head of brown hair and a matching beard. He ran one of the largest discount chains in the country and he was among her top five clients, if you ranked by sheer business clout, but he was also her mentor and someone she could let down her hair with, which she was about to do right now, before the tightly embedded hair clip gave her a migraine.

She reached into the back of her upswept do and freed the claws that held the heavy mahogany waves off her neck.

"Spanx are panty hose, Jerry."

"I know," he chided. "I have a daughter. But *you* should know by now that I don't have a thing for feet. Now, if you'd said earrings, that would be different. A woman's naked lobes make the back of my neck sweat."

"Earrings next, my love."

"You tease."

She laughed and was suddenly glad he'd called, even though she'd been trying desperately to close up shop and go home. She ran a private concierge service that had been growing like topsy up until very recently. But this had been another day from hell in a week of days from hell. She couldn't believe anyone could make her laugh, but Jerry had. He always did, which was why she'd taken his call at this late hour instead of letting the service put him through to Zoe, his own private concierge.

Jerry was one of forty-five top-tier clients, who paid up to fifty thousand dollars a year for Lane's Premiere Plan. They each had a private concierge devoted solely to their needs, who oversaw no less than six rotating concierges with different specialties, who were also at their beck and call around the clock. But Jerry wouldn't necessarily be able to talk freely with Zoe about his very spoiled daughter—and Lane owed him so much anyway. He really was more than a mentor, much more, but not in a romantic way. They flirted a bit, but he'd never even come close to making a pass at her. Sometimes she wondered why not.

She slipped off her clip earrings and shook her head, aware of the caress of her hair, cool against her burning face. It had been a hard day, a terrible day, possibly the worst of her career. Normally she would have been frustrated at having to deal with a sweet-sixteen party when it felt as if everything she'd struggled and sacrificed for was imploding. She would have done it, though, because that was her job description. She took care of all her clients, and Jerry was a vital one.

But right now, maybe she needed one client she could actually help.

"Seriously, Jerry, you should consider saying no to Felicity." She spoke softly, pleadingly, as she worked her skirt up, hooked her thumbs into the waistline of her ultra-stretchy Spanx and dragged them down. "I know how much you love her," she went on, making her case as she peeled off the panty hose, "but the Bone Dawgs have a criminal record, and more important, if you don't draw the line somewhere, Felicity will never learn to respect her limits—or others'."

"Lane, when did you turn into Mother Superior?"

"Actually, I was trying for Dr. Phil." So much for reasoning with Jerry. She stepped out of the Spanx and wanted to moan it felt so good. Her flesh was celebrating. Why was everything so tight? If stress caused water retention, then she was a dam about to burst. "How many are coming to this party?"

"Felicity hasn't given me the final count, but I'm estimating half her class at St. Mary's, which is a hundred, another twenty-five from her church group and that many again from company friends, my various clubs, colleagues and vendors."

Lane began to calculate, adding up numbers and aware that the amounts her clients were willing to spend on lavish parties could still shock her, especially with the country's struggling economy. Still, she had a job to do and a payroll to meet for her own employees, who now numbered several hundred around the country.

"Okay," she said, "let's say two hundred guests to allow for long-lost cousins, last-minute invites and party crashers. Kids love to crash these things. That's half the fun. Does she still want the Avalon ballroom in Catalina?

That means a charter cruise ship for transportation—and the talent will have to be flown in and flown out the same night, or put up at the island's luxury condos. The guests are staying over, aren't they?"

"Some will, I'm sure. As you said, whatever they prefer."

She undid the button of her skirt and tugged at the silk camisole. "We'll get a count when they RSVP. It's good of you to be this involved, Jerry." He could have had a personal assistant do it, or hired a party planner to work with his daughter. Most single dads with his bank account would have.

"It's for Felicity."

Anything less wasn't an option. His voice said that, unequivocally. Lane could hear rap music playing on his end and smiled. At times like now, she worried how far he would go to make Felicity happy, and whether he was trying too hard to compensate for what had happened when Felicity was twelve. Her mother, Jerry's ex-wife, had become despondent during their custody battle, knowing she was almost certain to lose custody of her child because of her drug use, and she had taken an overdose that proved fatal.

"This is going to be a great party, Jerry." Lane walked across the carpet, bare of foot and shoulder, aware of her image flickering from the glass doors of her bookcases to the office's wraparound windows. Her thoughts turned inward as the party unfolded in her mind. She could see revolving glitter balls, servers dressed like Bonnie and Clyde, drinks in crystal bathtub-shaped punch bowls, maybe even a fabulous antique car or two on display. It would be a twenties gangster theme, featuring a rapper band with no priors.

This was her forte, organizing and strategizing to create the client's vision. She pulled gently on the tattered green rubber band she wore on her left wrist, calming as she took in her surroundings. She loved this office. Despite the frenetic activity during the day, at night it was an oasis of calm and monastic order. Her burlwood desk was so highly varnished the gloss could have been liquid, and the room's muted lighting allowed her to see the bright twinkling lights of Century City, receding toward the Pacific coast.

"I'm thinking gangster theme, Jerry, but from the twenties."

Reaching up to unbutton her blouse, she continued to ask questions and make mental notes of Jerry's answers. It was oddly freeing walking around barefoot and taking off her clothes. She should do it more often…just strip down to nothing. She shivered as the silk blouse slid down her arms.

"Maybe a mix of past and present?" he suggested.

"Even better."

"Lane, are you all right? You sound breathless."

"Yes, fine. I'm changing clothes."

"In that case, put on the videophone."

"It's not that exciting, Jerry, believe me. I'm changing into my sweats. I'm going to get one of my concierge staff to drive my car home, and I'm going to walk."

"One of those days? Must have been a doozy if you're walking home."

"You have no idea. This day was spawned in the lowest level of hell and flung at me by the devil's henchmen on thundering steeds." She couldn't give him the details. It would breach client confidentiality, but she needed to vent. She was gut-level terrified—and she rarely allowed herself to feel anything resembling fear. She controlled it with a game she'd played all her life, a silly game that worked.

"Lane, I know what's happened to Simon Shan and Captain Crusader, if that's what you're talking about, and I don't know what to say. It's tragic. There's been little else on the news the last couple of weeks. I have a call in to Burt, but he hasn't returned it."

Jerry also knew the two men were her clients because he'd referred them both, Burton Carr, the activist U.S. congressman, whom he'd affectionately referred to as Captain Crusader, and Shan more recently. Simon Shan was currently the hottest ticket in town, even considering the mess he was in. Everyone had expected the next Martha Stewart to be a woman, but Shan, a London-based fashion designer of Chinese descent, had stolen her spotlight while no one was looking. He did everything with a focus, precision and freshness that made all the other lifestyle gurus look like amateurs.

He'd gotten his start by designing and creating his own unique casual look for women. His first full line was a smash, and he'd gone from there into makeup and accessories. Eventually he'd partnered with an upscale discount chain, the Goldstar Collection, and branched into furniture, linens, decor, parties, gardening, everything. He was also tall, lean and singularly attractive, creating great speculation about his sexual preferences—and an instant mystique. No one had counted on the next lifestyle icon being male, Asian and very possibly straight.

His downfall was drugs, but not just any old drugs. Opium. He admitted to having tried it once as a boy in Taiwan, where he grew up an only child to a doting mother and an authoritarian father. The opium use was little more than teenage curiosity, but his father had been outraged. He'd sent Shan away to a boarding school in London, not realizing it would change the boy's life forever.

Shan swore that was the extent of his own drug use. But several pounds of it were found in the trunk of his Bentley, and because he imported most of his furniture, textiles and other goods from Asia, he was also charged with smuggling the opium into the country. The charges had forced him to step back from his role as Goldstar's spokesperson. But at least he'd had enough money to hire the best legal help, and he was out on bail, awaiting arraignment.

The congressman's downfall had shocked Lane to her core. The feds had found child pornography on his computer in his D.C. office. Lane still couldn't fathom it. Even if Burton Carr was a pedophile, which she didn't believe for a second, why would he view child porn on his office computer? He'd always supported the fight for legislation to protect children, including the now-famous Amber Alert. He clearly cared deeply about people in general. On the national level, he'd worked doggedly to pass a bill compelling the large discount chains to offer benefits to workers, including heath care—and he'd cited Jerry Blair as one of the country's most progressive CEOs, and his company, TopCo, as an example of how a discount chain could—and should—be run.

Carr was one of her heroes. Actually, both men were.

"Lane?"

"Jerry, can we shelve the party discussion for tonight? There's plenty of time to iron out the details, and I'm really beat."

"Sure, but do me a favor, don't walk home. It's not safe."

"I've done it before, Jerry. The path I take is lit up like a movie premiere, and I don't live that far—"

"Lane, humor me, okay?"

"Okay, no walking tonight."

"I mean forever, Lane. Don't walk home—not tonight, not ever again."

"Well, geez, Jerry. I am thirty years old, and there are some decisions I feel qualified to make—"

"Yes, you are, but this is not a good one, Lane."

She was nodding to herself as he spoke. This was why Jerry Blair was a good CEO. He took care of people. He was one of the few people who'd ever taken care of her, and she loved him for it. She stopped short of telling him that, but with the words balling up in her throat, she said, "Uncle."

They said their goodbyes and as she hung up the phone, she felt the pain twist into sharpness. It nearly took her breath away, but she never had understood why her heart turned into a cutting tool at times. Loneliness, maybe. There wasn't time to analyze it. There never was.

Ignoring the ache in her chest, she went back to the gossip site and clicked on Jack the Giant Killer's byline. She had no choice. The paparazzo stalker was becoming famous for bringing down the infamous, especially since he limited his targets to those who abused their power and position. And he didn't stick to celebs, either. Jack had outed Burton Carr—and listed Carr as one of The Private Concierge's clients on the Gotcha site. And now Lane was terrified that Jack might have done it again with another client, someone she just signed yesterday.

Jerry Blair knew about the Carr and Shan scandals, but he didn't know about Lane's new client, and she hadn't told him. She wasn't sure she could—or should—tell anyone, including the police. Ned Talbert had signed his contract yesterday morning and late last night he'd killed his girlfriend, then killed himself. Lane had been struggling with disbelief all day.

She'd had three clients involved in felonies or capital crimes in just three weeks' time. And then there was Judge Love earlier this year. Love had presided over a popular television-courtroom show and was known for her toughness until her lurid private life became public, all of this thanks to JGK, as the Giant Killer had become known. Lane had found herself right in the middle of that scandal because one of her key people had decided to confront the Gotcha people personally. The site's owner swore that JGK operated under total anonymity, e-mailing or dropping his material at various specified locations. No one knew who JGK was, but Gotcha took pains to verify everything he gave them, including the raunchy Judge Love video.

Right now, Lane was terrified that her service would look like a hotbed of criminal activity. No one would come near her.

She clicked off the Web site and shut down her computer.

Everywhere she looked she could see herself, only she didn't look liberated in her undone skirt and flimsy camisole top. She looked exposed. She was heartsick about what had happened to her clients, including Ned. She knew them all as good men who couldn't have done what they were accused of, but sadly there didn't seem to be anything she could do to protect them. The problems were escalating, and Lane had to think of herself, as well. A concierge service *was* its clients. If the clients went down, the service went down with them.

She opened the drawer of her desk and pulled out Ned's application. She hadn't given it to anyone yet to process, and she'd handled the credit-card transaction herself. Her receptionist and assistant, Mary, had been out on a break, and Lane had been watching the desk. So, no one knew about Ned Talbert but her. And no one could know.

4

Rick prowled the darkened house using only a penlight. He wore latex gloves and slipcovers over his shoes the way evidence technicians did to avoid contamination. He was familiar enough with the place to find his way around in the dark, but didn't want to chance disturbing the crime scene evidence and signaling that someone had been here.

Not that anyone would notice, he suspected. It was just after midnight, and the guard had changed. The rookie had been replaced by a retiree. Sound asleep in a chair by the house's front entrance, the night-shift guy was doing a good imitation of a rusty buzz saw.

Rick had parked on a side street, walked over and let himself in through the back way, using a customized attachment on his pocketknife to jimmy the lock, rather than touch the knob, which should have been dusted for prints but didn't appear to have been. He was here to check out the crime scene, but he was also looking for the package he'd passed off to Ned all those years ago for safekeeping. And maybe the darkness would help him focus on his mission, instead of the countless reminders of his friend.

He'd identified the body at the morgue today. It was Ned without question. Rick saw the faded scar on his friend's chin even before he saw the bullet hole. When they were kids, he and Ned had believed they could do anything—jump off roofs and fly, walk on water—and they had the scars to prove it. Nothing daunted them, even when Ned missed a branch playing Tarzan, fell to the earth and split open his chin. They'd been eight at the time.

Rick turned off the light and stopped, needing a moment to deal with all of it, to breathe against the suffocating weight in his chest. He'd gone numb after his visit to the morgue, and he wished to hell he could stay that way. Scarred or not, the face he'd seen on the concrete slab wasn't his friend. It was a death mask with Ned's features. The body that had housed his larger-than-life spirit was an empty shell. He was gone.

Rick didn't believe in heaven and hell. He couldn't console himself with the belief that he would ever see his friend again. The Ned who'd been like a part of him had vanished, leaving Rick feeling as empty as the body in the morgue. He couldn't even hold a clear picture of Ned in his mind without having it replaced by a corpse with a bullet through its brain. There was no comfort to be found, even in his memories. That was why he had to find out what had happened. At least then he wouldn't be haunted by questions.

When he left the morgue, he'd driven straight over to the West L.A. station to talk with his buddy, Don Cooper, in homicide, who wasn't on the case but had confirmed that it was being handled by the big guns of the elite Robbery Homicide Division. Coop had heard unofficially that Ned's celebrity status in the sports world warranted the high-level involvement, not because they believed it was anything other than a murder-suicide. Coop also confirmed that a suicide note had been found at the scene, but the contents had not been revealed.

And then, for some reason, he'd volunteered the kind of gun Ned had used. None of this information should have been shared with an outsider, which was why Rick had come to Coop. He was a talker. One of these days Coop was going to talk himself right out of a job, Rick imagined.

Rick beamed the light over the leather chair where Ned had been sitting when he pressed the barrel of a full-size 9 mm Glock to his right temple and pulled the trigger. The chalked outline showed him knocked to the left by the force of the discharge and slumped over the arm of the chair.

Jesus, what had made him do that?

Rick's head swam with questions that were almost unbearable. Did Ned get that idea from him? Had the scene at the cabin triggered something in his friend? They'd done everything together as kids, and Rick had almost always been the leader, the instigator.

But Rick couldn't let himself believe that, despite the lacerating guilt he felt. Ned was an adult, his own man. He wouldn't have copycatted a suicide. Rick needed to start thinking like an investigator. What was Ned doing with a Glock? He didn't own a gun and had no use for them. He'd always said he could do more damage with a baseball bat. Rick wondered if anyone had checked to see if Ned had bought a gun recently or had a permit to carry the gun that was used. Or dusted the empty shell casings for prints.

Rick flashed the beam from the chalked outline of Ned's body to the woman's on the floor at the foot of his chair. According to Coop, she'd died in a sexually degrading position while partially naked and restrained. The cause of death was suffocation. She'd had a cheap grocery-store plastic bag tied around her head.

Rick had asked Coop if burn marks were found on her

genitals. He'd looked at Rick funny but hadn't asked any questions. He'd said he didn't know, but she probably hadn't died quickly. The condition of the plastic bag, plus the way the vessels in her eyes had hemorrhaged indicated the suffocation might have been interrupted several times, perhaps intentionally.

Rick breathed a curse word. This was all wrong. He knew it to the depths of his being. This wasn't a hero's death. Suffocating a bound woman and then shooting yourself was cowardly. Ned wouldn't have wanted to go out this way, or take her with him. He was trying to save Holly, not kill her.

Ned was drawn to self-destructive women, probably because of his mother. Her heroin habit had driven her to extremes, including hooking to get money for drugs. She'd died of an overdose when Ned was really young, and like a lot of kids with parents who screw up, he'd felt responsible. He'd been picking questionable women ever since, maybe thinking he could fix whatever was wrong. Or maybe they'd picked him. Nice guys like Ned were easy targets.

Rick looked from one chalked form to the other, trying to get a sense of the dominant emotion involved. Every crime scene had clues; the trick was to read them correctly. Murder was usually driven by fear or rage, but he didn't pick up either here. There was a methodical feel to these crimes—and that wasn't Ned. He'd said he was being blackmailed because of his sex practices, but he'd also said it was all lies. This crime scene said *he* was the liar. Only blind rage could have driven him to this. And why take his rage out on Holly? Unless he was being blackmailed *by* her.

Rick had no answers as he slowly flashed the beam around the rest of the room. The blood and spatter patterns were typical of self-inflicted gunshot wounds, and according to Coop, there'd been no sign of forced entry.

Rick saw nothing else that stood out, and with every passing second the risk of being discovered increased. But there was one last thing that had to be done.

He moved silently to the hallway that led to the master bedroom. He passed a writing desk on the way, and the beam of his penlight struck something small and shiny. The desk drawer was partially open and a high-gloss business card was stuck in the sliding mechanism on the side. Rick could imagine a technician opening the drawer and finding the card, along with other things to be bagged as evidence, then unknowingly dropping the card while closing the drawer. Or it might have been something else entirely. Someone may have been in a great hurry to cover his tracks and grabbed for the card but dropped it. The killer perhaps?

Rick fished the card out and held it under the light. The initials *TPC* were elegantly scrolled down the left side in gold leaf. Laddered across the card just as elegantly were the words *The Private Concierge*. On the bottom right was a woman's name, a phone number and an e-mail address. Lane Chandler.

The name was familiar, but Rick couldn't place it. He turned the card over and found a one-word question scrawled in what looked like Ned's handwriting: *Extortion?*

Was Ned accusing The Private Concierge of extortion or had he been looking for a surface to write on, grabbed the card and then tossed it in the desk drawer without realizing it had fallen down the side? And why hadn't homicide or the crime scene guys noticed it? Rick had spotted it in the dark.

Rick was running out of time. He continued down the hall to the bedroom and went straight to the maple armoire. The largest drawer had a secret compartment with a safe in the back, but Rick found it unlocked—and empty. Either Ned had moved the package, which he wouldn't have done without telling Rick, or the police had found it and taken it as evidence. And Rick couldn't avoid the other possibility—that certain people still had a vested interest in the contents of the package, and one of them had been here. But if that was the case, what connection did it have to last night's carnage?

Rick heard a scraping sound, metal chair legs against concrete. The officer was awake, maybe shifting position or getting up. He checked his pocket to make sure the business card was there, clicked off the penlight and headed for the back door. He'd watched Ned put the package in the compartment, but it was gone. And he couldn't risk taking any more time to search for it.

Monday, October 7
Two days earlier

Lane Chandler? Rick stared hard at the business card, aware that his eyes were tired and stinging. He rubbed them, massaging the sockets with his thumbs to relieve the pressure. It was six in the morning, and he'd been up and down all night. His mind wouldn't let him sleep for any length of time. There were too many questions, and primary among them was why her name had struck a chord.

He wasn't familiar with the concierge service, and he didn't know anyone named Lane Chandler, personally or otherwise. He'd heard the name somewhere, but he was exhausted and emotionally spent. He just couldn't seem to place it. He thought back, mentally sorting through the names of his clients over the years. He could check the actual files, but something kept him stuck in the chair in his cubbyhole of a home office, playing alphabet games.

It didn't sound real. Who had a name like Lane Chandler? A movie star, maybe.

L.C. What other women's name began with *L?* Not that many: Linda, Lydia, Lilly, Laurie, Leigh, Lucille, Lucy. Lucy?

Oh, Jesus. He rocked up from the chair and left it teetering. He didn't know any women, but he knew a girl named Lane Chandler. Or had known one. He'd arrested the little brat fifteen years ago. She'd assumed the name of a B-movie star when she ran away from home. She'd told Rick's partner, Mimi, that she'd picked some bit player from the old celluloid westerns with the stage name Lane Chandler. She liked the name, but not because the initials were L.C. That had been a coincidence. Taking on a man's name had made her feel stronger and tougher, like she could handle herself on the mean streets of L.A.

And then what had she done but trash herself on those streets?

Rick paced the room, feeling like he was in a cage, but maybe he needed the confinement right now. Where would he go if he wasn't hemmed in by these L-shaped walls? He might head south and never stop. South to the border. Run, don't walk. *Go, Rick, go. Get the holy hell out of here. Have some semblance of a life while you can. Meet a woman, fall in love for ten minutes. Give your heart away. It's the only thing you have left of any worth.*

Lane Chandler.

He slowed up and let his thoughts roll back a decade and a half. She was Lucy Cox. What a dangerously precocious kid that one had been, a real handful, the Jodi Foster of her time. Rick had picked her up for street prostitution—an open-and-shut case, given that she'd propositioned him. Blue-eyed and bold, she'd actually made him wish she was fifteen years older—and that had never happened before.

He'd been working juvenile vice since he'd signed on with the force, and dealing with drugged-out street urchins was enough to make any normal man want to put them in a straitjacket so they couldn't hurt themselves or someone else. They were sad, angry and desperate. Too often they ended up dead. But she wasn't one of them. She was something else, an underage madonna, luminous enough to light up skid row. The courts had put her in juvie, and Rick had helped make sure she didn't get out until she was legal, eighteen.

Rick walked to the window and stood there, shirtless, in the rising beam of light, letting it warm him. Jeans were all he'd bothered with this morning. There wasn't a woman around to complain about his bare chest—or appreciate it, for that matter. Hadn't been for quite a while. His last long-term relationship, and only marriage, ended ten years ago, for the same reason most law enforcement marriages ended. Criminal neglect. It wasn't that he didn't love her. He just didn't have the time or energy to love her the way she needed it. Couldn't blame her for that. He shouldn't have married in the first place, but he'd been young—and probably just selfish enough to want someone around on those interminable nights of soul-searching, someone to ease the loneliness.

The slam of a neighboring door brought his attention back to the view. His cubby was a converted storage room, and its only window looked out on the alley behind his house, exposing the back sides of a half block of badly weathered beach houses. The alley had little to recommend it, except bower after bower of glorious red and orange bougainvillea. Rick loved the stuff. It festooned the courtyard out front, too, and as far as he was concerned, it made his beach cottage look like a small palazzo.

Lane Chandler. God, he didn't want to go back there. It wasn't going to help anyone to dredge up that muck, least of all Ned. And there were so many other reasons not to pursue this investigation. A case like this could take months, years, even for a seasoned homicide detective, which Rick wasn't. You needed the right resources, computer databases, labs and technicians to investigate a murder. He had access to none of that, and he was running out of time. Everything pointed to murder-suicide. The police had already written it off.

But foremost among the reasons to let this investigation go was her, Lucy Cox, all grown up and running her own concierge service. Why didn't that surprise him?

He walked back to his desk, swept up her card, crushed it in his fist and dropped it in the trash. And then he left the room.

He got as far as the living room, as far as the doors to his beloved courtyard, before a realization stopped him. Like a bomb it hit him. What were the odds of so many seemingly disparate things converging on that one night at Ned's place? Rick had found Ned and his girlfriend dead, the package missing and Lane Chandler's card stuck to Ned's desk, all within the same time frame. Or what appeared to be the same time frame. The package could have been missing awhile, but Rick didn't think so. Ned would have mentioned it. And Rick suspected the card was recent, too. Ned wouldn't have let that slip, either. But maybe that was what Ned had been trying to say the night he showed up at the cabin.

What Ned didn't know, what no one knew except Rick, was that Lucy Cox *was* connected to that missing package. She was the catalyst for what had happened fifteen years ago—and the reason Rick had left the force.

If she really was Lane Chandler now, Rick questioned whether it was a coincidence that Ned had come across her somewhere. Had she approached him because she wanted the package herself? Why? He could think of people who might want to get their hands on it, but why her? Blackmail, most likely. And how did she know that Ned had it?

He turned and slammed back through the house, swearing to himself. He nearly took the door off the hinges as he entered his office, and the first thing he did was pick up the trash can. Now, where the hell was that card?

5

Priscilla Brandt hesitated at the bottom of the grand stairway and visually swept her living room with the acuity of a young, hungry bird of prey, missing nothing. The house was perfection, even to her critical eye. Fresh-cut irises stood in tall crystal vases, satin pillows were plumped and the Brazilian-cherry floors gleamed. Just the faintest whiff of lavender oil pleasantly stimulated her senses, along with the rippling piano runs of Mozart's *Adagio in H Minor*.

If you want your guests to think well of you, treat them well. If you want them forever in your debt, spoil them rotten and send them home with expensive gifts. If you have no money, cook exquisitely.

It was one of the many bits of wisdom in her sassy new etiquette book, currently at the top of the *New York Times* nonfiction list. Quite the coup for a former hash-slinger from the San Fernando Valley. Of course, the hash-slinging was how she'd put herself through college, but still, she had no real pedigree like the other mavens of manners, and at twenty-six she was a mere upstart compared to icons like Emily Post and Amy Vanderbilt.

Lineage matters only if you have nothing else of interest to offer.

She plucked an imaginary speck from the sleeve of her cashmere twinset and walked to the mirror over the fireplace to check her long chestnut waves for fullness and vitality, all signs of a healthy female libido, which was crucial in today's market, no matter *what* you were selling. She couldn't very well be outwardly sexy in her profession. She had to leave that impression in other ways, such as the slim, side-slit skirt and the snug fit of her sweater set, all belying the propriety of her cultured pearls. This was a lady, yes, but a tramp, as well, to anyone lucky enough to know her *that* well.

Feminine wiles are all about promise, ladies. Delivery is an altogether different matter.

Another of Priscilla's pointers. And within the hour she would be sharing more of her advice on national television. Another coup for the poor relation. The TV crew would be here soon to set up in the garden where she would be having tea with none other than national morning-show anchor Leanne Sanders, and Priscilla had made sure the grounds of her leased home in the Santa Monica hills were as perfect as the interior.

The trick was to be perfect without being perfectly boring. She had to be just witty enough, just tarty enough, to catch and hold the interest of a fickle public. But with impeccable manners, of course.

For Priscilla the payoff was more than book sales. She was in discussions for her own afternoon talk show, and it was with the very network about to interview her. So far the only stumbling block was the snot-nosed executive producer, who couldn't have been more than twelve, if his acne was any indication. Right in front of the network brass, he'd said he just wasn't "feeling" an etiquette show in the era of shock jocks and reality TV. Her material wouldn't be edgy or opinionated enough. The only thing he hadn't done was yawn. Pris would have had a breath mint ready to cram down his throat if he did.

She walked to the living room windows, pride swelling as she anticipated the beauty of the wisteria-covered arbor. The smile died on her red-matte lips as she looked out. "What the fuck?"

The crazy squatter was back and he'd turned her beautiful garden into a tent city! His crude cardboard shelter blighted the wisteria arbor where she'd created the perfect English garden for her outdoor tea. He'd been sneaking onto her property for weeks now, and she'd made the mistake of giving him money to get rid of him. Well, no more payola. She was going to kick his grungy butt off the property herself, not that she had much choice. She didn't trust the hired help not to rat her out to the tabloids.

She grabbed her cell phone from the writing desk in the hall and marched to the front door at a military clip. Someone had been giving the tabloids information about her, and she was going to put a stop to that, too. The rags had labeled her Ms. Pris, but now they were questioning whether it should have been Ms. Hissy Fit, simply because she'd taught a reckless teenage tailgater a lesson by letting him pile into the back of her new Mercedes. She'd publicly assailed him for riding her ass all the way to Burbank, and a gathering crowd had cheered her on, which seemed vindication enough. But there'd been no applause the following week when she'd made a waitress cry for serving cold food.

Okay, Ms. Pris had a temper. She was working on it. But this squatter was different, a clear violation of her rights. The porous greenbelt that ran from the house's car park to the garden forced her to walk on the tiptoes of her shoes to keep the high heels from sinking in. When she was done with this guy, she would go change into flats and freshen up again. She had time, twenty minutes—and she had another tip for her next book. Never wear high heels at lawn parties!

As she neared the cardboard tent, she saw a pair of grubby bare feet poking out the bottom and a pile of beer cans and trash next to them. She also saw something that made her blood boil. He'd been using her beautiful lawn for a toilet.

Another F-bomb rolled off her tongue. "Pack up your things and get out of here," she demanded.

He didn't respond and she kicked at the refrigerator box with the pointed toe of her heels. "Did you *hear* me?"

The box lifted off him and as the man roused and rolled toward her, Priscilla saw that he wasn't the transient she'd been paying off. He was much younger and fitter, with bright blue eyes shining through his shaggy brown hair— and he might not be so easily handled.

"This is *private* property." She brandished the cell phone. "You have two minutes to get your things and leave, or I'll call 911."

"Fuck off," he muttered, grabbing the box and giving it a shake, as if she'd soiled it. He turned his back to her and collapsed under his cardboard canopy, apparently intending to sleep off the rest of what was probably a liquid breakfast.

Somewhere in the base of Priscilla's brain, two wires touched, white hot. A circuit shorted out, sparks erupted and she began to tremble. There was no chance to curb the impulse. It was swift and lethal, animal rage. Her fists clenched, and her upper lip curled back, baring small, sharp incisors. Delicate nostrils flared, and a snarl rattled in her throat, as savage as anything heard in the jungle.

How dare he turn his mangy freeloading back on her! Counting to ten wasn't an option when some asshole was about to destroy the opportunity of a lifetime. *Her* lifetime. She dropped the phone and picked up a sculpture of an iron crane from the garden bed, her only thought to wale on this guy. She didn't even care if the crew arrived and saw her. He needed to be taught a lesson.

That snot-nose executive producer wanted edgy? Ha!

But as she raised the sculpture over her head like a club, a tiny voice of sanity—or maybe it was opportunity— intruded. There might still be some way to salvage this. If she could hit him just hard enough to knock him out, she could roll him onto the cardboard box and drag him out of here, an Indian carry. That way he couldn't fight her.

The horrible crunch of iron against skull bone made her wince, and just as quickly as rage had flared, it was gone. Fear flooded her, dropping her to her knees. Whenever she had these insane episodes, she was devastated afterward, shaken, afraid and deeply humiliated at what she'd done. This had to be her worst outburst ever. Had she killed him?

She pulled off the cardboard to find him slumped and unresponsive but still breathing. He was out cold. If she could get him onto the cardboard, she might still be able to drag him into the bushes where he couldn't be seen, but she had so little time left.

Moments later, bent over him and struggling to catch her breath, she realized it was no use. She couldn't even roll him over. He weighed as much as ten men. She sank onto the ground next to him, sobbing and furious. She should have killed him. Look at what he'd reduced her to.

Desperate, she searched for the cell and found it in the grass. She speed-dialed her manager, but got voice mail.

Her publicist didn't pick up, either. Didn't these people ever answer their damn phones? Why the hell was she paying them twenty percent of her hard-earned money?

Seconds later, she had Lane Chandler on the line, and the sound of her soft, melodious voice worked miracles. It calmed Priscilla like a dip in cool lake water.

"Priscilla, are you all right?" Lane asked. "How can I help you?"

Priscilla begged Lane to call the segment producer for the morning show and reschedule the taping. "Please," she implored, "do it now. Tell them I've had an accident."

"What kind of accident?"

Priscilla assured her it wasn't serious, just horribly embarrassing.

"I'll take care of it," Lane said. "Now, please, take a deep breath and calm down. Are you sure you're all right? I could call one of our concierge doctors if you need medical care. It's completely private."

"No! No doctors. I'll be fine. Just call the segment producer and get the taping rescheduled. No one else needs to know about any of this, all right?"

She clicked off and dropped the phone in horror, unable to believe what had just happened. Everything had been so perfect. It had felt like fate, the stars aligned. She'd never felt more poised or ready for anything. This was supposed to have been her shining moment. And he'd ruined it. *This was all his fault.*

She began to sob and swear and beat on the unconscious man, oblivious to the video camera trained on her. It was held by a silent, shrouded figure who was concealed by the same thicket of bushes where she'd been planning to drag the body. Priscilla may have dodged one bullet this morning, but there was another gun aimed straight at her.

6

Darwin LeMaster couldn't remember how to answer his cell phone. It was his own damn phone, too, the one he'd designed, patented and turned into a revolutionary new communications system, according to technology reporters. It came with one-touch concierge access, a GPS system, biometric fingerprint recognition and the ability to make not only secure, but untraceable, calls. The Darwin phone had made him a twenty-eight-year-old man of means and a phenom, whatever that meant, in the field of electronic networking.

BFD. He still couldn't answer it.

Right now, it was playing "Paranoid" by Black Sabbath at high volume, the equivalent of getting kicked in the head by a donkey, which was what it took to get Darwin's attention most of the time. But this was no ordinary call. From the moment he'd seen the incoming number in the digital display—*her* number—his brain had vapor-locked. What good was an IQ at the genius level if you couldn't take a phone call from a steaming-hot woman?

The noise stopped, and he breathed a sigh of relief. The call had gone to voice mail. But he also felt a body slam of recrimination. What kind of man was he? Sometimes he wondered if he even *had* a penis.

All around him in the cavernous, cluttered office that his coworkers called Command and Control Center 1, electronic equipment whirred, interrupted by mysterious intermittent beeping. The aroma of stale coffee sullied the air, wafting from the dozen forgotten plastic cups that were stranded wherever he'd set them when an idea hit. This morning's breakfast, a glazed doughnut with one bite out of it, had been abandoned to a napkin on the file cabinet next to his desk. Mostly he forgot to eat, but even when he remembered, he couldn't seem to gain weight.

He picked up the doughnut and bit a hunk out of it, chewing absently. Women worried about men who couldn't gain weight. It brought out the mother in them—and while his boss and longtime friend, Lane Chandler, didn't openly bug him about putting on poundage, she'd brought the doughnuts by this morning.

She *had* openly bugged him about sprucing up the command center, said it was the nexus of the entire concierge service and a selling point for prospective clients. She'd suggested professional organizers and decorators, but he'd been putting her off.

He rose and stretched, imagining a cat as he rippled the vertebrae of his spine. This was his lair, and he didn't feel like conducting tours. He'd been chided for being reclusive and secretive with his pet projects, and maybe his critics had a point. He had actually boarded up the office windows, preferring the eerie phosphers of LCD screens to natural light.

He could run the world from here. On the wall opposite his desk, several large GPS grids, glowing with red dots and streaming arrows, covered the most populous areas of the country. The electronic maps meant Darwin could locate any of their forty-five members with a Premiere

Plan and a fully featured Darwin cell, as long as they were within range and their phone was on.

He had also designed the circuitry necessary to scramble signals. If a Premiere member called in and requested a secure line, Darwin could hook them up with a couple clicks of his mouse, at which point the call could not be intercepted or recorded. Well, except by Darwin, of course. Any system was only as secure as the person who created it.

But no one worried about Darwin. He didn't have a *penis*.

He kicked a box of old circuit boards out of the way and dropped to the floor. "Give me twenty, you pussy," he grunted.

The homophobic drill sergeant who rented space in Darwin's brain got exactly seven military-style push-ups before Darwin collapsed. While he was lying there on the floor, surrounded by boxes of high-tech detritus and thinking about all the ways he needed to overhaul his life, the revolutionary cell phone sounded again. Sharp staccato bursts, each one more imperative than the last. The hotline.

He rolled over and stared at the ceiling. Thank God, a crisis. He didn't have to face the terrifying prospect of inviting a woman—make that the ultimate sexual-fantasy woman of the new millennium—to dinner and then maybe to his place, and then maybe to something approaching the sexual realm, like his bed?

A one-man Pluto shot would have been more realistic.

"Darwin, you have voice mail," said a come-hither female voice.

The phone was giving him a reminder, just as he'd programmed it to. If it had had legs, it would have jumped off the desk and strolled over to him. He would have to work on that feature.

He pushed to his feet, grimacing as he limped over to the desk, grabbed the phone and thumbed the Talk button. "What is it, Lucy?" That was her name from the old days when they lived together on the streets.

"*Please,* Dar, call me Lane," she said. "I need you. Can you come to my office right away?"

Lane unbuttoned her suit jacket and flapped the lapels to create a breeze. She liked to think that she'd come by her reputation as a cool customer deservedly, although right now she was anything but. Her face was flushed and her cleavage damp. Why did women always perspire *there* first? She really should plan for that when she was deodorizing in the mornings.

At any rate, she'd just run a crazed segment producer off at the pass and narrowly averted some kind of crisis. She didn't know *what* kind because Priscilla Brandt had hung up on her before Lane could ask. But at least Ms. Pris would get another shot at success.

Congressman Carr and Simon Shan might not.

Ned Talbert certainly would not.

"Hey, what's going on?"

Lane looked up to see Darwin shambling into her office, tall and floppy as an Olympic pole-vaulter, his mop of dark curls bouncing, and his baggy, worn jeans hanging on his narrow hips. He was nearly thirty, but he really hadn't changed all that much in the fifteen years she'd known him, except that he was a millionaire now instead of a juvenile delinquent—and so was she.

"Shut the door, Dar. Lock it, too."

His dense, expressive eyebrows lifted. "We have a receptionist out there," he said. "Why don't I tell the gray angel that we don't want to be disturbed."

The gray angel was their vibrant seventy-year-old receptionist, Mary O'Dell, who could have stalled a tactical squad of marines, she was so good. But TPC had an open-door policy, and anyone really determined to see Lane was unlikely to be stopped for long.

"I don't want Val barging in on us," Lane explained.

Darwin shut the door and locked it. Val Drummond had started in the mailroom and his fortunes had risen with the company's. He ran the administrative arm, but he was also handling concierge operations now that Lane was busy with the company's new expansion plan. But Val's promotion hadn't eased the tension between him and Darwin. Val was like the solid and steady but less gifted younger brother with a bad case of sibling rivalry. He was competitive with Darwin for Lane's time, and he seemed to resent that she and Darwin were much more than just the creative spark behind TPC. They were close friends with a bond that almost defied explanation, even to them…although, oddly, Darwin himself had been cutting ties with Lane lately.

But maybe it wasn't odd at all, Lane allowed. He had his eye on a sweet young thing he'd met at a comic-book convention. Seems they'd been friendly for a while, but now they were getting closer, and as much as Lane missed Dar's company, she knew it was good for a recluse like him to have someone in his life besides her.

Lane slipped off the jacket to her pantsuit and undid a button at the neckline of her blouse, still too warm to relax. It was time to tell him. This business was Dar's life, too, but it went beyond that. She trusted and confided in him as she did no one else.

"Well?" he said, perching on the arm of the high-back leather guest chair. "Are we going to end the suspense any time soon?"

She held him off a little longer, taking a detour behind her desk to the console that smelled of freshly quartered limes. She always had some there in a crystal bowl, as much for their tart essence as for the drinks. She poured a glass of ice water and held up the pitcher, offering him some, too. He shook his head, and she pressed the glass, cool and moist, to her check, aware that he seemed perplexed by his normally unflappable partner.

"You're going to say I'm crazy, but hear me out," she said at last. "I think we could be in trouble."

"You and I?"

"No, the service, TPC. Dar—" She was actually hoping he would laugh at her. "Do you think someone might be trying to damage this company, even to bring it down?"

He frowned. "You are crazy."

"Yeah, probably. I hope so." She took a drink, swallowing some ice chips with the water. The cold streaming into her chest cavity was almost painful. Maybe she *was* over-reacting, but the planned expansion into two more major cities had her spooked. She'd borrowed a small fortune to finance the move, and everything depended on being able to capitalize on the service's growing reputation. It had been relatively smooth sailing until recently.

Quickly, she brought Dar up to speed on what had happened. He already knew about Shan and the congressman, but he didn't know that Ned Talbert had signed on the dotted line the day he committed what was being called first-degree murder and suicide.

By the time she was done, Dar had fallen into the guest chair, apparently in surprise. "So, Ned Talbert was a client?" he said. "Wow, what is that now—three of our top clients?"

"Three in three weeks, and one of them is dead. It's surreal, a nightmare. But, listen to me now. I did something, well, rash. No one knew that Ned Talbert had signed, so I shredded his application." She hung her head at Darwin's disbelief. "Don't look at me like that. I panicked. I handled his credit-card transaction myself because Mary was out of the office—and then I forgot to give Talbert his copy of the contract, so I had all the paperwork."

She sighed and looked up, beseeching him to understand. "I didn't know what else to do. When the Burton and Shan stories broke, that sleazy gossip Web site reported that they were our clients. How would it look if they found out about Talbert?"

"Like all our clients are jinxed? Like we're the kiss of death?"

"Exactly."

"Why didn't you tell me before this?"

Thank God, she thought. He understood her impulse to save the company. He was a street kid, too, thinking with his wits, thinking survival. "I didn't want to believe it. I told myself I was being paranoid. Am I being paranoid, Dar? Two clients, maybe, but three? Can that be a coincidence?"

It raised a question that Lane didn't want to ask. Who would be next? She hadn't told him about Priscilla, but she was hoping that would turn out to be nothing. She was hoping it *all* would turn out to be nothing, just a figment of her overwrought imagination.

She walked to the windows that looked out on Century City and beyond that, the Pacific coastline, continuing to cool herself with the frosty glass and the sharp scent of lime. It was a bright fall morning with a hint of crispness in the air, but the weather wouldn't get chilly for another month, and at least half the people on the streets below wore shorts. This was southern California, land of perpetual flip-flops.

Darwin spoke over her thoughts. "Considering everything, you're one of the least paranoid people I know," he said, "and if anybody had a right to be, it's you, given where you've been and what you've done."

"Yeah, thanks for reminding me." He was trying to say she'd come a long way, baby, all the way from her distant, sordid past. She and Darwin had been runaways on the street when they met, both of them cold, hungry and sick. Darwin had needed medical attention. As his condition worsened, Lane had been forced to make some desperate choices. Although now she wondered if there *was* a choice when someone's life was at stake. The only people who knew about that time in her life were Darwin and the cops who put her in jail and threw away the key.

Darwin propelled his long frame out of the creaking chair and walked over to her, quietly relieving her of the ice water. She relinquished the glass without a word.

"Maybe it's bad luck and bad timing," he suggested. "Most celebs have a self-destruct mechanism that gets triggered just seconds after they hit it big. We've seen that happen."

She nodded, wanting him to be right. He wasn't as driven as she was—and didn't even want the expansion. It was Val who was pushing her to grow the company. She and Val were alike in that way, hungry, if that was the right word. But it was Darwin who had her heart, and her allegiance.

She fought the urge to brush doughnut crumbs from his T-shirt—and lost. He dodged her questing fingers. "Listen to me," she said. "Even if everything we're talking about is coincidental, we have to be on our toes—you and me. I'm not discussing this with anyone else, obviously. But the service's reputation is at stake."

He held the glass against his cheek as she had, apparently curious about the sensation. "Why would anyone want to bring this company down? And why would they go to such extremes to do it?"

"That I don't know, but we are a concierge service, and we take care of our clients. That includes protecting their privacy and their safety, if it comes to that. We can't ignore anything that could put them at risk."

"True, but it doesn't make sense. A competitor wouldn't want to hurt our clients. They'd want to steal them."

She shrugged. "So, maybe it's the paparazzi. Jack the Giant Killer. He's the one breaking all the stories—and no one seems to have a clue who he is. Why hasn't someone exposed *him* by now?"

Lane was angry about that. So far JGK had operated in total anonymity. Even Seth Black, the owner of Gotcha.com, swore he didn't know who JGK was, but despite that, Seth had been willing to give Jack his own byline and publish his exposés. Everything was done electronically, of course, to protect Jack's anonymity.

Dar seemed to be considering Lane's idea. "I suppose it could be some kind of payback, especially since Val and Seth Black tangled earlier this year over Judge Love. But even if Black and his henchmen are targeting us, how much damage can they do? What are the odds that our clients are going to keep screwing up on a grand scale?"

Again, Lane hoped he was right. But Trudy Love was another TPC client—and a perfect example of screwing up on a grand scale. She was an ex-judge who'd officiated over a divorce-court TV show and had made her name excoriating cheating spouses. Lane could do nothing to save her career once she herself had been caught double-dipping, a phrase Trudy had made a household word.

"Jack destroyed Judge Love's career with those pictures of her and that burly, tattooed biker who wasn't her husband," Lane reminded Darwin. She cocked her head. "And then Val tried to scare off Seth Black with a bunch of empty legal threats."

Darwin snickered. "So, Black is bringing down Val by destroying our clients one by one? Maybe even setting them up for the fall and then breaking the story? I hate to be the one to *break* it to you, Lane, but our clients are burying themselves. Do you really think Seth Black is capable of framing Ned Talbert for a murder-suicide?"

That was a stretch, she had to admit. Black was a vicious snitch, not a hit man, and Lane could prove nothing. It was just a gut feeling that her company had a bull's-eye on its back, but it was a strong one.

There were no more crumbs on Dar's shirt. She brushed at it anyway. "Just say you're with me, okay? We have to stay on top of this."

"Of course I'm with you. I'll do a background check on Seth Black and scour his site—and I'll check out JGK, too. If I can't find out who he is, maybe I can figure out who he's going after next."

She thought about hugging him, but he was saved by his cell phone. It was buzzing, as if he was getting some kind of alert. Darwin's personal phone was truly a one-man band. He hit some buttons and began to read the display screen.

"What is it?" she asked, alarmed at how pale he was.

"Video feed from the Associated Press."

"Feed about what?"

Darwin looked up. "Jack the Giant Killer just saved me some research. Here's his current victim." He flipped the cell phone so that Lane could see the screen.

It was hard for her to watch the stark news footage of Priscilla Brandt beating up a homeless person. Lane sat down on the console behind her, jiggling the water pitcher. Shock seemed to take hold, causing her to shudder and go numb at the same time. The acidity from the limes burned her nostrils.

"That's number four," she said under her breath. Priscilla had said the situation was embarrassing, not violent. It looked like assault with a deadly weapon. She could wind up in prison. Priscilla hadn't been with TPC six months, but Lane knew her background, and she'd sensed a desperation in Priscilla to succeed. Lane could relate to that to some extent. She'd fought her way out of the gutter, too, and maybe she'd done some questionable things along the way, but she'd never tried to kill anyone.

Lane went to her computer and pulled up the Gotcha.com Web site. Jack the Giant Killer's byline dominated the opening page. *Ms. Pris is Pissed!* screamed the headline.

"Listen to this," Lane said. "'Ms. Pris had a manners meltdown. This morning, Priscilla Brandt, author of a bestselling book on etiquette, viciously assaulted a homeless man. Apparently he camped out on her lawn, impeding her tea-garden interview with morning-show anchor Leanne Sanders, so Brandt knocked him cold with an iron statue, but couldn't drag him off her property. She shrieked obscenities and beat the homeless man with her fists. She then called Lane Chandler, her private concierge, for help.'"

Lane stopped, shaking her head in disbelief. She glanced over at Darwin, who was back in the chair, collapsed like a punctured tire. "Do you believe me now?"

7

She was legit. Her concierge service was first-class all the way. Rick's Internet search had pulled up countless references to TPC as the crown jewel of the private-concierge field, despite its fairly recent appearance on the scene six years ago. A large infusion of investment capital from an unspecified donor had launched the company, and a reputation for consummate perfectionism had kept it going. TPC was known for its round-the-clock devotion to making the lives of its clientele complete in every way.

Apparently there was nothing a TPC concierge wouldn't do, as long as it was legal, according to its founder and CEO, Lane Chandler.

She was legit, and successful.

Rick wasn't sure how he felt about that. It was always easier dealing with people when you had some leverage. In her case, doubled-jointed escorts and masseuses who specialized in happy endings would have been helpful. Of course, he always had her criminal past to fall back on.

Her company Web site described the boggling array of services offered and the different plans available. If you wanted round-the-clock attention with all the extras—and you had unlimited funds—the Premiere Plan was your baby. Rick found more than he needed to know about the company, but no mention of Lane Chandler's background anywhere, except the usual references to education, work experience, achievements and service awards.

She'd received a BA in business administration from Pepperdine on a full scholarship program. Highest honors, which didn't surprise him, despite her questionable start. He could still see the hungry glint in her mist-blue eyes. Funny how the soft-focus gaze and butterscotch voice had made her edges seem all the sharper, even at the tender age of fifteen.

A gossip Web site called Gotcha.com had broken stories about the messy scandals with some of TPC's clients, but Ned hadn't been mentioned among them. Rick also found references to the service's expansion plans, and the heavy debt it was carrying. Maybe she needed money. Now, *there* was a motive to go after the package Ned was holding. She could use the contents to blackmail the VIPs involved in the epic scandal her own arrest had caused. She seemed to be a magnet for scandal, no matter what she did.

But how did she know Ned had the package?

Rick sat back in his chair to think. He rested his feet on the desk next to a carton of take-out Chinese. He'd found it in the fridge, left over from before he went up to the mountain cabin. The rush of hunger he'd felt when he opened the refrigerator door had dizzied him. It had been over thirty-six hours since he'd eaten, and he'd wolfed a forkful of the pork lo mein, but couldn't get it down. His throat had closed up, and even a basic act like swallowing had been a challenge. He didn't know if it was grief, stress or…something else.

The pills, he told himself. Maybe he needed to lay off that garbage.

He'd entered into a specialized form of private investigation when he'd left vice years ago. Essentially he did things that law enforcement wouldn't—or couldn't—do. It had kept him busy and paid well. But, over the last few weeks, he'd closed all his open cases and informed his clients he was taking some personal-leave time. That was all they needed to know. All anyone needed to know.

Now, here he was, faced with the toughest investigation of his life—and as much as he wanted to walk away from it, he couldn't. He just couldn't. He had to do something. The question was, what?

His sigh was resigned. A talk with Ned's housekeeper might be the way to start. Less complicated than the Lane Chandler situation, which could easily take him places he didn't want to go. Ned's funeral arrangements were being taken care of by his attorneys, who were also handling inquiries from the press. The public knew Ned as a star outfielder, not as Rick Bayless's friend, so Rick had been left out of it, thank God. He could not have dealt with that right now.

Rick hesitated, listening. A loud *pop* came from somewhere in the house, launching him out of the chair. The carton of lo mein landed on the floor with a splat and Rick kicked it aside, taking care not to slip in the streaming juices. It sounded like a gunshot, and it had come from down the hall. He could see nothing through the open doorway, but someone was definitely in his house.

He slipped out of the small office, his bare feet soundless on the Mexican tiles. He crept down the hallway, his back to the wall, wondering if the intruder had found his gun. It was in the top drawer of the night table next to his bed, but the noise had come from the other side of the house, the kitchen, and he could hear a clicking sound coming from that direction.

Was the intruder reloading? That meant he'd come armed. Rick's gun was a Colt .357 Python with a cylinder that took six bullets. There would be five left before reloading was necessary.

An odd, breathy squeak made him hesitate. The clicking got louder, urgent. The squeak became a plaintive cry. What the hell? It sounded like a baby or an animal in distress. And suddenly he knew what had happened.

His heart jammed into high gear as he spidered up to the arch that opened onto his kitchen. He craned to look inside—and saw exactly what he'd hoped. *Yesssssssss.* The mousetrap he'd baited and set days ago had been sprung. Unfortunately, the mangy little creature pinned by the bar was still alive. He was caught by the leg instead of by his skinny neck, but at least he'd been caught.

Rick Bayless had won the war. He'd finally caught the cunning sneak thief that had been raiding his garbage and springing his mousetraps for months. The reign of the devil mouse was over.

Like most bachelors, Rick had never kept what you'd call a tidy kitchen. He routinely left the dinner dishes unscraped and unwashed until the next day or whenever he got around to them. Sometimes they waited until his housekeeper made her weekly visit. It was when she'd found the usually crusty dishes nearly spotless in the sink, and asked Rick if he'd done them himself, that he realized he had an ugly, hairy little dishwasher on his hands—and the war had begun.

He hated mice. He didn't like snakes, either, but at least most snakes ate insects, which justified their existence to some extent. Mice were scavengers and disease carriers. Can you spell bubonic plague? If Walt Disney hadn't turned them into saucer-eared heroes, no one would like mice.

But Rick's enthusiasm waned as he watched his nemesis roll and flail, trying to get his leg free of the spring-loaded bar. Amazing that he had a leg left. The bar would have broken his neck if he'd gone for the cheese first, instead of trying to spring the trap.

Not so clever this time.

Now Rick had to figure out how to quickly end this. The mouse's shrieks had become heartrending, and trapped animals had been known to chew off their limbs to escape. From the drying rack on the counter, he grabbed a large stainless-steel colander to contain the struggling mouse.

A gunshot was the quickest way to end an animal's misery, but that would be overkill for a mouse, literally. Drowning it was too much like torture and a cerebral concussion too brutish, but Rick had little choice. The concussion would be quick and painless. He should have invested in one of those live traps, but somehow this had turned into an epic war of wits, with the mouse trouncing him repeatedly, which had probably made him want the wretched little thing to suffer. Obviously, now he was getting soft.

He got a wooden mallet from the kitchen drawer where he kept his tools. But when he flipped the colander over, he found the mouse unconscious—or possibly dead. It didn't appear to be breathing, and there was no response when he nudged it with the mallet.

He pulled a pair of latex gloves from his jeans' pocket and settled on his haunches. He'd been carrying gloves with him since his vice days, as religiously as some guys carried condoms. You never knew when you were going to need the protection of latex.

He quickly had the mouse free of the trap, but it still showed no signs of life, and its leg was clearly broken. Funny how it didn't look so diabolically clever anymore. More like a defenseless creature that was caught up in the universal fight to survive, like everyone else. Food was survival. Cheese was food. It was simply trying to eat without dying.

Rick's thoughts took a grimly ironic turn. Maybe the mouse wasn't such a zero after all. It had cleaned up the place. Rick Bayless was the slob who'd left the dirty dishes. Besides, having somebody set a trap for you was no way to die. It just seemed wrong to be tempted with what you wanted most—and then killed for wanting it. Was that how Ned had died? Was he lured into a death trap?

His gut clenched at the thought. He shook off the questions. He had no answers. What he had was a dead mouse that needed to be disposed of. He left it where it was and headed down the hall to his bedroom to get a shoe box. Maybe he'd even give the devil mouse a proper burial.

By the time he got back, the mouse was gone. The trap was where he'd left it, and he could see a faint blood trail leading toward the refrigerator, but no sign of the mouse. It had regained consciousness and made a break for freedom, dragging itself across the floor. Or it had been faking the entire time.

Score one—or twenty—for Mickey. Rick had lost count.

8

Simon Shan walked over to the display of ancient ceremonial swords on his bedroom wall and removed a nineteenth-century jade-handled dagger. Other than a rare ivory mah-jongg set that had belonged to his grandmother, these weapons were the only heirlooms of value in the Shan family. They'd been passed down from father to eldest son for generations, and his father had told him that this dagger's blade was sharp enough to cut floating silk.

Simon ran the pad of his index finger over the edge, watching the blood rise to the surface and bubble. Amazing. He hadn't felt a thing.

Holed up in his spacious bedroom, he'd been considering the remains of his brilliant career. The media had made quite a fuss over his Eurasian features when he became a celebrity two years ago, calling them both exotic and patrician. Possibly that was why his face had graced the covers of five popular magazines this month alone.

The magazines were fanned out like a huge tiara across the cushioned bench at the foot of his bed where his former assistant had arranged them. He'd also been on countless talk shows and news programs, answering questions about his new gig as spokesperson and designer for the Goldstar Collection, one of the country's largest discount chains.

He'd been labeled the male heir to Martha Stewart and the next bona fide lifestyle icon. But that was then. Yesterday. Today he was a drug dealer. Two weeks ago, DEA agents had found half a million dollars' worth of opium in the trunk of his sports car. He'd been charged with dealing, possession, and with using his import-export company to smuggle in the contraband.

Today he was an exploding sun, a blindingly bright has-been.

He walked the length of his blue-and-green Olympic pool of a bedroom to one of the room's three bubble windows. He slipped the curved blade behind a light-blocking blind, moving it enough to look out at a typical Monday morning in Santa Monica. The sun was rising over the ocean, but he didn't dare press any of the remote buttons that would open his condo's custom blinds. Fifteen stories down, the paparazzi waited on the busy street with their zoom lenses. He could see them on the roofs of nearby buildings, as well.

They were probably hoping for a shot of him dirty, disheveled and strung out on his own alleged stash of drugs, which was why he'd taken extra care with his grooming, slicking his hair back from the widow's peak on his forehead and dressing in the black silk-blend turtleneck and unpleated gray slacks that were his signature look. If someone showed up at his door disguised as a deliveryman, or crawled through the air-conditioning ducts, Simon Shan would be ready.

He checked his left index finger. The blood had already dried in a perfectly precise line, and still he felt no pain. The skin didn't know it had been breached, and to his way of thinking that was more humane than a gaping, disfiguring bullet hole. He preferred Chinese martial arts and direct contact with his opponents, but if weapons were necessary, only daggers and swords should be allowed in civilized warfare. They required coordination, precision and courage. Guns were for cowards. Any idiot could pull a trigger, and too many did.

In motion, move like a thundering wave. When still, be like a mountain. The first two tenets of the Twelve Descriptions of ability came back to him. Ability was the literal meaning of kung fu in English, but Simon hadn't had to think about his martial-arts training in years. It would feel good to get physical with some slimy photog who stole pieces of a man's soul and auctioned them off to the highest bidder. It would definitely break the monotony.

The walls of his penthouse condo were closing in. He kept the televisions and computers dark to avoid the almost continuous coverage of his case, and the phone had stopped ringing, except for the press. For his part, he'd been avoiding all contact with the outside world. He'd chosen to isolate himself, and at first it had felt right, like protective custody. But now, the silence was deep and lonely. Painful. Today, he was going to break that pattern.

He opened the bedroom's double doors and walked down the long slate hallway to the kitchen, the dagger at his side. If the bedroom had always reminded him of a swimming pool, this hallway was a lap pool. The floor was flowing slabs of blue stone, cut and set so tightly that no seam could be seen, and the Oriental art on the walls featured black swans.

Recessed lighting haloed the brushed-steel and green granite kitchen. He'd had the oversize room designed to accommodate a cooking show, should he ever want to shoot out of his home. He'd envisioned parties featuring fusion cuisine, paired with the best California wines.

He attacked the pile of mail he'd been avoiding on the kitchen countertop, knowing it would be one rejection after another, some polite, some not. Events he was scheduled to host were being rescheduled, but with someone else at the podium. Parties in his honor were being postponed, forever. Even some interviews had been canceled, but most were being rethought along the lines of an exposé. Would he talk about the drug charges? About his guilt or innocence? About the disastrous impact on his future?

He wanted to talk about who had framed him—and how they could possibly have known where he was going to be that day, and when he was going to be there. But that would put him in the position of doing what all criminals did: swearing that they were innocent, crying that they'd been set up.

One reporter had done enough research on his past to ask probing questions about Shan's drug use when he was a teenager. He'd admitted to some experimentation and to getting caught, but he'd seethed inwardly at the insinuations that it had been more. He'd been educated in London, but most of his family still lived in Taiwan. They were people of honor, and this latest incident had brought them deep shame. Worse, his father seemed to believe the charges. The proud old man had stopped taking Shan's calls.

He slit open one envelope after another, skimming the contents, which were exactly what he expected. He was being uninvited from his own life, shunned. He had stopped reading the return addresses. He just wanted to get through all of it. Right now a clean counter would feel like a small victory.

He picked up another letter-size envelope, slit the top,

turned it upside down and shook it. Money floated out like confetti, hundred-dollar bills. He didn't count them. It was several thousand dollars—and he knew immediately who'd sent it.

His father had returned the money Simon had sent him. He'd been sending checks since he graduated from Oxford and got a job as a waiter to help pay his way through Cordon Bleu, the famous French cooking school. Now he was able to send a great deal more in the monthly envelopes, but this was his father's way of saying that his help wasn't welcome anymore. They would starve first.

Misery fizzed up into Simon's throat. It tasted brackish, and he fought the urge to be sick. He had to be strong. There was only one way to restore his family's name and their dignity. He either had to prove his innocence—or take his own life. There was no other way to stop the nightmare he'd brought down on them. When he was gone they could hold their heads up again. He knew his way of thinking would be alien to anyone not raised as he was. It was part of his culture.

Strong. Proud. Brave. He was a warrior.

"Simon…voice mail."

Simon looked around, confused. It sounded as if someone had whispered his name. A woman. Lane Chandler? A tiny flashing blue light caught his eye, and he realized he'd left his Darwin cell phone here in the kitchen. In his rush to shut off the phone, he must have hit the volume control rather than the End button.

"Simon, you have voice mail."

It was his cell, and whether or not the programmed voice was Lane's he didn't know, but it had always reminded him of her. Soft and soothing, slightly haunting. The kind of voice a man who liked women automatically responded to, vibrating up and down his spine. And Simon did like women, despite the media's speculation.

He set down the dagger next to the cell, contemplating both. One was ancient, the other ultramodern. Both had many uses, both were designed as protection, but in today's modern age, either could destroy a life in an instant. He drew in a breath, knowing the call was going to be ugly. Still, as long as he was cleaning up the mess, he might as well listen to his voice-mail messages, too.

His mailbox was full. He would have to call TPC to get the overflow, but he quickly screened all the calls he had by listening to the caller's name and the date stamp. There were several from his attorneys, his publicist, his TPC concierge and Lane herself, but right now, the only message that interested him was from Goldstar's chairman. It had come in two days ago.

"Simon, I apologize for the voice mail, but you haven't been answering your phone. Listen, my friend, that statement of confidence we discussed about believing in your innocence and standing by you…well, our lawyers and public relations people are advising against it. They're suggesting we keep a low profile, and that you do the same. The board has voted to put the launch of your products on hold until the outcome of your trial. That way you and your lawyers can concentrate on clearing your name, and we can all put this unfortunate incident behind us. Good luck, Simon. You have friends at Goldstar."

Simon pressed the End button. He picked up the dagger and touched the blade again. No pain. No pain at all. A second later, he whipped the dagger over his head and with a crack of his wrist, launched it like a missile at the kitchen's other doorway, the one off the hallway to the front door.

The tip of the blade stuck in the door frame, the handle quivering like the crossbar of an arrow. A strangled gasp came from the shadows of the hallway. Simon flipped on the overhead lights and strode toward the door. He was shaking. "Don't ever come up on me unannounced."

The tall, lithe creature he'd caught eyed him with a mix of fear and defiance. The material of her blouse sleeve was pinned by the knife blade, tethering her to the door frame. Simon didn't free her. He didn't trust her, either.

"I picked up the things you wanted," she said, pointing to the magazines that had fallen to the floor. "I thought I could leave them without disturbing you."

He unstuck the knife, ripping a chunk of lacquered wood from the door frame. His voice was frozen with rage at the world that had turned on him. "Give me another reason to think you've betrayed me, and you'll die by this blade."

9

"It's a go, Ashley. Sign the lease." A squeal on the other end of the line forced Lane to lower the volume of her earpiece. But she couldn't suppress a grin as she walked briskly down the Avenue of the Stars, toward the Santa Monica Mountains in the distance. She'd just green-lighted the plans to open the TPC branch in Dallas. She'd been putting it off for weeks, and she was as excited as Ashley, who'd been stranded in Dallas, scouting locations. Probably as nervous, too.

"Make sure it's the entire tenth floor," Lane said, "and we're good to go. Next step is getting the place staffed. You're going to be running the show, so put together your short list of contenders for the key positions and set up the interviews. I can be there this Thursday. That gives you four days."

"Will do! I'll have everything ready when you get here, and thank you so much for this opportunity. This is it for me, the ultimate, really. My dream."

"And your chance to make it come true," Lane said, congratulating her warmly, even though Ashley was really Val's choice. But that felt good, too. It was time to let go of the reins and give Val his head. He'd been pushing for the expansion, and he knew the staff better than she did, in terms of their leadership abilities. Besides, Lane was not the maverick that some people thought. She believed in teamwork. She'd played some beach volleyball when she was in college, and she'd admired the way the really good teams worked. One set up the shot, and the other one took it. That's what she and Val had just done, although he still didn't know it.

Lane excused herself, gently cutting the conversation short with Ashley. Lane's next call was to their receptionist, letting Mary know the Dallas move was official and to order champagne. Lane had decided the office needed something to celebrate, given their latest client fiasco—the frightening business that very morning with Priscilla Brandt. But Mary reminded her that Val was holding staff meetings all afternoon, so Lane's bright idea would have to be postponed.

She dropped her cell in her suit pocket and kept walking, oblivious to the fashion incongruity of white Nike Turbo Plus jogging shoes and a black spandex designer suit with a pencil skirt. She probably should have been a New Yorker. Walking was a requirement for her sanity. And today, she'd had no choice. She'd been stuck for too long, mired in doubt and indecision about the expansion. Walking helped clear her head and give her the perspective she needed to make decisions. It felt like she was moving forward in all ways, not just physically. She was charging, going somewhere.

But Jerry had told her never to venture out at night, so here she was, on her lunch hour, despite the obvious drawbacks of walking in L.A. at noon. Car exhaust, for one. It really wasn't a good idea to walk in cities where you could see the air you were breathing. Worse, it was the middle of the day, and hot. Her breasts were sweating again. And walking was costing her a fortune, no matter what anyone said about it being the low-cost alternative to health clubs. She was paying dearly just for the privilege of living close enough to walk back and forth to work.

But who'd have thought she would ever have a fortune to pay. Not so terribly long ago she was penniless and homeless. She attended high school classes in juvenile hall and later tackled college on a scholarship, supplemented by multiple part-time jobs, one of which was helping a professor who'd penned a surprise bestseller and desperately needed someone to organize his life. He'd been so thrilled with her efforts he'd referred his entertainment lawyer to her, who'd referred more clients. It had started like that, a chain reaction. And then she'd dragged Darwin, kicking and screaming, into the fold, and he'd invented his crazy "electronic bodyguard" phone, as he called it in those days. Finally, after two years of abject toil, she'd bagged her first really big client, who'd become another source of referrals, and ready cash.

And she hadn't stopped moving since.

Rick Bayless watched Detective Mimi Parsons take a huge bite of her PB & J on Wonder Bread, give it several distracted chews and then wash everything down with a slug of milk from a quart carton, which she'd probably swiped from the coffee room. She was glued to the tabloid magazine on her desk and hadn't noticed him standing not six feet away, observing her and the otherwise empty police-station bullpen.

Everyone's out to lunch, Rick thought, especially her.

At least she wasn't into health food, like the rest of southern California. She had snack packages of potato chips and chocolate-chip cookies lined up for her second and third courses. Not into highbrow reading material, either. The article was upside down to Rick, but he could make out the title from where he stood by the door, and it had something to do with a transgender female prison inmate giving birth to a fur-bearing baby of questionable species.

Not much has changed, he thought, smiling to himself. Mimi was still a mess. Her desk was stacked high with case files, unfinished reports and research data. Her blazer jacket was wrinkled and too large on her petite frame, not that he was any expert on fashion. Most notably, though, she was completely tuned out to everything but what held her attention at that moment. That's what had made her a stellar detective when they were partners, her avid, Peeping Tom–like concentration.

Rick had asked for Coop at the desk, but the clerk told him Don Cooper had been loaned out to the Palos Verdes Estates Police Department on a case. Rick figured that was apt punishment for Don's loquaciousness. Not much to talk about at PVEPD. A big case there involved victims of rabid squirrel attacks on golf courses. Occasionally someone got nailed by a runaway cart.

Rick had done a little more digging with the clerk, found out that Mimi was peripherally involved in the Ned Talbert case, and used all of his considerable stealth to sneak in here and surprise her. He and Mimi had done their thing fifteen years ago, working juvenile vice out of the downtown L.A. bureau. A year or so after he resigned, in part because of remarks he'd made that were critical of the juvenile-hall system, Mimi had called and told him she was switching to homicide. She'd sailed through the requirements, eventually transferred down here to the West

Side police station, and she'd been an integral part of their detective division ever since.

Rick had been instrumental in helping her get the job. She'd wanted out of the grinder, and he had pulled a few strings. Mimi actually did owe him for that, not that she'd ever admit it. Theirs had been a love-hate relationship, never romantic, sometimes trying, but always interesting.

He scuffed his feet, and she looked up, eyes narrowing at the sight of him. "What in the H are you doing here, Bayless? I haven't fired my gun yet this year. You're going to make me break that record?"

It was her way of saying hi. Rick nodded, unsmiling. His way.

He braved her suspicious, get-out-of-my-space glare and walked to her desk. Conversationally, he said, "I hear you're working with the Robbery Homicide Division on the Ned Talbert case."

She slapped down her sandwich, yielding to his rude intrusion. "And Ned was a friend of yours, I know. I'm sorry about that, I really am, but I can't tell you anything beyond what's been in the news, and you know it."

"So, you *are* working with RHD." LAPD's Robbery Homicide Division often took jurisdiction when homicides involved high-profile individuals or special circumstances, even if the crime had happened within the jurisdiction of another bureau. Ned's home was within the physical boundaries of the West bureau, which made the West L.A. station the occurrence division. So, fortunately for Rick, even if Robbery-Homicide was running the case, the West L.A. people would have been first at the scene, which meant Mimi may have had a near-virgin look at the crime scene.

"If I *was* working with them, that would be all the more reason I couldn't help you. Sorry."

"Who said I wanted help? Maybe I have some things to tell you."

"Yeah? Like?"

"Like Ned may have joined a private-concierge service just before he died. And *like* several other high-profile clients of that service have been accused of criminal acts. Big names, major shit, and all of it recent, *like* within the last month."

She glanced at the tabloid, which she so clearly preferred over his company. "What kind of criminal acts?"

"International drug smuggling and child pornography, for starters. Mimi, it may not be a coincidence that they all belong to the same service. It could be the link that connects them."

"Connects them to what, a serial killer? Are they all dead?"

"Not dead. Caught. Snared. They're all embroiled in career-ending scandals and most are looking at significant prison time if they're convicted. Maybe Ned wasn't supposed to die. Maybe he was supposed to have his career ended, too, and something went wrong. Someone should follow up on that. You, for example."

This was the moment when Rick would have handed her the TPC card with the word *Extortion?* on the back in Ned's handwriting, but he didn't want to have to lie to her about where he got it. And he wasn't quite ready to talk about the missing package, either.

"Where did you come up with this information? Do you know all these people personally?"

"Ned? Personally? I've known him since he was five, and he isn't into whips and chains. He's not a killer, and he wasn't suicidal. He had everything to live for, as the cliché goes."

"Did Ned tell you about this service? Did he have suspicions?"

Lie, Bayless. She's never going to get the significance otherwise.

He drew Lane Chandler's card out of his jacket pocket. "Ned was using this as a marker in a book he loaned me. Take a look at what he wrote on the back."

She glanced at the question Ned had scribbled on the back, her lips pursing as she turned the card over and continued to scrutinize it. "Not much to go on, Sherlock."

"Right, but Ned also paid me a visit at my cabin the night before he and his girlfriend were found dead. He said he was in trouble, that someone was trying to blackmail him. I had other things on my mind and sent him away. The next day, well, you know what happened."

She closed one eye, squinting at him. "So, this is about your guilt?"

"It's about follow-up, Mimi. Your specialty. You *need* to check this out—or get one of those RHD hotshots to do it."

Her expression said gimme a fricking break, but he knew Mimi, and she wouldn't have cleaned it up that much. "You know how they are, Rick. They're gods. The stink of the O.J. case will never go away, but they still walk on water. What do you think my chances are of getting them to go along with this? They'll laugh me off the case and loan me out to Palos Verdes."

It was a credit to Rick's years of practice that he didn't smile.

She held out the card, which he pointedly ignored.

"It ain't happening, Bayless," she insisted. "From what I hear, the case is being written up as a murder-suicide, and the lab results aren't even in yet. That's how sure they are."

Rick's jaw clenched so tightly he could hear a click in his ears. "How *sure* they are? How could they be sure of anything at this point? Maybe it's how anxious they are to be rid of this case. Did you ever think to ask yourself why, Mimi? Did it even occur to you that something else might be going on here?"

Mimi sighed. "I know cover-up is a buzz phrase these days, but it's a little early for that, don't you think? I was at the crime scene, and it sure as hell looked like a murder-suicide to me."

That's what Rick had been waiting to hear from her, but he didn't want to look too eager. Better to continue his rant a little longer. "And isn't that convenient for everyone concerned. They're not even going to bother with the lab reports? Either that came down from above, which raises more questions, or these guys are lazy."

Mimi shrugged, as if to say probably both. She peered at Rick. "If it were me, I'd write it off as a coincidence. Do you think it might be your history, not to mention *animosity,* toward the department that's causing you to look for conspiracies where there are none?"

"My *history* is exactly why I can't write it off." With that, he changed the subject. "Take another look at that card. Do you recognize the name?"

"Lane Chandler?" She shook her head. "Should I?"

"We booked her for prostitution when she was a juvenile living on the streets—fifteen years old, to be exact. She was calling herself Lane Chandler, but her real name was Lucy Cox."

Mimi rolled back in her chair, stunned. She stared at the card. "Holy shit, this is the kid that set off the firestorm. You might still be working in vice if not for her. Me, too, for that matter."

"I never shed a tear about leaving vice. The point is, Lane Chandler has a criminal past, even if she was a juvenile at the time—and we need to know what she's been doing since. Does she have an adult record, anything at all? I'd love to know how she ended up with clients like the CEO of TopCo and a hot commodity like Simon Shan."

"She represents Simon Shan?"

Mimi's eyes widened. Apparently Shan *was* a hot commodity. Rick didn't keep up with celebrity gossip, but he'd seen enough of it on Gotcha.com to know that Lane's service had become a lightning rod. The coincidence of so many clients in trouble at one company had not slipped Seth Black's attention, either. Of the bunch, Shan had been cited as the one with the most to lose.

That was before Ned Talbert died under gruesome circumstances, but Ned wasn't mentioned as a client of TPC, which meant the list had probably been made up before he joined—and Black had noticed the pattern even before Ned's death.

Rick added some more names. "U.S. congressman Burton Carr and Priscilla Brandt, who's hawking a book about manners. It's quite a list."

"Ms. Pris?" Mimi seemed impressed. "Still, the case is all but closed, and they're not going to open it up again because Ned joined a concierge service whose clients are having a string of bad luck. So, what do you think is going on?"

"I don't know, but I sure as hell wish I'd listened to what Ned was trying to tell me."

She scribbled down a note on her desk blotter, which was unlikely ever to be found again, given all the doodling already there. "Maybe I could do some checking on Lane

Chandler or Lucy Cox, just for old time's sake and because I'm kind of curious myself. Not that I owe you any favors. Because I sure as hell don't."

"Thanks," he said, deadpan. Better not to let her know that he was breathing easier. He lingered, wondering how to segue to his next concern.

She ripped open a bag of chips, about to wedge a few too many into her open mouth, when she realized he was still intent on something—her. "What? You hungry?"

"I was just wondering about the evidence from the crime scene. No big deal, but I left a package over at Ned's. I thought one of the techs might have picked it up."

"Rick, you're not really asking me to mess with the evidence, are you? Tell me you're not."

He shrugged, tilting just enough to grab a couple chips from her bag. He was taking a chance by tying himself with the package, but what the hell. Getting caught with his hand in a fifteen-year-old cookie jar was the least of his worries these days, especially with his gut telling him the package had been lifted before the police ever got there. Mimi might be able to confirm that for him.

"You could tell me if it's there, couldn't you?" he coaxed. "It's an old brown bubble pack, eight by eleven, unmarked but pretty beaten up. I'd like to have it back when the investigation's over."

"What's inside?"

"Personal stuff," he said, wondering if he could still blush. "It's a little embarrassing."

She heaved a sigh and picked up her sandwich, poking a bubble of red jelly back between soggy crusts. "Don't push it, Rick."

He nodded. "Right, I'll leave you to your lunch." He

had a feeling she would check. Yeah, definitely, Mimi was going to check. It was that Peeping Tom thing. Whether she'd tell him was another question.

10

Rumor had it that the King of Rumors was agoraphobic. Seth Black of Gotcha.com had been outed as housebound by rival gossip Web sites. That's what had given Rick the idea of staking out the man's surprisingly modest apartment in the Hollywood Hills area. Either online gossip didn't pay well—which wasn't likely since the gossip sites were now scooping the mainstream media and forcing the big guys to go to them for entertainment news—or Black was a frugal man. Possibly he was too housebound to relocate. Regardless, he'd broken Ned's murder-suicide story hours before the mainstream press had, and Rick was curious how the thirty-two-year-old agoraphobic got his information.

Rick bowed his head for a moment and dug his fingers into the aching muscles of his temples. He could feel the fatigue of his nonstop day. He'd been parked down the street from Black's place for going on two hours, but so far he'd seen no one except a telephone repairman, who got no answer when he knocked on the door of Black's ground-floor apartment. Rick had tried Black's number before he drove over, but the phone went right to voice mail. He was beginning to wonder if Black was home, and if this surveillance idea was a good one.

That morning, after Rick had the epiphany about Lane Chandler, he'd tracked down the address of Jenny Shu, Ned's housekeeper, and he'd gone over to pay her a visit. It didn't surprise Rick to find Jenny upset, but he hadn't expected a complete collapse. She'd been with Ned for years and Rick knew her well, so of course, he'd knelt down to hug the tiny Asian woman, and of course, they'd cried. Her sobs had ripped right through him, and Rick, who had been stoic until now, broke. Grief had washed through him until he shook, and Jenny had tried her best to comfort him. Maybe it was as simple as seeing someone else who knew and loved Ned.

Rick was sure his meeting with Jenny was a large part of what had exhausted him so completely. When they'd regained their composure, she'd patted his face and told him how sorry she was. She invited him in for tea, but he'd known he couldn't take her up on that. Reminiscing about Ned would have killed him. The pain she'd already touched into had almost killed him. He did manage to ask her about the package, but she'd seen nothing that matched his description, and he was satisfied with that. He couldn't ask her about what she'd witnessed when she arrived at the scene. Neither one of them could have handled that conversation. Maybe another time. Maybe.

After that, Rick had gone home to eat and get some rest. Good intentions, but somehow he'd found himself at the computer for another look at Seth Black's site. That's where he'd discovered that Black, with the help of Jack the Giant Killer, was routinely scooping not only the mainstream press, but all the other online sites, and that Black had been the first one to break the news on virtually every TPC client. From there Rick had gone to see Mimi, knowing in the back of his mind that a meeting with Black was inevitable.

Rick figured Black relied on the local paparazzi for pictures and salacious tidbits, but he had to be getting the more personal details from an inside source. A family member, friend or employee were the obvious ways, but given the nature of a concierge service, it only made sense that considerable client information was stored away somewhere, which had Rick wondering if TPC had a mole, someone intent on extortion as Ned's card had suggested. If clients confided in their private concierges the way they did in their hairstylists, there should be plenty of blackmail material to go around.

Still, drug busts? Child porn? That wasn't info you confided to anyone.

TPC had branch offices in San Francisco and Las Vegas, and according to the Web site they would soon be expanding across the country, but Rick was only interested in their corporate offices here in L.A. He'd found an employee tree with the names of some of the company's key players, but rather than run a background check on each of them, which would probably yield nothing, he'd decided to stake out Black's place to see who showed up. Even if the inside source wasn't a TPC employee, he was curious, especially about the mysterious Giant Killer. And Rick was betting that some of the really juicy stuff was hand-carried to Black since everyone knew that e-mail was no longer secure for anyone, including the country's chief executive.

Rick took a swig from a can of Coke that had gone flat. His last serious attempt at eating had been the Chinese takeout that morning, and he hadn't thought to bring any food with him. Maybe that's why he was perspiring and dizzy. It was warm outside, and hotter in the car.

He patted the front pocket of his jeans and realized he'd

left something behind this morning, a bottle of prescription pills. They were probably sitting on the nightstand at his place. He forgot them half the time anyway, and when he did take them, he felt like shit, worse than before. He ought to flush them down the fricking toilet, but he couldn't. He was dead without them. Well, dead sooner.

He shook off the morbid thought and focused on Black's place. There were still no signs of life, so to speak, but Rick had planned for that. He'd brought a five-by-seven envelope, addressed to Black, in case he needed a reason to go to the door himself.

He grabbed it and let himself out of the car.

Whoa, something was wrong. The cracks in the sidewalk appeared to slide back and forth as he approached the four-story apartment building, causing him to weave like a drunk. He stopped to get his bearings, and as he glanced up, he saw the mail slot open on Black's door. Someone was peeking through it from the other side, Rick realized. The slot was nearly at eye level and large enough to get a glimpse of a man's face.

Rick rushed over to the stoop. "Mr. Black! Seth! I need to talk to you. It's urgent." The slot banged shut and Rick heard the scrape of a sliding bolt, which meant there must be some way to lock it. He pounded on the door, hoping if he made enough noise Black would be forced to answer. He might not want his neighbors calling the cops, especially if he was trying to keep his work location a secret. There were also zoning laws.

Finally, the slot popped open and a gun barrel poked through. "Shut up, you fucking loony, or I'll shoot you!" Black hissed.

Interesting approach, Rick thought, moving out of Black's line of fire, which was severely limited, as was his intelligence, apparently. Rick decided to appeal directly to the man's entrepreneurial instincts, otherwise known as greed.

"I'm willing to pay for information," Rick said. "Any price you want."

"Yeah?" The gun barrel disappeared, replaced by eyes as black and beady as the suicidal mouse who'd taken over Rick's kitchen. "What kind of information?"

"Are you Seth Black? Can I see proof?"

"You aren't seeing anything until I know who you are and what you want."

Rick slipped a fake business card through the slot. It identified him as an IRS agent. There was a cell-phone number and an e-mail address, both of which were accounts in the fake name on the card.

"What do you want to know?" Black asked after he'd looked at the card.

"I want whatever information you can get me on a Century City company called The Private Concierge, and I'm particularly interested in its president, Lane Chandler."

"Is she in some kind of tax trouble?"

"I want to know about Lane Chandler's dark side and what's really going on in that concierge service. You call me with that kind of information, and I'll tell you what kind of trouble she's in. Share and share alike."

"You're crazy, man," Black grumbled.

"Maybe," Rick said, "but I pay well." He drew a hundred-dollar bill from the envelope he carried, which had four more of the same denomination inside. He slipped the bill and the envelope through the slot. It was all part of the cost of doing business.

"Geez," Black whispered, but with far less irritation in

his voice. "Yeah, maybe. We'll see. If I get something on her, maybe I'll call."

"You call, I pay. No maybes."

The slot closed and locked. Rick smiled. No one wanted trouble with the IRS. It was always easier to cooperate, just in case.

As Rick took a shortcut across the lawn and started back to his SUV, a flicker of movement caught his eye. Through a gate that led to the back of the building, he saw a shrouded figure flit out of his line of sight and disappear down an alley. Rick guessed it was a male by the height, and he'd just come out of the apartment building.

The rusty latch was jammed. Rick forced the gate, butting it hard with his shoulder. It flew open, and he broke into a sprint. When he hit the alley behind the building, he was already laboring. He stopped to scope the area out and catch his breath. Whoever he'd seen had a good head start. If he couldn't catch him, he might be able to ID his car, get the license-plate number. It was worth a try.

The block had several apartments, and the alley was covered parking with mostly empty stalls. Broken-down cars filled the remaining spaces, and debris from the Dumpsters stuck to Rick's feet as he ran, searching the shadowy crevices at the same time. A couple of tenants, trying to jump-start a car, turned to see who was coming by this time, and what the rush was.

Tenants or car thieves? Rick didn't stop to find out. Nor did he ask for directions. He'd learned from his years as a cop that they would almost certainly point him the wrong way.

The alley emptied into a quiet backstreet. Rick had no clue which way to go, and his vision was playing tricks again. He could see a small pack of dogs, probably trailing a female in heat, and some skateboarders on the opposite sidewalk, but there was no sign of a fleeing man in a hooded tunic and dark colors head to toe. Could it be Jack the Giant Killer he was after?

He headed east on a hunch and heard the roar of an engine. As he turned, a gleaming black car careened from out of nowhere and roared straight at him. It jumped the curb and grazed him, knocking him over the bumper before it tossed him to the ground. He hit, tucked and rolled, going with the momentum of the impact. He flipped at least three times, still doubled up to protect his head and his vitals. Jesus, what a day.

He forced himself to get up the second he stopped rolling, but the car was gone. No license number. He wasn't quick enough for that, but from the chassis it had looked like one of those expensive new luxury hybrid cars. Jack the Giant Killer was environmentally aware? A Jolly Green Giant killer? And wealthy at that.

Ah, life in southern California, Rick thought, groaning as he bent to dust himself off. He would have some bruises, but otherwise, he was okay, relatively speaking.

Lane glanced at her watch. It was 9:00 p.m., and she'd had a carnival ride of a day. Her triumphant walk on the Avenue of the Stars was over the moment she got back to the office. The police were waiting for her in the reception area, and they'd wanted to talk about Simon Shan, specifically his whereabouts at various times. Lane had insisted that TPC's client information was confidential. They'd finally gone, but she had a horrible feeling they would be back with a court order. Worse, she'd been accosted in front of prospective clients. A husband and wife real-estate-development team had arrived for their appointment while the police were still there, trying to intimidate client information out of Lane.

Little chance she'd see the couple again.

What she really wanted to do now was assume the fetal position and maybe suck her thumb. But she didn't have time. She had one last task, and it had become a religious ritual, possibly because it gave her a feeling of control, however illusory. Every night before closing up shop she used her cell phone's voice-activated recorder to review the important events of the day and update her to-do list.

Somehow, she would get through that ritual tonight, but first, she needed to breathe. She found the universal remote hiding under a stack of papers on her desk. The remote coordinated most of the electronic equipment in her office, and she used it to turn up the mood music playing on her sound system. The bluesy songs of heartbreak and loss soothed her for some reason, especially when she was stressed and overworked. But their magic wasn't working at the moment.

She scooped up her cell, left her desk and fell into the room's upholstered chaise, exhausted. No matter what she did to block out the whispering voices of doom in her head, she couldn't escape the fear that her company was under siege. And if it was, who was going next?

There were people who might want to harm her, enemies from her past, but she wasn't a threat to them now. If she'd meant to name names, she would have done it years ago. Surely they knew that. Now she had too much to lose herself. But the real question was why. If they did want to hurt her, why would they do it this way?

The Priscilla Brandt situation had deteriorated even

further this afternoon. Maybe it shouldn't have surprised Lane that an advice expert wouldn't take advice from anyone. Lane had urged her to consult an attorney, which had infuriated her. Apparently all of Pris's advisers had suggested the same thing, and now she wasn't taking anyone's calls, including Lane's. Lane had been trying to reach her all evening.

Some people created their own problems, and Pris might be one of them. Lane heaved a sigh and pressed the microphone icon on her cell phone's digital display, activating the system. Maybe she'd feel better once the record keeping had been taken care of.

She began to dictate: "Priscilla Brandt wigged out today and attacked a homeless man on her property. I did some short-term damage control by canceling her interview with the morning-show anchor. Long-term, the woman needs anger management, medical intervention and possibly a straitjacket."

Lane smiled at the thought. She spent so much time stroking egos and smoothing feathers that it actually felt good to say what she really thought. Also libelous, probably. Certainly, contract-breaching.

She jabbed the Replay button to record over the item. "Monday, October 7. Priscilla Brandt had a confrontation with a homeless man on her property…."

Lane's voice lapsed into a monotone as she went through the rest of the day's events. When she got to the to-do list, she used verbal commands to delete the things she'd done and add several new items. At the top of her list was the itinerary for her Dallas trip later this week. Next was a reminder to check in with clients who weren't in crisis. She owed Jerry Blair at TopCo a call to go over some ideas for his daughter's sweet sixteen. He'd finally hired the party planner she'd recommended, but she wanted him to know she was thinking about him and his concerns. She was also tempted to ask him for some advice. And maybe a good lawyer.

Lane had become so engrossed in her thoughts she didn't notice that someone had taken advantage of the office's open-door policy. The last of her staff had left an hour ago, and no one who didn't work in the building could get past the security downstairs. She'd thought she was alone. But she couldn't have been more wrong. A man stood at the doorway behind her, listening to her every word. He didn't work in the building, and he'd easily evaded the building's security. He was about to *invade* hers.

11

Priscilla Brandt marched from one end of her living room to the other, yanking open the curtains as she went. It was dark and she couldn't see what manner of monsters lurked outside, hiding in the bushes, but they could see in. So, let them, she'd decided. Let the paparazzi spy on her. Let the police arrest her. She was not going to be trapped in a boarded-up house like a cornered animal. She was not going to hide or cower or pretend to be repentant.

All right, she *was* glad she hadn't killed him, but that was all.

She tugged at the last column of drapes, which didn't want to open. The whole house was computerized, including the window treatments, which were programmed to open and close morning and evening, as well as adjust for daylight saving time. They could also be controlled by remote, but given her mood, yanking was mandatory. She would have yanked the devil's dick if she'd been able to get her hands on it.

Someone had caught her on tape this morning dealing with that stubborn mule of a homeless man, and then sold the footage to a muckraking gossip Web site. From there, the networks had picked it up, and all day long Priscilla had been forced to watch hideous clips of herself abusing a defenseless, unconscious person.

That made *her* the monster, of course. She'd been advised by her publicity people to call an attorney, avoid the press and say nothing, but that wasn't her style. And she'd *had* to talk to the police. They'd shown up on her doorstep, ready to cart her down to the station to question her. It was only because she'd hyperventilated and had to breathe into a bag that they'd agreed to talk to her in her home.

There was no one she could call. Her parents would have added to the embarrassment. They were free spirits who lived in a ramshackle double-wide on a scrubby patch near the California-Oregon border that technically put them in Oregon and saved them a buttload in state taxes. They didn't wear shoes and were the impetus for most of the Do Nots in her book. She'd had no time to make friends since she got to L.A., or do anything but focus on her career. Her road to success was the express lane, total and all-consuming.

So, she'd brazened it out alone, telling the police it was self-defense and the man had been harassing her for days, part of which was true. He had been harassing her, and she *was* defending her dream, damn it, even if this was a different guy. She'd even admitted to giving him money, explaining that she lived alone and was terrified of him.

Thank God, he'd gone away this morning. He'd regained consciousness well before the police arrived, hustled off her property and disappeared. Despite a thorough search of the neighborhood, they hadn't been able to find him, and no charges had been pressed against her. That was the only bit of luck she'd had.

Priscilla continued yanking curtains, and when she had

them all opened, the living room resembled an amphitheater with the audience hidden in the darkness beyond the windows. She poured herself a glass of an excellent French cab, swirled it and held it to her nose, taking in the hints of cherry and licorice. She advised people on how to choose wines. Mostly she was faking it, and any wine expert would have known, but the public didn't. She'd been elevated to the level of expert on many things, which could be the problem.

She coughed as the wine went down wrong. Maybe it was too much pressure for a pimply-faced kid who'd grown up in a border town and ate fast food with plastic forks. Maybe that's why she was cracking up, insulting people—and now, assaulting them.

Her Darwin phone rang, and she could tell by the ring tone that it was Lane Chandler, but she'd been fielding calls and advice all day, including from Lane, who'd joined the chorus in advising her to speak with an attorney. Apparently TPC even provided legal consults for its top-tier clients. But Priscilla didn't trust attorneys. She didn't even have an assistant, which made life hellishly busy, but she harbored deep fears of being exposed as a fraud and a hick.

Besides, Priscilla Brandt had done just fine on her own.

She left the wineglass on the bar and walked to the window, defiant, hands on her hips. Indignant tears welled. Let them look at her, the assholes. They were lucky she wasn't naked, wielding a bullhorn and staging a protest for privacy rights. They could try to destroy her, but she would never let it happen. She would even find some way to turn this debacle around and exploit it for the good of her career. But she wasn't about to do anything as ridiculous as going to rehab or donating time to a homeless shelter. Let the retarded, boozed-up movie starlets do rehab. *She* was an author.

Possibly she would turn this into a chapter of her next book. Not a catastrophe after all, but a life lesson. *Don't let the turkeys get you down. Shoot them and eat them with prune stuffing for Thanksgiving dinner.*

Her phone rang again, startling her. She'd left it on the bar, but she wasn't taking one more call tonight unless it was from Skip McGinnis, the kid who would be executive producing her talk show, provided he ever got his head out of his ass. If he was looking for excuses to drop the ball, he certainly had one after today's hot mess. She'd been calling him all afternoon, but kept getting his voice mail with that lying message about how important her call was to him. All she wanted was a chance to explain in her own words.

She rushed to the bar, but the phone's display said the call was from an unknown caller, probably the press. Damn McGinnis. This was humiliating. Every call that wasn't him felt like another rejection, and they were piling up. She should have let her manager call him. Let her collect the rejections.

She toyed with the phone, wondering what to do. The last couple of messages she'd left him might have been a bit snappish. She probably shouldn't have threatened to go over his head and have him fired if he didn't call back, but he couldn't have taken that seriously. Surely. Maybe she would try again, something humorous. To make up for the surliness.

She got his voice mail on the first ring, but the message had been changed. His voice was tight and furious. "If this is Priscilla Brandt, your show is as good as dead. And if I had my way your career would be dead, too. Don't. Call. Back."

Pris gasped and dropped the phone. How could he do that? Everyone who called him was going to hear that message. She felt her knees buckling and was afraid she would end up on the floor. It was all over. Tomorrow's papers would have the shots of her collapsing after Skip McGinnis rejected her via voice mail.

She pressed her palms to the counter and hung on. No, she wasn't going to give him that satisfaction. *No way!* In an act of symbolic defiance, she upended her wineglass and drained the entire thing. When the wine was gone, she banged the glass on the bar, shaking, but grateful that her nerve was coming back. No one was going to talk to her like that. There was only going to be one career in need of life support when this was over and that was *his*. Skip McGinnis, that pipsqueak excuse for a talk-show producer, was finished.

Rick Bayless was struck by two things as he listened to the woman who called herself Lane Chandler dictate information about her clients—the moody rhythm-and-blues track playing in the background and the tension crackling in the air. From his vantage point at the door of her office, he had a three-quarter view of her stretched out in the chaise. She was facing away from him, holding what looked like a high-tech cell phone, and he'd made a mental note of the names she mentioned, some of whom he recognized as VIPs of one stripe or another. Her comments were candid, as was her obvious annoyance with certain clients. But it was difficult to concentrate on what she said when his mind kept screening the image of a frighteningly seductive fifteen-year-old, who turned out to be as challenging as any street criminal he'd ever dealt with.

He'd taken her for older, eighteen at least. She'd stared right through him with her chilly azure eyes. They were as blue as jewels, and she was as bold and wary as any professional streetwalker he'd ever come across. She'd promised him his money's worth, anything he wanted, things he'd never dreamed of, whatever that meant. As he'd moved closer, he'd spotted her lean, wiry frame and gamine features—and realized he was dealing with a kid.

A kid? It had hit him like a bucket of cold water. He'd thought she was legal. And worse, maybe he'd wanted her to be legal because if he was being honest, he'd felt a flash of desire that was almost painful. Jesus, no kid should be out on the street having that effect on grown men. That could be why he'd been a little rough on her when he put her in the cuffs.

When she'd realized she was going to jail, the color had drained from her face. She'd begged him not to take her. She'd even tried to make him believe her sad story about a sick friend. Sad because they *all* had a sick friend. When she realized she couldn't talk her way out of it, she'd put up one hell of a fight. Ferocious didn't cover it, all the time shrieking that her friend was going to die. He used Tasers only to disarm kids with weapons, but he wasn't sure a Taser would have contained her.

Lane Chandler had grown up, but Rick's brain had no trouble making that transition. She'd been thirty-five at fifteen. The changes he saw now were all physical. He remembered a lean, starved, ready-to-spring body and a thick mop of dark brown hair that completely covered her face when she looked down. She could have set up housekeeping under that curtain of hair. But when her head came back up and the curtain opened, her gaze had scorched him.

Now, the mop had been brought under control. Sleek and glossy with mahogany hues, it curved toward her face like a whip, but it was still abundant enough that she had to comb it off her face with her fingers.

He wondered what she looked like these days. Still as cold and forbidding as a mountain fjord? Swim at your own risk? Or had the icicles been reserved for him, her persecutor? And what was that *music* about? "Unchained Melody," "Go Your Own Way," "Everybody Hurts" by REM? She didn't strike him as the type that would be heavily into heartbreak music, but those were the songs playing softly in the background. Did some guy just dump her?

He closed the door on the personal questions, concerned where they were taking him. The only one that mattered was whether or not she could have pulled off the gruesome alleged murder-suicide at Ned's place and escaped with the package. Rick had been working on a theory of his own about how Ned and Holly had actually died, and he couldn't imagine a woman like Lane Chandler accomplishing what he had in mind. Too much physical force required, especially in dealing with a man as big as Ned…unless she had an accomplice.

Lane's chin came up, and she scanned the office windows the way an animal sniffs the air, sensing another presence. He could see her profile, and the beauty that had been nascent then was evident now. The contours of her face had filled out, softening the angles and hiding the raw bones, the desperation. Her lips were parted, glistening. He wanted to think he'd done her a favor by getting her off the streets. That had been part of his goal. But now it forced him to consider another question. What a grim twist of fate it would be if by saving her, he'd somehow allowed her to cross Ned's path and be the instrument of his destruction. The thought made him ill.

He must have moved because she sprang up from the chaise.

"Who's there?" She spotted him in the doorway and began stabbing at the buttons on her cell. One of them lit up, flashing.

A panic button, Rick realized. She'd alerted security. The male voice coming from the phone's mouthpiece confirmed his suspicion.

"Ms. Chandler? Are you all right?"

Rick was on top of her before she could respond. He grabbed the phone out of her hand and fired instructions at her. "Tell the security guard you hit the panic button by mistake. Tell him everything is fine."

"Fuck off," she snarled under her breath. "Give me that phone."

He caught her as she lunged at him, spun her around and put her in an armlock. "Do it," he warned, applying just enough pressure to make sure she cooperated. "Or I'll tell him who you really are. I'll tell everyone, Lucia."

"What?" She craned around, as if she didn't know what he was talking about. Apparently, she didn't recognize him, either. But when he released her, she didn't hesitate. She took the phone from him and pressed the panic button.

"Sorry," she told the security guard. "I hit the button by mistake. Everything's fine."

"You sure, Ms. Chandler?" the guard said. "We found an exit door ajar down here on the first floor. The alarm didn't go off, which means there could be a problem with the system. Should I run up there, take a look around?"

She assured him that wasn't necessary, turned off the phone and tried to slip it into her jacket pocket. Rick took it away from her again, aware of the treasures it must contain.

"Who are you? And why did you call me Lucia?" Haughty and unflinching, she seemed determined to brazen it out. The years had softened her facial features, but little else. Inside, she was probably still as tough as a wire cutter, but that had to be mostly facade. A woman who'd built a successful concierge service from the ground up knew what people needed, inside and out. She played on those needs, had to. She personified the private concierge. Lane's early clients gushed her praises on the Web site, giving testimonials with the passion of religious converts. Apparently she'd saved them all in one way or another. Rick wouldn't have been surprised if she'd delivered some babies.

Her eye color seemed different than he remembered. It was still blue, but closer to royal than azure, and not nearly as sharp or crystalline. He wondered if this was part of her identity change, maybe contact lenses. But that could wait. Mimi hadn't gotten back to him with the Nexus-Lexus results, so Rick had no proof of any adult priors. And this wasn't the time to confront Lane about the murder-suicide or the package. But she was a woman under a lot of pressure—and he could apply more. Maybe she'd pop.

"Because that's your name, Lucia—Lucy—Cox. Is your mind racing yet? Just wait. If you're telling yourself that your juvenile records were sealed and no one could possibly prove what you did back then, don't be so sure. And in your case, it's not going to matter, anyway. The rumors will be enough to muddy up your professional reputation."

She stiffened, caught somewhere between outrage and

disbelief. He wondered how long it would take her to figure out that he wasn't a robber, a rapist or a blackmailer. He was the cop who'd put her in juvie—and made sure she didn't get out for a very long time.

Lane touched the tattered rubber band on her wrist, knowing that nothing could jump-start her frozen heart. The intruder had her cell phone and it might as well have been a weapon. At first she'd detected something familiar about his brush cut and aviator sunglasses, but it could have been the military thing, which was burned into the American psyche and a staple in plenty of action movies. All the bad guys wore metal-framed glasses, rode motorcycles and looked like RoboCop.

"Who are you?" she asked. "And what do you want?"

He studied the cell's display. "What kind of car do you drive?"

"I prefer walking."

"I'm sure the security people know what you drive. Shall I ask them?" He held up the phone.

"It's a Lexus hybrid."

"Nice, a social conscience." He nodded. "Where were you this afternoon at 4:00 p.m.?"

She hesitated, wondering if had something to do with her visit from the police about Simon Shan, but no, that had been earlier, when she got back from lunch. "I was right here, working. Do I need an alibi for something?"

"You might. Tell me about your clients—and start with Ned Talbert."

Lane had told no one but Darwin about Ned Talbert joining the service. Talbert may have told someone, but she thought it more likely that this man was trying to bluff information out of her. Still, that wasn't her greatest concern right now. She'd already begun to ask herself if he could be the person behind the assault on her company. There was no way to know what his motive might be, but clearly, he was after her, too.

There was a metal letter opener lying on her desk, but he would probably get there first. "I don't discuss my clients with anyone," she informed him. "And if I did, I'd have to have that person killed."

He tilted his head at her, as if she was a kid he'd caught in a lie. "Good thing your cell can't talk. You'd have to have it killed. Priscilla Brandt needs a straitjacket and the police are asking questions about Simon Shan. And oh, yes, Jerry Blair of TopCo has a very spoiled daughter about to turn sixteen."

He stopped, as if to say, "Do you get it, Lane? I heard everything, and I can use it against you. It would be like swatting a fly."

Heat crept up Lane's neck. Threats had the unfortunate effect of bringing out the street fighter in her. At the same time, she was aware that she'd put one of her favorite moody CDs in the music system. The Doobie Brothers soared into the chorus of "What a Fool Believes," and she let the music work on her, soothe her. She'd given up any hope that this man could be easily dealt with. He seemed determined to be her worst nightmare, another action-movie cliché, except that they weren't in a theater.

"What do you want?" she asked him. "Is it money?"

"I think that's my line, isn't it?"

By the disdain in his tone, he must have been talking about sex, but she had no idea why. "Listen, I have a business to run, people to take care of. Just tell me what you want."

"People, right—all your hotshot clients?"

"No, my staff. I employ hundreds, and they depend on me."

"Did Ned depend on you?"

Lane flinched as the intruder reached inside his leather jacket. He came straight for her, and she ducked down, ready to fight if she had to. He'd pulled out a wallet-size card, she realized.

"Maybe I'm looking for a private concierge," he said. He handed her the card, and then returned her cell with a mock-courteous nod. "I'll be in touch."

Lane glanced down at what appeared to be his business card. It had a company name and a phone number. She read the name Bayless Extreme Solutions with a slow-dawning sense of recognition, but she wasn't ready to let herself believe it. This wasn't possible. He was the part of her past she wanted to expunge, topping the list of people she never wanted to see again. How had he turned up in her life after all these years?

She wasn't sure how much time had passed, but when she looked up, he was gone. She was wet everywhere, filmed in perspiration. His card was twisted in her fingers, and the dampness at the back of her neck was icy cold.

Never, she thought. Never assume a bad day can't get worse.

12

Darwin didn't fear death, dismemberment or even a mild case of herpes. He did fear spitting on Janet Bonofiglio when he kissed her. He tended to do that when he got excited, but only if he was talking, and he and Janet weren't doing all that much talking right now. She was toying with the hair that had tumbled onto his forehead like a dark dust mop, pulling on the rubber-band curls and murmuring about how smart he was. He was trying not to suffocate from lack of oxygen.

He also feared not getting an erection or worse, getting one and losing control of it. The possibility of premature ejaculation with a goddess like Janet was unbearable. He'd waited much too long to have it all over at the speed of light.

"Darwin, sweetie, are you all right?"

"How could I be any better?" he squeaked. "I'm with you." He sounded like a horny teenager. Felt like one, too. This was asinine. He was nuclear waste, unstable, uncontainable and subject to detonation. She deserved better, but he didn't have any better, and he wasn't noble enough to tell her that.

She was sitting on his lap!

"Daaarwin, say something nerdy and cute. Did I ever tell you that Einstein is my favorite historical figure?"

"You mean like 'God is in the details' Einstein?"

"Yes," she breathed, "God is in the details. I love that. Now, do something with numbers. Big numbers excite me."

Big numbers excited her? Was she for real? "Pi equals 3.1415926535," he said, and then to dazzle her further, added, "Pi is the ratio of a circle's circumference to its diameter—and it goes on forever without repeating. I gave you ten digits, but it's possible to calculate an infinite number."

"Like a bazillion?"

"Yeah, like that. Pretty *exciting*, huh?"

She blinked and nodded. "I'll bet you're good at everything—programming TiVo, VCRs, remote controls? Can you fix computers?"

"I can build a computer," he said, "a computer that would make you gasp."

She bent to kiss his nose, but he lifted his chin and caught her mouth with his. Her soft and yielding mouth. This was nirvana. Maybe he should say that. She might like big metaphysical words, too. He could hear himself whispering excerpts from *The Way of the White Clouds* as they were building to simultaneous orgasms.

"Are you warm enough?" he asked her. "We could go back inside."

"Mmm, I'm fine right here. The view is beautiful."

They were out on the back deck of his hillside condo, overlooking the bright lights of Los Angeles, and she was fluttering her closed eyelashes and brushing her breasts against his skinny chest. Enormous breasts, and he was pretty sure they were real, too. Not that it would have mattered at this point.

He didn't understand the girl—or why she wanted to be

with him. She seemed inordinately interested in his brain, which always worked the way it was supposed to, unless he wasn't taking his meds, but he'd been an Eagle Scout there. He hadn't missed a dose since he met her, six months ago.

Tonight had been a long time coming, partly because of him and his male fears, like did her interest in his brain mean she had no interest in his penis? That would take the pressure off, but it would also kick the crapola out of his lifelong fantasy of sex with a Victoria's Secret catalog model.

Janet wasn't one, but she could have been. Easy. He'd first met her at a comic-book expo at the L.A. Convention Center. She was the ex-girlfriend of a graphic artist who was famous in comic-book circles, and Janet had inspired his series about the adventures of a heroine named Jezebel Truly. She was by far the most beautiful woman who'd ever caught his eye *and* smiled at him. He'd been so shocked he'd nearly fallen over a floor display of classic Superman comics.

"Maybe you've heard this one?" he said. "'We are just an advanced breed of monkey on a minor planet of a very average star.'"

"Carl Sagan." She beamed, pleased.

"Close," he assured her. "It's Stephen Hawking. He also said, 'But we can understand the universe. That's what makes us very special.'"

"Yeah? Cool."

"'To read is to voyage through time.'" He waited for her to guess.

"Stephen Hawking?"

"Carl Sagan." They both laughed. "He was talking about the ability to read books that are hundreds, even thousands, of years old."

"Wow," she whispered, shivering. "You are so smart."

"And you're cold. Let's go inside. I have a terrific way of keeping you warm, and it involves the mathematical formula for combustion."

His cell phone rang, dancing on the bistro table right next to them, but Darwin didn't even give it a glance. "Let it ring," he said.

She giggled—as good as a yes in his book. He was positioning himself to help her up when the ring tone went staccato, urgent. That was Lane, in trouble. He had to answer.

"Lane is calling," the disembodied phone voice announced. "It's urgent."

Darwin snatched up the phone and hit the Talk button. "Lane, this is not a good time. Unless you're dealing with a terrorist attack—make that Osama himself—I'm busy."

"Dar, I'm at the office. A man broke in and threatened me."

He jackknifed up, nearing knocking Janet off his lap. "Are you okay?"

"Yes, he's gone, but he left his business card."

"He threatened you with his business card?"

"Dar, I'm serious. You know this guy, too. It's Rick Bayless, and I think he could be behind the attacks on our clients."

"Rick Bayless?" He focused on the name, trying to place it. "The cop who arrested you back when we were kids?"

"Yes, but I'm not sure he's a cop now."

"Okay, tomorrow. I'll check him out first thing tomorrow. Or later tonight. I have company, Lane. *Commmmpany.*"

"No, this cannot wait. I need a background check,

some computer intelligence on this guy, anything you can find. He runs a company called Bayless Extreme Solutions. Dar? Please?"

Darwin glanced at Janet, who was hanging on his every word and batting her Miss Piggy eyelashes at him. Holy Mother of God, how could Lane do this to him? It was Sophie's Choice.

"Listen, Lane, you're safe, right? Nothing's going to happen tonight." Except right here in this condo, a lifetime first for Darwin LeMaster. "Call security and ask one of the guys to drive you home. Or hire a car. How about that? I'll call one of our limo services and have them send a car for you."

"You can't be serious. The cop who put me in jail when I was fifteen—and kept me there for three years on trumped-up charges!—just broke into my office! He *threatened* me."

Darwin let out a strangled moan and flopped back, nearly dislodging Janet again. "All right, I'll take care of it. *Slamdunkfuck!* Okay, sorry, I'm on it."

He continued to curse like a sailor under his breath, dropped a smile of apology on Janet and hung up without checking to make sure Lane could get home all right. But why was he worried? Lane was a street fighter. She'd saved his butt many more times than he had hers, and apparently she'd scared the guy out of her office.

"I'm sorry," he told Janet, boldly cuddling her. "That was my boss. She wants me to do something we call Net intelligence."

Janet's eyes got wide and deep blue, like they were going for a swim. "Net intel? Wow, sounds hot. Can I watch?"

"Actually, Net intelligence is what's left after you burn out your prefrontal lobe on a video-game marathon."

Janet didn't seem to get the joke, but her hopeful expression never wavered.

Darwin shrugged. The girl wanted to watch him surf the Net, sort through someone's dirty laundry, and who was he to argue? She seemed every bit as excited about that as she had been about making out. Maybe more. Not exactly flattering to his male ego, but he would take what he could get. And maybe make some serious points.

"You can watch, sure." He helped her to her feet and clasped her hand. "Come with me. You're going to love my home office. I call it Command and Control Center 2."

She wriggled her fingers in his grip and cooed, "You had me at command, Captain Kirk."

This was no longer a crush. Janet Bonofiglio felt like the proverbial moth to his back-porch lightbulb. She just wanted to sit and stare at Darwin LeMaster like some adoring kid. It was embarrassing. If she'd been harboring any doubts that he was a genius, they were gone, evaporated in the steam heat of her attraction to his brainpower.

Curled up in the chair next to him in the room he called Command and Control Center 2, she'd been watching him work on his computer intel for the last hour. His fingers moved over the keyboard at the speed of light, and he could make a search engine jump through hoops like a trained seal. Really, he was a ringmaster.

Wow, that was his name, she realized. LeMaster. Perfect.

She hugged herself, aware that he was totally absorbed in his work and not paying any attention to her. She liked that, too. It was cool for a man to have amazing powers of concentration. She just wanted all that amazing concentration focused on her. Or did she?

She gazed at him, her smile fading. She ought to

massage his shoulder blades. They looked tight. But she couldn't bring herself to do it. How weird was it that her only thought was about being a source of pleasure for him, when she was already contemplating the source of pain he almost certainly would be for her?

She'd been so badly screwed over by men. Her last boyfriend hadn't stopped at breaking her heart. He'd broken their legal and binding contract to split the proceeds of his publishing deal, even though she'd contributed the protagonist for his comic-book series. She hadn't had the money to take him to court or the kind of contacts who could have made things happen. She wasn't connected. She was SOL to the tune of about fifty K— and still bitter two years later.

Men had always taken advantage of her good nature, and a few other things. But Darwin did seem different. She loved his lanky frame and moist brown puppy-dog eyes. The slight cleft in his chin was hot, too. But could she trust this guy with her heart? Did he want her heart? Most men didn't. Various body parts, yes, but the heart always got overlooked.

She sighed, and he turned to her with an expression of concern. "Are you okay? I'm sorry. I get lost in this stuff sometimes."

"I know," she said, her smile sad. *Get lost in me,* she thought. "It's okay. I have to go, anyway." Aware of the regret in her voice, she gave him a quick kiss on the cheek, and laughed at herself. She was usually sleeping with a guy she liked by now. She couldn't even remember when she first met Darwin. It was ages ago at a comic-book convention, but they'd been just friends until a few months ago—and had their first kiss tonight. She wanted to go very slowly this time, and that seemed to be okay with him.

"Are you sure?" he said, "I won't be too much longer. No, shit, that's not true. This could go on all night. Sorry."

"I'm sure. I have to be up early tomorrow. The temp agency called with a job for me." She'd been doing temp work to make ends meet since the modeling assignments petered out. But she was also going to school and taking classes, hoping to reboot her life.

He looked as if he wanted to reach for her hand or stop her in some way. "When will I see you again?"

"Soon," she said, determined to sound reassuring.

"Like…how soon?"

She didn't want to lie to him, but she didn't know if she could trust him. Or herself. Or anyone. And she wasn't being completely honest with him, either. Revealing the real Janet, warts and all, was too big a risk. Why, she wondered, did it always have to be so complicated? She took his hand in hers, and felt her heart twist. "It'll happen," she said. "You'll see."

"You've reached Happy Carr's voice mail. This is Happy. If I haven't picked up yet, I'm probably out campaigning for my wonderful husband, Congressman Burton Carr, proud representative of the Thirtieth District. Leave a message at the beep, thanks!"

Burt Carr banged down the phone so hard he cracked a fingernail. Blood welled beneath the ugly fissure, but the pain was nothing compared to his impotent rage. Still, as he walked away from the phone and strode through the downstairs of his Benedict Canyon home, turning on the lights in one room after another, his eyes filled with tears. He was lighting up the place because it was so god-forsaken lonely in this huge five-bedroom house. And because he didn't know what else to do.

Whose side are you on, God? Are you going to let those bastards win this one, too? They've got everything else, all the money and the power. They don't need you. I do. We do. This country does.

Burt's life was unraveling. His wife had stopped taking his calls two days ago. She wouldn't respond to his e-mails, either, and apparently she'd decided not to let their kids talk to him. Even Burton Jr., his teenage son, wasn't answering his cell, at least not to his dad.

Burt had sent them all away to protect them from the ugly gossip and the press, who were circling the house like vultures. But he never thought his family would turn against him, too. He still couldn't comprehend it. He refused to believe his wife and kids could think him guilty of anything as evil and heinous as what the Washington, D.C., capitol police had accused him of. But they had plenty of evidence to back up their charges.

His congressional office had been roped off as a crime scene. They'd found porn on his computer. Child porn, but even worse, if that was possible. Little kids. There were pictures of toddlers hidden in passworded files on his computer at work. The public reaction had been so fierce and so immediate that he was being pressured to withdraw from the upcoming election, even though he'd vehemently denied the allegations and no charges had been brought. But there was an ongoing criminal investigation, and that was more than enough to make him unelectable.

Burt wasn't a perfect man. He worked too hard, spent too much time at the office and neglected his family. He was short-tempered, demanding and given to tunnel vision. He couldn't see anything but the goal, and that goal was whatever injustice he was trying to right at the time. Sometimes he used methods and tactics that were questionable, but he usually got what he was going after, and in his case, it was the bad guys, the takers, those who used their power unwisely and their wealth for evil gain.

He'd missed family anniversaries, birthdays and special events. He'd made lots of mistakes, and he wasn't good at apologizing. But perhaps his biggest mistake was taking on the powerhouse lobbyists and the fat cats of industry in this country. He'd been the prime mover in creating a nonpartisan congressional coalition that had pushed through legislation requiring big discount chains to offer health insurance and worker benefits. He and his coalition were now working on huge reforms, like the country's health-care system and legislation to penalize conglomerates that moved their plants and outsourced their work to other countries. In discussion was a truly controversial bill that would put a cap on egregious CEO salaries. Congressional hearings with some of those CEOs being called as witnesses were scheduled to start next month.

Burt Carr thrived on controversy and confrontation. He loved playing David to the Goliaths of big business. But this time he'd tweaked the lion's tail, and the roar could be heard far and wide. If the fat cats had a religion it was their corporate bottom line, and he had violated their First Commandment: Thou shalt not play Robin Hood. What we have succeeded in stealing from the poor is ours. Thou shalt not give it back.

It didn't matter, though. Even if he could clear his name, he would be forever tainted by these accusations. It was no accident that the child porn was on his computer. Someone had found a way to stop him simply by hacking into his hard drive and dumping the evidence. They wouldn't succeed, though. He might never win another election, but he'd find a way to fight corporate corruption and greed. Call him a crusader, but that's what he was born to do. He'd been a paperboy from the age of ten, and he'd witnessed so much petty crime against the poor and the elderly on his route that he'd organized the first Neighborhood Watch in his area.

Burt's aimless wandering through the house had eventually brought him back to his office where he came to a halt, the breath knocked out of him by the sight of a Carr family portrait that sat on his desk. It had always been there, but he couldn't remember the last time he'd looked at it. Now he would look at nothing else. It would haunt him, he knew.

The picture went facedown in a desk drawer, which he shut and locked. He didn't want to open it, even by mistake.

Gotcha.com was still flickering on his computer screen, boasting a hot update on the Burton Carr scandal. He sat down, clicked on the link and saw the blanked-out kiddyporn photos that were supposed to have been found on his D.C. computer. Jack the Giant Killer was taking credit for the pictures and swore they were the real thing, but that was impossible, unless the police had leaked them. Burt's computer had been taken in as evidence. Still, how many viewers of Gotcha would even think about that?

He shut down the computer, swearing not to go back to that site. He'd been obsessed with what was being said about him, but he was done with this garbage. It was turning *him* into garbage. The only thing more important than clearing his name and salvaging his projects was winning back the love and trust of his wife and children.

13

Lane was jarred awake by the shrill clatter of an alarm. She opened her eyes to darkness, unsure of anything except that she was fully clothed and sitting up. Where was she? Her heart pitched, and she reached out in panic to see if she could feel the walls around her, hemming her in. Confusion yanked her back to a time when she'd slept sitting up and fully clothed, in the black maw of a bedroom closet.

But this wasn't twenty years ago, thank God. She wasn't ten years old and sleeping in closets whenever it became necessary, for protection. She was in her own living room, and she'd drifted off on the sectional couch, waiting for Darwin's call.

The jarring ring drilled into her consciousness again. That *was* Darwin's call. She groped in her lap, looking for her cell, but it wasn't there. The noise was coming from somewhere else, somewhere lower, the floor.

She went down on her knees, following the sound, and found the black flashing cube under the coffee table. It must have fallen off her lap. "Darwin?" she said, fumbling with the Talk button. She sank to her side on the floor and closed her eyes, still groggy. She didn't wake up well, never had.

"Lane, sorry it took me so long," Dar said, his voice taut and hushed.

"What time is it?"

"Going on five in the morning. You're not going to believe this, but I can't find shit on Rick Bayless. The guy's a cipher. He left LAPD after that scandal over your arrest, and I have no clue what he's been doing since."

She and Dar had been living together on the streets back then, taking care of each other as best they could. Both had been misfits, Dar with his strange episodes and Lane with her witchy blue eyes and the stuffed giraffe she clung to as if it were a vital organ, although it was actually only a gift from her dad.

Dar had suffered from seizures that were later diagnosed as epilepsy, and Lane had become his protector. Most of the time she'd managed to distract the various gangs of street predators and lose them in the alley mazes, with Dar huddled in some alcove, where she would find him later. At times she'd been forced to fight, and she'd become good at it, using her starved appearance and lightning reflexes to outwit her enemies. But Dar's dire need for medical attention finally forced her out into the open, where the games were deadly.

She couldn't apply for a job without alerting the authorities, and she quickly figured out that the only thing of worth she possessed was her young female body, so she used it. And was caught the first time. Later, after she got out of juvenile hall, she found out that someone had actually followed up on her pleas. They'd checked on Dar, and he'd been sent to foster care, which in many cases was just another form of internment. Lane had found him through her probation officer, living in a Mormon family home with four other foster kids. Dar was the only person she'd tried to find.

"What about Bayless's company?" Lane asked.

"It's a name on a Web site. It goes nowhere, a maze with no exit and no contact information. I can't find a paper trail, financial or otherwise. No credit cards, no bills. He must pay cash for everything. I don't see how that's possible unless he uses prepaid credit cards, but they haven't always been available."

She struggled to get up. "You couldn't find an address, a phone number?"

"Not for Extreme Solutions. I did find the title on a house in Manhattan Beach. He bought the place ten years ago, the same year he got divorced. Looks like the marriage barely made it two years. Irreconcilable differences, of course, that's California law. No kids. He bought the house after they split up, and it's in his name as sole owner."

Interesting that he'd been married and divorced since he arrested her back then. She moved on all fours to the side table, where she'd left her tote bag lying on the floor. In the low light, she found paper and a pen in exactly the compartment they belonged. Thank God for organizational skills.

She made a note of the address and thanked Dar.

"Lane," he cautioned, "don't go over there on your own."

"Of course not. Why would I do that?"

"You're going, aren't you? Shit."

"Darwin, I'll be all right. My cell has a panic button, thanks to you, and it's working fine."

"Lane—"

She said goodbye, pressed the off button and blinked to clear her focus. Through a crack in the blinds she could see that the sky was already indigo blue. She needed a shower and some food, which meant the sun would be up by the time she got to his place, but that was fine. She preferred daylight, even if it also conferred some advantage on him. She wanted to see exactly who and what she was dealing with.

She didn't make a practice of hating people. There were ghosts from her past who could readily fall into the category of *hated,* and that would have sucked all the energy out of her. But she would make an exception for Rick Bayless. Him, she did hate—and for good reason.

Lane drove down his street and passed his house, surprised by the Spanish-style beachfront cottage. She wouldn't have expected Rick Bayless to live in a charming, bougainvillea-draped courtyard bungalow, but it matched the address Dar had given her. She continued on by, parking around the corner. She'd used MapQuest to find the place, and the detailed instructions had brought her straight to Bayless's front door.

It was still early enough that the entire neighborhood was quiet, except for the waves crashing on the beach. No one seemed to be up, except a few surfers, perched on their boards and waiting patiently for the next big wave. If Lane was lucky, Bayless might not be up yet, either. Catching him off guard should give her some kind of advantage.

She didn't carry pepper spray or a weapon for protection, but she had her Darwin cell, and it was keyed into the company's security services. One press of her panic button and the guards would track her using the phone's GPS system. If they couldn't get to her within a matter of minutes, they would alert a local security service.

Besides, she was pretty good at handling herself, and she'd always had good instincts for self-preservation. A few days after her tenth birthday, she'd run away from her feuding parents' home to live with her older sister, Sandra, who'd provided little care and no supervision. But at least the luxury hunting lodge in Shadow Hills where Sandra lived and worked wasn't a battleground.

Lane parked her car and made the walk back in just minutes. The fall morning was a bit chilly for the running shorts, T-shirt and sneakers she'd worn, mostly to have a ready excuse for fleeing the scene if she needed one. Across the street from Bayless's stucco cottage there was an old-fashioned boardwalk, facing the water. If need be, she could say she'd come here to run. Not that he'd believe it, but the police might.

Her first hurdle was his slide-bolted courtyard gate. She could see the slide bolt by standing on tiptoe, but it was too low for her to reach over the gate and open it. There was a bell, but he probably had a security camera, and that would lose her the advantage. Fortunately, the place was in need of some maintenance and the screws holding the bolt's metal plates were loose. All it took was some jiggling of the latch and the bolt plopped out of its wobbly cradle and hung there like a broken branch.

Lucky. She entered the courtyard and saw tiled benches, a bubbling fountain and flourishing pigmy palms. A low adobe brick wall facing the beach allowed him to sit in privacy and enjoy the view. His place was in need of maintenance, but the real-estate values alone would put almost any oceanfront property in the low millions, which meant he wasn't destitute—and probably didn't have blackmail in mind.

Maybe that should have reassured her. It didn't.

She checked the front door, which was securely locked, but there was also a set of French doors that gave access to what appeared to be the living room. She tried the knobs, felt one of them give a bit, and realized she could probably enter that way with a little effort. But breaking and entering?

She went back to the front door and rang the bell, reasoning that the element of surprise wasn't worth another jail sentence at the hands of Rick Bayless.

But two rings later, he still hadn't answered.

The loose knob on the French door gave way when she put some weight behind it. She pushed the door with her shoulder, and found herself in a haciendalike living room, decorated with colorful Mexican tiles, Indian rugs and an open-hearth fireplace. The house looked lived in, but not in a bad way. Her own place was a bit sterile by comparison, with much less warmth and color.

She waited and listened, planning her next move. She'd made some noise getting in, which would have roused most people, but she didn't hear any signs of life. Maybe he wasn't home. Or he was—and hidden away, waiting for her.

The house looked small from the outside, two bedrooms at most, but either the design was unconventional or someone had added on rooms, because as she slipped silently from one hallway to another, she feared losing her way. There was plenty of evidence of at least one male occupant. A khaki jacket and the leather coat she'd seen last night hung on the hallway coat tree. In the kitchen she found mail on the table, dishes in the sink and a bowl with what was left of some take-out Chinese food on the floor next to the refrigerator.

Lane moved closer. Was that meant to be pet food?

She saw movement out of the corner of her eye. It was all she could do not to scream as a tiny gray mouse limped to the safety of an opening between the refrigerator and the kitchen cabinets. As it disappeared, tail twitching, a horrible flashback assailed Lane. She'd awakened one morning in yet another musty closet. She'd had to find new ones when her hiding places were discovered. But this time she'd fallen asleep with half a cheese sandwich in her hand, and a mouse was gnawing away at the cheese. She'd let out a shriek as its razor-sharp teeth nipped her skin.

Now she backed out of the kitchen, shivering in disgust. Rick Bayless didn't run a very tight ship. His poor house pet was sharing its food with a scavenging rodent.

She found him in the last bedroom at the end of a strangely curving hallway. The arched door was hanging open, and she could see him sprawled on the bed on his back, apparently sleeping heavily. If he hadn't been breathing, she would have thought him dead. As it was, maybe drunk.

He was covered by a sheet, but everything she could see of him—head, shoulders, arms and feet—was bare. It was easy to extrapolate that he slept naked under that sheet, and she hoped to God he did. She wanted him as uncomfortable and vulnerable as possible when she confronted him. She wondered if he knew how it felt to be humiliated at the hands of someone who had all the power and control. Probably not, given that he was Mr. Big-Shit Extreme Solutions. Please, let *her* be the one to give him that experience.

She would also have greater odds of fending him off. Naked or not, he was bigger, stronger and probably faster than she was by twice. He was out cold. His mouth was open, his jaw slack, but the muscle definition in his neck, shoulders, arms and chest was obvious. Any advantage she had would not last long if things got physical.

She entered the room cautiously, aware that he could be faking to get her close enough to ambush, although he'd had plenty of chances, if that was his plan. An open bottle of pills had been spilled on the night table next to the bed. Lane's first thought was a drug overdose, her second, suicide. But that made no sense. If he'd wanted to kill himself, he would have taken all the pills. She inched closer to the night table. It looked like a prescription bottle, except that the label had been ripped off.

So, Mr. Big-Shit Extreme Solutions was a druggie?

Suddenly she had options. She could call the police and have him arrested. That would either put an end to his threats—or provoke him to carry them out. She still had no idea what his motive was, but an educated guess said that someone had hired him to damage her and her company, and her history with Rick Bayless was just a coincidence. He might even be the anonymous JGK, who was posting garbage on the Internet about her clients.

How interesting that he'd just given her the perfect opportunity to take pictures of him and expose his criminal inclinations on the Net. She would do it anonymously, with Darwin's help. Bayless would never know who'd outed him. She loved the eye-for-an-eye angle, but it wouldn't work unless he had something to lose, his reputation or his career. He wasn't a celebrity, but he did have a business, and pictures might come in handy regardless, if only as a way to back him off.

She'd put the Darwin cell in the zipper pocket of her shorts. It was a camera phone with wireless capabilities. She could take the pics and immediately e-mail them to Darwin. Even if Bayless was to catch her and confiscate the phone, he couldn't stop the transmission.

One last option came to mind. She could find his gun and shoot him, permanently eliminate him as a threat. This option had the most appeal by far, but she had to admit she wasn't quite rational where he was concerned. He'd put her through a degrading and terrifying experience, worse than anything those bastards at the club had ever done.

She glared at his unconscious form, wondering where the gun was. Most ex-cops had them around. The bedroom was relatively neat. That would make it easier to search, which she'd just decided to do. It was almost certain he had at least one gun, and probably several. Better she had the weapons than him. His clothes were hanging over the back of a chair. She quickly patted down the pants, shirt and jacket, but found nothing. The night-table drawer yielded only a wallet, various sets of keys and an array of sunglasses, plus other odds and ends.

Maybe in the closet, where he might have hung a holster?

She opened the first sliding door to a collection of sporting goods and stacks of storage boxes. Where the hell to start?

"Is there something I can help you find?"

Lane whirled at the sound of Bayless's voice. His eyes were open, and the sight of them made her legs buckle. She stepped backward, slamming up against the storage boxes. The mirrored glasses he'd worn in her office had hidden the cat-green color of his irises. Today it was vivid.

And worse, they were sharply alert, not drug hazed in the slightest.

She'd just lost her advantage. "I rang the bell, but no one answered," she said. "Your door was open."

"So, you invited yourself in?" He sat up, rubbing the dark gold thistledown that dusted his head and still peering at her. The scars on his face were evident, too, and even now, fifteen years later, they brought a flutter of fear. Her stomach tightened as she noticed the notch on his lower lip. She'd given him that scar.

"Watching your clients sleep," he said, "is that what a concierge does?"

"It can be arranged."

"How long have you been here?"

"I just walked in." Be careful, she told herself. This was the man who'd entrapped her, charged her with prostitution, cuffed her and grilled her for hours about contraband he'd found sewn in her stuffed animal. He'd roughed her up, called her names and threatened her, telling her he would never let her back out on the streets, he would keep her in jail until she was eighteen. And then he'd done just that, put her in jail and thrown away the key.

She wasn't sure her shaking legs would hold her. Fury and fear were coursing through her, fighting for control.

"What are you doing here?" He wrapped the sheet around him, as if he was planning to get up.

"You have mice," she hissed at him, stalling for time.

"I know. I've been trying to kill it, but it won't die."

"Too bad you're not a better shot. Apparently you did wing it."

"You mean the limp? That was a mousetrap. Didn't work, either."

Her laughter was bitter. "So, you've decided to kill it with fast food? High blood pressure and hardening of the arteries?"

"If it's good enough for me, it's good enough for the mouse." He shrugged. "Is this another one of your concierge duties? Inspecting for mice? Vector control?"

She breathed in, still shaking. Enough small talk. If she'd found his gun, he would be bleeding, dead, and that would be too good a fate for him. "You broke into my office. You threatened me. Why?"

He dragged the sheet with him as he got off the bed. Secured under the base of the lamp on his night table was a business card. He fished it out and flashed the front of the card, making sure she saw that it was one of hers.

"When did Ned Talbert join your agency?" he asked.

"He didn't." She didn't dare tell him the truth. It would draw her into the investigation of Talbert's death. "Are you investigating his case? Are you asking these questions in some official capacity?"

"Ned and I were friends, lifelong friends. I knew him better than anyone—and he didn't kill himself, much less torture and murder his girlfriend. Someone wanted to get rid of him, maybe her, too."

He turned the card over and showed Lane the word written on the other side.

"Extortion?" She shook her head. "That may be one of my business cards, but it's not my handwriting."

"It's Ned's handwriting." He fixed her with a burning stare. "If he wasn't a client, how did he get your card, and why did he suspect you of extortion?"

"I have no idea, but if you're accusing me of something, you'd better have more than a business card with a word written on it."

"I have plenty, Lucia—Lucy. I have your past stored

away in my brain, your time in juvenile hall and the sordid nature of your crimes. Those things I can prove since I was the arresting officer."

"What does my being busted for soliciting fifteen years ago have to do with Ned Talbert's murder-suicide case?"

"I don't know yet, but I'm going to find out. Meanwhile, I do know that several of your clients are having a run of bad luck. Judge Love, Simon Shan, Congressman Carr, Priscilla Brandt and the late Ned Talbert, may he rest in peace. Ned is gone, and the others probably wish they were."

Lane didn't know what to say. It didn't seem likely he was the Giant Killer, but somehow that made him seem all the more menacing. "If you're going to make idle threats, then I'll make some real ones. I'm not without friends, Mr. Bayless, people with power and influence, people who get things done. My enemies are their enemies."

"Really? Friends in high places?" He dropped the sheet and casually walked to his closet. "In that case, maybe I'd better get dressed. Don't feel you need to stay, unless you'd like to help me pick an outfit."

"You need more than fashion advice, Bayless. *You* should be in jail for what you did to me, but I'd settle for a frontal lobotomy and chemical castration."

Lane turned on her heel and left the bedroom, not stopping until she was out of his house. Apparently she was wrong. He hadn't been hired by someone. He was doing this for himself—and his friend Ned.

That made it personal, and much worse. Now their history mattered. Everything mattered. Her head swam with confusion and lack of sleep. Her temples throbbed. This was all such a fricking mess—and Mr. Extreme Solutions was hung. Of all things, she did not need to know that.

14

Rick studied his reflection in the bright lights of his bathroom mirror, wondering what Lane Chandler might have noticed when she got a good look at him. There were no obvious signs of dissipation, but she must have seen the spilled pills. He'd only taken two, but the damn things had hit him like a hammer, and she'd probably jumped to the wrong conclusion. Regardless, he had to keep up the pressure. He needed information from her, and his only leverage was the threat of exposure. Whether he could actually ruin her or not was beside the point. What mattered was that she thought he could.

He stepped back, satisfied that he looked formidable enough to get things done, even if she sicced her big bad friends on him. *It only mattered what they believed, not what was true.* Maybe that was why her accusations had disturbed him. She'd called him everything but a child molester. He wondered why she'd stopped at that. Obviously she had no knowledge of the risks he'd taken back then on her behalf. He'd jettisoned a law enforcement career because of her, not that he had any lasting regrets. It had seemed like the right idea at the time, but maybe it was true that no good deed went unpunished.

He'd just come from the shower and was still dripping.

The towel he'd knotted around his waist caught some of the runoff, but he needed to get dry, and dressed. At least he didn't have a head of shaggy cougar-brown hair to blow-dry. He'd shaved most of it off years ago for a variety of reasons, but the side benefit had been incredibly low maintenance.

Moments later, he had on a pair of denim jeans and a sage-green crewneck sweater he'd taken from a pile of clean laundry that had yet to be put away. His mind was still on Lane Chandler as he sat on the bed and scooped the pills back into the bottle. He'd thought about her over the years, wondering how she might have turned out, but never guessed she'd be a hot success in a business that required her to cater to the whims of the rich and famous. Not that he hadn't seen the seductive side of her personality, along with all the other sides. And she'd had plenty of opportunity to learn, with her older sister running that exclusive hunting lodge in Shadow Hills. Glorified whore-house is what it was.

When he had the pills cleaned up, he grabbed his keys, wallet and sunglasses. He assumed Lane had been looking for his gun in the closet, but he kept the Colt revolver in the slot between the mattress and the bed frame. He tucked the gun into the waistband of his jeans in the back, and headed for the front door, aware of the numbness and tingling in his left leg. It felt almost like a limb that had fallen asleep from lack of circulation.

His stomach rumbled as he passed the kitchen. He was actually hungry, but he'd grab something on the way. He needed to see Mimi about that background check on Lucy Cox. Lane Chandler's threat about friends in high places had made him think there might be something to the conspiracy theory that had been cooking on a low burner in his brain—and that she might be involved. Now he needed to find out who her "friends" were.

Val Drummond was waiting in Lane's office when she showed up at 10:00 a.m., three hours late for the meeting they had first thing every morning. At Val's insistence they met on the stroke of seven to update each other and hold planning sessions, or whatever was necessary for that particular day.

He glanced up from text messaging and raised an accusatory eyebrow. "Killer traffic?"

"Have you been here since seven?" Huffy, Lane dropped her tote bag on her desk with a bang, knowing it could scratch the gleaming surface—and that would bother him more than it did her. Val had a way of making her feel like a loser, even though it was her company. She couldn't imagine him putting a scratch in anything, knowingly or otherwise. He simply didn't make mistakes. Everyone else did, but not Val. It was galling, but it also made him indispensable. Mistakes were fatal in a concierge service. You were only as good as your reliability.

"I asked our garage security to let me know when you drove in." He still hadn't lowered the eyebrow. Possibly it had its own rigging, like a sail. "Wouldn't want to keep you *waiting*," he added.

"I'm sorry, Val. I rarely miss one of our meetings unless I'm traveling. This was an emergency." She'd already decided not to tell him about her morning encounter with Rick Bayless, or the night before. Val was a worrier, and there was nothing he could do anyway.

"Something you want to talk about?" He clicked off the cell and settled back in the guest chair, his legs uncrossed so as not to wrinkle his chocolate-brown slacks. An apple-green cashmere sweater over an aqua dress shirt finished his outfit.

The look was masculine, elegant. So was he, his skin as rich and brown as the slacks, his hair slicked back with pomade to control the curl. He would have worn a tailored pinstripe suit if he could. But Lane didn't want such formal clothing in the corporate offices. They weren't a brokerage or a law firm, where stress and tension underscored the aura of power. TPC offered comfort and service, but in a more relaxed manner. Everything about the service said calm and in control. Only the world outside was flustered and disorganized.

She moved her tote to the floor, undid the buttons of her garnet-red wool blazer and sank gratefully into her comfortable executive chair. "I'm okay. Let's get on with the meeting."

Val tapped some buttons, bringing up a new screen. "First up, damage control."

"For us—or the clients?" She probably should have had her cell at the ready, too. She kept her to-do lists on it, as well, but she'd had a rough morning, and she didn't feel like trying to keep up with Val today. That's why she'd hired him, to be organized and efficient. Let him.

"Both," he said. "Seriously, it's only a matter of time until someone, and it could even be one of our clients, starts to wonder about this contraption Darwin invented." He tapped the phone he was working on. "And I'm wondering about Darwin."

"What do you mean?"

"He's totally territorial when it comes to our Premiere clients and their phones. He's always insisted on servicing them exclusively, and he's secretive about what he's doing. It's ridiculous."

"But the Premiere clients have the phones with all the extra features that only Dar understands. He invented the phone."

"And he needs to start training people who *do* understand those features." Val nearly came out of his chair. "What if something happened to Dar? Our Premiere clients would be without service? The whole company would go to hell?"

That was a bit of an exaggeration, but Val was clearly upset, and he was making a good point.

"We have a world-class tech-help department that covers all our other clients. It's working beautifully, and we need to do that for our Premiere clients. Let's face it, Lane. Without our name clients, we're nothing."

"Have we had complaints from the Premiere clients?" Lane still didn't quite understand his vehemence.

"Not that I know of, but this—" he waggled the Premiere version of the phone with all its extra features "—is an accident waiting to happen. We can track these people, we can listen in on their conversations and eavesdrop on their text messages. God knows what Darwin designed this thing to do. It's a time bomb."

Now he was going too far. "Please tell me you've not suggesting that we're spying on our own clients. That's simply not true. Even if we could do those things, Val, we wouldn't. It's *illegal.*"

"We can track and locate our Premiere clients wherever they happen to be."

"Yes, of course, but that's for their protection. If they're lost or having car trouble—any kind of trouble—we can respond immediately to their needs. The GPS function is for their convenience, as is every other feature of the phone. Val, we're talking about high-profile people, the kind who get kidnapped."

He settled back in his chair, only slightly contrite. "I know that, but Darwin's got all kinds of shit on these phones, and even though he's secretive as hell about what he's up to, he's very lax about security. I'm just afraid it's going to look like we're tracking people, maybe even setting them up."

"*What?* Why would we do that?"

He shrugged as if to say he didn't know. "I'm just saying, if the media spotlight ever gets turned on this agency, that's how it could look. Don't kill the messenger, okay?"

Lane was stunned, possibly because she feared he might be right. Val was the detail man, the cautious one, and often an alarmist. Plus, he was jealous of Darwin, which Lane had never understood. Val was the one with the prestigious degrees. He had the only Ivy League MBA in the company. Lane had gone to school locally on scholarship and Darwin had no higher education at all. Dar had taught himself the electronics necessary to customize their phone system, and Lane had always survived on her wits—and for better or worse, another powerful motivator, desperation.

"Let's not borrow trouble," she said. "We have enough spoiled food on our plate as it is. Let's talk about something we can actually solve."

"Oookay." He clicked some buttons on his keypad, bringing up his phone's PDA function. "Let's see, here…ah, Simon Shan. I think we should recall the bodyguard he requested."

"She's not doing a good job?"

"Shan seems happy with her, but I'm concerned about his having asked for someone full-time to live at his place, and a woman to boot. That could backfire, especially since the police have already been here, asking questions."

"You mean it could look like we're providing him with female companionship, rather than professional security services?"

Val nodded. Lane had to agree it could be a problem, but she didn't want to disrupt Shan's life any more than the devastating opium bust already had. "Let me think about that. Meanwhile, what else do we have to deal with? Have the gossip Web sites broken any more horror stories on our clients?"

"Nothing since Pris Brandt, and that was yesterday. We're on a lucky streak."

Not really. She hadn't told Val about Ned Talbert. He didn't know the baseball star had briefly been a client before he died. Val had enough to deal with, so Lane was keeping certain things to herself, like Ned Talbert and Rick Bayless. Besides, she might be able to pull a few strings and take care of the Bayless problem herself.

Val's phone had been beeping throughout the meeting, indicating that calls and messages were piling up. Lane was grateful it wasn't her. Val was now the glue that held things together. He oversaw every facet of the service, and TPC would have come to a standstill without him. Lane had been so busy this last year, working on the expansion plan for the service that she hadn't had time for the day-to-day operations. Val took care of all that.

She still interviewed new clients buying in at the Premiere level, and she worked personally with many of them, but for the most part, she'd turned the client services, which were the heart and soul of the company, over to Val. It hadn't been an easy decision, and she still feared something may have been lost. Val lived and breathed his work, but in a different way than she did. It wasn't about the clients as much as it was about him, his advancement. And he bridled at the idea that a concierge was a servant in the true, positive sense of the word, service being an honorable calling. Lane had always stressed humility, graciousness and courtesy in the time-honored tradition of the Clefs d'Or, the original professional organization for concierges, formed in France in the late 1920s. Val preferred the idea of a concierge being a hip, go-to kind of assistant, but he'd been willing to compromise, and he'd done exceedingly well in blending the two.

Lane was pleased with the administrative team he'd picked and with the work his client-services group had done in hiring and training concierges. Most important, their clients weren't complaining.

"Have we heard anything from Priscilla Brandt or her people today?" Lane asked. "What's going on there?"

"Apparently Priscilla believes she can handle the situation herself. I spoke with her publisher yesterday and recommended a spin doctor but got nowhere."

"She needs a head doctor, Val, not a spin doctor. Therapy."

But Val had already moved on. "Trudy Love wants out of her contract."

"Her contract with us?" Lane asked, wishing she didn't have to be reminded of that mess, too. Judge Love was the first casualty of the gossip Web sites, featured by Jack the Giant Killer earlier that year in a brutal online exposé, complete with zoom lens close-ups of her open-air dalliance with a biker so heavily tattooed that he looked clothed when naked. The judge had no tattoos.

Val had been so enraged he'd met with Seth Black, the

owner of the Web site, to confront him, probably thinking he could scare him off. Val had done it on his own, without consulting Lane, and she'd already told him never again to take the bait these vultures dangled. Sadly, it was too late. They'd been prime targets of Gotcha.com ever since.

"Her show has been canceled," Val explained. "She's broke, can't even get a paralegal job, and go figure, she no longer needs our services. *I can't imagine why.*"

He was bitter, and Lane understood why. They were all at the mercy of a relentless and ubiquitous enemy. "Release her, of course, and wish her well. No, never mind, I'll do that. I may have a job lead for her."

As Val went down his list, Lane felt her stomach flutter. At first she didn't recognize it as anxiety, but as she watched him tick off one task after another, she wondered at the wisdom of having given him so much control. Darwin was her cocreator and partner in spirit, but workwise, he was now primarily a troubleshooter. It was Val who literally ran everything and that was a lot of power to have in one person's hands.

"How are the expansion plans going?" he asked her when they'd finished with his list.

"Oh, I haven't had a chance to tell you!" She was thrilled to have some good news to report, especially since he'd been bugging her. "I gave Ashley the go-ahead, and I'm heading to Dallas on Thursday. So, it's full steam ahead with the expansion plans. As soon as you get your butt out of here, I'm back on it. All work, all day, all expansion plans."

He grimaced, but it was really his futile attempt to hide a grin. She smiled back, and actually felt a moment of relief, of lightness. But as she fell back in the chair and Val stood up, she noticed movement in her periphery. The door had been ajar. Now it was closed. Not the door to her office. She'd closed that when she arrived, despite the open-door policy. This was the door to Lane's bathroom. Someone was in there, and they'd heard every word that she and Val said.

15

Simon Shan felt as if he were being pulled apart. Literally. Forces at the center of his being had gripped him, and they were tugging and plucking, grabbing at him, drawing long and hard, as if he were a tree being uprooted from the ground.

A moan slipped through his teeth. *Stop. Let go.*

He twisted and turned, struggling to push his attackers away, but he couldn't make his arms move. Somehow he knew it was one of those dreams he'd had as a child where he desperately wanted to wake up. He was being chased by monsters or eaten by ravenous fanged creatures. But if he could think about dreaming could he *be* dreaming?

A sharp sensation pierced his consciousness. Pain? The creatures were upon him, mauling him, feasting. He could feel their wet tongues, their teeth, but he couldn't move. They'd pinned him to the bed, and they were going to eat him alive. Another stab, but not pain this time. Pleasure? He cried out in confusion.

Shan woke up with a start. He opened his eyes and saw the room, the bed…the woman. More confusion rocked him. What was she doing?

She was bent over him like a yogi in a meditative pose, but this was no trance. Her mouth was fixed tightly on his hardening penis and her fingers gripped him at the base of his shaft, pulling and tugging him into the deep hot well of her mouth. Her soft, suctioning lips.

What? Paradise? Yes. This was bliss, whirling him into its vortex. Quicksand, sucking him under. Death, swift and sweet.

He jackknifed up, grabbed her by the nape of her neck and pulled her off him. A rope of black satin tangled in his fingers. It was her coiled hair.

She was the ravenous fiend! He could see that now. She was the enemy.

"What are you doing?" Holding her at arm's length, he railed at her for defying him so outrageously. "I told you not to do that, slithering around like a snake. I told you I would kill you if you did."

"I want to help," she whispered, shaking her head and seemingly unable to say anything else. Her mouth was still open and wet, her eyes wounded and yet woozy with carnal lust. The sight of her made him ache and harden, but he didn't want her to know. He was so deeply ashamed of his burning loneliness.

She found the courage to confront him. "Would you kill me when I only want to help you?"

"What do you mean, help?" he asked harshly.

"Be your comfort, your ease. Life is hard."

"Comfort me with your mouth on my *dick?*" He was furious at her and enthralled by her at the same time.

"In whatever way that I can." She stroked his thigh. "If this brings you ease, why not?"

The silk of her skin and the grace of her touch were too much for Simon. Her voice was like liquor, throaty and raspy, deep with fire. Only her face, neck and hands were visible, all long and pale and soft. She was wrapped in a red kimono that enveloped her from shoulders to feet, but she was dangerously sexual, as only a woman could be, glowing with lust, oozing juice like ripe fruit.

He'd never seen her naked. Perhaps he never would, but he knew it would be devastating. It was entirely possible that her intent was to confuse and distract him, to weaken him so that his enemies could destroy him. She could so easily be a spy, but he didn't have the strength to fight her off. Her gentle fingers sapped him of everything human and strong. All his energy flowed into the organ she caressed. Nothing was left to stop her onslaught.

Keep your friends close—and your enemies closer. He didn't know the origins of that saying. He doubted it was Asian. But it was very bad advice when your enemy was a beautiful, sensual woman.

She bowed her head, as if calming and centering herself. As she bent toward him, her eyelashes fluttered over his thigh and her blushing cheek grazed his penis. He flinched, racked with desire. He would have killed to have her, fought armies and mythical monsters. *He would have killed.*

She rose up and left him wanting. She kissed him on the mouth, and desperate, he clutched her face and kissed her back. Rage flared through him, rage at his own weakness. How could he have let himself lose control like this?

Tears welled in his eyes and she saw them. Her eyes filled, too.

"Let the anger melt away," she implored. "Let me help."

Spent, Simon lay back, naked and exposed to her, surrendering all. At least he wasn't reduced to asking her for anything. She knew what he wanted, what he would have begged for if he'd had to, and soon, with her sweet, greedy little mouth, she was on him again, deeply, pulling.

This was no dream. She had won. She took nothing, gave everything, yet she had won. He was helpless. She was going to make him explode with pleasure, blow him to pieces. He should have killed her, made good his threat. *Please, God,* he thought as pleasure furled and swelled in his groin. *Please give me the strength to destroy my enemies. And the wisdom to distinguish them from my friends. Don't abandon me to this woman.*

Lane put her finger to her lips, signaling Val to be quiet. She rose from her chair and darted over to the bathroom adjoining her office. Either she was hearing things or there was someone inside that room.

Val seemed startled at her rush. "Wow, Lane, you must really need to pee."

She shushed him again as she strained to listen at the door. She couldn't hear anything at the moment, but the door had been ajar when she arrived at her office a half hour ago, and she'd just seen it close. "Excuse me," she called out. "Is someone in there?"

Lane gave the door a sharp rap. A shuffling noise could be heard inside. The door creaked open, and Lane stepped back, aghast as she saw who it was. "Sandra?"

Her sister hovered in the shadows of the unlit bathroom, smiling sheepishly. "Sorry," she said. "This is awkward, isn't it? Sorry, *really.*"

"What...what are you *doing* in there?" Lane hadn't spoken to her sister in at least five years and hadn't seen her in fifteen. "What are you doing *here?*"

Sandra hunched her shoulders, clearly uncomfortable. "Visiting? I was in the area, and it didn't seem right not to stop by and say hello. I should have let you know I was here, but, well—"

She clutched her short blue denim skirt at the waist, as if she was holding it together with her hand. Lane recognized the formfitting blouse and pointy-toed red pumps as staples of hostess work in cocktail lounges and casinos—and wondered if that's what Sandra had been doing since their hunting-lodge days. Her long dark blond waves were probably hot off the curling iron. There were a few lines around her eyes that hinted at her forty-plus years, but other than that she looked very much the same, a pretty, seemingly ditzy mantrap. *Seemingly* being the key word.

"I'm sorry," Sandra said, "did I catch you at a bad time?"

Lane didn't know how to answer the question. She had to wonder why Sandra hadn't called first. Maybe she thought she wouldn't be welcome, which wouldn't have been too far off the mark. Lane had decided several years ago, after Sandra turned down the last of Lane's many invitations to visit, that she had to stop extending herself to a sister who clearly didn't want to be part of her life. They hadn't spoken since. They didn't even exchange cards.

There'd been another reason for the estrangement. Lane had just picked up her first high-profile clients, and it looked as if her concierge service might be a bigger success than she'd ever imagined. She needed everything to be squeaky-clean. A criminal record and a shady past, which included a sister who'd run an exclusive men's club along with her gangster boyfriend, would not have looked good. Sandra hadn't seemed to want a relationship, so Lane had let it go, gladly.

"Actually, Val and I were just finishing up our meeting,"

Lane explained, stepping back to let her sister enter the office. Sandra didn't move. "Is something wrong?" Lane asked.

"My zipper's broken. Your receptionist let me in your office to use the bathroom. Of course, I told her that I was your sister, and it would be fine— But I couldn't get the zipper fixed, and then this gentlemen showed up—" she pointed to Val "—so I decided to hide out in the bathroom. Sorry, embarrassing."

Lane might have thought it funny except for the sensitivity of the discussion she and Val were having. Sandra could have signaled that she was here, but Lane decided not to bring that up. Her sister was clearly mortified. It could wait until Val was gone and they were alone.

"Can I help with the zipper?" Lane asked. "Or possibly you'd like some pins?"

"Pins! Yes, safety pins, thank you."

While Lane went to get the pins from her desk drawer, Val introduced himself to Sandra. They exchanged a few words about the lovely fall weather, and then Val made excuses about work obligations and left, promising to get back to Lane later. Lane was not happy about this surprise visit from her sister, but at least it had cut short Val's character assassination of Darwin. He was always more than ready to blame Dar for the service's problems, and even though he'd made some valid points this time, he kept putting Lane in the position of referee.

She sighed as she scooped up a handful of small safety pins and returned to the bathroom. She would have to talk with Dar again.

"Are you still living in Shadow Hills?" She handed Sandra the safety pins and turned on the bathroom light, letting her sister deal with the broken zipper. Back in their

Shadow Hills Hunting Lodge days, Sandra had been responsible for the lodge's team of women hostesses, and
that had required some quick zipper fixes on many a night.
No pun intended, Lane thought, remembering the wealthy
and privileged men who frequented the luxurious
compound, nestled in the foothills of the San Gabriel
Mountain Range. And the media tsunami when the truth
about the place came out.

"You probably heard about Hank dying in that car
accident, right? He was driving his prized preowned cer-
tified Ferrari and he slammed it right into the side of a
cliff, just about head-on. Of course, without Hank around
to manage the lodge, the owners shut it down. Just as
well, I suppose. It was failing badly, anyway."

She sighed, but went on pinning her skirt, as if to say
that was all the emotion Hank was worth. Lane agreed.
She'd known about the accident. News of the spectacular
crash had even made the *L.A. Times*. Hank had piled up
his car three years ago, after the hunting-lodge case was
dropped, but people who knew him were quoted as being
surprised that it hadn't happened sooner. He'd driven like
a maniac, risked his life on a daily basis—and that was
one of the man's *least* offensive traits.

"With Hank gone, I went to work in a casino for a
while," Sandra said. "But I hated it. Since then I've been
managing a restaurant in the Valley. To be honest, I need
a change, but it's difficult when you're my age." She
glanced up from her repair work. "I guess you officially
changed your name to Lane Chandler, huh? I always
thought you'd outgrow your penchant for that silly name.
Wasn't he just a second-rate actor in cowboy movies?"

Lane's smile was rueful. That second-rate actor was responsible for the few pleasant memories she had of her

time at the lodge. She used to watch the videotapes of the old westerns they played in the bar. When the guests went out hunting, she would sneak into the bar, and Willy, the bartender, would play movies for her. She'd loved *The Lone Bandit* and *The Outlaw Tamer.*

"Maybe I was looking for a role model," Lane said defensively. "Chandler was always being mistaken for a bad guy and on the run from the law, but somehow he found the real villain and saved himself."

Obviously, Lane could relate to the misunderstood-loner role. And maybe taking on the name of a toughened survivor had conferred some kind of protection on a kid who'd been forced to look out for herself from the time she'd run away from home at ten. It had not been a pretty childhood, and her long-lost sister had done little to make things easier.

"Have you been in touch with Mom?" Lane asked, knowing it was a touchy subject. Their mother had always favored Sandra, but had wasted no time disowning her when Sandra got involved with the shady boyfriend and the lodge. She'd also written off Lane when she ran away, declaring that she was as bad as her trampy older sister, and the two of them deserved each other. Lane had been told by the public defender at her trial that her mother had signed over legal guardianship to Sandra, and would not be attending the trial. And then, as it turned out, Sandra hadn't shown up at the trial, either. All of that had come as a blow to Lane, but not a surprise.

"Are you kidding?" Sandra snorted. "She'd put a restraining order on me if I tried to contact her. What about you? Does she know how high and mighty you are these days?"

"Hardly high and mighty" was all Lane said. She

already regretted bringing the subject up. Sandra had finished with her skirt, so Lane ushered her into the office and suggested they have a seat. "Would you like something to drink?" she asked. "Coffee?"

Sandra didn't want anything to drink. Nor did she seem to want to sit down, so Lane remained standing, too. "How long are you staying?" Lane asked her.

"Oh, didn't I tell you? I'm not going back. L.A.'s my new home."

"Do you have a job, a place to stay?"

Sandra smiled. "Actually, I was hoping you could help me with that."

Exactly what Lane feared. Sandra had come to stay, and that was the last thing Lane needed right now. Her sister was the type who in her anxiousness to please everyone was loyal to no one—and Lane didn't trust her. The timing was also peculiar. She'd waited fifteen years just to show up when her little sister's business was under siege?

Lane was still bitter that Sandra hadn't come to her aid when she was alone in L.A. and at the mercy of the police and the juvenile courts. Of course, there had been extenuating circumstances. Lane was told that Sandra had been in an accident at the lodge and had ended up in the hospital. Lane had always wondered if her sister might have been in a worse situation than she was. Sandra had been at the mercy of her thug boyfriend—and all those VIPs she betrayed at the Shadow Valley Hunting Lodge.

"Sure you don't want anything to drink?" Lane said, walking over to her desk, "because I think I could use a little something something right about now."

16

"Mimi, it's Rick Bayless, your former partner and proud reference for your current job. I'm sitting outside 1663 Butler Avenue in my Jeep. The palace guard won't let me in. They say I need an escort, and you don't want the job."

"That's right, Bayless. This may come as a shock, but I'm not in the escort business, even for you. You're lucky I answered the phone."

Detective Mimi Parsons's voice cracked like a whip in Rick's ear. He really was parked at the curb outside the West L.A. Community Police Station in his car, and he probably *was* lucky she answered the phone. Someone had alerted the duty officer not to let him past the reception desk, and that had to be Mimi. Now, if only she wouldn't hang up.

He kept his tone easy and conversational, which *wasn't* easy for him. "Anything come up on LexisNexis for Lucy Cox or Lane Chandler?"

"Nothing," she snapped. "I ran all three names, Lucy, Lucia and Lane. Looks like she's kept her nose clean since she got out of juvie."

"Or she hasn't been caught. What about the package, Mimi, my personal stuff?"

"What about it?"

This was where Rick would have pinned her to the back of the chair with a wooden stake through her heart if he were there in the bullpen with her. It was also where he would have started talking louder and drawing attention to his own presence. Probably why she didn't want him around. He had no doubt it was stressful dealing with a man who had nothing to lose. Thank God. That was the sole pleasure he got out of this investigation.

"Did you check out the evidence room?" he asked.

She spoke tight against the mouthpiece, her voice hushed. "There's no fricking tattered bubble-pack envelope in evidence, Bayless. End of story. Your package isn't there. Now, are we done? I have a case to close."

He assumed she meant Ned's case, and that pissed him off more than he could possibly say. Good thing he couldn't, because she would have hung up on him for sure—*before* he'd given her his theory on what happened that night.

Rick rolled up the car window to eliminate all street noise. "I have one last thing to say on this, Mimi. Let me say it and you won't hear from me again."

She muttered a four-letter word, which he took as a yes. "Let's be clear on one thing," he said. "I'm not conceding that my best friend shot himself in the head, but if he did, and I stress *if,* I think he was forced to do it."

"Someone forced Ned to kill his girlfriend and then himself?"

At least she'd asked the question, which let him wedge in a bit more of his theory before the ax fell. "No, the perpetrator forced Ned to kill himself to stop the perpetrator from torturing her."

"So, who killed her?"

"The perp did, afterward. That was the plan. He restrained both of them, Ned and Holly, and he forced Ned to watch the torture. When it got too much for Ned, the perp gave him an ultimatum. Kill himself and save the girl."

"Would Ned do that?"

"Yes—"

"Interesting theory." She cut him off before he could tell her about Ned's background, his dead mother and sister and his savior complex. "Okay, so if Ned was restrained, forced to watch his girlfriend being tortured and then murdered in a way that made it look like suicide, why were there no signs of restraint on his clothing or body? No duct-tape residue, no rope fibers?"

"You can restrain people without rope, Mimi. With Saran Wrap, done right, it's impossible to get free."

She cut in again, really annoyed now. "If there was Saran Wrap involved, it was from Ned Talbert's porn stash. I can't and won't give you the details of what happened, Bayless, but your buddy had a trunkful of dildos and ball gags in his house. He had enough kinky shit to start his own sex shop. You do the math."

The loud click in his ear was the sound of the ax falling. Mimi was gone. Obviously, she thought he was extrapolating from thin air, that he didn't know any of the details of Holly's death. But Coop had revealed some of the preliminary evidence for torture through gradual asphyxiation. He shouldn't have, but he had. And the porn stash Mimi had mentioned meant nothing, unless you were looking to confirm your theory of murder-suicide and close the case. Whoever killed Ned and Holly could have planted the sex toys, *would have,* for that matter.

Rick squeezed his eyes shut and rubbed his forehead,

trying to focus his thoughts. Damn drugs were messing with his mental processes, too. At least he'd sown the seeds. If Mimi closed the case the way the brass obviously wanted her to, it wouldn't be with an easy conscience. She was a damn good detective, and Ned's and Holly's deaths would haunt her. Not the way it haunted him, but she wouldn't fall asleep quite as quickly at night.

Burton Carr's sixteen-year-old son answered the front door, rocking and shambling, ducking his head, apparently desperate to avoid eye contact. Burton could hardly bear to see his namesake so acutely uncomfortable. He tilted and craned around the boy's six-foot frame, trying to see who else might be in his sister-in-law's house. Burton's wife and the rest of his family had to be hidden in there somewhere.

"No one's here but me," Burt Jr. said, blinded like a sheepdog by the thick wedge of auburn hair that had fallen onto his face.

Burton's foot hit a clay pot on the brick porch, and the sound was like the clang of a cymbal to his frayed nerves. His sister-in-law and her family lived in an old-fashioned rambler in the heart of the San Fernando Valley. She fancied herself a great gardener, and she had flowers blooming everywhere. Wind chimes going, too. Burton had always hated wind chimes. The clinking glass hurt his ears.

"Son, it's me, your dad. Look at me. How's your sister, Beth? And Andy, how's he doing?" Andy was the youngest, just nine, and Burt was most concerned about how he might be handling the upheaval in his life.

"They're both okay. They're with Aunt Gloria. Shopping, I think."

"Where is your mom?"

His son peered at him through burnished strands. "She's sleeping."

Burton's heart began to race. His wife was in there. That meant he had a chance. He always had a chance when he could get with people and talk to them, especially her. She knew him better than anyone, and she'd forgiven him a great deal in their years together. By now she should know enough not to give credence to what his opponents put out about him, but they'd never done anything like this before, never accused him of such heinous crimes.

Accused, he thought. He *wished.* Someone had framed him.

"Let me in, Burt," he said to his son. "Your mother and I have to talk. You know we do."

His teenage son rose to his full height, looming large and trying to intimidate his own father. The sight made Burton wobbly on his feet. He wasn't frightened. He was ill, sick at heart. It should never have come to this.

"I told you," Burt Jr. said. "Mom is sleeping."

"Burt, please—"

"She doesn't want to see you."

"But, son, I didn't do what they're saying. You have to believe—"

"Dad, I know you didn't do anything bad."

The boy began to shuffle again. He tried to shut the door, but Burton thrust out a hand to stop him. "You do?" he said. "You know that?"

"Yeah, sure, it's okay."

"Thank you—" Burton's voice cracked so badly that he could only whisper the rest. "Thank you for that." He reached for his son's hand. All he wanted to do was touch the boy, but Burt Jr. flinched and reared back.

"Please, leave us alone now," he said, and shut the door.

Burton Carr, distinguished U.S. congressman from the Thirtieth District, collapsed on the doorstep of his sister-in-law's house. He dropped to his knees without even giving a thought as to how that might look. He'd been in public service his whole life, as had his father and grandfather before him. He'd served eight terms in Congress, sixteen years. Burt Jr. was born the year he was elected to his first term, and he was as proud of the office now as that day. Before that he'd been involved in state politics, and everyone had told him he was destined for greatness. He wondered what they thought of him now, those people who'd believed he was anointed.

He had believed it, too.

He didn't see the shrouded figure in the car across the street. He didn't see the camera with the zoom lens or hear the rapid-fire clicking. He was focused on the screaming pain inside—and what he could do to stop it. His own son had become the gatekeeper, denying him access to his family. Was there a pit of despair any deeper than that? He didn't understand how any of his family could believe him capable of such things. His wife had been with him over twenty years. His children were his blood, and blood ties were stronger than any other, weren't they? Who was closer? Who knew him better?

But as he finally found the strength to get up off his knees and walk to his car, he realized that perhaps they *didn't* know him, perhaps no one did. He had never taken the time to show them who he was. He wasn't even sure he knew himself. Was that his sin, he wondered, that his facade was so good, so convincing, no one could possibly recognize him without it? Possibly hidden under the crusader's mask for all these years was a monster.

He pulled a handkerchief from his pants pocket to blow his nose and wipe the wetness from his eyes. And still he did not hear the clicking of the camera.

Jerry Blair was a strange dude. Rick spotted that right away. He was wearing sunglasses in his office—and doing something weird with his thumbs.

Rick had set up an afternoon appointment, on false pretenses, of course, with the man who ran the discount giant TopCo. Rick had arrived early and spilled some gourmet coffee on his designer suit—a disaster!—hoping the gushy, overly solicitous receptionist would give him the key to the executive washroom. She'd done just that, and it was Rick's ticket to roam the halls of the inner sanctum.

He found Blair in the huge corner Office of the President, a room with glass walls and vertical blinds that made it easy to observe him through the slats. A large man with a heavy head of hair and a beard, Blair was nearly horizontal in his executive chair, his hands resting on his chest near his sternum with his thumbs pressed together. His eyes were probably closed, but Rick couldn't tell because of the sunglasses. Some kind of power nap?

"Mr. Fletcher? Mr. Blair will see you now."

It was the nervous young woman who'd given him the bathroom key. When he'd arrived, Rick had given her his phony real-estate-developer card. Bob Fletcher was the assumed name.

"Great," Rick said, pretending to be confused about where he was. He handed her the key and followed her lead to the door of Blair's office. Rick's research had turned up information about a parcel of land near the Foothill freeway that Blair had been trying to acquire for another store, but the owner wasn't budging. Rick figured presenting himself as a real-estate developer with personal ties to the property owner would get him a quick audience with Blair, and the ploy had worked.

Rick had also found an article on eligible L.A. bachelors that described Blair as charmingly eccentric, divorced, and raising a teenage daughter to whom he was devoted. A later article described Blair's ex-wife's death from a drug overdose and speculated that she'd grown despondent over their protracted custody battle. Despite the rumors of feuding, Blair's halo hadn't been tarnished by the dark tragedy. He'd been called a local business hero, who was above the health-care and benefits fray because even his part-time workers got benefits and a profit-sharing pension plan. TopCo paid well over minimum wage and people flocked to work for the chain.

The article delved into his personal life, mentioning past romances and insinuating that he and Lane Chandler might have been more than business acquaintances. Blair had coyly described Lane as a good friend and spoken highly of her concierge service. Rick was curious how close their friendship was. Close enough that Lane could call on Blair to do her dirty work?

Rick entered an unpretentious office with the requisite high-gloss mahogany desk and matching furnishings. A world map of TopCo locations hung on the wall behind Blair's back. The CEO was now sitting up, seemingly ready to do business. He flipped up his sunglasses, letting them rest in his hair, and revealing large, disarmingly gentle brown eyes. His Web site bio said he was forty-five, and Rick supposed he was attractive enough with his neatly trimmed beard and crisp white dress shirt. Rick didn't consider himself any judge of male beauty.

"Bob Fletcher, is it?" Blair rose and extended his hand.

"Nice of you to come by on such short notice. I always appreciate a man who's ready to do business."

"Thanks." Rick took his hand, surprised at the strength of his grip. "Are you light sensitive?" he asked as they both sat down.

"Oh, the sunglasses? Migraines. Day in, day out. I just live with them. It's not fair, is it? Seems like some of us struggle with pain and discomfort from the day we're born. Others just sail through."

Rick doubted Blair knew anything about the pain *he* lived with. "Character building?"

"Yeah." Blair snorted. "Fuck that. Just give me a skull that doesn't feel like a Christmas nut being cracked. Can I get you anything? Coffee, tea? I can't touch either. Even small amounts of caffeine—deadly."

"I'm fine," Rick said. "And by the way, Ms. Wright and SOOS, her Save Our Open Spaces group, send their love."

Blair fell back in his chair, his fingers steepled, sizing Rick up with an intrigued smile. "Tell me more. Apparently you have more influence with her and her band of no-growth cronies than I have. She's been laughing at my efforts to buy her out for the last two years."

Rick lied through his teeth, letting Blair think he had an inside track with the avowed no-development activist who owned the prime piece of land Blair wanted and was refusing to sell it at any cost. She and her wealthy neighbors wanted to keep their area pristine, which meant no discount stores and the middle-class riffraff they attracted. Not that Rick blamed them. There were enough chain stores to go around.

"You really believe she could be persuaded to change her mind?" Blair asked.

"People can always be persuaded once you know their blind spot." And that *was* Rick's specialty. Blind spots.

Blair looked skeptical. "You're not suggesting anything illegal."

Rick assured him he wasn't. "I've discovered in dealing with people that the key is to listen carefully, especially when they tell you what kind of person they *aren't*. It's almost always who they are. Likewise, pay attention to what they say they *don't* need because it's what they do."

"Sounds like good information to have." Blair nodded. "And what did you discover in listening to Bindy Wright? What does she need that she won't admit to?"

Rick smiled and sat forward. "Actually, *I* have a pressing need. I've invited Ms. Wright and several key members of SOOS to opening night at the Ahmanson. The play's a comedy about overzealous developers, but it has a surprise twist the good activists might appreciate. I need the best seats money can buy, and I'm considering TPC, a private-concierge service that I'm told you use."

"Lane Chandler's service?" Jerry looked more curious than surprised.

"Yes, Lane Chandler, impressive woman. I met with her the other day, and she suggested I speak with some of her clients. She specifically mentioned you." Rick had a feeling this would get back to Lane, which was fine with him. He wanted her to know he was right behind her, every step of the way.

"Well, you're right, Lane is impressive." Blair finessed a card from a silver box and handed it to Rick. "I'm sure she gave you her private number, but just in case. TPC is the best by far. You would know many of its clients by name."

Rick thanked him for the card. Nice bonus. "I may already know of two clients—Simon Shan and Priscilla Brandt? Both have had some serious problems lately, haven't they?"

Jerry shrugged it off. "Just coincidence. Lane is the best in the business. If you want your third-row-center seats, she can do it."

Rick slipped the card in the breast pocket of his jacket. What was this guy, her pimp? He could feel a simmering dislike for the man, the thought of which actually annoyed him. He had no personal interest in Jerry Blair. What he didn't get was Lane's interest, beyond Blair's big-fish status. And he knew there *was* interest because he'd heard the fond note in her voice as she dictated herself a reminder to call Blair and express her support for the upcoming party for his daughter.

"Is something wrong?" Blair asked.

Rick had to think fast. "Were you doing some kind of meditation earlier? I couldn't help but notice through the blinds." It could have gone either way, but Blair appeared pleased at the question.

"Meditation is for bringing things down," Blair explained. "I like to bring things up. What you saw me doing was pressing my thumbs together over my sternum. The combination of three heartbeats, all in sync, one in each thumb and the third in your chest, is very energizing. You should try it, my friend. No offense, but you look a little frayed around the edges."

Before Rick could answer, a flushed and angry teenage girl burst into the room, her sun-streaked ponytail flying. The receptionist was hot on her heels, apologizing. "Mr. Blair, I'm sorry, Felicity wouldn't let me buzz you."

"Would you get out of here," the teenager snarled at the receptionist. "He's *my* father and I have unfettered access to him. It was written up in the custody ruling."

No one bothered to explain to Felicity that custody was no longer an issue, Rick noticed. Her mother was deceased. Blair nodded to the receptionist to leave, at which point Felicity turned on her father.

"Dad, you canceled the Bone Dawgs! How you could do that? I checked their Web site, and they're performing somewhere else the night of my sweet sixteen!"

Blair rose. "Felicity, as you can see I'm in a meeting."

She glared at Rick, as if noticing him for the first time. "So? I'll bet he doesn't lie to and deceive *his* daughter. You never even told me. This is *so* humiliating. When my friends find out, I'm going to kill myself."

"Felicity, don't talk like that."

"Oh, yeah, because of *Mom,* right?" She rolled her eyes. "She probably OD'd because you were so sneaky and stingy in the divorce settlement."

Blair went ashen. He seemed speechless, helpless. Rick wanted to step in and help the man fend off his own daughter, but he couldn't interfere. This was private, and tragic. His ex had been busted for possession and dealing while they were married, but Blair's high-powered lawyers got her off with a slap on the wrist. Of course, those same lawyers eviscerated her during the divorce settlement. Apparently she became despondent and turned to drugs again when it became clear she was going to lose her daughter, too. The media speculated that it was suicide, but the coroner called it an accidental overdose. At any rate, Blair had been raising his daughter alone ever since, or trying to.

Felicity threw up her hands in disgust. "Oh, never mind. I'll find a band that will make the Bone Dawgs look like computer geeks—and you'd better not try to stop me, my dear devoted father, or I *will* kill myself."

She stormed from the room, leaving thundering silence in her wake.

Blair gathered himself together enough to apologize to Rick. "She never really recovered from her mother's death," he explained. "I hope you'll excuse her—and me. I'm afraid our meeting is over."

Blair asked Rick to let himself out and then he disappeared through a door that might have been a conference room. Rick took a moment to scope out the office. The far wall was covered in plaques and commendations, and there were several framed photographs of Blair's daughter on the console behind his desk. Rick also noticed a large black umbrella and a jacket that looked like a rain slicker hanging on a hook behind the office door, but neither raised any red flags. It rained occasionally, even in southern California.

Migraines, power napping and an abusive daughter? Jerry Blair didn't strike Rick as a man who had the balls to run his own life, much less a giant like TopCo. And that charmingly eccentric reference telegraphed gay. He really did wonder what Lane saw in him.

17

Lane stole into her desk drawer and pulled out a bar of dark, succulent Spanish chocolate. She broke it and offered half of her treasure to her sister. The fragrance of the rich chocolate liquor filled her senses.

"I need a hit," Lane said. "How about you?"

Sandra's smile held a touch of nostalgia, as if she was reminded of the kid sister who had shown up on her doorstep all those years ago. It was almost a moment.

Lane wished she and Sandra had actually shared some moments as sisters, but they'd never been close, and Lane had always felt responsible. Their parents fought and bickered constantly, and it was especially difficult for Lane because she was part of the problem. Their mother believed their father favored Lane over Sandra, and she railed at him about it.

Lane had no idea what to do. She adored her father and worried about him because of his heart condition, but she couldn't hover or spend much time with him without antagonizing her mother. Sandra moved out at seventeen, the day she graduated high school. She couldn't bear all the fighting, but it only got worse after she left, and that's when Lane knew it was up to her. She'd caused the rift, and the only way to heal it was to leave. Once she was out of the house, her parents would remember how they must have loved each other before she was born, and they would find their way back to each other.

Sadly, the fighting didn't stop after Lane ran away. Her mother had already disowned Sandra for running off and making a mess of her life. She just as quickly washed her hands of her youngest daughter. Lane never got the chance to tell her father why she really left, and the following year he died of congestive heart failure. Lane regretted to this day that she hadn't been with him. He was the only reason she'd stayed at home as long as she had.

Lane discovered from a returned Christmas card that her mother had remarried and moved with her new husband to a retirement colony in Mexico. The scribbled note from her mother on the unopened envelope said she was moving to Mexico, and she'd signed it with her new name. At times it just didn't feel right to Lane that so much pain hadn't taught them all some lessons and brought them closer. At least she'd begun to understand that the problems between her parents had existed long before she did.

And thank God for this stuff, she thought, breaking off a bite-size chunk of the candy bar. She didn't eat chocolate the way normal people did. She bit off the corners first, then nibbled around the edges, reveling in the pungent mix of flavors as long as possible. With the first piece in her mouth, she could taste cocoa that she imagined was from beans as rich and black as French-press coffee, a luscious apricot tang and possibly a hint of wild strawberries. But each melting bite got better. Chocolate was her balm. Sadly, it was also her friend, her lover and her consolation.

"What did you mean that you aren't going back?" she asked her sister.

Sandra tucked the wrapper around the piece of chocolate, seeming to steel herself. Whether it was against the candy or the question wasn't clear. "I can't work in any more establishments where everything is for sale. I need a fresh start—and I was hoping it could be here."

"Here? The Private Concierge?" Lane couldn't keep the shock out of her voice. She should have stepped up. Sandra was her sister. But as relieved as she was that Sandra wanted something better for her life, the timing couldn't be worse. Even if she hadn't meant to, Sandra had brought everything bad with her, the past. And Lane couldn't be sure that she hadn't meant to.

"A job, maybe?" Sandra studied the chocolate, apparently too uneasy to look at Lane.

"Sandra, I don't know. Things here are a little tough right now."

"Tough?" She gave the opulent surroundings a suspicious glance. "I would never have guessed."

"Not finances, other things. We have a lot going on."

"I could help you with whatever's going on. I'm incredibly organized, you know that. And I work very hard."

Weirdly, it was true. In their hunting-lodge days, Sandra had often looked as if she'd been dressed by a bag lady, which made her seem flighty and disorganized, but Lane had always suspected that was a defense mechanism. It was Hank, Sandra's crazy, controlling boyfriend, who'd talked her into taking the job supervising the hostesses at the lodge, and in those days, Sandra had been so insecure and eager to please him that she would have done anything—except become a hostess herself, which was a euphemism for call girl. An attractive woman was live bait at the lodge, so Sandra had made herself just un-attractive enough, which was actually a brilliant subter-fuge. In reality, Sandra had a steel trap for a mind, and she'd quickly worked her way up to managing the entire lodge, while letting Hank think he was in charge, of course.

Lane tossed what was left of her chocolate in the trash and turned in her chair to look out the window. She snapped the band on her wrist, trying to decide what she could share with her sister, certainly not her clients' troubles. She wasn't even sure that Sandra could be trusted to keep their own past under wraps, which would make it very dangerous to have her around. Lane had to come up with another plan, perhaps find Sandra a job somewhere else, with one of the many companies TPC had a relationship with, although that might come back to haunt her, too.

"What is that green thing on your wrist?" Sandra asked. "Are you still wearing a rubber band to ward off evil spirits? You haven't changed so much after all."

Lane glanced down at the frayed green band she'd just snapped, amused that Sandra thought it had something to do with evil spirits. Maybe it did. "Probably not," she admitted, turning the chair around. "And you? Have you changed?"

Lane hadn't really meant anything by it, but heat flooded Sandra's face.

"What are you trying to say?" She tugged at the neckline of her blouse, narrowing the gap. "I did the best I could back then. If you're such a big shot now that you don't approve of me or the way we lived, then just say it."

Lane's face colored, too. "No, I was just— Nothing, forget it."

"You're my sister," Sandra said, "and I've never asked you for anything. I'm asking now—and I'm not too proud to remind you that I helped you when you needed it."

She meant by taking her in and giving her a place to stay, Lane realized. Her sister must be desperate. She'd just played the guilt card, and with no apologies whatsoever. Her tone was defiant enough to make Lane wonder what was happening in Sandra's life. Lane didn't want to think about whether this had something to do with their years at the lodge—and the way everything had gone up in flames after Lane took off for Los Angeles—but she was forced to.

Running away had felt like Lucy Cox's only option at the time. She was a late bloomer, and still more string bean than sexpot, but the men had begun to take notice. She'd slept in the closet to avoid one of them. Twice, he'd come into her room at night, using the excuse that he was lost. And she'd been warding off Sandra's sleazy boyfriend since she was twelve. But she couldn't tell Sandra, who'd deluded herself into thinking she was in love with Hank. When Lane had finally taken a stand against Hank, threatening to tell her sister, he'd given Lane an ultimatum. It was her choice. She could either put out for him or for any of the members of the lodge who might be interested. One way or the other, she was going to earn her keep.

That's when Lane had started making her plans to run. She'd had no way of knowing that someone had been using the lodge's security cameras to take hidden videos and still shots of the VIP clientele. Even the men's used condoms had been collected, and whoever had done it had sewn several of the pictures and the condoms into the guts of Lane's favorite stuffed animal, a tattered giraffe that had been a Christmas gift from her dad. It was the one thing she took with her when she ran.

Lane was fairly certain Sandra had done the stashing, possibly for blackmail purposes, but more likely as leverage against Hank, should she ever need to back him off. But Lane had stonewalled the police when they'd questioned her, swearing she knew nothing about the contraband, even when it became clear that things would go much easier for her if she ratted out her sister.

The D.A. at the time must have believed he had the case of a lifetime. At daily press conferences, he tantalized the media, calling the suspects men of wealth and prominence, but withholding their names. He would reveal nothing until his case was solid, which included the testimony of fifteen-year-old Lucy Cox. She'd become a cause célèbre, and he was going to use her to prove that the lodge was engaged in prostitution with underage girls, even though she'd sworn to the D.A. and anyone who would listen that she'd never been a hostess.

But then, miraculously for the suspects, the stuffed giraffe and its contents were stolen from the evidence room, and the case was thrown out. Everyone walked away scot-free, except Lane, who was tried and convicted of solicitation, assault on an officer of the law, attempting to escape and everything else they could throw at her, including a trumped-up drug charge, with Rick Bayless prominent among the witnesses against her. The lodge was shut down, and all the VIPs went back to their privileged lives, but several mysteries remained unsolved.

The thief who stole the evidence was never found, and no one had any idea where that evidence went—or where it was now. It was still prime blackmail material to Lane's way of thinking. But she had actually tried *not* to think about it over the years. She wanted to believe her beloved stuffed animal had been destroyed by whoever took it, and the nightmare was over. Yes, there had been prostitution involved, but none of the hostesses were underage. It was all adult and consensual, except for Hank, who'd tried to force himself on her, and who had later died in a rather glorious car accident. She didn't know what happened to the other man, the one who'd come into her room and terrified her.

Lane felt a chill at the back of her neck. Hank's murder was unsolved, too, and there were still suspects galore. Of course, everyone thought Sandra had killed him. Battered girlfriends were always prime suspects. But Sandra's alibi had stood up—and Hank had many enemies. Any one of the lodge's VIPs would have had reason, and it made sense that they'd waited a few years to disassociate themselves from the lodge and the scandal. As the manager, Hank knew all the kinky details of their extracurricular sex lives, and may well have been the person collecting the blackmail evidence against them.

Many people had reason to want him dead, but the leads had all been blind alleys, and the police had finally given up. In reality, they should have talked to just one more person. Too bad that they hadn't, because Lane Chandler might just be the only person who could help them solve that crime.

Lane snapped the rubber band hard enough to feel its sting. The back of her neck was filmed with perspiration, icy cold. This wasn't going to work. As much as she might want to help her sister, she couldn't give Sandra a job— or let her stay. It would be far too dangerous.

Wednesday, October 9

The foothills of the San Gabriel mountains were haloed with a buttercup-yellow glow as Rick approached the ticket windows at Dodger Stadium in Chavez Ravine. The morning sun would soon be up and bathing everything in its glow, including him, and he wanted to be gone before that happened. To the left of the ticket windows, high on one of the concrete walls that housed the stadium, were murals of the greats who had played at the field. Rick recognized Sandy Koufax, Jackie Robinson and Pee Wee Reese. Today, Ned's image was up there, too. His portrait had been painted on a huge canvas backdrop, which now hung over the murals.

Rick was gripped by sadness as he looked up at the familiar grin lighting up Ned's handsome face. Beneath the portrait, in a roped-off area of the parking lot, were impressive floral bowers and bouquets from various dignitaries and organizations. But just as showy were the small mountains of stuffed animals, strewn flowers and homemade posters from the fans.

Rick walked over to a small poster and bent to read it. "Ned Talbert, R.I.P. an innocent man. Hell, if he was going to kill anybody, it would have been the refs for all those shitty calls against the Dodgers." Dodger management had held a memorial service here yesterday. Rick hadn't come. He'd had to choose between the chance to check out Jerry Blair and the service, but the decision had not been difficult. Rick wasn't in the right place for celebrating Ned's life and his baseball career, but he was glad others had been, lots of them, if the tributes were any indication. He'd been afraid the murder-suicide story might taint public opinion, but apparently the Dodger fans weren't ready to believe everything they saw on the news.

Rick noticed a security guard in his periphery. The man was watching, but keeping his distance, perhaps trying to give the early-bird baseball fan his moment. Still kneeling on the concrete, Rick bowed his head, as much to keep the guard away as to clear his thoughts. He'd had another sleepless night, filled with questions that went nowhere. Nothing came together, and that made him wonder if he was on the right path. He'd been focused on Lane Chandler to the exclusion of everything else, like one of those homicide dicks, so convinced he had his killer he ignored evidence that didn't make his case. Not unlike what they were doing in Ned's case.

Rick didn't know why his friend had been stripped of everything human and decent—his future, his honor, even the dignity of death—or who had a reason to want Ned remembered as a heinous killer and a coward. But if Ned's demise had anything to do with the package his friend had been holding for him, then he, Rick, was all the more responsible.

He hadn't come here to say goodbye. He would leave that for another time and place, somewhere he and Ned had shared their lives, not this big, impersonal shrine. Rick had come because he had something to say, a vow to make. To himself. Whoever had done this to Ned and Holly was the heinous killer and coward, and it was up to Rick to ensure that the killer be remembered that way. Man or woman, Rick intended to hunt the person down and strip *him* of everything that was human and decent.

He touched the ground to steady himself, then rose and walked away from the tribute without looking back. Ned did not die with a smile on his face, and Rick needed to keep the pain of his death fresh. The horror and fear Ned must have felt were always with Rick, a torturous reminder of what his friend had gone through. No one should leave this earth that way.

Rick had found himself hoping his theory of how Ned and his girlfriend died was wrong. It was excruciating to think about, and there was still too much he couldn't explain, even to his own satisfaction, like the lack of evidence that Ned had been restrained. Still, if your goal was to stage a murder-suicide, you'd do anything, whatever it took, to camouflage those restraints. Rick had tossed out the idea of Saran Wrap, but it wasn't that far-fetched.

Possibly even Mimi was coming around. He'd promised not to contact her again, but he'd had an e-mail from her this morning saying she wanted to meet him at a bar on the west side to discuss their last conversation. Rick's mouth tightened with a grim smile. Good.

Simon stepped out of the shower stall and reached for a towel. The steam in the room was thick, despite the apartment's excellent ventilation system, but the water was already chilling into beads on his body. He had the air-conditioning on high. He wanted to feel that shock of cold air after the hot shower. Possibly it would calm him, like the hot and cold baths once used in insane asylums.

The irony of that idea amused him as he cleared a circle in the fogged mirror and studied his dark eyes and golden skin tone. The wear and tear of so many sleepless nights was showing, but he could see the resolve in his eyes, the determination that had turned hard and focused. The hounds may have thought they'd run him up a tree, but he wasn't their big-game trophy yet.

His hand brushed something on the bathroom counter, and he was startled by the small Chinese puzzle box that sat on there. Had he forgotten to return it to the safe last night? That was incredibly reckless of him. Inside was a tile from the rare ivory mah-jongg set left by his paternal grandmother. In the game of mah-jongg, wind tiles were inscribed with Chinese characters for the four compass directions representing the four winds. This precious ivory tile was inscribed with the Chinese word *dong,* which meant east. His father had broken up the ancestral set to give Simon the tile when he left Taiwan for boarding school in London. He'd told Simon that the tile would remind him where he'd come from, and it would one day bring him back.

Simon concentrated on the intricate steps to open the box, reassured when the lid came open, and he saw the tile safe inside. As he closed the box, he felt the back of his neck begin to tingle, ultrasensitive. It was almost as if he'd picked up a warning signal. He wrapped the towel around his waist, aware that she must be somewhere nearby. That was probably the reason for his prickling skin as much as the cold. He'd become so sensitized to her presence he could register it as he would a change in temperature.

He'd had no contact with her since yesterday when she'd surprised him with that surreal blow job. Afterward, he'd banished her to her room, but he still hadn't decided what to do about her. He wanted to talk with Lane Chandler first, and probably in person. He didn't know who to trust at this point, and Lane's service had provided him with the female bodyguard whose name was Jia Long, which meant beautiful dragon in Chinese.

Long's credentials couldn't be faulted. She'd been

trained by Israeli martial arts experts, had worked in international intelligence, including Scotland Yard, and her résumé described her rather mysteriously as an escape artist, skilled in the use of exotic concealed weapons.

Simon had a little test in mind, for Lane, and for his bodyguard, as well.

He pushed open the door and saw her at the end of the hallway that led to the master bedroom. She quickly averted her eyes. She was on her knees, her head bowed, holding something in the palms of her hands. He walked toward her, wondering why his legs should be shaking at the sight of a kneeling woman. He had the upper hand. He was on his feet, towering over her.

"What's this?" he asked, meaning the ornate metal object she held. Before she could answer, he saw that it was the key to the guest room door. When he was decorating the condo, he'd found an antique door with panes of frosted glass that had reminded him of the sliding doors in his family home in Taiwan. He'd bought it immediately.

"It's the key to my room," she said. "It can be locked from both sides. I brought this so you could lock me in."

"Why would I do that?"

"Because you'll never trust me otherwise. Please, lock me up for as long as necessary, I beg you."

His vision went pale for a second, turning her bowed body silvery white. Trust her? That was something he could never do. He didn't dare, and yet he sensed that she was sincere. He actually believed her.

Maybe that was exactly what she wanted.

"You were sent to protect me," he said. "How are you going to do that if you're locked up in your room?"

She looked up, perplexed. "How can I protect you if

you don't trust me, if you won't put your life in my hands? It's not possible."

Simon wanted to laugh, but his throat was suddenly hoarse. He would lock her up. God, yes, he would lock her up. But he couldn't imagine any room that could contain her. It would take a bank vault and a straitjacket at the very least.

18

For Seth Black, knowledge wasn't power, information was. Information was a rush, a high. It broke him out in a sweat—and he had the feeling he might be sweating a lot today. Besides, what else did he have in his claustrophobic, radioactive, wired little world? Nothing. There were no signs of a fancy car, a mansion or a girl in his life. Information was it. His Prozac.

He worked out of his living room, and if he'd ever let anyone inside this landfill of a one-bedroom apartment, they would have reported him to the health department as a pack rat. He *was* a pack rat, but that was only half the problem.

He distracted himself by clicking the mouse that rested beneath his fingers. On his computer screen, a video replayed of a shrouded figure leaving The Private Concierge offices via a back stairwell. The figure exited the building through an emergency door, and according to the videographer who got the footage, the figure had been spotted making the same exit a half-dozen times already that week. He'd never been seen going in, however, which led Seth to think that the figure went in the normal way, through the front door like every other employee. In other words, the mystery man worked for TPC.

Seth whooped and slammed his hand down on his desk. It hurt a little, but what the hell. He was on the trail of the Giant Killer! Jack, himself. No one was more curious about Jack's identity than Seth. Jack had made Gotcha.com piles of money with his amazing scoops, and Seth was not ungrateful, but he wanted a little control over the guy, just a little.

His laughter turned into a cracked giggle as he pushed his glasses back up on his nose. Information again. Knowing Jack's identity would be Seth's ace in the hole, whether he used it or not.

Seth was scrolling though the rest of his e-mail, checking out the death threats he routinely received, when someone rapped at his door. He nearly knocked over his chair and was halfway down the hall toward his bedroom before he could stop himself. *Whoa.* What was he doing? This was ridiculous. He pressed a palm against each wall of the narrow hallway and bent forward, fighting the nausea. He was going to be sick for sure.

Who the hell was banging on his front door? He'd given his videographers explicit orders to use the drop slot. He'd had the receptacle built into the wall of his porch because he didn't like answering the door. Well, shit, he *couldn't* answer the door. Even thinking about it panicked him. And he'd been adamant that everyone use the slot. The sign he'd put out there had a big fat red arrow pointing to it. But some idiots couldn't wipe their butt with either hand.

The pounding stopped, leaving Seth so wobbly he wanted to sit down on the floor and cry. Thirty-two years old, a full-grown man with a bad complexion and a receding hairline. Nice visual.

He was just catching his breath when the banging started up again. *What?* Delivery people rang the bell and left the packages at the door. Seth's elderly neighbor lady usually brought the stuff in. He'd given her a key, and he paid her to help out with things, like groceries and supplies. So, who was out there now, trying to drive him nuts?

This had to stop. He whirled around in anger, but froze where he stood. He was going to have to open that door— and he hadn't done that in months, years? He'd lost track.

He surveyed his living room. The walls were stacked high with household supplies and electronic equipment, all in boxes. These days he worked out of boxes rather than open the door to furniture movers. He owned the whole apartment building. He was rich. He could easily live somewhere else—except that he couldn't.

When he reached the end of the hallway, he turned and backed toward the front door, feeling his way through the booby-trapped living room. A circuit board he'd been working on was sitting on the floor by his desk, the guts hanging out, wires exposed. If he stepped in that, he'd fry. Of course, he should have unplugged it, but sometimes he liked to live dangerously. How else was he supposed to prove he wasn't a whining, sniveling pussy?

Walking backward was hard. Seth Black was no Michael Jackson. He would have tried to ignore the knocking, but it was loud, insistent and repetitive. He tripped over a cord and nearly landed on his butt. That really pissed him off. Growling, he heaved himself up and made a dash for the door.

He ripped open the old-fashioned mail slot he'd had cut into his door when the panic attacks started. "Hello?" he shouted, unable to see anyone. "Who's there? What do you want?"

"It's me!" a small voice squeaked. "I'm down here."

A kid? Curious, Seth actually unchained the door and opened it a crack. Sweat was pouring down his face and his fingers felt like chopsticks. He couldn't get them to work.

The grinning face of a prepubescent girl greeted him. "Want to buy some Girl Scout cookies?" she cooed.

She was sitting on the steps, apparently waiting for him to come to the door. But Seth was immediately suspicious of her freckles and impish red curls. And when she stood up, proud as punch in her plaid school uniform, and showed him a box that looked like cookies you could have bought at any store, he figured this had to be some kind of scam. He'd heard about kids who pretended to collect for the United Way and then used the money for drugs.

"You nearly kicked down my door for this?" he snarled at her. "You could have killed me!"

Her eyes got round as saucers, but Seth wasn't buying her parochial-school act. He hauled off and slammed the door so hard the walls vibrated and boxes fell.

He could hear the little girl crying, but he didn't give a shit. Kids shouldn't be allowed to sell fake Girl Scout cookies door to door. Kids shouldn't be allowed to sell anything. Look at the trouble she'd caused with her squeaky voice and ham-hock fists. How could a little twerp like that pound so loud?

He made it to his desk and collapsed in the chair. He was hollow, breathless. It felt as if his lungs had been yanked out of his chest. His heart was clanging like a five-alarm fire bell, scaring the shit out of him. This was it, the perfect storm. The roaring in his ears was a tornado funnel that would suck him up and spit him out. There would be nothing left of him but the plugged sebaceous glands and the pimples he hated.

The circuit board sat open on the floor, wires exposed. A terrible urge overcame him, and in that second he understood why people drove their cars into trees and swallowed too many pills and did crazy, reckless, suicidal things. They did it because the pain was too great. They couldn't live with it.

He didn't want to die. He just wanted to stop this panic attack.

He dropped to the ground, his hand hovering over the wires, crazy thoughts flooding his brain. Electroshock therapy, Seth Black style. It would be excruciatingly painful. It might even kill him, but it would be pain he had chosen. That was the difference. His choice. His pain. Anything to take control away from the demons.

He was still hunched over the wires moments later when a tiny white card floated down and landed on his arm. He could have shaken it off, but something stopped him. It was the business card that IRS guy had left him, along with the five hundred bucks.

Seth plucked the card from his arm, accidentally crinkling it as he settled back on his haunches to have a look. Nothing there he hadn't seen when he read it the first time. Just a company name, a cell-phone number and e-mail address.

Odd that he already felt a little calmer. The clanging had stopped, and his breathing was okay, although he didn't really understand why. Money both thrilled and soothed him, but it couldn't be that. IRS agents didn't have access to enough money to produce a sneeze, much less this effect.

But this guy had been throwing money around pretty good, as Seth remembered. Possibly he wasn't an IRS agent? Seth smoothed the creases from the card and began to laugh. It felt like some kind of a sign. It had to be, because he was almost afraid to let go of the damn thing.

Dar felt his forehead, wondering if he was getting sick. He had several brand-new Darwin phones opened up on the clean room table, their guts on display. Works of art, all of them, as exquisitely designed as the most intricate electronic spiderweb, but he didn't even feel a flutter as he gazed at them. They could have been peeled potatoes for all he cared.

Was he hot? Perspiring? Allergic to the tuna salad he'd eaten for lunch? There had to be something wrong with him. It wasn't just that he couldn't respond to the naked beauty of his phones. He couldn't even get turned on by the real problem. These phones all had a flaw.

Luckily they'd been caught before they were issued to any clients, because every one of these babies was setting off airport-security sensors, and Darwin had no idea why. He hoped the cause was as simple as the extra batteries or the power strips, but normally that kind of mystery would have taken possession of his mind until he'd solved it. Today, he just didn't care. Nothing called to him. Nothing excited him. Not faulty phones, not even his new project, which dealt with earthquake prediction through measuring patterns in the tidal flow.

He left the room, pulled off his disposable lab jacket and his gloves and stuffed them in the trash. He'd been inspired by the work of a maverick geologist who'd tied earthquakes into the tides, but right now Darwin couldn't have cared less about predicting earthquakes. Maybe an earthquake would get his pulse going.

He crossed the hall to his office and keyed open the door. He didn't always bother to lock it, but this morning he'd noticed that the Dodgers cap that sat on his gooseneck desk lamp was on the floor. Maybe he'd knocked it off himself. But he wasn't wearing it when he left last night. He didn't even like the Dodgers.

"What *do* you like, Darwin?"

It was a rhetorical question he'd been asking himself since Janet walked out of his place night before last—and his life, apparently. He wasn't sick. He was Janetless. He hadn't heard from her since then, and he hadn't called because she'd seemed to be asking him not to. She'd said it would happen. "You'll see," she'd said. He had no idea what that meant, but it had sounded like she wanted some space.

"Darwin, you have a text message."

Darwin wheeled around. His phone was talking to him. It was lying on his desk, and he hadn't been able to hear it in the clean room.

He rushed over and picked up the phone, hit the button to bring up the screen and saw the words that filled the display.

imusm. tonite? watch movies on your big-screen tv? xoxo J

"J? Janet?" His heart began to clatter. "I m u s m? What does that mean?"

He squinted at the texting lingo, trying to interpret it. "I m you? I miss you? S m? Sadomasochist? Silly man? No! So much! I miss you so much."

Darwin gasped. She was saying she missed him and wanted to watch movies with him tonight. He quickly typed in his response.

my big screen and i await u. xoxo D

Darwin flipped the phone into the air, sending it so high that it nearly hit the ceiling before it stalled out and started to drop. It did three somersaults on the way down, and he caught it behind his back. He had a date with the woman who loved all things big. Things were looking up.

Mimi had wanted to meet for drinks at a cellar bar in West L.A. Rick didn't like the idea of a bar where you took an elevator down to a dank subterranean room with low ceilings and no back exit, but Mimi was definitely calling the shots. He would have trekked to a polar substation in Antarctica to find out what she wanted to talk to him about.

"An apple martini for the lady and a beer for me," he told the hovering cocktail waitress. "Whatever you have on tap." He wasn't sure how booze would mix with the drugs in his system, but hell, all it could do was kill him.

"Are you okay?" Mimi asked as the waitress left. "You're perspiring."

Rick touched his brow with the cocktail napkin. "This could be Hitler's bunker. It's hot in here," he lied. It was a beautifully air-conditioned lounge, designed to look like a Roaring Twenties speakeasy. The female help wore practically nothing, and he was enjoying himself. He hadn't been in a dark bar with a woman in a long time. It made him want to feel that spark again—or anything resembling that spark—even though Mimi wasn't necessarily the girl of his dreams. And vice versa, he was sure.

Mimi pulled a laptop computer out of her battered briefcase. "So, here's what I have on Lucia Cox, aka Lane Chandler. You ready?"

"Uh, yeah." She'd told him she'd found nothing on Lane, but she must have gone back for a second look. He was more than ready, but there was this one thing. He still needed to tell Mimi what he knew about Ned. "Give me five minutes first, okay? Maybe less."

She scowled. "This is *not* about the Talbert case, right?"

"No, this is personal, deeply." Rick knew he might not get another chance at this kind of time with Mimi. She'd insisted on meeting him here because she didn't want him at the police station, where everybody knew him as Ned's friend. She couldn't have it look as if she was passing him information, even if it was only about Lane Chandler.

The waitress showed up with their drinks, and Rick held back on his information, letting Mimi drink some of her odd green concoction and hoping she'd mellow out before he started.

After a moment, she glowered at him, her lips still on the straw. "Okay, what is it? Let's get this over with."

He signaled a time-out. "You asked me if Ned was capable of killing himself to save a woman, and the answer is yes. Ned was born to rescue women, and he was fatally attracted to damaged goods. He'd been carrying a load of guilt for years because he couldn't save his mom and his sister. Yeah, if anybody could have been manipulated into killing himself in a situation like that, it was Ned."

"He actually believed the perp wouldn't kill the girl if he killed himself?"

"Maybe, maybe not. It was the only way he could stop the torture, and that's what he had to do. Afterward, the perp killed the girl anyway, which was the plan all along."

Mimi shook her head, frowning at her drink as though it was a urine sample. It did look like a little like overripe pee. Rick was certain he'd never be able to drink anything green again.

"You met Ned when he came to the department's charity 10K run," Rick reminded her. "Maybe you got a feeling about him? He didn't torture women, Mimi. He saved them." Rick confessed his first theory, which he hadn't shared with her before. "I thought he might have killed Holly by accident, some game they were playing with ropes and plastic bags, and then he shot himself out of remorse. I could almost make myself believe it, except that Ned didn't like guns. He didn't own one—and it wasn't in him to torture anyone."

"And I'm supposed to do *what* with this information? Tell the brass I knew Ned and he was too sweet to commit the crime?"

"Just consider it. The guy deserves that much. He had an aversion to guns and a need to save doomed women. It needs to be known." He let that sink in. "And if you should decide to share this information with the powers that be, please take full credit for it."

"Or full blame when they tell me I'm crazy."

She yanked the straw out of her drink, picked up the glass and took a slug. After several minutes of brooding silence, she said, "Do you want this stuff on Lane Chandler or not?"

Rick could read people, but he had no clue whether he'd gotten through to her. "I want it," he said.

All business, she booted up her laptop and pulled up a file. "It occurred to me that Lucia Cox was probably on probation for some time after she left juvie, and I could track her that way. Turned out I was right. The girl had an interesting life, but she kept her nose clean."

"No adult priors?" Rick asked. "No record at all?"

"Clean as a whistle. She went to the equivalent of a vocational high school in juvenile hall. When she got out she worked at a low-rent L.A. hotel, where she had to do everything from staff the registration desk to clean the rooms. Her probation officer stayed in touch with her even after she was off the rolls. He had some concerns about a night job she'd taken."

"Which was?"

"A bouncer at a sports cabaret, which is a nice way of saying titty bar." Mimi shrugged. "Apparently the job paid well. She worked at the hotel during the day and the bar at night to come up with the money to put herself through college. The officer was impressed enough that he helped her get a scholarship, but that bouncer job must have been someone's idea of a cute promotional trick. She wasn't big enough to strong-arm anyone, although she was fast. You remember how crazy she got when we tried to take her in."

Rick did remember. She was fast—and desperate. She swore her friend was sick, and she couldn't leave him on the streets. When Rick tried to get the cuffs on her, she fought her way out of his hold and cut his lip with the open lock. Come to think of it, he owed her for that.

"Looks like she may have been one of the entertainers at the bar, too," Mimi added, peering at the screen. "Not a dancer, some kind of nightclub hypnotist gig. Don't ask me how that worked. But listen to this, she also volunteered at a hospital, holding preemies. Her voice soothed them. This is all from her former probation officer."

Preemies? As in babies? Rick shook his head, but he wasn't entirely surprised. She undoubtedly could be hypnotic and soothing when she wanted to, and yeah, she could probably rock babies to sleep. Babies of all ages. He'd Googled her service, going all the way back to when she was a company of one. Her ads had the mark of an amateur and she'd probably written them herself, but they promised the sun, the moon and the stars. There wasn't anything she wouldn't do to make her clients' lives easier and more rewarding. Hire her and your life would be transformed. She would be your genie in a bottle.

Lane Chandler, miracle worker.

That was one of the consumer remarks, praising her dedication. Rick didn't know how much of that was promo, strategically placed by her, but the consensus seemed to be that Lane Chandler was a woman who could solve any problem.

Interesting that they were both in the same business. He solved problems, too—and she had become one.

"When did she legally change her name?" he asked Mimi.

"As soon as she was off probation. It was like she couldn't wait to kill off Lucy Cox."

Interesting. Rick had already formed an opinion of Lane Chandler, and he doubted she would find it flattering. But it didn't dovetail with what Mimi was telling him. The adult woman sounded complex, possibly with conflicting personas—Lucy, Lucia, Lane—but he had the feeling there was a thread running through it all, a dominant character trait that tipped the scale and defined her.

He couldn't seem to get a read on her from the investigative angle, but maybe if he thought of himself as a potential client... He'd done that fifteen years ago when he'd mistaken her for a grown woman. He still didn't know how a fifteen-year-old had managed to be that seductive and mesmerizing. She'd changed everything since then, even her eye color, but he wondered if she'd really changed anything at all.

19

Case Notes. Wednesday, October 9, 11:00 p.m.:

Her real name is Lucia Cox. She changed it to avoid any association with her criminal past. But she hasn't left her past behind. She's still selling what everybody wants. She's just found a way to make it legal.

Lucy Cox knows how to take care of people. Gender is irrelevant. She is equally skilled with either sex. With men, she provides balm for the ego, a soft, knowing hand for aching muscles and a sharp mind for detail. It's sexual, of course. Everything she does is sexual without actually being sexual. But the promise is there. Always.

Lucy will take care of you.

With women she is knowing in a different way. She's compassionate, a listener, a sister. She not only meets their needs, she anticipates them, and that quality of empathy is irresistible to women. They love having their minds read. They love being known. The less a woman understands herself the more she wants to be understood....

Rick paused, pen in hand, aware of his quickening pulse beat. This was getting too personal. And that was the problem. It *was* personal.

He continued to write.

Is that true of everyone? Do any of us understand ourselves? Aren't we always a step or two away, for our own protection? Who can look in the smoking mirror and not be charred? We can't look at our own infantile needs, our rage for love and approval, our blind rage when we're rejected. We would die, like the basilisk from the Bible.

Is that what Lucy sees that we can't? Does she know us that well? What are her naked impulses? Does she have them?

Women are coddled in a different way than men. It's more subtle, but she does coddle them, speaks to them in ways that only they can hear, sees the secret needs that others miss. Perhaps that's sexual, too. It's not entirely clear with Lucy. It's only clear that she can see what people lack as if she were psychic, feel their deepest pain.

Consider the power this gives her. And what power does to people.

He set down the pen, unable to write as fast as his thoughts were coming. She'd had the power at fifteen when he put her in jail. She was thirty now. She'd been free and on her own since eighteen, and it wasn't hard to imagine that she'd planned her steps carefully, including choosing the perfect profession. She had some of the country's highest-profile people in her care.

He settled back in his chair, bemused by what he'd written. He was looking for that one unifying element of her personality that would explain her and mesh all the contradictions. He'd pegged her as a fixer, a problem-solver like he was. But there was no seduction involved in what he did, no emotion. It wasn't personal. She dealt in fantasies, dreams. He dealt in reality, and often, night-mares. He completed assignments for people. She completed people, insinuated herself into their lives.

How had she insinuated herself into Ned's life? And why did he want her there? Or did he?

Extortion?

Reflexively, Rick opened and closed the rings of the binder in front of him. He'd used the case-notes approach because that was how he'd kept track when he was in law enforcement—and he still had Lucia Cox's file. But in those days his notes had been an accumulation of facts about the crime, not behavioral profiles of the suspect. This read like the psychological autopsy of a D.C. madam.

He'd been trying to sort out his thoughts about Lane Chandler and catalog what he knew. But if he'd been hoping to produce something orderly and logical, bullet points leading to a conclusion, this wasn't it. What he'd written read more like free association—and it was about Lucia Cox, not Lane Chandler.

Odd that his office felt chilly but the back of his neck was damp. Could be the drugs, but it was probably his frustration. She still eluded him, despite all his research. She was his only link to what happened at Ned's that night, and knowing who she was seemed vital, but maybe he was deluding himself about her importance. He'd begun to confuse her with her alter ego, Lucia Cox—and he kept going back to his encounter with a fifteen-year-old kid, as if there was something unresolved. Maybe this wasn't about Ned. Maybe it was about him.

He picked up the pen and wrote one last line in his notes. **The woman who promised to transform others' lives had done quite a job on her own.**

A scraping sound caught Rick's attention. A week ago that noise would have sent him down the hall to the bedroom for his gun. Now he knew exactly what it was. Quivering against the baseboard of the far wall in his office, a small, gray, furry thing with big, black, shiny eyes stared at him. As soon as they made eye contact, the creature blinked and disappeared behind a stack of bins. Damn mouse was taking over the place.

Rick couldn't kill him now. No way. Having a suicidal mouse around the place was like looking into the smoking mirror. Rick saw himself, and it was not a welcome sight. What had happened to the man who thought all he wanted was to cut ties and let the boat drift out to sea? Sappy as it sounded, he now saw a man who had somehow found the will to live, despite the odds against him, and even if all living meant was limping around like a wounded mouse, trying to find a second of meaning in whatever time was left. He saw a man both stupid and stubborn. He saw a survivor.

Lane sat on her living room couch with her white terry caftan flowing around her like a prom dress and her feet tucked under her butt. She'd balanced her lightweight laptop on the arm of the couch, and she was inputting some last-minute changes to the itinerary for her trip to Dallas at the crack of dawn tomorrow. She'd spoken with Ashley today, who assured her that she had several strong candidates lined up for the key positions.

That was the good news. She'd also spoken with Jerry Blair, who'd told her about a visit he'd had from a real-estate developer. The developer said he was considering joining Lane's service and that Lane had told him to contact Jerry for a recommendation. Lane didn't recognize the man's name when Jerry mentioned it, but she knew who he was by the description—close-cropped hair and aviators that hid striking green eyes. Lane had pretended she knew the developer and thanked Jerry for the recommendation. What else could she do?

Rick Bayless was becoming quite the stalker.

Lane was achingly tired, which made an early-morning trip seem all the more arduous. She'd been looking forward to getting away, until her sister materialized, hidden away in Lane's office bathroom. She'd put Sandra up in a good hotel until she could figure out what to do with her. She'd also loaned her some money, and now Lane was rethinking her decision to ask Sandra to find work elsewhere, as far away as possible.

Lane didn't want to go through a wrenching family fight right now, and she was almost certain there would be one, given Sandra's state of mind. Besides, it might make more sense to have her sister close until Lane figured out what she was up to, if anything. Sandra was smart under all the fluster and bluster. She might be one of the smartest women Lane had ever known. There must be something she could do at TPC that would keep her busy and out of trouble. Meanwhile, she did bear watching, if only because her timing was suspect.

Lane grabbed her cell, intending to leave Val Drummond a message to find something tedious and boring for Sandra at TPC, perhaps in accounting. She tapped out the speed-dial code, but got a message that service was unavailable. Probably just a temporary glitch, but she wanted to get the chore taken care of and go to bed. According to the display, it was midnight.

She unwound herself and went to the dining room to look for the cordless phone. It was on the sideboard, where she last remembered leaving it, but as she reached for the phone, a shadow crossed the room. Someone had moved past the windows of the French doors. There were no lights on in the room, and she could see her dimly lit roof garden outside, but not well enough to make out details.

She told herself it could have been a bird. There was a fountain in her garden, but she'd never heard of birds taking midnight baths. Still, she was reluctant to call security. It was probably nothing, but the flickering shadows were making her heart jump. Even her legs felt weak.

There was a control panel by the French doors, and one of the buttons turned on the sprinklers outside. If something was out there, she might be able to scare it away. She found the panel, but had to feel her way to the right button. She did not want to turn on the lights or the sound system.

She counted over from the left, found the fourth button and pressed it, relieved as the sprinklers came on. The sound of running footsteps brought her to the window. She saw someone heading for the fire escape. The figure looked tall enough to be a man, but moved fast, with catlike agility. For a second she thought he'd leaped over the side of the wall, but he must have gone down the fire escape. She had to call security now, but she couldn't stop shaking.

Her first thought was that someone was trying to burglarize the place, but her mind didn't want to stop at that scenario. Crime was infrequent and rarely violent in a neighborhood like this. Still, you never knew. She was probably lucky she hadn't been raped or murdered. Her next thought was of him, Rick Bayless. He'd been spying on her in her office, so why not here?

That bastard. Anger burned through her fear.

Her enmity toward Bayless came surging back, as real and palpable as the day he'd arrested her. He had terrorized her. She'd told him nothing when he questioned her about the pictures and condoms he'd found hidden in her stuffed animal. There'd been nothing to tell. She had no way of knowing how any of it got there. But he didn't believe her.

He'd slammed his hand down on the table and called her a liar. She'd been so good at not showing fear that he'd upped the stakes, trying his damnedest to scare her with stories about what they'd do to her in juvie. She'd never understood his fury—it was almost personal—or why he'd called her street trash, said she was no good, a waste of his time, worthless. She'd lost it when he got in her face and called her a whore. She'd slugged him with her fist.

She now believed that's what he'd wanted. He considered his cut lip an accident and wanted to be sure he had something solid to pin on her. Later, when the judge read the charges against her, there were not one but two counts of assault against a police officer. Talk about bait and switch. Talk about entrapment.

He wasn't an officer, he was a monster. He'd warned her he would throw away the key, and he had. She'd been charged with eight felony counts, six of which had nothing to do with the solicitation for which Bayless arrested her. He'd thrown in resisting arrest, attempting to escape and whatever else he could come up with, including a drug

charge because he'd found some capsules in her pocket—
pills she'd bought from a street vendor who swore they
would help Dar. Turned out they were nothing but table
sugar, but somehow Bayless had made the drug charge
stick, and Lane had done three years in juvenile hall.
Three *years* in a hellhole with hard-core gangbangers and
drug dealers when she would have been out in six months
at most. And all because she'd offered him a blow job.

She'd definitely picked the wrong guy, but she had no
experience spotting cops, and she'd never solicited anyone
before. He hadn't believed that, either. Nor had he
believed she needed money to get medical help for Dar.
He'd just dragged her into jail and thrown the book at her.

She walked back to the table, her legs unsteady, and
picked up the phone. She needed to call security. She
needed to report this, but for some reason she didn't. Why
wasn't she calling? Maybe she didn't want the guards to
see what a furious, shaking mess she was. Her pulse was
pounding and her hands trembling, but it wasn't fear, it
was rage. She hated admitting how deep it went, even to
herself.

Darwin LeMaster's office was a mole labyrinth.
Sandra's flashlight beam passed over piles of clutter that
were several feet high, creating the illusion of an underground network of tunnels and paths through the darkened
room. From where she stood at the doorway, it looked as
if the clutter was mostly boxes of electronic junk and
stacks of computer magazines and comic books.

She didn't know how anyone could work in such chaos.
It was midnight and everyone had left TPC's corporate
offices long ago. Lane had told Sandra she would be
working at home tonight, so Sandra had felt safe in

making her move, but she didn't know where to start. His computer, of course, but it looked as if he had a half dozen of them sitting around the room on various perches. There were two on his desk alone, but that narrowed it down. She would start there.

Gingerly she made her way along the path that led to his desk, using the flashlight beam to guide her. She'd checked all the offices first, to make sure no one was around. If anyone had been, her story was going to be that she'd lost her wallet today when Lane was giving her a tour of the place, but she didn't want to disturb anyone this late at night. She'd already told the security guard that, and he'd been very courteous about letting her in and offering to help her search.

She'd convinced him there was no need. She would make a quick check, retrace her steps and be on her way. If he was watching her now on a security camera, he wouldn't see much beyond the beam of her light. Should that make him suspicious, she would say she couldn't find the light switch, and in this obstacle course of an office that wasn't hard to believe.

But she doubted he was watching. She'd saved Darwin's room for last, and she'd seen the raunchy magazine that had been lying open on the guard's desk, hidden, he thought, behind the high counter. By now his attention must have wandered back to the "article" he was reading on the world's sluttiest sorority sisters.

Sandra let out a despairing sigh. It was a shame. People took no pride in their work anymore, none at all. All you had to be was average nowadays to beat ninety percent of the competition. She considered it a sign of the times. The American dream was no longer within the reach of the average man, and he was starting to figure that out. The system was rigged. Rigged to the great advantage of those who already had the dream, and if Joe Blow wanted any part of his share, he had to be just as ingenious and cagey as, say, those Enron dudes. Actually, cagier. Most of the Enron dudes were in jail.

Sandra sat down at Darwin's desk, wishing she had something to cover the seat of his chair. It looked as if a wad of gum was stuck to the outside of the metal webbing that supported the arm. Ugh. At least she could tell what computer he was using by the keyboard. The keyboard to her left was so thick with dust it made her wonder if the cleaning people were ever allowed in here.

Darwin was clearly an eccentric, but that could work in her favor.

She switched on the computer to her right and whispered thanks under her breath. It was password protected, but he hadn't activated the biometrics security measures. It didn't require his fingerprints to boot up the machine, just a password. That would give her a fighting chance.

She hadn't been quite honest about her employment plans. She had worked at a casino and managed a restaurant, but she'd also been taking computer-science classes, including software programming, and she was damn good at it. That was going to be her new career, until it became clear that she had to come here to Century City.

Now for the password. She checked the scribbles on his desk-calendar blotter and opened the drawers, searching the contents with her flashlight. She even checked under the desktop and the seat of his chair. People often stuck things they were trying to hide to the underside of surfaces, and it was amazing how often they wrote down their passwords. But apparently Darwin hadn't done that. She saw nothing stuck anywhere except that disgusting gum.

She tried to give the gum a wide berth as she bent to feel under the chair again, but something scraped her arm. Curious, she turned the flashlight beam on the gum and realized that it was holding a crumpled sticky note to the metal webbing under the arm. It took careful work to free the note from the webbing and the gum, but when she smoothed it out she could read all but the last character of what looked very much like a password string.

How's that for security, she thought with a disbelieving shake of her head. Just as she'd always said, people were incompetent. And in this case, careless, too. Sandra's good luck was very possibly her sister's downfall.

She turned her attention back to the computer and typed in what she had of the password, quickly running through all thirty-five characters in the alphanumeric alphabet for the missing letter or digit. Unless he'd gotten really fancy, those were the only possibilities. As it turned out, she didn't have to go very far. The addition of the letter *D* brought up the hard drive, which contained his programs and data files.

"Excellent," she whispered. "Now we're in business." All that was left was to introduce a virus in the form of a security patch that would download automatically to all the Darwin phones.

20

"Who's there?" Rick heard the hush of someone's breathing. He felt the bed shake, as if something heavy had bumped into it, and in his groggy, half-drugged state, he thought it was her again.

"Lane? Wha the hell?" The words came out slurred, confused.

The bed jolted, knocking him into the brass bars of the headboard. Rick's eyes flew open to a sea of black. It was night, his bedroom. The room was dark. He struggled to make sense of the simplest things. When he tried to get up, something locked onto his ankles and pinned them down.

He grabbed for the headboard and missed. A pair of massive fists dragged him off the bed. He hit the floor hard, a direct blow to his tailbone. The pain made him gag. A flying kick to his chest knocked him back against the bed. Acid foamed up from his gut, mixing with the blood in his mouth. This son of a bitch wasn't playing games. His intent was to maim or kill.

Rick rolled to his side. He launched himself in the direction of the attacker, hoping to knock him off his feet. Another blow grazed his shoulder, and he caught the guy's leg, upending him. The floor shook with his weight. Rick still couldn't see, but knew he was dealing with a big guy, a giant.

Rick rocked to his knees and pounded his fists into the man's gut, searching for his most vulnerable area, the groin. He had to put this guy out fast. A shadow loomed in front of him. His attacker had rolled to his side. He was getting up. Rick heaved himself up, too. He connected with a right to the man's jaw. He heard a bone crack and ducked as a swing came his way. Maybe he had a fighting chance here. Maybe this wasn't his last night on earth.

He plowed into his assailant, knocked him backward and waled on him like a punching bag. He felt him stagger—and heard someone from behind him shout.

"I've got him! He's mine."

Shit, there were two of them. As Rick turned, something exploded over the top of his head. He sank to his knees, fighting to stay conscious. Another blow to the back of his skull put him down, flat on his face.

Fists came at him, pummeling him. Rick doubled up to cover his vitals, but a heavy boot landed one kick after another. They were going to beat him into submission— and not stop until he was dead.

The pain blotted everything out, except the voice of one his attackers. "You should not have fucked with her, man," he shouted at Rick.

The words echoed in Rick's head as he passed out.

Something was wrong with Pris's cell phone. She could dial out, but no one she'd just speed-dialed was answering the phone, and she wasn't getting a voice-mail prompt. It was well after midnight, but that shouldn't have been a problem. You could leave messages around the clock.

She was in her bedroom with the curtains closed, all of her voyeuristic impulses exhausted. Even her temper was spent. Mostly she was confounded. She couldn't even leave a message, and she had something big to tell her team of handlers, every one of them. Big, like momentous. She'd planned to do it privately, via e-mail, but she had a local television interview scheduled tomorrow, and if she had to go public she would.

She rose from the chaise where she'd been watching a pay-per-view movie and decided to try one more time. The person she really wanted to talk to, the only one she thought might still be on her side, was Lane Chandler. Perhaps Lane could be her liaison to the others, a surrogate manager—and mother.

Pris pressed the concierge button, which should have given her direct access to Lane. She'd already tried several times, getting everything from dead air to messages that all the circuits were full and she should place the call again later. This time the phone rang and Lane's message came on. But once again, no voice-mail prompt.

Pris stared at the phone, not knowing what to think. She could always try the landline, although it had no concierge button. But that wasn't the point. Lane not only wasn't answering, she was somehow blocking her voice mail. Had she blocked everyone or had Pris been singled out for this appallingly rude treatment?

It was the last straw. Really, the last one. Pris had endured one rejection after another. If she'd had the energy, she would have stomped the phone into shrapnel, a million plastic pieces. As it was, all she could do was shake her head and try to swallow over the anguished lump in her throat. She was going to cry and she hated tears…unless of course, they could be put to good use.

Thursday, October 10

Lane dashed down the steps of her building, threw her purse and briefcase into the backseat of the waiting airport limo and swung herself inside. The doorman was putting her suitcase in the trunk. She checked her watch and reminded the driver she was running late, calling out thanks as he shut the door.

She'd overslept and unless this was the fastest trip to LAX in history, she was going to miss her flight. "Please," she said as the driver got in, "hurry!"

He glanced into the rearview mirror, his eyes hidden behind dark sunglasses. "Not a problem, ma'am. Buckle up."

Lane did not buckle up. She was going to try to get some work done on the way to the airport, and she needed the freedom to move around. She opened her briefcase and took out the résumés Ashley had e-mailed. Lane had decided to extend her trip overnight in order to interview several candidates with management potential. There was one very hot prospect, a woman that Val Drummond himself had met and recommended, and Lane wanted to be prepared with the right questions. Good management people were rare.

Moments later, she looked up from her laptop, where she'd been putting together the interview questions, and was immediately disoriented. Where were they? She'd never seen this side street, and they should have been on the freeway by now. "Excuse me, Driver? We're going to LAX, right?"

"Count on it."

Something about his tone made Lane uneasy. She checked her watch. She hadn't been working fifteen minutes. "Where are we?"

He didn't answer. Instead, he turned down another

street she didn't recognize. Was he lost and didn't want to admit it? They were in an industrial area that was sparsely populated with large warehouse-type buildings. Maybe he was taking a back way to the airport.

Lane saved her file and put the laptop back in her brief-case. The limo was actually a town car, but still very spacious, and she was quite some distance from the driver. His seat was separated from hers by a sliding window that had been left open wide enough for them to talk.

"Are you having trouble finding the airport?" she asked, feeling very much at his mercy. "My cell phone has GPS, and I can find out where we are. What was the name of that last street? Aviation Way?"

"Put your cell phone away, ma'am."

"What? I'm trying to help."

"Put the fucking phone away!"

The car screeched to a halt, throwing Lane into the back of the driver's seat. The cell phone flipped out of her hand. Stunned, she pushed herself back, only to see him rip off his glasses and turn around.

"Put the phone away and do what I tell you!"

Lane gaped at him. Her driver was Rick Bayless and his battered condition told her she was in big trouble. Cuts and bruises mottled his face and neck. His cheekbone bulged as if it might be broken.

"What happened to you?" she asked.

"Yeah, like you don't know. I was attacked in my sleep by thugs. They told me I shouldn't fuck with you, Lane. So, do you know what I'm going to do now? I'm going to fuck with you *big-time.*"

His eyes shimmered with anger. They made her think of something pale and deadly, something laced with acid.

"Who attacked you? And why do you think I had anything to do with it?"

"I know you did."

She heard a click and realized he'd locked the doors. She snatched up her cell phone from the floor and dropped it in her purse. "There, I put it away, just like you said."

"Good. Now shut up, *just like I said.*"

He started the car and pulled out, throwing her backward and spraying rocks in their wake. Where the hell was he taking her? Her mouth had gone tacky dry. She couldn't swallow, and her pulse was a trip-hammer. God, how she hated that feeling. She remembered the way he'd tried to scare her as a kid. He'd been one mean son of a bitch, and she had despised him for it. But she wasn't a kid now. They were both adults.

"Listen, you can quit trying to intimidate me," she said. "Let's talk about this—"

"Try? You haven't seen me *try,* bitch."

"Bitch?" She gasped the word. "How dare you?" Whatever had possessed her to think this asshole was an adult? He was a third-grader, calling names and bullying people.

"Take off your clothes," he said, looking over his shoulder to make sure she understood him.

"Don't be ridiculous."

"Take them off." He pulled a gun from inside his jacket and held it high. "There's one bullet in the chamber," he said, spinning the cylinder with his thumb. "Think this could be your lucky day?"

"You wouldn't do it." Her voice caught, and she was sure he heard it.

With a flip of his wrist, he had the gun upside down and the barrel aimed right between her eyes, all while he continued to steer with his left hand. She wasn't certain he could actually shoot the gun that way, but she wasn't taking any chances. She knew why he'd chosen this road. There wasn't another human being to be seen.

"Get naked," he ordered. "Do it now or this gun goes bang."

"But why? Why do I have to take my clothes off?"

He hit the gas pedal and the car surged. "To discourage you from making a premature exit. I don't have time for preferred detainment methods, like tying you to the bumper. Make sense?"

Lane couldn't believe it. He was insane. The only thing stopping her from crowning him with her briefcase was their rate of speed. They were sure to crash and die if he let go of the wheel.

"So do it," she said, calling his bluff. "Shoot me."

A horrible dry click sounded, punctuated by Lane's shrill scream. He'd pulled the trigger! The chamber had been empty, but he'd pulled the fucking trigger. She collapsed backward and started to kick off her high heels. She was shaking from head to toe, but even in shock, her brain was working. Could she use the heels as a weapon?

He wheeled the car around and headed back in the direction they'd come. Lane nearly fell over as she struggled to get out of the jacket to her wool jersey pantsuit. Everything was made so damn small these days.

"Are you done yet?" he asked.

"Give me a minute! It's not easy getting out of your clothes in a careening car." She undid her slacks, maneuvered them down to her ankles and pulled them off. "Done," she said.

"Hand them over."

Lane tossed jacket and pants over the seat. His window

was down and as the cool air hit her bare skin, she shivered. "I'm freezing," she said, hugging herself.

"Where's the rest of it?"

"The rest of what?"

"Lose the underwear."

She was wearing a camisole bra and Spanx Power Panties. Furious, she yanked the camisole over her head and then peeled off the Spanx, which was no easy deal. She slapped the unmentionables into his open palm, and watched in shock as he tossed everything, every stitch of her clothing, out the window of the car.

That suit had cost her a fortune! "Where are we going?" she asked as he pulled onto a freeway entrance ramp.

"The airport. You have a flight to catch."

She drew up her legs and hugged them to her body, trying to get as much coverage as she could. "I can't get out of the car like this."

"Yeah, that'll be awkward, especially since you're going to have a welcoming party. Someone tipped the people from Gotcha.com that a big name was going to show up. Should be great publicity for your business."

"You can't be *serious.*"

"You'll be thanking me when you get to security. You won't have to take anything off."

He laughed, and something snapped inside Lane. It was almost a physical sensation. A nerve in the base of her neck went red hot. It was the fuse on a stick of dynamite, and when the fire hit the powder, she was gone. She didn't care anything about her nakedness, his gun or the consequences of her actions. She had never thought of herself as a cold-blooded killer, never imagined in the darkest corner of her mind that she could happily take a life. But all she wanted to do was rip his head off and fling it out the window, ditch it without a second thought, the way he had her clothes.

He was still laughing as she lunged at him, but he must have seen her coming. The security window rocketed up. Her head hit the tempered glass with enough force to dent it, and the world began to spin off into outer space. She crumpled on the seat, fighting the glittering light that flooded her vision. But there was nothing but darkness behind her closed eyes. A strange taste filled her throat, as rancid as bad peanuts—and just as suddenly that was gone, too.

21

Did we have sex?

It was Darwin's first thought when he opened his eyes that morning and saw Janet sleeping at the other end of the couch, her head buried in a feather pillow and her bare feet buried in his armpits. Damn intimate having a woman's feet in your armpits. Normally it would have meant other bare and intimate things had happened, except that they were both fully dressed…and sadly still very much relationship virgins.

It had been her idea to sleep over, and the sex he'd thought was a certainty—how could you spend that amount of time together horizontal and not have sex?—turned out to be watching big-screen TV, cuddling-and-getting-to-know-each-other time.

Also, perpetual-hard-on time for him.

"How long did we sleep?" She yawned, stretched and inadvertently tickled him with her toes. "Is it late?"

"Nineish," he said. "Wish I could play hooky, but my boss went to Dallas this morning, and the rest of us are expected to hold the fort."

She sat up, her angelic face nearly hidden with sexy, messy blond hair. She shook it out of her eyes and frowned at him. "Oh, poop, do you have to go right away?"

"Yeah, I really should, but—" Darwin couldn't quite figure out what she was doing with her blouse, but it looked like she might be unbuttoning it. "Actually, I have some time."

"Perfect." She flopped on top of him, rolling to her side to nuzzle in the curve of his neck and make odd little cooing noises. A moment later she popped back up to stare him right in the eye. "Darwin, this has been lots of fun, and you're a great guy, but—"

Here it came. He was about to get dumped. He wasn't boyfriend material. She wasn't into him that way, but she would always want him as a friend friend. Friend friend? How many times was he going to have to hear this BS from women?

"I think it's time, don't you?" she said.

"Time for what?"

"To get closer…you know."

A bit churlishly, he said, "No, I don't. Should we maybe show each other our vaccination scars? What do you mean?"

"This." She wriggled suggestively.

"Oh, yeah, *closer.* Definitely, we should do that. Like now, you mean?"

A roll of her eyes and a flutter of those Jessica Rabbit eyelashes. "Yes, like now." She pressed a kiss to his surprised lips, and then she actually nipped him. Darwin could feel the sharpness of it streak all the way to his groin. It was seismic, the precursor of an earthquake. And it was *excellent.*

"Can I use your bathroom to freshen up first?" she asked. "I feel a little grungy."

Dar helped her off the couch. Hushed by male admiration, he watched her sashay out of his living room and disappear down the hall to the master bedroom, which was large and lavish, but mostly unfurnished. He hadn't had a clue what to buy when he found his cliffside home in the Hollywood Hills last year, so he stuck with the important stuff, like a bed. His parents had tossed him out when he was twelve because of his behavioral problems, which turned out to be undiagnosed epilepsy, and he'd lived mostly on the streets and in foster homes after that. Any house with indoor plumbing would have been lavish to him. This place was positively palatial.

He needed to shower and shave, but he'd have to wait until she was done. The house had several bathrooms, but all his gear was in the master. He and Janet had been sleeping on the couch in the great room, which was a combo family and kitchen area.

He found the remote on the floor and turned on the TV as he walked the considerable distance to the fridge. Tiled with large slabs of golden South African slate and furnished with buttery leather pieces, the great room was his second favorite room, although if this was where the closeness was going to take place, it stood a good chance of becoming his first.

He helped himself to some bottled water and hooked the door with his bare foot to shut it. His neck was kinked from the way he'd slept, so he rolled his head from one side to the other, making himself dizzy as he headed back to the couch…which was still warm from their body heat, his and Janet's.

He liked the sound of that, *their* body heat.

He sank into the couch like a stone, drank some water and surfed the morning shows to see what was going on in the world that he and Janet had totally tuned out. Maybe another TPC client had bitten the dust.

He should probably be feeling guilty about the string of disasters befalling his service's clients, but he'd never run into a distraction quite like Janet. And besides, lately he'd been feeling superfluous at TPC with Lane running the expansion and Val doing everything else. He wasn't sure what his role was anymore. He'd even thought about leaving and starting his own company, although not a concierge service. Something on the cutting edge of the communications field, where he could continue to create and be useful.

Meanwhile, though, he'd found other ways to entertain himself, like Janet. She kept him preoccupied and out of the kind of trouble that came from having too much time on his hands. His brain was always running at full speed, scrounging up things to do, some of them with the potential to be dangerous, he supposed. He'd always had the problem of coming in for a landing once his imagination took flight.

"Stop traipsing around like hookers—"

Darwin hesitated and backed up a couple channels to see who was talking about hookers. He'd heard a woman's voice and it had sounded familiar.

"—and selling yourself short, ladies."

It was Priscilla Brandt. Darwin nearly spilled the bottle of water he'd tucked between his legs. She was on a network show! He didn't recognize the woman doing the interview, but Priscilla looked great. She was as mouthy as ever, and maybe a little strung out, but hot. Definitely hot.

The interviewer wrinkled her nose. "Are you calling American women hookers?"

"It's in my book," Priscilla said, shamelessly plugging her debut tome on manners. "I'm telling them to stop *dressing* like hookers and selling themselves short." She turned to the camera, her eyes sparkling a little too brightly. "Put on your pearls and your finest hosiery, ladies, and let him wonder how he'll ever afford you."

"I see, very nice." The interviewer glanced at her notes. "It says here that you've just fired your agent, your manager and your public relations people because they're not supporting you in your time of need. Is that true?"

Pris smoothed her glossy chestnut tresses. "Does it say that I fired my private-concierge service, too?"

"Now, what is a private-concierge service? Our audience might not know."

"You tell me," Pris said. "This one advertises itself as a transformative experience, how about that? They say if you join, your life will be richer, fuller and better than your dreams." She made a scoffing sound. "I can't even get them on the phone. Now, *that's* bad manners."

The interviewer's eyes gleamed. "Would you like to share the name of the service?"

"Why not? They're not doing me any favors. It's called The Private Concierge. Big deal, huh? I had high hopes for Lane Chandler, the owner. She seemed like one of those rare compassionate souls, but she's abandoned me, too. I've left her a dozen voice-mail messages since last night, and she hasn't returned one of them. It is my full intention to sue for breach of contract."

The interviewer gasped and so did Darwin. He wondered if Lane was watching. While she was single-handedly trying to expand their business, Priscilla might just wreck it. Single-handedly.

He grabbed his cell, which was right next to him on the occasional table. Normally one button would get him through to Lane directly, but tonight he was getting a no-

signal message. It had to be a cell-tower situation, which
was weird because he'd never had a problem with reception at his home.

He hoped that was all it was. Otherwise, Val would be
on his case—and maybe even Lane. Dar's gut tightened as
he thought about the unfairness of that. Why was he the
whipping boy when things went wrong? In reality he was
the one who'd been advising caution. He'd gone along
with the branch offices in San Francisco and Vegas, but
when Lane began talking about growing the business even
more, Dar had warned her they were already moving too
fast—and this was well before their clients had started imploding.

TPC had been nicely in the black at the time, but going
national and opening up branch offices in Dallas, Chicago
and New York, which was Lane's grand plan, would
require that they borrow heavily. Dar had wanted to take
the time to stabilize and solidify their financial position.
He'd wanted a safety net that would allow them some
margin for error. But Val, the anal-retentive bean counter,
had done nothing but egg Lane on. And she'd been determined, so now they *were* deeply in debt. Sometimes he
wondered if the insecurity of Lane's past made her unable
to settle for the status quo, ever.

A bloodcurdling scream obliterated his musings. It had
come from the master bedroom. Janet? He dropped the
phone and ran.

FREE Merchandise is 'in the Cards' for you!

Dear Reader,

We're giving away FREE MERCHANDISE!

Seriously, we'd like to reward you for reading this novel by giving you **FREE MERCHANDISE** worth over **$20.** And no purchase is necessary!

You see the Jack of Hearts sticker above? Paste that sticker in one of the boxes on the Free Merchandise Voucher inside. Return the Voucher promptly ... and we'll send you valuable Free Merchandise!

Thanks again for reading one of our novels – and enjoy your Free Merchandise with our compliments!

Pam Powers

Pam Powers

P.S. Look inside to see what Free Merchandise is **"in the cards"** for you!

What would you prefer...

Romance OR Suspense?

Do you prefer spine-tingling page turners or steal-your-heart stories about love and relationships? Tell us which type of books you'd enjoy – and you'll get

**2 Free ROMANCE Books or
2 Free SUSPENSE Books**

with no obligation to buy anything.

OPTION 1
Romance

Get 2 FREE BOOKS that will capture your imagination with modern stories about life, love and relationships.

FREE!

FREE!

OPTION 2
Suspense

Get 2 FREE BOOKS that will thrill you with a fast-paced blend of suspense and mystery.

REMEMBER: Your Free Merchandise, consisting of **2 Free Books** and **2 Free Gifts**, is worth over $20.00! No purchase is necessary, so please send for your Free Merchandise today.

Plus TWO FREE GIFTS!
We'll also send you two wonderful FREE GIFTS (worth about $10), in addition to your 2 Free "Romance" or "Suspense" books!

YOUR FREE MERCHANDISE INCLUDES...
2 FREE Romance **OR** 2 FREE Suspense books
AND 2 FREE Mystery Gifts

FREE MERCHANDISE VOUCHER

| 2 FREE ROMANCE BOOKS and 2 FREE GIFTS | OR | 2 FREE SUSPENSE BOOKS and 2 FREE GIFTS |

393 MDL ESXY
193 MDL ESYC

392 MDL ESYN
192 MDL ESYY

Please send my Free Merchandise, consisting of **2 Free Books** and **2 Free Mystery Gifts.** I understand that I am under no obligation to buy anything, as explained on the back of this card.

FIRST NAME   LAST NAME

ADDRESS

APT. #   CITY

Order online at:
www.Try2Free.com

STATE/PROV.   ZIP/POSTAL CODE

◄ DETACH AND MAIL CARD TODAY! ▼

(FM-MI-08)

Offer limited to one per household and not valid to current subscribers of Romance, Suspense or the Romance/Suspense Combo. **Your Privacy** – The Reader Service is committed to protecting your privacy. Our Privacy Policy is available online at www.eHarlequin.com or upon request from the Reader Service. From time to time we make our lists of customers available to reputable third parties who may have a product or service of interest to you. If you would prefer for us not to share your name and address, please check here. ☐

NO PURCHASE NECESSARY!

The Reader Service - Here's how it works:

Accepting your 2 free books and 2 free mystery gifts places you under no obligation to buy anything. You may keep the books and gifts and return the shipping statement marked "cancel." If you do not cancel, about a month later we'll send you 3 additional books and bill you just $5.49 each in the U.S. or $5.99 each in Canada, plus 25¢ shipping & handling per book and applicable taxes if any.* That's the complete price and — at a savings of at least 15% off the cover price — it's quite a bargain! You may cancel at any time, but if you choose to continue, every month we'll send you 3 more books, which you may either purchase at the discount price or return to us and cancel your subscription.

*Terms and prices subject to change without notice. Sales tax applicable in N.Y. Canadian residents will be charged applicable provincial taxes and GST. Offer not valid in Quebec. All orders subject to approval. Books received may not be as shown. Credit or debit balances in a customer's account(s) may be offset by any other outstanding balance owed by or to the customer. Please allow 4 to 6 weeks for delivery. Offer available while quantities last.

If offer card is missing, write to The Reader Service, 3010 Walden Ave., P.O. Box 1867, Buffalo, NY 14240-1867

BUSINESS REPLY MAIL

FIRST-CLASS MAIL   PERMIT NO. 717   BUFFALO, NY

POSTAGE WILL BE PAID BY ADDRESSEE

The Reader Service
3010 WALDEN AVENUE
PO BOX 1341
BUFFALO NY 14240-8571

NO POSTAGE
NECESSARY
IF MAILED
IN THE
UNITED STATES

22

Lane woke up in a room she didn't recognize, lying on a bed surrounded by what looked like mosquito netting. She didn't seem to be tied up or restrained, but she might as well have been blindfolded. He'd removed her contact lenses and the world was a blurry watercolor mural. Large objects like dressers and chairs were distinguishable, but not much else.

This had to be his place. She doubted he would have taken her anywhere else, but the thought of being alone with him in his house made her heart thunder. She could still hear the dry click of his gun discharging. God, terrifying. And ordering her to undress at gunpoint? She could be dealing with a psychopath.

She was covered with a sheet and probably still naked underneath. But that was the least of her problems right now. It felt like someone was pounding nails in her skull. Each kick of her pulse brought blood—and pain—rushing to her injured head. She closed her eyes. *Lane, calm yourself.*

Moments later, she raised her head gingerly, grateful her neck wasn't broken considering how hard she'd hit the security window in the limo. She could move her fingers and toes. Everything seemed to be working, but she couldn't rule out other injuries, including a concussion.

Pale light was seeping from behind the shaded windows. She couldn't tell whether it was morning or afternoon, but at least it was still day.

She told herself to lie quietly and listen for anything that would tell her where she was and who might be around. Somehow she had to get up and find her way out of this place. She could hear muted noise coming from outside the windows, but it wasn't nearby. Most likely it was people on the boardwalk across the street or kids on the beach. The interior of the house seemed strangely still and explosive, but that was her nerves.

She wondered if he was sleeping. Or gone. She could only hope.

The aching became a deep, pounding throb as she sat up. A pull against her wrist distracted her for a moment, and she saw that the green rubber band was still there. She'd left it on in her rush to get undressed. Odd that he hadn't taken it off.

Dizzy, she braced herself, slowly swung around and put her feet on the floor. Before doing anything else, she pulled the top sheet free to wrap around herself after she got out of the netting. She couldn't find an opening, so she slid to the floor and crawled under it, trying not to move her head too much. Everything she did made the throbbing worse.

Once she was free, she steadied herself against the nearest chair and took another look at the room. It seemed to be a fairly typical spare bedroom, except that the architecture and decor were old-style Spanish. The doors and windows were arched, the walls were stucco and the terracotta floors studded with Mexican tiles.

No sign of her belongings anywhere, but that didn't surprise her. Rick Bayless wasn't running a hotel. He'd brought her here because he believed she'd sicced thugs on him to scare him off. It wasn't a bad idea. She wondered who'd done it, and how she was supposed to convince him that she hadn't.

She got herself over to the windows, but they were locked with a bolt mechanism that she couldn't release. Exhausted from the effort, she made it back across the room to a large armoire by steadying herself against the furniture. But there was nothing inside the armoire except boxes of his papers and old manuals from the police academy, a couple of broken table lamps and various other odds and ends. No clothing, which meant she was leaving this place in a sheet and a rubber band.

She checked the dresser, too, startled at the sight of herself in the mirror. Her shiny dark hair looked as matted and unkempt as a wet dog's. The purple circle under her left eye was probably the start of a shiner, and the splatter of spots on her face was...what? Dirt? Blood?

She moistened a finger with spit and scrubbed at the spots. Her stomach was rolling. She couldn't tell whether it was from pain, hunger or the sight of her own blood, but she was getting sicker by the minute. Closing her eyes made everything roll. Nothing was going to help, she realized. She just had to keep going, move.

The door to the room was unlocked, which seemed almost too convenient, but it was her only option. A series of short hallways took her to a kitchen that she recognized from her prior trip to the house. Bayless himself was sitting in the living room when she got there, gazing out the front window at the ocean beach across the way, and apparently waiting for her.

She studied him with a sense of disbelief. How could he look so freaking serene? He'd kidnapped her, harassed her at gunpoint, assaulted her with a security window, and now he'd taken her hostage. That was enough to put him away for the rest of his natural life.

He glanced over at her as she swayed on her feet— bloody, sick and wrapped in a sheet. "How are you feeling?" he asked, as nonchalant as if she'd had a bout with the flu.

Anger snapped her backbone into place. "I feel like shit, thanks."

"You look better than you did."

"Too bad I can't say the same for you." She wasn't the only wipeout in the room. He had some battle scars, too.

"So, what am I doing here?" she asked him. "Being held for ransom?"

"You're free to go, but the sheet stays."

He expected her to drop the sheet and walk out the door? No, of course he didn't. He knew she wouldn't make it two blocks naked, blind and on foot in the big city. If she was picked up for indecent exposure, there would be more bad press, the last thing she needed, which also explained why he didn't seem concerned that she might report him to the cops.

"Well?" he pressed, obviously enjoying himself.

She ripped away the sheet and made a dash for the door, getting there just seconds before he did. She wrenched the door open and he slammed it shut, trapping her awkwardly with her back to him.

"I forgot how quick you are," he said, straddling her with his arms to hold the door shut.

"I forgot what a liar *you* are!" She whirled around, glaring at him. She should have kneed him in the groin and crippled him for life, but she couldn't catch her damn breath. It didn't even matter that she was naked. That's how badly she still wanted him to pay for what he did all those years ago. He'd baited her until she slugged him, trumped up charges against her and then walked away and left her to rot in a prison.

Was he looking at her breasts? "Get me that sheet, you sick bastard."

He matched her, glare for glare. "Not quite sick enough to hire thugs to beat you to a bloody pulp."

"I didn't do it."

"Who did?"

"Someone else. I want that sheet!"

"You'll get the sheet when I get the truth."

They eyeballed each other, locked in a stare down, nostrils flaring, chests heaving.

Defying him to stop her, she crouched down and covered herself as best she could. He conceded with a harsh sigh and walked away. A moment later, he tossed her the sheet, and she sank into the nearest chair, woozy, her head throbbing, and cursing herself for not going out the door while he had his back turned. He'd given up. He might still let her go, if she could find the strength. But her insides were heaving, and she felt as if she was going to.

"I have a concussion," she said. "I'm dizzy and sick to my stomach."

"You don't have a concussion. I checked the lump on your head before I left the bedroom. It's a hematoma, a big word for a bad bruise."

"I see—and you went to med school where?"

"I'm an ex-cop. We know something about concussions. I also checked to make sure your pupils weren't dilated and your breathing was normal. You're going to be fine. Unlike me, who's going to be dead in two months."

"What?" She glowered at him. "What's that supposed to mean?"

"It means that a month ago I was given three months to live."

"What kind of utter crap is that?" She almost didn't want to dignify it with a response. "Given two months to live by who?"

"You mean by *whom?* A neurophysiologist. That's a big word for a doctor. I have a congenital disorder, named for the doctors who discovered it, Burke, Harnett and Stone." He pointed to a bottle of pills on the table next to the chair where she sat. "It's a disease with an identified genetic contribution, meaning it runs in families. Fortunately, it's rare, and by rare I mean that you're about as likely to get it as you are to win the California lottery. I just pulled the lucky ticket."

Even with her blurry vision, Lane could see the half-empty prescription bottle of pills. This one had an intact label, unlike the torn label she'd seen on the bottle next to his bed the night she broke in. Her heart did a funny half skip, but she refused to be sucked in by whatever game he was playing.

"You're not dying. Dying men don't abduct women, threaten them with guns and drive like psychopaths. *That's* a big word for a fucking maniac. What is this? A pathetic ploy for sympathy?"

"Yeah, is it working?"

"I'm all broken up, can't you tell?" She thrust her hand from the folds of the sheet. "Give me your gun. I'll put you out of your misery."

"You're all heart, Chandler."

"Whatever I can do to help, Bayless. You've always been so good to me." If he was dying, she was Mother

Teresa. Hmm, not a good analogy. She *was* Mother Teresa. Well, sort of. She did dedicate herself to the care of others.

"Spare me the sob story," she said. "I forgot my violin. Are we through now? Can I go?"

"No, you can't."

Her voice went shrill. "Okay, I believe you're dying. Boo hoo. What am I supposed to do about it?"

"Shut up," he warned her. "Forget that I ever told you. *Just shut the fuck up.*"

Lane caught back a retort. She wasn't handling this right. Whether he was telling the truth or not was irrelevant. She ought to be playing along.

He came back into her range of vision, and she expected to see anger that his crazy plan wasn't working. Cold psycho fury. But instead, his lips were pursed and his expression thoughtful, as if he was considering her plight. His image was still fuzzy, but she could make out the lunar green eyes and the strange shimmer of his hair. His buzz cut looked like a golden halo in the light.

Looming over her, he reminded her of one of Darwin's comic-book heroes, contemplating the fate of the doomed damsel. But that was a trick of her lousy vision. He was a classic bully, cold, hard and probably a coward at heart. She wondered what it would take to break his spirit the way he'd tried to break hers. More than anything, that's why she couldn't forgive him. He'd ripped away everything that was good about her and made it sick and twisted, when he was the sick one.

"Forget the thugs who attacked me," he said. "If you want out of here, just tell me what you know about Ned Talbert. Your business card was at the crime scene, and he'd written the word *extortion* on the back. Why?"

She considered her next move. Would he be satisfied if she admitted to part of it, something that made sense, given what he already knew? It was unlikely he'd go to the police now, after what he'd done to her.

"Mr. Talbert was curious about my service," she said. "We had a brief meeting. I told him about our various plans, and he left to think it over."

He nodded. "Excellent. See how this works. You tell me the truth, and I let you go. I'll even give you back your suitcase. When and where did this meeting with Ned take place?"

She knew exactly when it was, the day before he died. How could she forget that? "Sometime last week. He came to my office on Avenue of the Stars. You know the one," she said pointedly.

"Somebody wanted Ned out of the way. Who? Why?" His voice was different now, taut. "I don't know," she said. "Why would I know? I only met Ned that one time."

He closed the distance between them and knelt at her chair. His eyes were pulsating. It felt as if she could feel his heart beating. He was angry and frustrated, but it was much more than that. He was desperate. Lane knew that feeling well. She'd been desperate to help a friend once, too. She'd thought Darwin was dying, and she would have done anything. She *had*.

He yanked on the sheet to get her attention. "Something was missing from Ned's place—a package with the evidence from the hunting-lodge case fifteen years ago."

"The evidence? How did Ned get that? It was in the stuffed animal in my knapsack, the one that disappeared from the evidence room. That's why the case was dismissed, wasn't it?"

He ignored her questions. "I need to know who took

that package from Ned's place. Whoever did it killed him and his girlfriend—and tried to make their deaths look like murder-suicide."

"And you think I know who did it?"

"I think you know something."

"Why would *I* know anything?"

"Lane, one night you barge into my bedroom and tell me you have powerful friends. The next night I get assaulted by thugs who warn me not to fuck with you. What am I supposed to think?"

He still hadn't told her how he knew Ned had the evidence. She suspected Rick had something to do with that, but she didn't want to open another can of worms. She had to get out of here, catch the next flight to Dallas.

"Listen to me—" She touched his arm, but he pulled away. "I don't know who beat you up. I had nothing to do with that or the missing package. *And I don't know anything about what happened to Ned.*"

He got up, breathing out an obscene word.

"Please, I have to go," she said. "People will be looking for me when they find out I missed my flight."

"Let them look. I'm out of time."

"Out of time? Why?"

He closed his eyes, exasperated. "I told you, I'm dying."

That ridiculous dying ploy again. She wasn't going to believe that, even if it was true. She had no reason to think he was dying besides some phony pills. He *wasn't* dying. He couldn't be. That would change things, and she didn't want them changed. *This man had pointed a gun at her and pulled the trigger.*

She struggled to get out of the chair, the sheet billowing around her. "You have to let me go. My business is in trouble. Someone is trying to sabotage it, and to be honest, it won't take much. I'm deeply in debt."

It cost her every shred of pride she had to reveal that, especially to him, the vice cop who'd sworn that she would never amount to anything. He'd predicted she would be back on the streets, selling herself as soon as she got out of juvie.

He studied her now, unmoved by her last-ditch attempt to reach him. If anything, there was contempt in his expression.

"You asked for the truth," she said, her voice low, burning with shame. "That's the truth. I'm in trouble. You can understand that."

"Ned is dead, and I'm going to be. How much trouble are you in compared to that?"

The reality of it came as a shock. Her concerns did seem petty next to his, except that he wasn't dying—and his icy indifference allowed her to hold on to the resolve to defend herself. "I don't know anything!"

"It *can't* be a coincidence that I found your card at his place and the package was missing. You know something."

"Why are you doing this?" she shrilled at him, feeling as if she was going insane. "What do you want? Money? How much? I'll get it."

His expression changed. At first there was disbelief in his narrowing eyes, as if she'd surprised him with the offer. But as his gaze flickered over her the disbelief faded, burned away by anger—and something even darker that she didn't understand.

He almost looked as if he hated her. *Passionately hated her.*

"You're not offering sex?" he asked, his voice eerily quiet. "Isn't that what you do?"

Lane struggled to breathe normally. *Sex with him? He would have to kill her first.* She wanted to scorch him with her withering disdain. But the gauntlet had been thrown down. He'd call her out.

She whipped open the sheet enough to walk, and went straight for him, fueled by all the burning indignation a fifteen-year-old girl's soul could contain. Because that's what she became every time she was around him, a frantic child, trying to hold her own with a monster determined to break her. But he hadn't broken her, and she couldn't let him think he had. Even if he killed her, she couldn't let him think he'd won.

The moment she got within range of him, she slapped him hard. Her open palm hit his bruised cheek with a loud, moist pop.

"That's for throwing my clothes out the window," she said, her voice trembling and her hand stinging. "That was an Armani fucking pantsuit."

He didn't react to the blow, not even a flinch, but she wasn't done. She reached back to slap him again, but he blocked her hand. He grabbed it hard, and Lane felt the iron in his grip, but she didn't hesitate for a second. Tears burned her eyes, but that didn't stop her, either. With the fires of vindication burning in her heart, she got in his face, just the way he had hers—and spit at him with all the force she could muster.

This time he did flinch, much to her gratification.

"That was for calling me a whore," she said, "and making me feel like one."

23

The screams sent Darwin running to find out what the hell was going on. He burst into the bedroom, but didn't see Janet. The screaming had stopped, but he could hear muffled noises coming from his walk-in closet. The door was open.

"Janet?" He found her in there, standing by the center island and clutching his favorite digital camera, the one with the fastest shutter speed and the powerful zoom lens. She was madly clicking the arrow key and viewing the snapshots stored in the camera's memory.

Darwin's heart sank as he realized what she'd found.

"Janet, don't. Give me that, please."

She looked up at him, stricken. "How could you do this?"

She thrust the camera at him. He took it, knowing what he was going to see. Shots of Janet from the front, bare-breasted, as she hastily changed into her Jezebel Truly outfit behind a ComicCon booth. Janet from the rear, bending over in short shorts to drink from a water fountain. His beautiful Janet, with her tongue all over a vanilla ice-cream cone. God, had that sight given him a religious experience.

"Did you take these?" she asked, her voice trembling.

He wished he could lie. She probably wanted him to lie. Maybe if he claimed he'd swiped the camera from some paparazzo-stalker dude… But he was the stalker. He'd accumulated a vast collection of Janet and her alter ego, Jezebel Truly, over the few years. All taken without her knowledge, and most before he'd even met her. Last night he'd snapped a dozen or so while she was sitting on his toilet with the bathroom door ajar.

His camera was fast and silent, perfect for stealth shots, as he liked to call them. But he wasn't doing it to hurt her. It was his tribute to her ethereal beauty.

"Why didn't you tell me you wanted pictures?" she rasped, apparently unable to speak. "Why didn't you just tell me?"

Tears welled in her velvety brown eyes. Whether or not he'd been trying to hurt her, she was hurt. And furious.

Miserable, he hunched his shoulders. "I don't know."

"What are you, some pervert voyeur? Were those pictures going to show up on the Internet?" she demanded to know. "YouTube, maybe?"

"No, of course not. You're beautiful. You're perfect. I was trying to capture that."

Laughter burst out of her, strangled and thick. "Apparently my ass is *really* beautiful. There must be fifty pictures of it. Darwin, I'm sorry. I can't stay here."

"No, Janet, let me explain. I'm the one who's sorry."

She shook her head, furiously blinking away tears. Her lip curled, quivering as she tried to talk. "I must have a sign on my back that says exploit me, *please*. My ex-boyfriend used my image in his comic book and when the series hit big-time, he cut me out of our deal *and* his life. He kept everything for himself. I didn't think you were that kind of guy."

"I'm not! Janet, I'm not. These pictures were for me. No one else would ever have seen them."

"Not even me? How long were you going to keep them a secret? Darwin, that's sick."

Darwin bowed his head, crushed. He had no idea how to defend himself because he *had* done it. He'd taken the pictures. All he wanted was to have her with him, some kind of permanent memento that no one could take away—and now that was *all* he would have, a camera with some snapshots that seemed sordid after her reaction to them. Maybe they were sordid. Maybe he was. All he knew was that he'd lost the only woman who'd ever shown any interest in him as a man.

He was silently raging, fighting with himself as she marched past him. The crack of a door slamming shut made him groan aloud. His despair was so great that he sank to the floor and sat there, helpless, his spinning mind deflecting thoughts of everything but Janet, and what he might have done to salvage their relationship.

Mired in his own misery, he'd forgotten all about Lane and Priscilla and the television show. His boss and best friend might as well not have existed. Nor could he hear the buzzing of the landline handset, still off the hook and lying on the couch in the great room.

Darwin couldn't hear anything but the wrench and thud of his own heart.

Rick dropped Lane's hand and wiped the spittle from his face with the sleeve of his shirt. Braced, Lane waited for him to retaliate. Only when he turned away from her did she draw a breath. It felt odd, staring at his back as if she had somehow wronged him.

"You didn't believe me," she said without bothering to

explain what she meant. "My friend was unconscious. He could have died. I thought he had—and I will never forgive you for that."

He was quiet, but Lane could almost hear what he wasn't saying. *My friend* is *dead, and you're the only connection I have to his killer. Why won't* you *help me?* Could he possibly think this was some kind of retaliation?

"I took you off the streets," he said. "I did you a favor."

She shook her head, even though he couldn't see her. "You really believe I'd still be on the streets if not for you? You thought I didn't have any decency in me at all?"

"I know what happens to kids on those streets."

He turned to her, his eyes blazing with emotions she couldn't read. Anger and frustration at being misunderstood, maybe even some guilt. She couldn't look at him. She didn't want to know about his problems. She had more than she could handle on her own.

She walked to the window, wondering what he saw when he gazed out at the ocean. Probably that would depend on whether you were dying or not, she realized. Something tugged in her chest. How bizarre that her memories of him had driven her to make something of herself. At the age of fifteen, she'd been shocked and awed by the big tough policeman in the mirrored sunglasses. She'd seen him as the enemy, but she'd also felt some grudging admiration, and possibly even a touch of hero worship. And then he'd destroyed her. In the most personal way, he had destroyed her.

Maybe he had been trying to help her back then—to set her straight or something—and he'd just chosen a very unfortunate way to do it, by making her believe that she was as bad and unworthy as she feared.

She was tugging the rubber band on her wrist, an echo of the tightness in her chest. But when she glanced down, she saw that her hand was smeared with blood. Had she cut herself? She rubbed at the smear, but couldn't find any wound. If it wasn't her blood, it had to be his. But she hadn't hit him hard enough for that. It was barely a tap.

Shit, he was bleeding. Her heart went cold. "Rick? Are you okay?"

She turned, but he was gone. He'd left the room without saying a word, and she didn't know what to do. Follow him, find out what happened?

She scanned the room. Her suitcase, briefcase and purse sat in an alcove by the front door. Maybe they'd been there all along, and she'd missed them. Obviously, he meant for her to go. He was far wiser than she was. Whatever was wrong, she had to believe that he could handle it. She had a dangerous tendency to want to rescue men in crisis. It had started with her father, and then carried over to Darwin. Some women were hopelessly drawn to convicts. Maybe she was hopelessly drawn to wounded-warrior types. Not good, though. Not smart.

When she gathered her wits, she went to her purse, fished out her cell and checked the time. She didn't try to check her messages. There wasn't time, but the cell seemed to be working now. Thank God he hadn't thrown her purse out the window. She was still connected to the world. She would miss her luncheon meeting with Ashley and one of the new prospects, but she could make the afternoon and dinner meetings, and everything else could be rescheduled. She had a spare outfit in her suitcase, and she could clean up in the club room at the airport, even shower if there was time. She also had a spare pair of contacts.

She opened the suitcase, pulled out the pantsuit and dialed up the taxi. It would be here before she was dressed and ready.

* * *

From an arched window on the second floor, Rick watched Lane get into a taxi and leave. *Was he okay?* Had she really asked that question? He had never been less okay—or so torn and confused about a woman.

She thought he was a sadistic SOB, trying to terrorize her. He'd taken her hostage this morning, but what had been on her mind—and was clearly tormenting her—was what he'd done fifteen years ago. Yes, guilty. He *had* tried to terrorize her back then, but not for the reasons she thought.

What were his reasons? That was the question eating at him now. He'd briefly mistaken a teenage girl for an adult, and in a moment of weakness, he'd been slammed by pure lust, pure need, pure something. It had been powerful—and it had appalled him when he'd realized she was a kid. He'd been trying to help her, just as he'd said, but maybe he had overreacted because of his attraction to her. Was that why he'd come down so hard on her?

He hated to think so. He didn't know what would have happened if she'd been older and he hadn't been wearing a badge that day, but he knew there were plenty of men out there without badges. He knew he couldn't leave her on the streets. So, he'd crossed the line with some of those charges against her, probably most of them, but he'd been trying to protect her from herself and others—

Others like him?

Outside, the light had turned the ocean into a burning chrome surface. The surfers had long deserted the beach, unable to catch a decent wave, and the sun worshippers had taken over. Rick wished life could be that simple again. He wished there really were do overs.

What if she hadn't needed his protection then?

What if she needed it now?

She probably thought he'd removed her contact lenses to blind her. That was only part of the reason. He had wanted to see the actual color of her eyes—the stark turquoise that froze you and then melted you down like runoff in the summer. He hadn't seen the blue mists today. She'd been too outraged. But he'd seen her eyes—and remembered why she'd felt like a fist to his gut.

He'd ruled out relationships when he got his death sentence. He hadn't planned on ruling out sex, too, but that's how it had come down so far. Odds were he would never have a woman in his bed again, never smell the lingering scent of her on his sheets. He'd accepted that, but it would have been nice…

Even if that woman was her?

Aw, no. Don't go there, Bayless.

She'd hired thugs to beat the shit out of him!

He picked up the sheet from the floor and without thinking brought it to his face. He couldn't help himself. He felt a jolt of longing as he breathed her in. The cords of his throat tightened.

Christ, his mistake for bringing her here. What was he thinking? She had nothing to give him. Nothing but pain—and dark reminders.

Moments later the sheet was in the trash, and he was scrubbing his face with cold water from the tap in the kitchen. He noticed the blood on the sleeve of his shirt and he pulled the shirt off, too, wadded it up and stuffed it in the garbage can with the sheet. Maybe he could be rid of every trace of her. But the blood was his, he knew. A nosebleed. Another symptom?

He heard familiar skittering sounds. The rodent, again. He really should have clocked the hairy little beast when he had the chance. He didn't even look around to see where it was now. He wasn't in the mood for another soul-searching experience with the smoking mirror. He did not need to see his own naked impulses at this moment, God forbid.

What he needed to do was write.

He got himself a fresh shirt from the bedroom, and when he reached his office, he saw that he'd left the binder with his case notes lying open. He settled heavily in the chair, picked up the pen and began to write.

October 10, 11:15 a.m. I'm dealing with mysteries that try the soul—my friend's death, my own—but the one that takes hold of my mind as I fall asleep at night is her. I beat the crap out of her fifteen years ago…

He had no idea how long he'd been writing when a faint high-pitched sound caught his attention. Not the mouse. It was his spare cell phone, the one he used for his other identities. He'd been working so intently, he hadn't heard the signal beep until now. He must have voice mail.

He checked the phone and saw that he did have a call, but there was something else he had to do first. He grabbed his primary cell and tapped out Mimi's number, but the call went immediately to her voice mail.

"One more favor, Mimi," he said, "and this is the last one, ever. See if you can find out if Lucy Cox actually had a sick friend, as she claimed. Maybe her probation officer or someone who remembers her from juvie would know. Thanks. I—"

He'd started to say he owed her. But what was the point?

He checked the voice mail on his other cell and discovered a day-old message from Seth Black. Rick was mildly surprised as he listened to Black's request. He wanted to talk with Rick about TPC, the concierge service. Black had come across some new information, and he had a theory about what was going on.

It was a vague message, but then Rick's offer to pay for intelligence had been vague. He'd left Black a card with a fake name and this number, and apparently Black had decided to follow up. It would be interesting to see whether he had anything of value—or if he just wanted put the squeeze on Rick for more money.

"Lane?" Sandra moved quietly through the rooms of her sister's condo, slipping from one to the next. She hadn't been able to reach her sister by phone and didn't know whether she'd left on her trip to Dallas that morning or not. Sandra was torn. She'd been anxiously awaiting this opportunity, but she was almost as nervous about getting caught going through Lane's place as she was about why her little sister wasn't answering. Lane could be a snot when she wanted to, but it wasn't like her to blow off multiple voice-mail messages.

Sandra had been calling since early morning on the pretext of wishing Lane well. She'd also wanted to know if Lane had come to any decision regarding their talk about a job, but her real intention had been to make sure Lane was gone and the coast was clear.

Sandra had finally called Mary, the receptionist at TPC, to get Lane's flight information. Sandra then called the airline, and by pretending to be Lane and using her confirmation code, she was able to find out that Lane had not boarded the flight. That information forced Sandra to get creative. She'd driven her rental compact over to TPC and told Mary that Lane was having problems with her phone. She'd fudged a little, saying she'd managed to reach Lane, and that Lane had made arrangements for a later flight, but needed something from her home and had asked Sandra to pick it up and bring it to her. Sandra would need the key.

Mary had bought every word of it.

Sandra had thought she might find Lane at home, ill or unable to call work for some reason. But her sister's luxury rooftop condo was quiet. No one was home, and Sandra didn't know Lane's whereabouts. Most likely she'd caught a later flight and was in the air right now. That's why she wasn't returning calls, but it was odd that she hadn't notified Mary, or someone, of her change in plans. That wasn't like Lane at all. Although—Sandra sighed, remembering—she'd had that nasty habit of running away as a kid.

Sandra began her snooping in earnest in the master bedroom at the end of the long entry hall. It was clearly Lane's room, and her sister's decor was a bit austere for Sandra's tastes, although she did love the silvery Venetian mirror propped against the wall by the walk-in closet. The rest of it looked like a page out of the *Restoration Hardware* catalog. Sandra wasn't into hardwood floors, mission-style rockers or high-gloss brass telescopes.

The telescope sat on a dark cherry console and was pointed out the window at the Santa Monica Mountains in the distance. If Sandra had owned a fancy place like this, she would have pointed the scope the other way, toward Century City, where Lane had her business. On a good day, you might even see a movie star coming out of the Creative Artists Agency or catch a glimpse of Leanne Sanders, the stunning local morning-show anchor, sneaking into the glass-enclosed Hyatt Regency bar with one of her entourage. It didn't seem right that Lane had ended up working with celebrities like Judge Love on TV, and Simon Shan. That really should have been Sandra. She had a much better way with people.

The graceful sleigh bed and matching dark cherry dressers were closer to Sandra's idea of how decorating money should be spent. She flopped down on the bed, not surprised at how hard the mattress was. Lane had been pretty anal, even as a kid. If she hadn't been so antsy about the activities at the hunting lodge, things wouldn't have had to end in a total flipping disaster. But Lane was Lane. She'd always been an independent brat, even to the point of changing her name.

Sandra had never understood how their father could have preferred his youngest to his more outgoing and beautiful older daughter. She still felt resentment, but she'd more than made up for the lack of male admiration after she left home. Plenty of men had found things to appreciate in Sandra, and still did.

She glanced at her cell to check the time and see if any messages had come in. She really shouldn't dawdle, although she wouldn't have minded dawdling in such a grand place as this. Why should Lane have all the fun?

Before leaving the bedroom, she gave it a thorough going-over, searching the closets and dresser drawers, even lifting the sofa pillows and the area rugs to check underneath. She examined the hanging art, which looked like pretty pricey stuff, as well as the various accent pieces. She even helped herself to an engraved pen and letter opener, souvenirs from Lane's writing desk.

Her last act was to use the camera function of her cell phone to take pictures of everything she'd just inspected. She would go through each room this way.

Sandra checked her phone repeatedly as she scoured

the rest of the house. As focused as she was on her mission, her mind was also on Lane. The flight to Dallas was only a couple of hours. She might even be there by now, but no call. Sandra had no illusions about her relationship with Lane. They weren't close, but her sister wouldn't have ignored several urgent messages. She would have found a way to call back.

Sandra was becoming very concerned that something had gone wrong, and she'd been promised—guaranteed—that wouldn't happen. Nothing was supposed to happen to Lane. Her sister was off-limits, no matter what else went down. That was the deal.

24

Even Simon Shan was aware of the hush that fell over the reception area as he walked into TPC's corporate offices. Nothing could be heard but the soft *plishing* sounds of the fountain, which was actually a wall of water, streaming over a backdrop of black agates. The young lady at the door, greeting visitors with fragrant stalks of white botanical orchids, hesitated, her hand hovering in midair.

"Beautiful, but no thank you," Shan told her. She seemed reassured by his courtesy. The receptionist, a normally graceful older woman who sat at the midpoint of a frosted-glass counter, wasn't. The pen slipped out of her hand, but she didn't even appear to realize that she'd lost something as Shan walked up to her.

It was a little embarrassing. The media had been trying to cast him as a sinister figure in his slate-gray slacks and black turtleneck, and apparently the smuggling charges against him only added to his allure. Today's *L.A. Times* had suggested that all he really needed was an eye patch. Maybe they had him confused with an Asian Johnny Depp.

He reached inside his leather jacket and took out his translucent-blue Darwin phone. "Either my cell isn't working or there's a problem with your system," he told her. "No one responds when I press the concierge button, and Lane Chandler isn't answering her direct line, either."

The receptionist rose to her feet, her fingernails clicking against the desk's glass surface. "I'm so sorry. We are having a problem. All of our Premiere clients were notified by e-mail this morning, and I believe we attempted to deliver a replacement phone to your residence, Mr. Shan, but no one answered. We have backup phones available here if you'd like one. The system's creator, Darwin LeMaster, is personally working on the problem right now."

Still a little flustered, she tucked some runaway silvery tendrils of hair back into place. "Is there anything else?"

"Yes, may I speak with Ms. Chandler, please?"

"Again, terribly sorry. She's traveling today and tomorrow, but Val Drummond, our executive vice president, would be happy to help you with whatever you need. And of course, we can offer you that backup phone. It doesn't have all the features of the Darwin phone, but it will connect you directly to your private concierge. Who *is* your concierge?"

Shan shook his head, very disappointed in this woman's lack of understanding. "My concierge helps me with hotel reservations. She has nothing to do with the company's policies, nor should she. I don't need to speak with my concierge about the invasion of my privacy by a bodyguard assigned to me by this service."

"Oh, no! Of course not." She sprang up and hurried in the direction of Lane's office, gesturing for him to accompany her. "Would you mind waiting in Ms. Chandler's office while I fetch Mr. Drummond? I can get you something to drink, coffee, tea? We also have fine wines and spirits."

Simon didn't want anything to drink, but as always, he was pleasantly soothed by the quiet elegance of Lane's office. Orchids seemed to be today's theme. Sprays of them in pale yellow and white filled a crystal vase on her desk and one on the credenza. He breathed in their heady fragrance as he walked over to the windows to take in the view.

He'd barely sat down in one of the guest chairs when Drummond appeared, his hand extended as he walked over to Simon.

Simon rose and only reluctantly shook his hand. He'd never met Val Drummond, but didn't like him on sight. Too put together and pretentious. A man should never walk around looking like a clothing ad. Drummond was actually wearing a herringbone-print jacket with an ascot. All he needed was a stick pin, and he could have been mistaken for a London pimp.

"Please, Mr. Shan, sit down and make yourself comfortable. Mary tells me your bodyguard has been inappropriate. My deepest apologies. Of course, she'll be replaced as soon as we're done here. And I plan to contact the police once I know how she's invaded your privacy. Perhaps we can bring her up on charges."

"No need for the police," Shan said, rapidly losing faith in Mr. Drummond's common sense as well as his sense of style. "You can probably imagine why I don't want them involved. I am under investigation."

Drummond colored. "Yes, right. Well, then…can you tell me what she did?"

"Let's just refer to it as trespassing on private property." Shan hoped he wasn't blushing, too. *I woke up from a dream to find her ministering to my cock in the most exquisite way imaginable. She's as supple as a cat and as beautiful as a piece of Oriental porcelain, and I think she's trying to kill me.*

Drummond's forehead wrinkled, signaling that he wasn't comfortable with ambiguity. "Well, of course, we'll terminate her," he said. "And I'd like to offer you a complimentary six months' extension of your service to make up for any inconvenience. No, make that a year. And of course, a replacement bodyguard. A male, perhaps?"

Simon pretended to deliberate. As far as he knew, Jia Long was still locked up in her room, serving her self-imposed sentence. He'd checked the door before he left this morning, and it was locked tight. Supposedly she'd been in there since offering up her key—and her freedom—yesterday morning. But that didn't mean much when your résumé described you as an escape artist, which was why Simon had knocked on the door to tell her he was going out. He wanted to hear her respond. He also wanted to dangle the bait.

She'd come to the door, speaking through it and expressing concern that he would go out without her as his security detail. She'd offered to go out for him. He'd thanked her, but said he was going to speak with Lane Chandler at TPC and could be whisked there and back in a limo without ever stepping outside. He wouldn't need protection for this outing, although he might go for a brief walk on the Avenue of the Stars, if there weren't any paparazzi around.

"I believe I'll continue to work with Ms. Long for now," he told Drummond. "Possibly I overreacted and should speak with her myself."

"Mr. Shan, are you sure? That's not your responsibility, and it's not how the service operates. We're here to make your life as stress free as we possibly can. Ms. Long has obviously crossed a line."

"True, but that may be exactly what makes her a good bodyguard." Simon had no intention of letting Jia Long go just yet. He'd come here to tell Lane Chandler his suspicions about his bodyguard as a possible saboteur and observe her reaction. But he'd changed his mind when confronted with Val Drummond, whom he knew little about.

"I'd like you to leave it to me," Simon said.

"Well, of course, if that's what you prefer. But you will contact me immediately if there are any other problems?"

Simon agreed, but before he could rise from the chair to leave, Drummond was approaching him, offering him a replacement phone. "This is me," he said, pointing to the red concierge button. "Press it night or day, and I'll respond personally and immediately."

Simon nodded, though he had no intention of pressing Mr. Drummond's button, ever.

Moments later as Simon left the building through the revolving doors at the front entrance, he took the time to stop and look up and down the street. He'd hired a limo from a company other than TPC, trying to control for some of the variables, and he'd called the driver moments ago with a change in plans, asking to be picked up out front rather than the garage. He wasn't hoping to foil the regular paparazzi as much as to see if Jia, who knew exactly where he was going to be, was out there waiting for him.

Of course, she wouldn't show herself. But that didn't mean he might not spot a shrouded figure in some parked car, idling taxi or recessed door front. A shrouded figure the media had made infamous by labeling Jack the Giant Killer.

On the advice of his criminal attorneys, Simon hadn't

told the police that he'd been framed for the drug-smuggling charges. It would have made him look more guilty than innocent, the attorneys had told him. Shifting the blame was the first refuge of con artists and sociopaths, they'd said. *And besides, you're guilty. Let us deal with that. It's why we make the big bucks.*

They hadn't actually said that last part out loud. They didn't have to. Simon had understood on a gut level that they believed him guilty, and worse, that he would never convince them otherwise. He could only imagine their amusement if he'd told them what else he suspected, that he'd been framed by the paparazzi, specifically the monster who brought down one big target after another, Jack the Giant Killer.

Simon had no proof of this yet. The pictures that had shown up in the media so far could have been taken by any monkey with a zoom lens and the agility to hang from the limbs of trees. And Jack hadn't taken credit for Simon's downfall, as he had for some of the others. But there were other factors that Simon had become aware of, links to TPC clients. No one might be taking JGK seriously, but Simon had to. He wasn't so certain he wasn't living with her.

Rick blinked, trying to bring the front door of Seth Black's apartment into focus. He'd been sitting in his car, zoned in on Black's place for the last fifteen minutes, and his vision had suddenly gone haywire. Weird, bright lights were blighted by grainy black spots. He could have been looking at the aurora borealis through a patch of black mold.

He ripped off his sunglasses and pressed the pads of his fingers into his closed eyelids, hoping that would help.

Sweat chilled his forehead, and his stomach flipped like a pancake. Nausea. Great. What else could he look forward to today? He'd eaten that morning, forced down a banana and a protein bar, but that was early, before the incident with Lane, and it was now late afternoon. Maybe he just needed some food.

If only he could convince himself that was the problem, but he knew better. He was getting worse. The symptoms were kicking in, and that really pissed him off. Death sucked. People who wrote platitudes about not appreciating life until faced with death must have been living really shitty lives. He fished the prescription bottle out of his jacket pocket and squinted at the fuzzy label. He'd started taking the damn pills again, *as instructed,* but for what? To go blind?

Sure, he'd been one of those idiots who prided himself on never going to the doctor, never taking pills. But he *was* taking them now. He was doing what he was supposed to, being the good guy, so where was the gold star? Whoever kept track of this good-guy stuff clearly wasn't paying attention. Just like they hadn't been paying attention when Ned and his girlfriend were tortured and murdered.

Christ, who did keep track? Anybody? Was there a ledger somewhere? A day of reckoning? Was there any cosmic justice at all?

Rick was of the suspicion that anything you wanted done you had better get done while the getting was good, and that was right here on earth.

He lowered the car window to get some air. His chest was tight, but that was anxiety. Panic set in whenever a new symptom appeared, but it wasn't death he feared, it was the helplessness. He couldn't make his eyes work right. What was next? His bladder? The joy of adult diapers?

Half-blind or not, he'd come here for a reason. He would sit tight until his vision cleared up enough to pay Black a visit and find out what he'd meant by his theory about TPC's clients. Rick had also wanted some time to see who might be coming and going before he went to the front door. Since it was broad daylight, and he would have been easy to spot parked on the street, he'd found a deserted alley across from the building and stationed himself there.

So far there'd been no activity at the apartment, including any sign of the crazy in the black hooded sweatshirt who'd tried to run him down the last time he was here. The assailant had fit the description of Jack the Giant Killer, and Rick wouldn't have minded being the one to end Jack's reign of terror, but he didn't expect lightning to strike twice. And he hadn't accepted the media's assumption that Jack was a man. The lean build and average height they described didn't rule out a female.

Rick's vision was about ninety percent there when he let himself out of the car a short time later. But something was still off, and he knew it the moment he put his feet to the ground. The pavement seemed to roll beneath him as he headed across the street, and the apartment door had an odd greenish halo that grew brighter as he reached it.

He ignored the aberrations and rapped sharply, listening for footsteps inside and waiting for the mail slot on the door to open as it had before. But no one came, and it was dead quiet inside. He rapped again, waited for a response, and then used his fist. The door shook under the impact.

Rick glanced around to make sure he wasn't attracting unwanted attention. He could see two women getting into a compact car down the street. Other than that, the area appeared to be deserted. He called out Black's name and banged again. He had to be in there. He was agoraphobic, housebound.

When no one showed, Rick used his cell to call Black's number, but apparently he wasn't answering the phone, either. Maybe he was sick. Rick spotted a narrow concrete walk that wound around the side of the building, and took it, watching his step as he checked the windows and the back entrance. But everything was locked up tight, and no one responded at the back door, either. He pulled an old receipt from the pocket of his jeans, intending to write a note and drop it through the slot before he left, but he only got as far as the scrubby hedges that lined the front walk.

Something came at him like a freight train, but Rick never saw what it was. First, the sidewalk shifted and his shoe slammed down hard on the edge of the concrete. And then a powerful force seemed to snatch him up and throw him onto the walk. When he tried to get up, he was knocked down again. It felt as if someone had come up from behind and clubbed him. But there was no one around. Everything was out of kilter, and Rick was rolling like a clown in a barrel, but he could see well enough to know that he was alone. No one had attacked him.

When he stopped rolling, he pulled himself to his hands and knees, hanging on to hedges and anything else he could reach to keep from falling over. He began to crawl toward the street, but it took all the strength he had just to get to the curb. Even the paved road was rocking like a boat in a storm.

It felt like an earthquake, but he knew it wasn't. His body was going nuts on him. He just needed to get across the street and back to his car. He couldn't go down in the middle of the road like some drunken bum, passed out in plain view of anyone who came by. He didn't want to die this way—

That was his last thought as his arms gave out from under him and he collided hard with the cold, unforgiving asphalt, face-first. Bones cracked and cartilage snapped, and he felt all the air rush out of his lungs, leaving him empty, gasping. An instant later the bright lights in his brain went out.

25

Lane stepped out of the hotel shower, her skin red and steaming. Heat poured off her dripping body in waves as she grabbed a towel and wrapped it around her wet hair like a turban. She'd cranked the tap up as hot as it would go, nearly scalding herself before she got it adjusted. And then she'd let the needles sting and pummel the tension out of her body.

Nothing could release her mind, but at least she wasn't physically tied in knots. It had been a long day, starting with being kidnapped at gunpoint by a man who claimed to be dying. Everything from that point on had been anti-climactic by comparison, thank God, but she was still trying to get herself back into concierge mode, which in her world meant calm and in control.

With Ashley's help, she'd been able to reschedule all of her interviews here in Dallas—and several of the candidates had impressed her. Afterward, she and Ashley had gone out for a late dinner, reviewed the résumés and discussed tomorrow morning's interviews. Lane had just two more people to see before she caught a flight back to Los Angeles. Not such a terrible day, considering how it had started.

She grabbed a terry hotel robe from a hook, slipped her

feet into matching slippers and snuffed out the aroma-therapy candles she always brought with her. As she left the lilac-scented room, she turned the light off, but left the fan on to dehumidify the air. Every little thing helped, she told herself, echoing one of her own self-help tips. Simple measures and simple pleasures to buffer the stress.

She'd made sure to ask for a room with a sitting area, and this one was spacious and inviting. A cozy alcove housed a writing desk, and a pair of white louvered doors opened onto a small balcony. The music playing was a CD by Tears for Fears, with one achingly melodic tune after another. Soothing, at least to her. She always brought her own music or made sure the hotel could provide it. And all her service's clients could expect the same treatment. Their favorite flowers were cut, elegantly vased and waiting for them on arrival. Plus, a bowl of fresh seasonal fruit, cheeses and crackers, or whatever else they might specify. Having some of the comforts of home eased the tension of traveling. But that was normal tension.

Knockout drops might not have done it for Lane tonight.

She sat on the bed and picked up her cell, hoping that Darwin had worked out the technical problems by now and that Val had been able to calm their Premiere clients' concerns—and provide backup cells to whoever wanted them. Her phone wasn't working, either, but she'd been in a plane and out of touch most of the day, anyway. When she reached the hotel, she'd e-mailed Val from her laptop, and he'd brought her up to date, as of that morning, including his meeting with Simon Shan.

Odd that Shan would refuse to let Val switch out the bodyguards, but Val had probably made the right decision not to insist, given all the pressure the service was under right now. Lane would contact Shan herself when she got back.

Meanwhile, she might be getting more done because her phone hadn't been ringing every two minutes. At least she was able to bring up her voice mail, which meant Darwin must be making some progress. She skimmed her messages, vaguely disappointed by the time she got through the long list. There was an older message from Darwin that she hadn't heard before, telling her he had new information about Rick Bayless, something that would blow her mind. She wondered if Dar had come across what she had learned that morning, that Bayless was dying. Lane also had several messages from Sandra, which surprised her. She didn't know her sister cared that much. There were at least twenty calls from Mary, who did double duty as her assistant, relaying messages from clients who couldn't get through to Lane. She forwarded each of them to Val, which Mary should have thought to do. Possibly she'd been a little flustered over the Shan incident. Jerry Blair was the last one in Lane's queue. He was still in mortal combat with his daughter over a hip-hop group. But all in all, nothing very interesting, which made her wonder what she'd expected.

Her own shocked laughter caught her off guard. It took her another moment to process the possibility that some-where in the back of her mind she might have been looking for a message *from* him, rather than about him. Rick Bayless? Why would he be calling her? Checking to see if she got here okay? She needed *her* head checked. If he had anything to say, it would probably be more of the same. Threats and intimidation. Or his specialty, bullying.

He'd never bothered to explain how Ned had ended up

with the hunting-lodge evidence, which brought everything he said into question. And yet he seemed utterly convinced that Lane knew something about it. He was clearly obsessed with his friend's death, maybe even enough to fake a terminal illness in order to get information. But even if he wasn't telling her the truth, there was something desperately wrong with Rick Bayless. She could see that. He was in human turmoil, and that tugged at her, dammit. Maybe it was grief for his friend or survivor guilt. What stuck in her mind was the way he'd looked at her when she'd made her desperate offer. The hatred she'd seen in his eyes. It had something to do with her, but it wasn't her he hated. She'd just realized that. He never had, even back then. He hated what she was doing, selling herself.

It was a gut feeling, but strong enough that she felt the need to find some tangible way to confirm it. But that was impossible. Still, there were other things she might be able to confirm. She glanced over at her TPC tote bag, where she kept her laptop. She would look up the condition he'd mentioned and find out if it even existed. What had he called it? Barnes Harnett Stone syndrome? Or Burnes? Something like that. If she racked her brain, she might even recall the name of the medication he was taking.

Darwin heard a sound that made his heart jump with hope and fear. The tremulous sigh had come from the doorway of his office. He almost couldn't make himself look up from the computer. He so wanted it to be her. But he was also out of his mind, trying to figure out what had happened to his phone system and wondering if someone had hacked in and sabotaged it. Clearly his security algorithms had failed, and worse, he hadn't done enough penetration testing to discover the system's vulnerabilities. He was kicking himself for that now.

He had the phones up and running again, for the most part, but he still hadn't found the flaws. Plenty of tech-happy schoolkids screwed with networks just for fun. They hacked into Web sites and e-mail because they could. But he could also be dealing with a case of bungled electronic espionage by someone who meant to pirate his programs but not necessarily destroy them or leave any footprints behind. That could have been perpetrated remotely from anywhere in the world by anyone with the skill to do it. But Darwin had a hunch it was more personal than that—and closer to home.

When he did look up a moment later, he saw the fair Janet, hovering uncertainly. She'd pressed her thumbnail to her lips, which made her look even more nervous than he felt.

"I couldn't find you at your place, so I came over here to your office," she said. "Excuse me, I meant Command and Control Center 1." She held up a pizza box in one hand. "The security guy let me come up. I kinda bluffed my way in, though, told him I was delivering some pizza."

Darwin's stomach clenched. He didn't know if that was about pizza or Janet. "Yeah? Great." That was all he could manage his throat was so dry.

It seemed hours before she said anything. He was almost afraid he would be forced to find something else to say, but suddenly it happened. Words came forth from her beautiful, perfect mouth.

"Sorry I freaked," she said. "I thought you were going to sell the pictures or something, and then I realized you don't have to do that. You have plenty of money—"

"Well, yeah, some." Please, God, just take me now, he

thought. This was so lame. She really did deserve better than him. She deserved a man who could speak, and who didn't sneak around and take pictures of her.

"Could you eat a piece of pizza?" she asked.

At his nod, she walked to his desk and set the box down on a lopsided tower of how-to tech manuals on digital-cellular security. There was no unused space. Darwin remained in his chair, wordstruck. Did this mean she'd forgiven him? She still hadn't said why she was here.

"Janet, are we okay?" he asked. But she didn't seem to have heard him. She was looking around his cluttered cavern of an office, her eyes widening in awe, as if just realizing that he must be up to something wondrous and, to her, probably a bit mysterious.

"Wow," she whispered, "what are you doing?"

"Looking for a needle in a cosmic haystack." He kept the details as simple and understandable as possible as he explained that his system may have been penetrated—and then he watched her eyes light with excitement. How many women in this wide world were turned on by computer weirdness, Stephen Hawking quotes and the infinite degrees of pi? Only this one, as far as he knew. Lane was happy to leave the technical stuff to him and never hear another word about it.

"What kind of pizza is that?" he asked.

"Goat cheese and sundried tomato."

Darwin swallowed back a choking sound. He hated goat cheese. He probably hated sundried tomatoes, too. He wasn't sure what they were—or why anyone would do that to a tomato.

"My favorite," he said as she gave the box a push toward him. "You having some, too?"

She nodded. "I'm ravenous."

"Then come on over here," he said, a twinge of possessiveness in his tone. "Sorry, I only have this one chair. The others are loaded up with important shit."

He grinned. She smiled. "We'll manage," she assured him.

As she perched on the arm of his chair and draped her arm around him, her breast softly brushed his cheek. He felt a surge of energy and optimism unlike anything he'd ever known. After he'd wolfed down some food, he would puzzle out what had happened to his state-of-the-art cellular network. Could be he'd gotten too fancy for his own good. But with this woman at his side and some goat-cheese pizza in his belly, he could do anything.

Rick opened his eyes to a pair of beady black orbs staring back at him. A quivering nose. Whiskers. It was all the proof he needed that he was dead. He had died lying there in the road in front of Seth Black's apartment, and now he'd come face-to-face with a vampire bat or something equally satanic, which must make this hell.

Or his house.

The room was dark, lit only by moonlight seeping in through the glass doors. It was an effort to move anything, even his eyes, but he could make out the area rug he was lying on, the Mexican tiles set into the floor and the clay pots in which his palms grew. And the courtyard doors. This was his house. He even remembered how he got here.

A little girl had found him half on, half off the curb in front of Seth Black's place, and she'd wanted to get help, but he wouldn't let her. What got him moving were her tears. She was obviously frightened by the crazy, bleeding man, and he'd had to convince her he was okay. He didn't want the police or the paramedics involved. It might have been someone he knew.

When he got himself into a sitting position, he found that his equilibrium was better. He was dizzy and weak, but that feeling of being flung to the ground was gone. Once the little girl saw that he was okay, she got very chatty. She told him about the bad man in the corner apartment, which would have been Seth Black's. Said he'd yelled at her when she tried to sell him some Girl Scout cookies—and then she'd put the squeeze on Rick.

He couldn't remember how many boxes of cookies he bought, but she'd gone away skipping and singing, to tell her mom. He'd left all but one box on the side of the road and made it back to his car, amazed that he could walk upright. The rearview mirror told him he'd done some damage to his face, possibly even broken his nose, but that was nothing for a guy who hadn't expected to wake up.

The little girl had also told him something else of interest. She said the bad man had a visitor earlier that day. School had started late that morning, and on her way there she'd seen someone all dressed in black go into his place, a tall man wearing a hood. She couldn't see his face, and she wasn't certain about the time, but she gave Rick the name of her school. He would check it out.

It sounded as if JGK had been there sometime that morning. Rick had read JGK's byline on Gotcha.com. Black claimed he didn't know the paparazzo's identity, but that may have been hype. Maybe they were buddies and had gone somewhere together, which put Black's agoraphobia into question.

It had been a rough drive back to his place in the busy late-afternoon traffic, but Rick had made it. He'd even gotten inside the door, but not as far as the couch, where he'd been planning to collapse. He'd blacked out again and hit the deck in the middle of his living room floor, obviously several hours ago.

Get up, Bayless. You did it before. You can do it again.

His first effort was a wipeout. He didn't seem to have broken anything, but sharp, shooting pains kept him flat on his face. He tried again, moving one limb at a time, and aware of the numbness in his left leg, which may have had something to do with his second fall. He used the nearest wall for leverage, and when he made it to his feet, he felt the triumph of a kid passing his driver's exam. Crazy. Triumph from standing on his own two feet?

He turned on the lights and made his way to his office, using the walls to steady himself and vowing to throw away the damn pills. Flush them down the toilet. His doctor had said there would be side effects, but this was no way to live, even if you were dying. Especially if you were dying. He'd actually seen two doctors. He'd gone for a second opinion and had another battery of tests that had confirmed the first diagnosis. The drugs he'd been given were the only ones available for his rare condition, and there was nothing either one of those doctors could tell him now. He had no intention of going back until he couldn't function on his own. But he wasn't there yet, dammit.

The prescription bottle was on his desk, next to the open binder. *I'm dealing with mysteries that try men's souls, my friend's death, my own. I beat the crap out of a fifteen-year-old kid, not physically, but I roughed her up emotionally and obviously did some lasting damage....*

He shut the binder, took the pills and went to the kitchen. Everything that didn't serve him was going in the trash tonight, and that included his guilt about her. He'd been trying to help her. If he hadn't been a vice cop who'd heard a million excuses, he might have believed her about the sick friend. He regretted that now, but he couldn't do anything about it. He couldn't do anything about the grudge she was holding, either.

But he could do something about these fucking pills.

He considered the garbage disposal, but didn't want to take the chance of gumming it up, so he ripped the label off the bottle and dropped it in the trash, aware that it was not the right way to dispose of medication. You didn't have to be an ex–vice cop to know that unused drugs could leach into the water supply and landfills. There was also the problem of addicts going through Dumpsters, and pushers looking to resell drugs.

But Rick didn't have the energy to take the pills back to the druggist or to search for a municipal disposal program. He just wanted to be rid of them. He closed the lid on the garbage can and turned to see his hairy beast of a roommate hovering in the corner, watching him. Mickey was getting damn brave. Obviously he knew a softie when he saw one.

Rick glared back at him, hoping to scare him off. "What?" he said. "You looking for food?" Rick had nothing in the house. The creature was starving, probably. Teach him. He'd picked the wrong guy to mooch off.

Mumbling his displeasure, Rick limped off in search of the Girl Scout cookies. He found the box on the living room floor, where he'd dropped it. He hadn't noticed before but they were peanut butter, his favorite.

His stomach rumbled at the thought of the sweet, crunchy cookies. His mouth began to water. He was starving, too. Mickey peeked from around the side of the couch. The beast had followed him, limped all the way from the kitchen. They were in fine shape, the two of them.

Rick dropped to one knee and sat on the floor, groaning all the way down. When he opened the cookies, he found them hopelessly broken. Easier to eat, he reasoned, offering a broken piece to Mickey, who crept up and began to nibble it off the floor.

Rick had never seen food disappear that fast. "One of us has an appetite," he said dryly, supplying Mickey with a handful of cookie pieces. He also took a handful for himself and began to munch.

Man and mouse, eating together, staving off starvation. It was a special moment. Rick almost smiled. And for one moment, he allowed himself to think about who would feed this mouse when he was gone.

26

God didn't seem to be listening to Burt Carr's prayers. He stood next to the desk in his den, his hand on the phone he'd just hung up. It was the chief of staff from his D.C. office telling him that the congressional hearings to investigate CEO compensation had been postponed indefinitely. Some of the worst offenders had been asked to appear and explain their excessive compensation packages, but Burt had also invited some model CEOs to testify, including Jerry Blair of TopCo.

They had pared their salaries and given back their annual option grants to shake things up and inspire their troops. Leaders like that were role models for integrity and fair play, and Burt wanted the business community—and the country—to understand how it could be done. The bill he was drafting would provide incentives to companies that based compensation on productivity and gave shareholders a say in deciding executive compensation.

Health-care reform was in trouble, too. Without Burt's leadership the other members of Congress were buckling. Nearly everything his nonpartisan coalition was trying to accomplish was in jeopardy. And there was nothing he could do. Many people had been involved in drafting the legislation on health-care reform, but when it came to searching out support and rallying the troops, he'd been the coach, the team and the cheerleading squad. Health care was his baby, his football. And now he was benched.

He'd refused to resign or pull out of the upcoming election, even though he knew many of his colleagues on both sides of the aisle wanted him to. They were horrified at the thought of an accused child molester in their midst. But he wasn't guilty, whether anyone believed him or not, and he'd agreed only to a leave of absence until his case was decided.

He went back to his desk and turned on his computer. No one would take his phone calls, including his own family. The computer had become his only outlet, but what an outlet it was. The World Wide Web was well named. It continued to grow exponentially, had the tentacles of a mythological sea monster and it gave people like him a very large reach.

He was going to appeal directly to the people. And once again, to the highest authority there was. He'd been working on setting up a personal blog, one in which he represented only himself and would be free to say whatever his heart and mind directed. Some honesty was in order, some self-scrutiny, and most of all, some hope for a different kind of politician, one who didn't play the games and was beholden to no one but the ideals he believed in and the people who'd voted for him.

Burt pulled the computer keyboard in front of him and started his blog with the desperate plea he'd made just a few days ago.

Whose side are you on, God? Are you going to let those bastards win this one, too? They've got everything else, all the money and the power. They don't need You. I do. We do. This country does.

As he continued to write about the crisis in the House of Representatives and what it could do to the country, he felt a premonitory chill. Gooseflesh crawled up his arms, bringing a painful shiver. For the first time perhaps, he recognized how dangerous this crusade of his was. A lot of people had a lot to lose—those CEOs and their multimillion- and even billion-dollar packages, the giants of the health-care industry, the insurance companies, the pharmaceutical industry and the HMOs. A politician who not only didn't play their games, but vowed to expose them to an already disgusted public, was a threat indeed. It may have gotten him ruined. It could well get him killed.

Jerry Blair was one wily coyote.

Jack the Giant Killer had been tailing the TopCo CEO since he left his Brentwood estate fifteen minutes ago. Blair had seemed to be heading toward downtown L.A. on the Santa Monica Freeway until he'd made an abrupt exit on Crenshaw, going west, and then taken several more turns, finally pulling into the parking lot of an internet café.

Even weirder, Blair was driving a junker. The CEO normally drove a Beamer Z4 Roadster 3.0, but this morning he was behind the wheel of a lowered silver and black Trans Am that had to be at least thirty years old and looked as if it had been pimped out by a crew from the *Monster Garage*. The dents had dents. That was why Jack had almost missed Blair when Blair had come barreling out of his gated Brentwood compound.

Plus, Blair was in disguise. He was known for wearing sunglasses, even inside, but today he had on one of the baggy-bottom jogging suits and the wide headbands that rappers had made popular. Jack had spotted the bizarre outfit when Blair went into the café—and wouldn't have been surprised to see gold chains.

Now Blair was using one of the café's computers, possibly because he was up to something he didn't want on his personal or work computer. Jack, loitering in the fruit-juice bar next door, was watching Blair through a connecting wall of windows, and strategizing plans for tracing the CEO's movements on the Net. It wouldn't take long, but it did require getting to the computer as soon as Blair was done, and before anyone else had logged on. Jack had to be ready to move the instant Blair got up, and then there was the problem of losing Blair when he left the café.

Jack's chance came when Blair took a bathroom break. Blair had logged off, which probably meant he was leaving after the pit stop, and that might give Jack just enough time. Less than a minute later, Jack logged on to the computer with a credit card, brought up the browser and clicked the down arrow on the navigation bar. A menu dropped down with the history of the most recent Internet addresses used. Jack brought up the first one and frowned. Blair had been reading a California congressman's blog?

A blog on politics? Not a porn site?

Jack skimmed the congressman's post, beseeching God not to abandon him and his constituents to the heathens— and looked up just in time to see Blair head out the door to his car. Fortunately the computer was situated where Jack could see people leaving, but could not easily be seen. Jack didn't even bother to log off. The credit-card bill could be straightened out later.

Blair drove the junker back to the Santa Monica Freeway and took the on-ramp headed toward L.A., but once again, he detoured unexpectedly, taking the Harbor Freeway south to the 103rd Street exit. And now he appeared to be headed into the dark heart of Watts, where the riots had broken out in the sixties, and thirty years later, the police were caught on videotape beating a man named Rodney King, which ultimately triggered another riot. There was supposed to be a gentrification project going on around here somewhere, wasn't there? Jack didn't see any sign of it.

Talk about a wild-goose chase on steroids.

Blair's ultimate destination was a graffiti-splattered warehouse in a neighborhood that had to be gang owned and run. Jack would have been reluctant to enter the warehouse under the protection of an armed guard, but Blair was giving him little choice. This was beginning to look like a big, sexy story.

Blair had left the Trans Am in the driveway and entered the building through an unlocked door next to the garage door. He was carrying a very suspicious-looking combination-locked briefcase. Jack followed him, surprised to see that the interior had been refurbished with steel beams and glass skylights, and subdivided into what looked like offices and lounges. The space was beautiful, but cold and sterile, like something out of a video game.

Blair had just entered an elaborate glassed-in recording studio and was already involved in an animated conversation with some pretty tough-looking customers. He seemed to know these guys, and Jack recognized a couple of them by the logos on their jackets as members of an up-and-coming hip-hop band.

That's when Jack saw the money. The suitcase Blair

had been carrying was lying open on the table. Jack couldn't see the bills' denominations, but there had to be tens of thousands of dollars in the case. Jack tried to get close enough to listen, but the lingo was almost indistinguishable. Still, it didn't take long to figure out that Jerry Blair had dressed up in ghetto chic and come there with the intention of bribing these people with vast sums of money. But it wasn't for drugs or illegal arms, Jack realized with slow-dawning amazement. It was to play at his daughter's sweet-sixteen party.

Laughter would have alerted the band's security detail, who were milling around the studio and not doing a very good job of securing anything. Otherwise, Jack would have been howling. Wild-goose chase? That was the least of it. Jerry Blair was clearly nuts. But at least he'd brought the right car into a neighborhood like this. At this very moment, Jack's was probably being rifled of everything but the McMuffin box left over from breakfast.

27

Lane knew something was wrong even before her taxi had pulled to the curb in front of her office building. There was a crowd milling at the entrance, and some of them had the look of reporters. She had no clue what was going on, but her gut told her this was not good. She stashed the papers she'd been reviewing in her briefcase and got herself organized for a quick exit from the cab. She'd come directly here from the airport to meet with Dar and Val about the phone problems, and her luggage was still in the trunk.

The doorman spotted her inside the cab, rushed over and opened the door to speak with her. "Ms. Chandler, the police are upstairs," he said. "They're waiting to talk to you. I'll have the driver ride you around to the garage entrance, and you can take the elevator up from there."

"What's happened?" she asked him, scanning the crowd to see if there was anyone she recognized. "Why do they want to talk to me?"

"I don't know, ma'am. I just thought it would be better if you didn't have to deal with this mess at the front door."

"Yes, thanks." Lane wondered why someone hadn't called to alert her that the police were there. It could be a problem with her phone again, but she'd checked when the plane landed, and she had several messages, some from her staff, but none had mentioned a problem with the police.

If it had just happened, there wouldn't have been time to warn her. Her stomach tightened as she considered another possibility—that her staff might have been ordered not to warn her, say, if the police wanted the element of surprise. No, that was too paranoid, even for her. She hoped something hadn't happened to another one of her clients. That seemed the strongest possibility.

She dashed out of the taxi as soon as the driver pulled up to the elevator in the garage. She tipped him, told him where to leave the luggage and then watched the floor numbers light up as the car ascended. She played one scenario after another in her head. Val's message about Shan and his bodyguard came back to her. Had something happened since yesterday? Pris seemed another likely victim, for some reason. But it could be Burton Carr, or someone on Lane's staff. It was open season on TPC.

She entered the reception area, feeling like a wrinkled mess from her flight and juggling her briefcase and purse. Maybe she expected chaos of some sort, but the room appeared deserted except for the lovely gray angel, Mary, who was seated where she always was, midway between the spread wings of the frosted-glass counter.

Not smiling, though. Mary looked glassy-eyed with worry—and stuck like a pinned corsage to her chair. Even the softly cascading sheet of water behind her had an odd, hushed sound, more sinister than tranquil.

Lane approached her. "Is everything all right, Mary? I was told the police were here."

"Over there." Mary nodded toward the waiting area behind Lane.

Lane turned as a petite fortyish woman in a severely cut gray blazer and navy blue slacks came forward. "Mimi Parsons, West L.A. police," she said, pointing to the badge on her belt that identified her as a homicide detective. She gave Lane a quick look at the badge and then closed her jacket. "Are you Lane Chandler?"

"I am. Is there a problem?" Lane glanced past the detective and saw a balding man in a badly cut navy-blue suit, who was probably her partner, loitering near the coffee bar. He'd helped himself to a cup of TPC's gourmet brew and was watching a video introduction to the company's concierge services.

"Do you mind telling us where you were this Thursday morning?"

"Yesterday morning? I was on my way to Dallas on business." Lane answered without hesitation, even though the question—and the detective's manner—disturbed her.

Parsons cocked her head and peered at Lane long enough to make her wonder if this had something to do with Rick Bayless and his kidnapping attempt. Did the detective know about that? Had something happened to Bayless? Lane said nothing more.

"Can anyone verify your whereabouts?" Parsons asked, frowning deeply.

Lane figured her for years younger than she looked. She had rather attractive, naturally wavy brown hair, cut short with peekaboo bangs, but the frown added decades. "Why would they need to?"

The man ambled over, opening his jacket to show his badge as he joined Parsons. He was also homicide. Lane was too rattled to catch his name, which wasn't like her. She always caught names. It was her business. But this one was obviously the good cop and Parsons the bad. He actually smiled as he introduced himself.

The ploy didn't work. Lane was all the more on guard. The detectives who'd come to talk about Simon Shan had not started by asking her where she was at any particular time.

Lane's arms were cramping from the weight of her purse and briefcase. She set both on the counter. She felt anything but cool and unflustered, but they didn't need to know that. She'd already decided not to invite them into her office, although that would be the polite thing to do. She wasn't giving them any reason to prolong their visit. And she wanted a witness to everything that was said.

Poor Mary was still statuelike in her chair. An electronic switchboard took care of the phone calls, so her job was to greet people, direct traffic and assist Lane when necessary, all of which she did beautifully. Lane gave her an encouraging smile, and turned back to her inquisitors. "Before we go any further with this, I'd like to know why you're here."

Parsons exchanged a glance with her partner. Her tone hardened. "Do you know a man named Seth Black?" she asked Lane.

"He runs a celebrity-gossip Web site, doesn't he? I know *of* him."

"You've never met him? Never been to his place of business?"

Lane gave it some thought. "Not that I remember. Why would I have been there? I didn't do business with him."

Her partner spoke up. "Well, in a way you did. He broke stories about some of your biggest clients, didn't he? He's destroyed a few careers, maybe even a few lives? He couldn't have been one of your favorite people."

Lane shook her head. "Generally speaking, I don't like people who destroy others, but I don't know this man. I don't know where he works, where he lives—"

The partner cocked an eyebrow, wrinkling his bald skull. "You don't know where he lives?"

"No, of course not. Why would I?"

"Seth Black was found dead in his apartment this morning. Somebody didn't like him enough to murder him."

"Murder?" Now Lane wished she'd taken them into her office. The wall of water behind Mary was beginning to sound like waves crashing on rocks. "What does this have to do with me?"

Parsons moved in. "Are you missing something, Ms. Chandler? Something of value, possibly from your office or purse?"

Her impulse was to say no, but that would make her look guilty, because she hadn't been in her office since Wednesday night. So she said nothing, and the partner handed her an eight-by-ten photograph. His smile had taken on an evil glint.

Lane instantly recognized the ballpoint pen in the enlarged snapshot. She could even read her own name. It was one of a set of two identical pens that Val had given her for Christmas. She kept one of them in her desk here at the office and the other at home in her writing desk.

Lane wanted to cover her ears to drown out the noise of the waterfall. What had ever made her think cascading water would be soothing? She also wanted to go to her office and see if the pen was still in her desk drawer. But she knew better than that. They would follow her.

"Am I under suspicion? Are you charging me with something?"

"No, just putting you on notice. You'll be hearing from us again, and meanwhile, don't do any more traveling."

Detective Parsons handed her a business card. "In case you remember something you think we should know."

Lane was grateful her hand was steady as she took the card. Her legs weren't. She was also grateful the counter was behind her for support. As the two detectives walked out the door, she sat down on the counter and heard something crack. It sounded as if she'd broken the glass, but when she turned around, she saw Mary, facedown and apparently out cold. The gray angel had fainted.

If he'd had another bottle of pills he would have trashed them, too. It had now been forty-eight hours since Rick jettisoned the miracle drugs the doctor gave him, and he was feeling halfway human again, which was probably better than he looked. He was still pretty beaten up, and his face had taken the worst of it, but the cuts had started to heal and so had the nose he'd mistakenly thought was broken. That told him he'd made the right decision.

And now he had business that wouldn't wait. Lots of it, actually.

He slowed the Jeep to check street signs, reminding himself not to miss his turn as he drove through the quiet residential neighborhood. It was early, not even seven on a Saturday morning, and most folks were probably still in their beds, but Rick had a good reason for the early start. He had no idea how much time he had now that he was off the meds, but he had to make it all count, every minute.

He'd made up his mind—if he had any choice in the matter—that he wanted to go out doing something that had meaning for him, rather than wallowing in self-pity or even cashing in his own ticket. That last option had really begun to appeal to him. But then the wounds had begun to heal and it had seemed like a sign, except that he didn't believe in signs. People wanted to believe they'd been saved for some special purpose. That was ego. The way Rick saw it, he and the gimpy mouse were too stupid and stubborn to die. If there were any signs, they were all bad, but he and Mickey had been ignoring them. Then again, maybe they'd both been saved by Girl Scout cookies.

When Rick woke up this morning, the reason for his existence had come to him. It was simple. Pieces of the human puzzle were missing, his puzzle. He had unanswered questions. Wasn't that what got everybody up in the morning? Maybe people only went willingly once they had all the answers. He needed to know the truth about Ned—and he might even bring down a giant killer while he was at it. He hoped that would let Ned and Holly rest easy. It was the only thing that would allow Rick Bayless to go quietly.

Today's first stop was another shot at Seth Black, who hadn't responded to any of Rick's attempts to call him. Rick hadn't been able to leave a message because Black's answering machine had been full. But as he turned the corner onto Black's street, he saw the yellow tape and the patrol cars sitting out in front of his apartment building. He recognized some of the crime scene people and one of the two detectives, Mimi Parsons.

They'd roped off Black's place. Rick's mind flashed back two days to when he'd pounded on the apartment door but got no answer. He pulled his Jeep over to the curb, safely hidden by an even larger SUV, and wondering if he should let himself be seen, especially given the cuts and bruises on his face. He turned on the car radio at low volume to catch any breaking news, and then he dialed up Mimi on the cell. She answered on the first ring.

"Mimi, this is Rick. Got a minute?"

"Actually, no. I'm working an active crime scene."

"Anybody I know?"

"Where you been? It hit the airwaves last night. The guy who ran that online tabloid, Gotcha.com, was drowned in his own toilet. Or maybe he was electrocuted and then drowned. We won't know what actually killed him until the prelim comes in."

"Electrocuted?"

"Yeah, it looks like he grabbed some live wires."

"He fried himself?"

"Maybe, but he didn't drown himself. There's evidence of force."

Seth Black dead? There were plenty of people who might want to dust the scandalmonger, but Rick couldn't help but wonder if this had some connection to the voice mail he'd received from Black about TPC. "When did it happen?" Rick asked.

"Rick, gotta go. Listen to the news."

She clicked off, and Rick switched to a twenty-four-hour news channel. Within moments they were reporting on the gruesome death. Rick was shocked by two things: the estimated time of death, which was Thursday morning, and the person who was being questioned in connection with the crime, Lane Chandler.

There was no information about why Lane might be considered a suspect. Actually, the official sound bite from law enforcement was courtesy of Mimi herself, who referred to Lane as a person of interest. But Rick knew something that neither the media nor Mimi Parsons knew.

A little girl had seen someone entering Black's apartment on Thursday morning—and it couldn't have been Lane. She'd been with Rick.

28

"Excuse me, that's my machine!" Priscilla Brandt scooted over to confront the stocky older woman who had removed Pris's towel from the Thigh-Clops machine. The nerve. Pris had only been gone long enough to grab a drink from the juice bar, and she'd clearly marked her territory with the monogrammed towel she'd brought from home. This was a coed fitness club, and she didn't like thinking about where the house towels had been.

"Oh, sorry," the woman said, gingerly settling herself in the bucket seat. "I didn't see anyone using it."

Pris held up her blueberry blitz. "I dashed over to the juice bar to get this. The service here is dreadful, isn't it? They're supposed to bring drinks around so people don't have to abandon their machines in the middle of a set. By the way, I only had two sets, ten repetitions each, to go. It would just take a sec."

Pris was lying. She intended to be on the Thigh-Clops until she no longer had the strength to spread her legs, but first she had to get this porker off it. She waggled the drink again. "Hydration is very important."

"Yes, it is," the woman said pleasantly. "I won't be long."

Pris was trying desperately to be polite, but she couldn't believe the interloper wouldn't give up the machine. "I am in a bit of a hurry."

"Me, too," the woman chirped as she fumbled around with the gears and the settings. She obviously hadn't used the machine before, which meant it would take her forever to get her frumpy self organized, if she ever did.

Pris was now dead certain that Satan had sent this person to tempt her into another act of violence, in the name of civility, of course. The woman's Stepford-wife smile and the bright, singsong voice couldn't be for real.

"I'll be done soon," Satan's mistress promised. She was now struggling to get the pads of the thigh press between her legs, where they belonged.

No one should have to witness this, Pris thought, frustration burning holes in her self-control. "Soon?" she muttered under her breath. "Not likely. There's enough thunder in those thighs to run a power plant."

Someone within earshot chuckled, and Pris glanced behind her at the buff young trainer who'd given her some tips on the chinning station. He'd told her to tuck her butt under to relieve the strain on her back. And then he'd snapped said butt with his towel. Cheeky brat.

"I love me some thunder," he said, glancing at Pris's thighs, which weren't as trim as they could be. That was why she needed the damn machine back. Actually, she needed a Thigh-Clops in every room of her house.

Pris heard huffing and puffing. Satan's mistress was now red-faced with determination and squeezing away on the inner-thigh press. She must have heard the exchange and decided to take it personally. Her smile had been replaced with a flamethrower glare, which she aimed at Pris.

It was one of those awful moments of truth. When someone directed every atom of their being into intimidating you, you really should walk away. That would have been the mature way to handle it, but Pris knew a little bit about intimidation herself—and this rude porker was not going to give up the Thigh-Clops, ever. She was going to make Pris wait if she had to kill herself doing it.

"Do you know who I am?" Pris asked.

"No clue. Paris Hilton?"

"I'm Ms. Pris, the auth—"

"I don't care who you are," the woman wheezed. "You're not getting this machine. And don't give me that look, you skinny little bitch. I need Thigh-Clops more than you do. I could breathe on you and knock you over."

Pris was appalled. The only sane course was to dismiss the woman as a lowlife, but Pris burned to mail her a copy of the etiquette book with some anthrax inside. Then, an idea struck. The top floor of the club was arranged in a circle. The woman would probably leave as soon as Pris did. But Pris would only pretend to leave. She would round the circle, come up on the machine from behind and seize it as soon the woman left.

It worked. Moments later, concealed by a stack of workout pads, Pris saw the woman abandon the Thigh-Clops. Pris made her move, breaking into a jog. She had to get there before anyone else did. But, to her shock, the woman turned and began to lumber back to the machine, too. She must have seen Pris in the mirrors on the walls.

Maybe it was inevitable that Pris and her nemesis would get fatally entangled trying to take possession of the Thigh-Clops. Pris got there first, but the other woman shoulder-butted her out of the bucket seat and promptly sat on her, nearly squishing the breath out of her. That's when Pris went for the woman's hair. She had to. It was dislodge her or die.

Pris was oblivious to the crowd that had gathered. Nor did she notice the figure in the hooded sweatshirt, who'd stopped working out with the free weights in order not to miss a moment—and who had a cell-phone camera at the ready, recording every flying fist and foul word.

Jack the Giant Killer wasn't a regular member of this exclusive fitness club, but enough money greasing the right palms could get you in the door of just about any celebrity bastion. You didn't have to rub elbows with the wealthy to gain entrance to their private playgrounds, just with the poor bastards who toiled to serve them. That was your ticket in, because they didn't like the spoiled, self-indulgent celebs any better than Jack did.

Jack turned away from the scene with a smile—and a sense of achievement that made all the effort worthwhile. Only a true champion of the underdog could appreciate the satisfaction that came from meting out justice to bullies and blowhards, even anonymously. Jerry Blair had been an exercise in futility, but Ms. Pris never disappointed. Some people begged for boundaries like out-of-control children, and Jack was happy to supply them. Ms. Pris had just sealed her own fate. She would be the next giant, albeit a baby one, to go down.

Someone had been in Lane's condo. It was a suspicion that grew stronger as she walked through the kitchen and dining area. Nothing seemed to be missing, but things weren't sitting just right, as if someone had moved them and failed to put them back. Lane noticed a crooked mirror above the dining room console, a vase of cut flowers on the wrong table and an off-kilter area rug. Normally she had a good eye. In her business, it was imperative. Things couldn't be off, even a little.

She told herself it could have been the cleaning lady, and that she, Lane, had been too distracted by her crazy life to pay attention. But when she got to the entry, she stopped in her tracks, jarred by the sight of an open door. She hadn't noticed it last night. She'd come home exhausted from her trip and vibrating with nerves after her encounter with the police. But now, in the strong morning light, the open guest-closet door was hard to miss—and to explain away. She'd barely had time to have guests since she bought this condo. The closet hadn't been used since her housewarming, and the door was always shut tight.

She turned in a circle, aware that she hadn't changed out of her cotton sleep shirt when she got out of bed. It didn't make any sense that an intruder would still be in the condo this morning, but it was a terrifying thought. Someone had planted one of her engraved pens in a dead man's house. She'd checked her desk after the detectives left TPC, and the pen was gone, so of course she'd assumed whoever had taken it from her office had planted it at the crime scene. But the pen was part of a set, and Lane kept the second one here.

She hurried back down the hall and checked the writing desk in her bedroom. The second pen was missing, too. She almost never used it. It was one of those heavy, gold-encased pens, good for making first impressions, but little else. Had she moved it, put it in her purse and lost it? She couldn't remember.

The thought that someone had broken into her condo

as well as her office was terrifying. Maybe it was panic, but she could still feel the intruder's presence, and it gave her gooseflesh. The homeowners' association manager sometimes let repair people in, but never without clearing it with Lane first. And since today was Saturday, she couldn't do much beyond leave the manager a message.

She went back to the living room, gave it a thorough going-over and then doubled back down the hallway to check the guest bedroom. She didn't see any other signs of an intrusion, but she was still rattled. Just a few days ago she'd thought she heard someone out on the roof garden. That may have been how an intruder got in, probably while she was in Dallas. She could remember thinking it was Rick. But what reason would he have to try to frame her for a murder?

She felt compelled to search the roof garden, too, but she wasn't certain what to look for. The police would have recognized signs of forced entry, but she didn't want the police involved now. She needed to figure this out on her own.

Indian summer had returned with a vengeance, Lane realized as she opened the patio doors. The birds chirped feverishly from their perches in nearby trees, and the enveloping warmth helped to calm her nerves. Maybe there was some logical explanation for the missing pens. She could hope.

The patio doors and windows showed no signs of force, and she didn't see anything else amiss as she walked the perimeter of the roof garden, searching the limestone tiles and stucco walls as if it were another crime scene. The fire escape explained how someone could have gained access to this area the other night, but not how an intruder got inside her condo. But these were questions for an expert.

She needed to talk with the building's security people, and they could only be reached through the homeowners' association.

As she finished her inspection, she stopped to admire the flowering hibiscus bushes and the other potted plants. Her favorite part of the garden was the wrought-iron arbor. It dripped with verdant green clematis vines that bloomed well into fall, producing clusters of tiny milk-white flowers that saturated the air with sweetness. Deep green bowers shaded a set of woven cane chairs and a granite fire pit. But the focal point was a wall fountain that spilled into a reflecting pond made of stone. Lane hadn't stocked the pond with fish, mostly because of the reminders it would evoke.

Just the sound of the tumbling water brought back images of the creek-fed lake where she and her father used to fish when she was a child. They would float on the lake in their little rowboat, their lines sunk deep in the water, half-asleep in the hazy summer sun, and watching the dragonflies skate the surface of the lake. The fish bit rarely, but that wasn't the point. What mattered was that her dad was still strong enough to fish. Just sharing space in the boat was made precious by the knowledge that their summer idylls would soon be coming to an end.

Lane wasn't with her dad when he died. She'd believed she was the reason her parents fought so bitterly, and that they might have a chance to reconcile if she was gone. She'd thought it was her fault that her father seemed to prefer his youngest daughter's company over that of anyone else, including his wife. He'd loved to tell Lane stories and share his outdoor pursuits with her, things his wife didn't enjoy, such as fishing, and Lane was enough of a tomboy to savor every second of it. Theirs had been a special relationship, and Lane was still devastated that she hadn't been there to say goodbye to him. She had done what she thought was right for him and her mother at the time, but there was no way she could have known that her parents' problems had started long before she was born.

She'd told Sandra that she couldn't bear to hear her parents fighting anymore, and Sandra had understood, and allowed her to stay. Sandra had left home for the same reason, but the sisters had been on opposite sides in the warring household, Sandra siding with her mother against Lane. The family rift had created a barrier that existed to this day.

Lane sat in one of the cane chairs, aware of the wiry braids against the backs of her bare thighs. She'd put the cushions away to preserve them from the weather. Now she would have some lovely cross-hatching on her backside, but she didn't care. This was a good place to think.

She'd returned Sandra's phone calls last night and told her about the incident with the police at the office. She'd also mentioned the possible break-in at her condo, but Sandra hadn't seemed surprised or particularly concerned. She'd said she was glad Lane was all right, but had made up an excuse to get off the phone. Lane had been stunned, and hurt. There didn't seem to be any way to bond with her sister, but clearly she, Lane, wanted to. Otherwise, why would she be feeling this welling emptiness, the gaping hole that nothing could fill, as she liked to call it?

Lane sighed. Emotional pain. It was the reason God made chocolate.

The doorbell startled her. She glanced through the clerestory windows into the living room and beyond to the entry, wondering if maybe Sandra had decided to come over after all. Lane had overslept, so it was probably around ten.

"I'm coming," she called out as the doorbell rang and rang. All she could see through the front door's peephole was a pair of mirrored sunglasses. She didn't know anyone who wore aviators except Rick Bayless, did she? "Who is it?"

A male voice shouted back. "Open the door so we don't have to yell—unless you want your neighbors to hear us."

Bayless, definitely. She flipped the dead bolt, but left the chain lock on. He pushed his glasses up on his head, revealing cuts, bruises and a squint that did little to dim the neon green of his eyes. He was dressed in olive-drab pants and a white T-shirt, both of which could have been military issue. The only thing missing was the dog tags.

No one would ever have known this guy had a terminal illness with an unpronounceable name. But Lane had done research in Dallas that verified everything he'd said. The syndrome was rare enough that only one medication had been developed, but all it could do was slow the progression, which was usually rapid once the symptoms set in. The brain stem failed to recognize signals from the nerves, which ultimately shut down the vital organs. The motor skills went first, then the lungs and heart. He was living with a time bomb, his own body.

It was hard to believe. And maybe that was good because she desperately didn't want to believe it. She needed a reason not to do anything stupid, like trust him.

"It's important," he said. "I need to talk to you about Seth Black."

"I can't. I'm expecting someone—uh, my sister, Sandra. Besides, what's there to talk about? Someone murdered Black, and they think I did it."

"I know. I'm your alibi." Lane stared at him, letting that sink in. "Are you going to let me in?" he pressed.

"Hang on," she said. "I'm not dressed. I'll get a robe."

"Lane, you're fine. I've seen you naked. It doesn't matter."

She winced. "Could we keep that between ourselves, please, unless you want *me* to tell the neighbors that you kidnapped me at gunpoint."

"I really wish I hadn't had to do that."

"Kidnap me?"

"Yes." He grimaced rather convincingly. "Desperate measures."

Right answer. But no way was she entertaining him in a T-shirt—and she didn't have a bathrobe. She was behind on her laundry and both her robes were in the hamper. "What do you mean you were my alibi?"

"Seth Black died Thursday morning, sometime shortly after 7:00 a.m. You couldn't have done it. You were with me."

"How do you know when he died? The news says the medical examiner's report hasn't come in yet."

He shrugged, as if to say I have ways.

Her legs actually began to shake as a frightening possibility hit her. She stared at him, dumbstruck. "Oh, my God, someone framed me with that pen. Was it you? You broke in here, stole the pen and planted it in a dead man's apartment. Did you have him killed, too?"

He looked as though he might laugh at that. "Think about what you just said. Why would I frame you for a murder and then provide you with an alibi?"

"So I'll owe you. You've set it up so I'll have to bargain with you. You want me at your mercy…but it won't work."

"Why not?"

"Because I don't know anything about your friend *or* how he died."

"That's a fucking lie, Lane. My friend *joined* your service the day before he was murdered. He signed a one-year contract to the tune of fifty thousand bucks for a Premiere membership. Why did you lie to me about that?"

Lane froze. She had no idea how he could get that kind of information, unless possibly through some police connection. She'd destroyed Ned's application herself, before anyone else saw it. The only one she'd told was Darwin. She'd also been the one to run Ned's credit card because Mary had been away from her desk.

"You have no proof of that," she said.

"All the proof I need is right here." He flashed a copy of Ned's credit-card statement that included the TPC charge. It was hard to miss with all those zeros.

"Get in here," she said, unchaining the door. "The neighbors will hear you."

He smiled darkly, flicking his glasses back on his nose as he entered. "Ned had an online account, and since I was the closest thing to family he had left, his password was a no-brainer. It was my initials and birth date."

"All right, I *confess,*" she said, being intentionally dramatic. "It's true I didn't tell you, but I wasn't covering up a crime. I didn't tell anyone. I was trying to protect my business. I was afraid of the repercussions of another disaster for a TPC client, especially something that horrific." Imploringly, she added, "Concierge services operate on word of mouth. Publicity like that could destroy me."

He folded his arms, clearly skeptical. "That's it? You didn't want it getting out that Ned was a client?"

"Yes, that's it, I swear." To her relief, he didn't dismiss

her answer out of hand. But it was hard to read him because of those damn sunglasses. Even now she wondered about his stoicism—and what had made him that way. He was like one of those reinforced-steel briefcases with the combination locks and the silver reflecting surfaces. No doubt he'd seen bad things on the street. She'd seen them herself, but probably not the carnage he'd had to deal with. So few kids made it, nearly all of them ravaged by drugs. Cleaning up after that must have been a pretty damn disillusioning way to make a living.

She was sure he hadn't done it out of love for troubled youth, given his bullying ways with her, although maybe that was standard operating procedure with drug-addicted runaways. But she hadn't been using, despite what he may have believed. She'd experimented a bit, mostly to keep from being ostracized by the other kids, but she'd been too worried about keeping herself and Darwin alive to risk messing with drugs.

"Why are you so obsessed?" she asked him. "Your friend is gone, and you don't have much time left. You ought to spend it doing something you've always wanted to do."

Her gaze strayed to his mouth. It was nothing more than a glance, but he eyed her suspiciously. "What makes you think there's something I've always wanted to do?"

"You mean there isn't? I don't believe you." Something possessed her to walk over and rip the metallic glasses off his head. "You just won't admit it."

He squinted at her fiercely. "Why did you do that?"

"It's harder to lie when people can look you in the eye, isn't it?"

"It would be *if* I were lying."

He was so implacable that she felt a defiant impulse.

Someone really should shake this man up. Her heart surged, propelling heat all the way to her fingertips. The rush of blood electrified her arms in a painful way. She managed to fight off the impulse for all of about ten seconds. She wanted to shake him, even slap him, anything to get a response. But for reasons she could not have explained, she slipped her hand behind his neck, curled her fingers in the soft blond bristle that was his cropped hair and kissed him on the mouth.

He unleashed a surprised obscenity, but Lane ignored him. For such a hard-set mouth, his lips were easy and sweet. They made her clutch deep down, and gasp at what she was doing, kissing the cop who'd arrested her. Her mouth watered, the way it did when she ate chocolate. But chocolate had never made her heart kick and race like this. After an astonished moment, they both stepped back and stared at each other.

"What the hell was that?" he breathed.

"Bizarre, huh?" A nervous giggle lodged in her throat, but she had no chance to say anything else. He caught her by the shoulders and hauled her back to him, kissing her until they both stumbled backward and bumped into the wall. Lane was only absently aware that they were endangering her favorite sculpture, a Chinese porcelain horse. The end table it sat on had been pushed aside and was teetering on two legs, but she couldn't focus on the impending accident. Even the crash didn't bring her back to her senses.

Their bodies clung so tightly she could feel him hardening against her, and that shocked her, too. She started to push him away, but he pulled her back, as if he couldn't bear to let her go, and his mouth moved so beautifully over hers. Heat poured off him as he ran his hands down her back and gripped her ass, igniting a sweet little fire. But she could feel other sensations, a chill racing up the back of her legs, the exposure.

"Rick," she murmured, "what are you doing with my shirt?"

The cotton material was bunched tightly in his hands, revealing everything, including the fact that she wasn't wearing any panties. He glanced at the dark nest of curls as he let go of the material. "Sorry," he said, and then he actually blushed, deeply.

"No, it's okay. I'm just—" This was the big bad cop? Amazing. There was hope for him yet.

"You're just what?"

"Surprised! Look at you. You're alive. You're flushed with life."

He stepped back from her, shaking his head.

"No," she said. "Help yourself. Focus on yourself. Maybe there's some way you can beat this disease."

His dazed expression grew confused, cold. "Beat this disease? What was that? A mercy kiss? Show the dying guy that life is worth living?"

"No, of course not." She tried to think how to explain, but she was confused, too, and it was already too late. She could see his bewilderment turning to anger and worse, suspicion. *Oh, God, no.*

"Don't do me any favors, Lane, Lucy, whatever the hell your name is."

He picked his glasses up off the floor where she'd dropped them. She wouldn't have dared try to stop him. He was already too far gone, cold and remote. He put the glasses back on, letting her see her startled expression reflected in the lenses before he turned and headed for the door.

She winced as the door banged shut behind him. She wondered fleetingly if he was angry enough to withhold the alibi and throw her to the wolves, but then her mind snapped back like the rubber band on her wrist. He couldn't have been more wrong about the mercy kiss, but he hadn't given her time to convince him. Maybe he didn't want to be convinced, and if so, that was just as well. Maybe it was just pity she was feeling. Whatever this flaring pain was, she could not allow herself to get involved with a man she was doomed to lose.

29

You don't have much time left. Spend it doing something you've always wanted to do. What a fucking cliché. As far as Rick was concerned, people who said that to the dying should be killed. What did they know about having months, maybe weeks, to live?

Caught in the snarled traffic on Pacific Coast Highway, he noticed the gray skies and the heavy mist rolling in from the ocean. The weather had sneaked up on him when he wasn't looking. It had been sunny and balmy when he left Lane's not fifteen minutes ago, and now it was about to pour.

She didn't understand. Ned might be alive except for him. If Rick had to spend time all the way down to his last minute searching for the truth, he would do it. But enough noble self-sacrifice. He was starting to sound like a religious martyr.

Rick pulled to the side of the road and slammed out of the car, ignoring the drizzle. The traffic had stopped moving, and Pacific Coast Highway had turned into a parking lot. In drought-stricken southern California, drivers were so freaked by wet pavement they slowed to a crawl.

He could use a walk anyway. Maybe the rain would

cool him down. Otherwise, he was going to drive back to her place and do something stupid.

The kiss had been interesting. Her pity he could do without. And he had to wonder if there was something karmic about that pep talk of hers. Years ago he'd been trying to verbally slap some sense into her, and he'd been just as overzealous. She would probably argue more so, but she'd seemed bent on self-destruction back then, selling herself on the street. He still didn't get it. She could have gone to a shelter or called 911 for her sick friend. His theory: she didn't trust anyone—and had been determined to prove she could do it all on her own, without help.

He strongly suspected that was still true.

He shook the rain off his shoulders and kept walking, aware that he was wearing nothing but a T-shirt. Maybe he'd catch a cold, expire and end all this soul-searching agony. He tried doggedly to get his mind on Ned and what had to be done next, but apparently his mind wasn't done with Lane Chandler because it kept taking him back to her—and a mystery that had nothing to do with Ned.

She had changed in every way he could see, but his gut kept telling him she hadn't changed at all. She was still selling herself short, and he didn't understand why, especially now. She had beauty, intelligence, natural sensuality, everything. He could see all of that promise in her fifteen years ago. She was a budding femme fatale, possessed of a voice that could calm the soul and excite the mind. She promised respite and relief of the kind every man craved…and she had sparked a longing in him for something he could never have.

He might never forgive her for reminding him that he could still feel that spark. He didn't want those feelings now. He didn't want to feel *anything,* but that was damn near impossible around her.

Someone honked at him as he dashed across the highway to get to a little coffee shop. He was soaked and some steaming-hot coffee sounded good. Maybe then he could exorcise Lane Chandler and focus on what came next. There was another woman he needed to think about. Holly. Ned's dead girlfriend.

Moments later, as he sat at the counter, nursing a mug of freshly brewed black coffee, he mentally reviewed the steps of his investigation, starting with the night he'd broken into the crime scene at Ned's place. He'd come across nothing that disproved the RHD's position of murder-suicide, but he'd been hampered by the darkness and his need to find the package. He'd made no progress with the package, but at least he knew the police hadn't found it.

He had found Lane's business card that night, which had gotten him into the current mess. A check of Ned's online credit and bank accounts had yielded nothing, except that Ned had joined Lane's service. Rick had also looked at satellite photos of Ned's house on the night he'd died, thinking he might see a strange car or person in one of the views, but they'd shown no unusual activity.

There was no sign of forced entry or a third party present, and the preliminary coroner's report had found that no drugs or alcohol were involved, but there was sexual paraphernalia and signs of physical torture, including the burn marks that Ned had mentioned the night he came to the cabin.

Rick sipped his coffee, grateful that it was hot and strong. He needed to focus. Everything seemed to support murder-suicide. The times of death created the only discrepancy, but that had been explained away, too. Ned had died of the alleged self-inflicted gunshot wound some time before Holly died of asphyxiation from the plastic bag. It appeared that her death had been a long, drawn-out affair. He'd given her just enough oxygen to revive her whenever she was close to death, but then apparently at some point, he'd mistaken her unconsciousness for death and shot himself, overcome by remorse.

Disgusting. The idea was so repellent it made Rick sick to his stomach. Ned wouldn't hurt anyone, much less torture a woman in such a violent, sadistic way. Never. He had no reason to do it, and the investigators hadn't come up with any convincing motive, as far as Rick was concerned. The rough-sex stuff wasn't Ned, either, despite the corroborating evidence.

Rick needed to look at Holly. His gut was telling him that she was a link to something everyone had missed. He didn't know how deeply they'd delved into her life, because Mimi was keeping a tight lid on any information about the investigation, especially where Rick was concerned. Maybe she'd been taken to task by her superiors. She wouldn't even return Rick's calls at this point.

Mimi—and the RHD—had never considered Holly as anything other than a victim of Ned Talbert. Rick wondered if it might be the other way around, simply because Ned had always been drawn to women who were damaged. Rick just hoped to God he could keep his thoughts trained on Holly long enough to get something done.

His bodyguard was still in her room. She hadn't been out of there in over forty-eight hours, unless she had the gift of invisibility, which seemed possible. Simon had taken to listening at her door for sounds of activity, but since yesterday it had been silent. He'd questioned whether she was inside, and then he'd begun to wonder if she was ill. Given her credentials, she should have no problem taking care of herself, but he didn't know if she was eating or sleeping, and something about her was almost pathologically fragile. It didn't make sense.

He stood at the kitchen counter, eating his lunch of scrambled eggs and prosciutto out of the pan he'd prepared it in—and wondering if he should take something to her. The cell phone rang as he was washing the dishes moments later. The service had delivered his new Darwin phone yesterday, and all the flashy extras seemed to be working again, including the screening feature that allowed him to hear voice mail as it came in. He'd actually turned that feature on this morning. He had to fight the instinct to isolate himself because isolation was not a good move when you couldn't trust your own bodyguard. Even he could see that.

"Mr. Shan, pick up your phone! Pick up your phone, Mr. Shan," the caller demanded. "This is Upton Yorty, and you have a choice. You can talk to me, or you can plan on an extended stay in Club San Quentin, say, twenty to life? Somehow, I doubt they'll have your silk bed linens there."

Simon grabbed one of the linen kitchen towels from his collection and dried his hands. Upton Yorty, or Up Yours, as everyone called him, was the head counsel on Simon's defense team, and a belligerent old bastard, but with the best acquittal record in the history of the California bar.

"Mr. Yorty," he said, pressing the speakerphone button.

"Mr. Shan, it's about time we met. I'm sorry it has to be under these circumstances, but you've ignored all my prior requests for meetings."

"Yes, my apologies. I've had phone problems that included lost voice mail, but that's all been fixed now." He could also have said that Upton Yorty was not an easily accessible man himself. Simon had been speaking with the other attorneys on the team while Up Yours flitted around the world, dealing with international business moguls, heads of state and other more prestigious clients.

"First the bad news," Up said, his voice booming from the speaker. "We weren't able to move back the court date on the arraignment and bail hearing. We're on the calendar for Friday morning at ten. Today is Saturday, so that's less than a week away."

"And the good news?"

"There is none. I'll be back in my office Tuesday afternoon, and I'd like you there for a sit-down with me and the rest of the team. I've gone through your entire file, the police and lab reports, the prosecution's evidence and our own investigator's reports. We have all the cogent details, but the team hasn't agreed on the best possible defense, and time is now an urgent factor. In other words, we have the trees, Mr. Shan, lots of trees, but no forest. Your defense team is lost in the woods and we need to know where the hell we're going."

Simon agreed to the meeting, thinking how much he wanted to tell Up Yours where to go. The other attorneys had assured him everything was on track and running smoothly. If his defense team now needed him to be their compass, he *was* in trouble. But Yorty was known for his courtroom theatrics. Maybe Simon had just gotten a sample.

Simon moved around the gleaming kitchen, putting away spices and setting things straight, and very much aware that his mind had already gone back to her.

Compelled, he slipped down the hallway to listen at her door. He was wondering whether to unlock it when her voice startled him. She was on the other side, talking to him.

"Have you come to tell me you trust me?"

"Are you all right?" he asked her.

"Answer my question."

He used his key to unlock the door, but by the time he got it open, she was on the other side of the room, pulling a silk kimono around herself and tying it.

"No," he said, aware of the distress in her dark eyes. "I didn't come to tell you I trust you."

"Then why don't you send me away?"

"I don't know," he admitted. "Why don't I send you away?"

She turned around, facing the wall. "Leave and lock the door behind you. I only want to help you. Come back when you believe that."

Simon shut the door. He didn't lock it.

Burt Carr hadn't slept or changed clothes in thirty-six hours. He'd been too busy fielding questions on his blog from a concerned public—and too grateful that most of them believed his declaration of innocence and his claim that he'd been framed in order to stop his investigation and his bid for reelection. He was wild with missionary zeal. These were his people, and together, they would change things.

He closed his eyes to a strange pattern of white dots and flashes. Eyestrain, probably. Exhaustion. His fingers fell away from the keyboard and he dropped back in his chair, heaving a sigh and letting the ball of tension in his chest dissipate. The lights were still blazing in his house night and day, and he was still afraid of the loneliness that would overwhelm him should he turn them off, even one of them.

Some time later, the phone on his desk rang. Burt opened his eyes, groggy and confused. He couldn't imagine who would call him this late on a Saturday night, except perhaps his wife. He grabbed the handset. "Hello, Happy?"

"No, I'm not happy, Burt. And this isn't your wife, either."

An icy chill came off the man's voice. Burt shivered reflexively, trying to collect his thoughts. "John Fuller?" Under any other circumstances, Burt would have known the voice of the Democratic National Committee chairman immediately, but it was late, and this was not a run-of-the-mill call.

"Yes, Burt, it's John. I just came home from a benefit dinner to a stack of e-mails about your blog. What's that all about, Burt? Some of us are wondering why you'd want to be Moses shouting from the mountaintop right now. You're in a pretty precarious position. I would think you'd want to sit tight until you've dealt with the very serious charges against you."

Burt almost harrumphed. As if he needed to be told the charges were serious. "The blog isn't about me, John. It's about my work, *our* work. Things still have to be done. I'd feel responsible if health-care reform got derailed because of my situation. And the hearings on CEO compensation need to go forward. The people of this country are crying out for change."

"That may be true, Burt, but now's the time to step back and let your colleagues in the House get things done. I'm sure you'll be hearing from some of them. The boys are uneasy about this grassroots movement of yours. It's a risky business getting millions of people riled up and storming Congress with e-mails and petitions. It makes us all look bad, and the boys don't like it, Burt, especially with an election less than a month away."

The boys were a small cadre of powerful senators and congressmen from both parties who often collaborated and cooperated when the stakes were high and compromise was needed to move important legislation. They'd been so successful in greasing the skids they'd become nearly invincible—and a grassroots appeal to the masses like Burt's was a direct threat to their control.

Burt rubbed his eyes. The coiled phone cord suddenly looked like a double helix, dividing in two. He was tired, too tired to be having this conversation. At moments like this, he actually wondered whether the "boys" might have had something to do with the porn found on his computer. Many of them had big corporate positions and board chairmanships awaiting them when they left politics. It was a politician's equivalent of a golden parachute, and one of the ways they were rewarded for their loyalty to their various special interests. It was also everything that Burt detested about American political life.

"Can I be candid, John?" he blurted, knowing he should not utter another word, but unable to stop himself. "If I really believed that my esteemed colleagues always had the best interests of their constituents in mind, I would be happy to step back and let things take their course, but it doesn't work that way. Too often the constituents are last on the list. That isn't right, John. The people elected us to represent them. They deserve their due."

"What are you saying, Burt? You don't trust your own

colleagues, the fine men—and women—who've always had your back, no matter what you asked of them?"

"I couldn't have put it better myself, John—and I've never asked anything of my colleagues that I wouldn't ask of myself."

Fuller let out a snort of frustration. "Burt, don't be foolish," he said. "You've lost your wife and children. There are people who could see to it that you lose everything else."

"I don't care about anything else." Burt slammed down the phone. But in the seconds it took to catch his breath, he realized that wasn't true. He cared very much about his cherished projects, and especially health care. It was the most important work of his career, and would have been his legacy.

He covered his eyes, hiding them from the bright lights. If only he could turn the computer off and rest, but there was so much to do. The system was no longer working. It wasn't just the poor being disenfranchised, it was the country's bedrock, its hardworking middle class. People couldn't afford gasoline to run their cars. Next it would be food, clothing.

Oh, yes, Burt Carr was filled with the spirit of change. He intended to make Robin Hood look like a slouch, and if he had no Merry Men left, he would rally more hardworking, dissatisfied folks to his cause, a revolution of the oppressed. He wanted this country to make good on its promises to every man, woman and child, and he would go up against anyone, the boys of Congress, the chairman of the DNC, or God himself, to see that it did.

30

Sunday, October 13

Val Drummond awoke with a smile on his lips. What a great dream. It wasn't about sex, but almost that good. He'd just killed his Darwin cell phone. He'd snatched up the screeching, jabbering hunk of black plastic and flung it like a missile out the window of his office. A sense of freedom had washed over him as the cell disappeared from sight. Thank God for silence.

Brrring brrrring brrrrrrring. Val, you have an urgent message.

Val sat up in bed like a shot. The phone was really ringing? It wasn't a dream? "Gimme a break!" He rubbed his eyes and tried to read the display on his digital clock, but the sun was shining so brightly he couldn't see the time. He'd drunk two beers and crashed last night without even taking off his clothes. Of course, he'd forgotten to lower the sun-blocker shades.

He knew it was Sunday morning, and he'd been hoping to sleep in. He'd been fielding all the panicked VIP calls since Lane hit the papers as a person of interest in the Seth Black case, and his cell had been ringing off the hook.

He scooped up the phone and squinted at the display, but couldn't read it, either. "Drummond," he said without having any idea whom he was talking to.

"How can I help?"

"Maybe you could get me into a witness protection program?" The woman's voice was faint and squeaky, as if she were being strangled. "I need to be someone else, *anyone but me.*"

"Excuse me? Who am I talking to?"

"It's Priscilla Brandt, and someone hacked into my phone. As of this morning, my voice-mail messages are all over the Internet! I thought these phones were supposed to be secure. Foolproof, you said."

Her voice shot into the dog-whistle register. "I ought to sue, dammit. I'm going to sue. This is your fault!"

"Easy, Priscilla, let's take a breath and start over. Tell me what happened. I'm sure we can straighten it out."

She rattled off a Web address. "Type that into your browser. It will take you to a site where you can hear me screaming that TV producers are bloodsuckers just like the paparazzi, and that Skip McGinnis, the idiot-child executive producer who rejected my television show, should be electrocuted and drowned like Seth Black. And I really do believe that, Val. These people are parasites who feed off the talent and fame of celebrities. They have no loyalty to anyone or anything. It's all opportunistic horseshit."

Val winced. Technically, he was probably in the same class as the worthless parasites she wanted exterminated. "Is that the worst of it?" he asked.

"I wish. I don't know what nationality McGinnis is, but he looks like a lily-white Wasp elitist pervert, so I pretty much covered the waterfront, coming up with every awful

insult I could think of. I left out Islamo-fascist terrorist.
I'm not that crazy."

Jeez, what was it with celebrities and racial slurs? He
didn't know how the hell he was going to straighten this
out—or if he even wanted to, given how she'd bashed TPC
on that morning talk show.

Meanwhile, he could hear her muttering and getting
herself even more worked up. He had to do something to
calm her down, and if concierge work had taught him
anything, it was how to do damage control. When in doubt,
lie through your teeth, just make sure you're smiling when
you do it.

"Priscilla, you have nothing to worry about," he said.
"I'll make a few phone calls, one of which will be to the
best publicist on our referral list. The man is a genius with
image rehab, not that you need it, of course, but as long
as we're fixing things, let's do it right. I'll also set up a
consult with one of our best attorneys, and I'll fire off a
call to Darwin about the security issue with your phone.
We need to consider the possibility that whoever compromised your voice-mail system may have added offensive passages to make it a bigger story."

"Nice try, Val, but I said every word. If anything, they
edited it. I can really be a fishwife when I get going."

She said it, not me. Val subdued a smile. He'd dealt
with enough narcissistic clients that it didn't break his
heart when one of them ate a hunk of crow, whether it was
good for TPC or not. The Priscilla Brandts of the world
needed to be exposed, and Val was secretly overjoyed
that it had happened via one of Darwin's cell phones.
That little bastard was going down, too, finally.

"*Yesssssssss,*" Val said, unable to contain himself. Two
birds with one cell phone.

"Val? What was that noise? Are you laughing?"

"No, of course not, that was a sneeze. I must be getting a cold, probably the rain—"

"You think this is funny? I guess you like seeing us uppity white folks get put in our place, right? Well, you and your whiny black friends can have a good chuckle on me. Go right ahead."

You don't want to mess with me, uppity bitch.

Val held his tongue and went into damage-control mode again, doing his best to convince her that her predicament was top priority to him, and he would do everything he'd told her and more to resolve it. He also promised to have Lane call her personally.

"Yes, have her call me," Priscilla said. "I want to thank her."

"Thank her for what?"

"For electrocuting that Seth Black creep. I just wish she'd done it sooner."

The woman needs a straitjacket for her mouth, Val thought as he hung up the phone. Something had to be done about Priscilla Brandt, and fast.

Jack the Giant Killer wasn't expecting to see Lane Chandler show up at Pris Brandt's place, but apparently someone was. The gates opened immediately for her hybrid Lexus.

Jack sat in the back of a rental van, parked across the street, watching through the van's windows as the gates closed and two hulking security guards resumed their position on each side of the entrance to the private lane. Jack hadn't seen these guards around before. Miss Pris must have hired them after the voice-mail leak this morning.

Now the whole world knew what a venomous little snake she was. Jack took sincere pleasure at that thought, and at how freaked she must be at the random assaults. Maybe this would teach her to play nice? Jack's only regret was that she'd become paranoid enough to hire security. It would have been fun to see her reaction from inside the gates, up close and personal, but that was too risky now. It would be more difficult to get to her, but where there was a will—

Jack wanted Priscilla Brandt to know that she wasn't any better—or safer—than anyone else in this world. She could be picked off as easily as the homeless guy who'd camped on her lawn. All it took was someone good and sick of the high and mighty getting their way—and of her vile temper, in particular.

Jack assumed Lane Chandler had made the trip to do damage control, which meant it would soon be time for more damage to be done, something no one could control. Not unlike Lane's own predicament. Apparently someone was trying to frame her for Seth Black's murder, unless she had actually killed the guy, which Jack doubted. Seth had legions of enemies. The gossip sites were already hinting that Jack might be involved, given that JGK had taken down a number of Lane Chandler's clients. Jack could take credit for the clients, but not for Seth Black's murder or framing Chandler.

Wouldn't it be interesting if JGK actually had some competition? Lane Chandler was definitely a target, and Jack was as curious as everybody else about who had the concierge lady in their rifle sights.

Lane found Priscilla Brandt sitting on her couch with a butcher knife in her hand. The area was littered with feathers and pieces of foam stuffing, and several decorator pillows lay around her, hacked to pieces and gutted. She'd clearly been on a rampage, and Lane was almost afraid to go near her.

"Priscilla?" Lane's voice was soothing and calm, despite her alarm. "What happened? Are you all right?" Lane was very aware that she needed to get closer to Pris, if possible, needed to touch her and make contact. She also knew a move like that could backfire.

The other woman looked up, her eyes glazed and distant. Lane couldn't tell if she'd been crying or raging. Probably both. Now she just looked shell-shocked.

"I've never been given anything," Priscilla said, speaking in a flattened, aching tone. "I've slaved and sacrificed for everything I have, and now someone is trying to take it all away. They're out to destroy me, and I don't know why."

Lane wondered if Priscilla really didn't realize that her outbursts might have made her some enemies. Lane had discussed the situation with Val, and he seemed to think Pris could survive this latest debacle, but only if she stopped upchucking in public.

"No one is going to take anything away," Lane said, infusing her voice with conviction.

Pris dropped the knife and fell back, collapsing on the couch. A spasm gripped her, and tears flooded her eyes. Lane went to her immediately. She picked up the heavy knife with its gleaming executioner's blade and slipped it under the couch, out of sight.

Gently, she touched Pris's arm. "Val called and told me what happened. We'll take care of you, Pris. You have the entire service at your disposal, no charge, and please consider accepting a lifetime Premiere membership, also at no charge. We haven't determined how your voice mail was breached, but if it was due to a security failure on our part, we intend to take full responsibility."

Pris began to wail about everyone thinking she was a bitch and a bigot and her career being over. Lane's grip on her arm tightened.

"Who might want to hurt you, Pris?" she said, bringing the conversation back to practical matters. "You need to make a list of suspects. We'll hire an investigator to get to the bottom of this, but we have to start somewhere."

"I don't know anyone who'd want to hurt me, except maybe Skip McGinnis himself." She seemed genuinely baffled. "Or that god-awful Jack the Giant Killer person. Those scavengers live off other people's misery, and they should all be killed. Don't ever regret what you did, Lane. It was a public service."

"Priscilla, I didn't *kill* Seth Black, and I don't believe he deserved to die, no matter what he did to me or my clients."

Pris rose from the couch and began searching the room, probably trying to find the knife. Lane was glad she'd hidden it.

"That's where you're wrong," Pris said quietly, but with enough deadly menace in her voice to make Lane shudder. "Look at the damage they've already done. They have to be stopped."

Lane wondered if Pris had anything personal against Black, or just a vendetta against all gossipmongers. Lane had little doubt that Pris was capable of almost anything, including drowning an entire litter of kittens, if she wanted them out of the way. Priscilla Brandt was one of the scariest people Lane had ever dealt with. Her eyes had turned bloodred when she was searching for the knife.

Lane would see to it that Pris had the best investigator money could buy. And she would also find her a therapist, a specialist in anger management, if Pris would go to one. But she actually hoped Pris would not accept the offer of the lifetime membership. The woman was a disaster waiting to happen, without any help from the paparazzi at all.

31

Simon quickly scanned one text message after another, skimming the slanderous comments about him. He was reading messages that had been published as breaking stories on Gotcha.com—news flashes that updated the readers to the latest scandalous details in what the gossip Web site was calling the "Simon Shan Drug Bust Story!"

Gotcha had scooped every other Web site with the drug bust, and the messages dated back to the very first one.

Simon had found them on Jai Long's cell phone. Or to be technically accurate, on a small storage device called a SIMmate that Jai used to save her text messages. She also had one of those fancy dual-slide phones with a full Qwerty keyboard and a large enough screen to compose and send lengthy messages. It had made Simon wonder why a bodyguard needed such sophisticated equipment.

Now he knew.

Simon glanced at his watch. He needed to move fast. It was Sunday evening, and he'd ended the standoff with Jai by sending her out for some much-needed supplies. His goal had been to get her out of her room so he could check things out, and even though she'd taken her cell phone with her, she hadn't taken the storage device. So he'd borrowed it just long enough to insert it in the USB port of his own computer—and voilà, he had access to her entire cache of saved text messages.

But she could come back at any time, especially if she had any questions about why he'd suddenly sent her out. Simon's brain was buzzing as he read through the rest of the messages. Had he found the smoking gun or was this merely another piece of the puzzle? He couldn't be sure whether Jai had actually authored the messages or just copied and sent them, but why did she have them on her cell and who had she sent them to? He would need access to her phone to see where they'd gone. Little chance of that, but his gut told him he was getting closer, warmer. And maybe he was getting hot.

Lane hadn't even made it home from Priscilla's before she got an urgent phone call from Val, asking her to meet him at TPC. He wouldn't say why, but promised to explain everything when she got there. He'd also called Darwin, who was on the way.

Lane didn't like being kept in suspense, especially if it had anything to do with the Seth Black murder, which was very much on her mind. She no longer suspected Rick of setting her up, but someone had—and she needed to take her own advice and come up with a list of suspects. *This wasn't going to go away.* As far as she could tell, the police seemed quite content with her as their prime suspect, although so far they were only calling her a person of interest, and she'd heard nothing from them since they showed up in her office on Friday.

The streets of Century City were empty as she turned onto the side lane that would take her to her building's underground parking. Normally the light weekend traffic would have been a pleasant break. Today it just seemed sinister.

Lane wanted to dismiss the Seth Black murder as an aberration and go back to solving other people's problems, as she had been doing most of her life. She honestly didn't know why anyone would want to pin his murder on her, unless the crazy who was stalking her clients had decided to focus on her instead. She'd done nothing about an attorney, thinking hiring one would be premature and could make her look guilty. Still, she probably ought to find a private detective for herself, as well as one for Pris.

But she doubted that's why Val had called an emergency meeting on a Sunday afternoon. He'd asked her to come directly to Darwin's office, and he'd sounded intense. She had a bad feeling this was about Priscilla's stolen voice mail.

"We have a saboteur in our ranks. Darwin, the self-named boy genius, has been screwing around with his own system. Guess who caused the voice-mail leak?"

Not the words Lane wanted to hear from Val Drummond as she entered Darwin's office. Val was sitting on the edge of Darwin's desk, holding what looked like two thick manuscripts. The pages were three-ring punched and secured with aluminum posts. Darwin was nowhere around.

"What?" It was all Lane could get out.

"We have a saboteur in our—"

"I heard that much, Val. Why would Darwin do something like that?"

Val glanced around Lane at the doorway. "He's right behind you. Ask him."

Darwin stormed into the room, his hair moplike as always and his jeans hanging on his slender hips. "I didn't leak anything," he said, clearly incensed. "That's total bullshit."

Val got up, looking self-important, and dropped the manual on Dar's desk. A cloud of dust rose from the impact. "These are the tech manuals for the Darwin phone. I got them off his computer."

Dar muscled around Val to look at the printouts. "He broke into my computer to get these. Someone's been messing with my encrypted files, and now I know who! That's electronic espionage, in case you didn't know, Val."

Lane could only assume the manuals were Dar's top-secret plans for the phone, possibly the design or the programming. Even she hadn't seen them.

Val moved away from the desk, conceding the space to Darwin, but nothing else. "He's the only one who understands the network he created," Val said. "That's why I downloaded the manuals. We've had a serious security breach, and I wanted to know why. No crime there."

"How do we know *you* didn't cause the breach?" Dar countered. "You rip off my encrypted programming files, and now you're trying to make it look like I'm responsible?"

Val bristled. "Your sheer negligence alone could have caused the problems. You keep your damn password stuck to your desk chair, and you're so stupid in love with that girlfriend of yours, you can't tell time anymore. You're not even here when you're here, buddy."

Dar said nothing, but he looked a little guilty at the mention of his girlfriend. Lane wondered how that was going. She'd lost touch with Dar lately. They used to have heart-to-hearts on a regular basis, and he was always the one she would go to with problems. Sandra might be a blood relative, but Dar was her brother. Lane could talk to him about anything.

Val pointed at the manuals. "If I understand these things, you can capture the content of our Premiere clients' voice mail, listen in on their live conversations, and you're tracking them with the GPS system. That's an invasion of their privacy."

Dar snarled in outrage. Lane had to block him or he would have gone after Val. "The system wasn't designed to spy on our clients! E-mail and voice mail get lost and deleted by mistake. I have to be able to retrieve it. It's for the convenience of our clients."

"I understand that, but what about the *content* of that voice mail?"

"What about it? Our clients' phones aren't bugged, and *no one* is listening in on their conversations. I'm surprised you'd even suggest it. The only one here who's violated anyone's privacy is you. You broke into my secure files."

"There's plenty of blame to go around," Lane told them both. "I've been preoccupied myself, but it's time to get focused, all of us. Let's get the problems fixed. Dar, the security breach has to come first. Until we know who leaked Pris's voice mail and how it happened, none of our clients is safe. That has to be your first priority. And if *you* can't solve the problem, we're going to bring in an electronics-forensics expert."

Dar conjured up a dramatic frown, but Lane stayed firm. "I'm giving you twenty-four hours before I call in the experts. This isn't a video game, Dar. It's a crisis, and the future of the company is at risk."

Her gut twisted as she realized it was true. She wasn't just pep-talking her two key people. TPC really could go down. She could lose her company.

"Val," she said, "what if we held one of those motivational meetings, the way we used to, bring everyone together, the entire corporate staff, including the concierges. They deserve to know what's going on, don't you think? Not all the gory details, of course, but it's public knowledge that several of our clients are in trouble. We could admit that the service has taken some hits and these are hard times, but if we hang together, we can pull out of it. Ask for their help and support. What do you think?"

He looked skeptical. "It might be a little early for that."

"Okay, but let's talk about it and be ready with a plan. Meanwhile, I'd like you to continue overseeing the concierge operations and the business end of things. I'm going to back-burner the expansion plans for now and get involved with the troubleshooting here, so I'll be backing you up."

Now Val was furious. "You're not going to do *anything* about him?" He flipped a thumb at Dar. "The phones are his baby, and he won't let anybody else near his gobbledygook electronics stuff. In my book that makes him responsible for everything that's gone wrong. We need to get forensics in here *now,* Lane. It's going to take a team of experts to figure out what the boy genius there has done."

"Easy, Val." Lane used her best, calming voice. "It's Dar's system—his creation—and he gets the first shot at fixing it." She didn't mention that Dar had been with her from the beginning and was a partner to her in every way but financial. It was her company only because she'd come up with all the money through loans and one very significant angel.

Val's jaw clenched, going white at the edges. He'd always been the solid, steady one of the two, Dar the creative spark and the idea person. But Lane needed both of them now. They all needed one another. When word got out that a Darwin phone had been breached, Lane fully expected their Premiere clients to panic, and some would quit the service. It would be one more blow of the wrecking ball, and she didn't know how long a floundering, deeply-in-debt company like TPC could hold up.

Lane hesitated at Darwin's door, aware that he'd locked himself in to work on the voice-mail problem, and wondering if she should interrupt. She'd been working in her office since the meeting with Dar and Val, reorganizing the Dallas expansion plans and compiling a huge to-do list that would start with contacting clients personally, including Jerry Blair, who was on the brink of his daughter's birthday bash. But Lane needed to talk to Dar about something that had nothing to do with the phones. It was about Rick Bayless.

Dar had left her a message when she was in Dallas that she couldn't return because the phones were out. Maybe it was old news now, given everything she'd learned about Rick on her own, but she really couldn't assume that. No, she really couldn't.

One more thing about Bayless. This'll blow your mind. Call me back. Dar.

She rapped on Dar's door. He didn't answer, so she opened it a crack and saw him glued to his computer, frantically typing in strings of numbers on the keyboard. He really did look like a mad scientist. His eccentricities were one of the things she loved about him, but they also made him unpredictable. As did his medical condition. She wondered if he was faithfully taking his seizure meds. That might account for some of his erratic behavior lately.

Her thoughts flashed back to how she'd met him. She'd

been sleeping in a downtown L.A. shelter whenever she could get a bed, but the nights they were full she'd been forced to search the streets for somewhere to stay. One night, late, she'd come upon a group of kids her age, watching a younger boy writhe around on the ground. They told her he was tripping on drugs, and then they wandered off, leaving him there.

Lane had stayed with him, grabbing him when he thrashed and went stiff. He'd vibrated in her arms like a tuning fork. In his lucid moments, he'd begged her not to call the paramedics. "I'll be okay," he'd told her. "I took some bad shit, but you can't tell anyone. If the cops find out, I'll get jail time."

Lane had agreed, mostly to keep him calm, and when he'd come out of it, he'd seemed okay. They'd begun hanging out together after that, at first for safety reasons. Kids alone were always more vulnerable. But it hadn't taken her long to figure out that this strange little thirteen-year-old named Darwin didn't take drugs, bad or otherwise. Whatever was wrong with him, it wasn't that.

"Dar, can I come in?" She rattled the doorknob to get his attention.

He looked up and managed a wan smile. "Get your butt in here," he said. "I'm in over my head."

"We can bring someone in to help," she suggested as she joined him at the desk. "There's no need to wait."

He sat back and rubbed his eyes, which were probably strained to the max. Lane's heart twisted. He looked so much like the boy she'd befriended all those years ago. Dar had never really grown up like everyone else. He lived in a world of computers, comic books and virtual reality. She hoped he wasn't in trouble.

He glanced up, one eye still squeezed shut. "I can do it. I just need a break. My brain is fried."

She wanted to hug him and tell him it would be okay. Instead, she dragged a wheeled stool over to his chair and sat down. Whatever he'd wanted to tell her about Bayless could wait. She needed some time with her friend. "Taking a break is a good idea, Dar. Let's catch up, okay?"

He threw up his arms, stretched and rolled his neck, making loud cracking sounds. "Sure. What's going on?"

"You first," she insisted. "How are things going in your life, generally, I mean? It's been ages since we talked."

"Things are okay, other than this mess."

"Everything good with you and—what's her name, Janet?"

He looked wary. "Fine, why?"

"I don't know. You seem a little reluctant to talk about her."

"Well, I'm not stupid in love with her, if that's your concern. What is Val's problem, anyway? He just won't get off my ass."

"He's probably worried, Dar, as I am. You haven't been yourself lately. We really haven't seen very much of you."

Dar nodded wearily. "Yeah, I know." He glanced at Lane, and a grin surfaced. "Okay, I'm smitten. This boy is pretty far gone, but isn't it about time I met someone and had a life outside this cave? What's wrong with that?"

"Nothing." Lane breathed an audible sigh of relief. "That's wonderful, Dar. I'm thrilled for you. You deserve some happiness."

She rolled over and planted a kiss on his cheek, which brought a bright blush of color to his face. She further embarrassed him by telling him she loved him and that he'd better take care of himself, eat right, get some rest and all the various other guilt trips that kindred spirits can lay on each other.

He brushed her off, but gallantly brought her fingers to his lips and kissed them. "What about you?" he said. "Someone might as well have pasted a bull's-eye on your back. Any idea who set you up, or why? Not that I'm sorry Seth Black is toast. He was one of the gossipmongers who tried to ruin Janet's reputation when her artist boyfriend reneged on their comic-book deal."

Dar had fiercely protective instincts. Lane remembered how he'd stayed awake nights when they were on the streets together, keeping watch so she could sleep. She'd done the same for him, but he'd always insisted she sleep first, no matter how tired they were. Now he had someone else to protect, Janet.

Lane toyed with the green rubber band on her wrist. "I have no idea who would want to set me up," she said. "Anyone could have taken that pen from my desk."

Lane had made a suspects list, as she'd advised Priscilla Brandt to do, but so far the only person on Lane's list was her sister. The timing of Sandra's reappearance was still troubling to Lane. She seemed secretive, as though she had some covert purpose, but Lane wasn't any closer to knowing what it was. She'd decided to keep Sandra around so she could watch her. Maybe she should start by returning Sandra's voice-mail messages. Her sister probably thought she was in jail by now.

Dar smiled at the frayed band. "You still got that thing? I'm amazed it hasn't disintegrated." He was suddenly serious. "I'm sorry I haven't been here to support you. That's not right. We've been friends too long."

She nodded. "We'll get through this, and so will the service. But we have to stay on our toes, Dar. We all need to be more careful about security around here. Seth Black is gone, but his Web site isn't. Someone else will take over, and there's that Giant Killer guy. He's made a career out of picking off our clients. He's still out there."

"Yeah, I hear you."

Dar seemed uncomfortable. He was tapping his keyboard restlessly, and he wouldn't look at her anymore. Maybe he just wanted to get back to work.

She changed the subject. "Before I go, Dar, I've been meaning to ask you about Rick Bayless."

"What about him?"

"You left me a voice mail saying you'd found something on him that would blow my mind."

"Damn, I totally forgot. Get this—Bayless was a suspect in the hunting-lodge case."

"How is that possible? He was the arresting officer." Lane didn't believe it. "There wouldn't have been a case without Rick. He was the one who found the evidence that was hidden in the giraffe I had stuffed in my backpack."

"No, I don't mean a suspect in the prostitution case. Bayless became a suspect when the evidence disappeared. And not only a suspect, *the* prime suspect. But the case was a huge embarrassment at that point. The D.A. just wanted to be rid of it, and they had no proof that Bayless stole anything. He was never formally charged, but he quit the force shortly after that, and the rumor was that he'd made some kind of deal to avoid prosecution."

"Why would he steal evidence that *he* found? That doesn't make sense." Still, she had wondered how Ned Talbert came to have the evidence.

"No idea, but be careful, Lane. He's not your ordinary private investigator. He takes on stuff no one else will touch, things law enforcement can't do, like covert stuff for the military."

Lane had already had some personal experience with Bayless, and she knew something Dar didn't know—that he was terminal, which made him more dangerous rather than less. That was information she would keep to herself for now. She didn't want to distract Dar from his task. And it *would* be a distraction if he knew where she was going when she left here—straight to Bayless's house.

32

"**Y**ou asked me to call when Ms. Chandler left, sir. She just drove off."

"Excellent, thanks," Val said, speaking into his earpiece headset. He'd slipped a hefty tip to the attendant in the building's garage to let him know when Lane picked up her car—and to keep his mouth shut about it.

Val verified that Lane was leaving with his own eyes as he stood at the window of his office and watched her drive away. He'd expected her to head up Avenue of the Stars toward her condo on Empyrean Way. Any sane person who'd just spent an entire Sunday in the office would be on their way home now. But she was driving east toward Santa Monica Boulevard and the 405 Freeway. And she was driving fast.

None of that mattered. She was gone. Now he could make his move.

He went back to his desk and picked up the document that he hoped would blow the lid off this little company—and finally get Val Drummond the recognition he deserved. The document was nothing more than a three-page, single-spaced transcript of several voice-mail messages. Val had brought it with him to the meeting this morning with Lane and Darwin, but when he'd seen the

way Lane had leaped to Darwin's defense, he'd decided
not to use it. He wanted to confront Darwin on his own,
without his mommy there to protect him.

Val wanted the boy genius to sweat. Maybe even beg
and plead.

Val heard the papers rattle and realized his hand was
trembling. He'd been waiting years for this confrontation. It would prove who the better man was, finally, unequivocally. *He* was indispensable, not Dar. Why couldn't
Lane see that? He wondered what it would take for her to
get it. Would she have to lose her company? He could
arrange that. Val Drummond could arrange it. She had
underestimated him for far too long.

He glanced at his watch as he left his office. It was after
six, and he didn't want to miss Darwin. Val was also
seething from Lane's other slight. She'd made the mistake
of closeting herself with Darwin in his office this afternoon, and excluding Val. He'd never been invited to their
closed-door sessions or their two-person secret society, for
that matter. He was always odd man out, but they didn't
hesitate to dump all the work and responsibility for running
the place on him when it suited them. And faithful mutt
that he was, he did whatever he was told. He'd been a team
player even though he wasn't allowed on their team.

Well, fuck that. Dar was roadkill, and he deserved to
be. He was a careless slob. Of course, Val had done
nothing to discourage Darwin from his carelessness. And
he was happy to use it against him now. But he needed to
strike another blow quickly, while Dar was down.

Val hesitated at Dar's closed door, hearing voices. A
woman was in there with him, and since it couldn't be
Lane, it had to be Dar's bimbo girlfriend. Val nodded,
deciding it was a sign. Dar had so little respect for the

company's security he was throwing a party for two in his office while he was supposed to be figuring out how their client's voice mail had been compromised.

Val opened the door without knocking, hoping to find them horizontal on the desk, but no such luck. Dar was glued to his computer and his girlfriend was sitting on the floor, cross-legged, serene amidst the chaos, and chatting with someone on her cell. That was the conversation Val had heard.

Val gave Dar no warning as he stuck a transcript of Priscilla Brandt's pirated voice mails in the space between Dar's face and the computer screen.

"I hope you can explain this," Val said. "I found it sitting in your printer tray yesterday morning when I came by the office to get some papers I'd been planning to work on this weekend. That's just plain sloppy, Dar. You need to do a better job of covering your tracks, man."

Dar glared up at him, his eyes bloodshot from hours of peering at the screen. He looked half-demented, and Val had a moment's doubt about the wisdom of what he'd done. "What the fuck is that?" Dar growled.

"A transcript of one of Priscilla Brandt's voice-mail messages. It came off your computer."

Dar's bimbo girlfriend snapped her phone shut. "Leave him alone," she said. "He's under enough pressure."

"Aw, what a shame." Val smirked at her, but secretly he was pissed. Now Dar had another protector? How did a bobbleheaded geek like him get these women running interference for him?

Dar ripped the transcript out of Val's hand. "You came up with this yourself, you asshole. Priscilla's voice mail is all over the Net. All you had to do was copy this and print it."

Val's chortle was triumphant. "Check the date. I found it in your printer tray yesterday morning—Saturday—the day before her voice mail went public. Who hacked into her system and leaked those messages if it wasn't you, huh, Dar-baby? What were you trying to do, impress your girlfriend?"

Dar's chair flew backward, spinning in circles as he sprang up. Val broke for the door, but Dar caught him halfway there, bringing him down with a full-body tackle. Val tried to kick the little bastard off, but Dar was ferocious. He climbed all over Val, growling and snarling, pummeling him.

The girlfriend grabbed Dar's leg and dragged him off, pleading with him to stop. Val marveled at her strength. He kicked his way free of Dar's grasping hands and scrambled to his feet.

"Stay away from me!" Val warned, pulling his cell from its belt holster and thrusting it in the air. "I'll call the cops."

Dar snorted. "Call them! You can tell them about my alleged wiretapping, and I'll tell them you murdered Seth Black." Val let out a howl of outrage, but Dar outshouted him. "You went to Black's place and threatened to kill him when he was harassing Judge Judy Love on his Web site."

"That was years ago—and all I did was *talk* to him. TPC was just hitting its stride, and he was picking off our best clients. I told him to back off, that's it."

"Right, but he didn't back off. He went after us with a vengeance, and you've always hated him for that. You wanted to be the big hero, save the company, and he made you look like the pathetic blowhard you are. I told you to stay away from him! I told you it would backfire."

"You're afraid of your own fucking shadow, man. Somebody had to do something."

"So you electrocuted him?"

"Don't be ridiculous." Val flipped him the bird, disgusted. "You'd do anything to take the heat off yourself. You're desperate." He gave himself a shake, straightening his clothes. "This isn't over, genius. It's just begun."

Sandra was beginning to feel like a professional break-and-enter artist. She'd had no trouble getting inside Darwin LeMaster's fancy-pants house. An unlocked utility-shed door had let her into the garage and from there, the laundry room. But she was a little concerned that the place might be booby-trapped with security devices.

She knew the coast was clear, but she didn't know for how long. Darwin was holed up at TPC, trying to fix the phone system. Good luck, she thought, smiling. His girlfriend was with him, apparently for moral support, which he was going to need.

Sandra crept through the house, using a penlight to find her way and careful not to turn on any lights. She was looking for a home office, but what she found in Darwin's master bedroom was an elaborate electronics setup similar to the Command and Control Center at TPC, although his bedroom's decor was much better. Possibly he allowed this place to be cleaned once in a while.

She really couldn't imagine why Lane gave Darwin so much rope. Sure he had a genius IQ, but that didn't mean he was smart. Brains and smarts were two different things. The ability to string mathematical equations across a blackboard didn't mean much in the real world. He probably couldn't warm up a can of soup, but obviously Lane hadn't figured that out yet. She wasn't too damn smart, either, considering that she'd brought all this on herself.

"How very convenient," Sandra murmured, rubbing her hands together as she saw the blinking power light and realized his computer had not been turned off. "Looks like this system isn't any better protected than his other one."

Lane's knuckles stung from pounding on the weather-beaten door. She shook her hand to ease the pain and then pressed her ear to the blistered wood. It was getting dark and there were no lights on inside the house, but she could hear muted noises. They sounded like moans—and knowing Rick's condition made that all the more frightening.

She debated calling 911. He might be dying in there. But she was certain he wouldn't want her to, nor did she want to explain who she was or why she was at his place. First, she had to get inside and find out what was going on, and then she would call, if necessary.

She left the front door to check the courtyard and found one of the French doors ajar. It surprised her that someone in Rick's line of work would leave his house unlocked, even if he was home, but there was no time to think about it. She let herself in—and nearly stumbled over a body on the floor.

"Oh, my God." Lane backed out the door in shock. A man was lying on his side, his back to her, his hands and feet tied with what looked like an extension cord, and his mouth covered with duct tape. It could have been Rick, except that this man's hair was longer and darker. From what she could see, he wasn't badly hurt, but he must have been making the moaning noises.

She could also see that the place had been ransacked. Cabinets were turned over and drawers pulled out. The sofa and chairs had been stripped of their cushions and the linings slashed. Someone had been searching for something.

The man was trying to talk to her, frantically mumbling and jerking at his bonds. Lane had to step over him to get in the house. "If you want me to help you, hold still," she said.

He *was* hurt, she realized. One eye was purple and nearly swollen shut. The cuts and bruises on his face and arms didn't appear to be serious, but there was blood everywhere, soaking the front of his white T-shirt and jeans. She didn't see a head wound, but he must have one.

Lane had never seen him before. He looked young, maybe early twenties, and he was clearly frightened. His eyes were bright, darting.

She knelt next to him, warning, "This is going to hurt," as she ripped off the tape.

He gasped from the pain. "Untie me, please," he blurted. "My friend needs help."

"Is Rick your friend? What happened to him?"

"Yes, untie me. I'll show you. Hurry!"

Lane had barely loosened the extension cord on his wrists when the man sat up, pulled his hands free and quickly untied his own feet. "Take it easy," Lane said as he sprang to his feet. "You could be in shock."

She got up, too, hoping to calm him. But the man swung around and all she could see was a huge fist coming at her. It grazed the side of her head and the force of his swing knocked her off her feet again.

A sofa cushion buffered her fall. She sat there a moment, fighting off dizziness and a hot, stinging pain. "What the hell was that about?" she said to no one. The man had vanished.

She wasn't even sure which way he'd gone. When she got to the French doors, she saw Rick coming through the courtyard gate. "Are you okay?" she asked him, weak with relief. His mouth was bleeding, and it looked as if the scar on his lower lip had been opened. "What happened here?"

"T-two guys," he said, trying to catch his breath. "They jumped me when I walked in the front door. I got one of them, but the other one took off while I was tying up his friend. I couldn't catch him with that head start."

"You got one of them?" she said, just realizing what she'd done. "The guy in your living room?"

He took one look at her pale face and shot past her into the house. She could hear his groan of frustration. "Where is he? What did you do?"

33

Lane swayed on her feet. Maybe she'd been hit harder than she realized. She was thinking she ought to sit down, when Rick grabbed her by the shoulders and guided her to the only upright chair in the room.

"Are you okay?" he asked, standing over her. "Did he hurt you?"

"It was a hit and a miss," she said. "Never mind, I'm all right."

"Are you sure? All right enough that I can yell at you?"

Lane winced, aware that she probably deserved it. "That dirty rotten liar said he knew where you were. That's the only reason I untied him. I thought you'd been kidnapped or something."

"Yeah, you wish."

Was that a touch of irony in his voice? Somehow she'd expected more anger, more gnashing of teeth and foaming at the mouth. And possibly more demands at gunpoint. He didn't look pleased, but he did seem at least as concerned about her as he was about the man he'd lost.

"You're the one who's hurt," she said. "Your lip is bleeding."

She reached out to touch his mouth, and he rocked back on his feet. "Ouch!"

"I didn't even touch you," she protested.

"No, it's something else." He pressed a hand to his rib cage. "I may have cracked something. It was a pretty good fight."

"Pretty good fight," she muttered. *"Men."*

He turned, still clutching himself as he inspected the trashed room, and Lane saw the oozing wound on the side of his head. That must have been how the other guy got so bloody, she realized. It was Rick's injury, not his.

"You're been hit," she said. "Let me look at that. You're probably in shock." She didn't say it, but that would explain how he'd fought off two men and captured one. Even men who weren't terminal couldn't do that.

"Stay where you are," he insisted, turning to glare at her.

Oookay, not going up against those mean green eyes, even if he was bleeding. She changed the subject, but only to distract him. "Was it the same men who ambushed you before?"

"I didn't see them the first time, which is why I took the trouble to tie the guy up. I was hoping to ask him his name, and a couple other things."

"Maybe if you'd stuck a Post-it to him that said don't untie me?"

"Damn, why didn't I think of that?" He went over to the upended sofa, leveraging himself against the wall in an effort to get the heavy piece of furniture back in place.

"What are you doing?" she shrilled at him.

"Redecorating." Using his arms and legs, he lifted the sofa and quickly let go as it bounced into place. He tried not to grimace, but he was clearly in pain.

"That's it," she said. *"You* stay where you are. I'm getting something to clean you up." This guy needed a keeper.

When she got back from the bathroom with a damp cloth, a dry towel and some bandages, he was back on his feet and inspecting the room. "Take off that shirt and sit down," she said, putting some steel in her voice. "You're not strong enough for detective work. Do you want me to call 911 and get you medical help?"

It was a threat, and he knew it. "Do not call." He pulled off his T-shirt and let it drop. Groaning, he picked up a cushion and tossed it in the nearest chair, where he sank down heavily. "Feels like a cracked rib," he said.

Lane had expected to see some muscle wasting and physical deterioration, based on the research she'd done on his disease. She saw none. Cracked rib or not, terminal or not, he was in fighting shape. She'd heard about six packs. Now she knew what all the fuss was about. It took an effort not to notice that even bruised and bloodied, he possessed more than a few of the attributes of a male underwear model. She made the effort.

She perched on the chair arm and leaned over him to clean the wound on his head. "I'm guessing you don't want me to call the police, and I won't," she said, "but that's only if you tell me what's going on. Who were the intruders and why did they ransack your place? What were they after?"

"I don't know."

Yeah, sure. "Is it true that the DNA evidence in the hunting-lodge case was stolen and you were a suspect? Did you take the evidence?" She sat back to look at him. "Rick, did you take it? Is that why they broke in?"

She took his glaring silence as a yes. "Why would you steal evidence that could have put those bastards in jail? Did they pay you off?"

The silence wore on, and she let it, but he wasn't

getting off the hook. She was close enough to breathe on him, close enough to hurt him.

"Because they were going to crucify you," he said at last.

"Who? The men from the lodge?"

"No, the prosecutor's office, the press, the public. Everyone who feeds on news about beautiful little girls being sexually exploited—in this case, by wealthy, high-profile men. It would have been a media circus and you would have been center ring. I'd seen it happen before."

He shifted his weight and winced. "The victims in these situations are almost always destroyed. Usually they're ground down to nothing before they ever get caught. You weren't. You were salvageable, I thought."

"You did it for me? To protect me? I thought you hated me."

"I hated what you were doing."

"And that was enough reason to risk your career, and jail?"

"I'd been on the streets all my life, dealing with hopeless kids, even as a kid myself in the neighborhood where I grew up. Ned had a mother and sister who OD'd on drugs. Maybe I was at the breaking point when you came along."

His voice was harsh, possibly with emotion. Still, she wasn't sure she bought that. "What about the hunting-lodge suspects? They walked because of you."

"They would have walked anyway. The case wasn't going to stick. The hidden-camera pictures weren't good enough for identification purposes and the DNA was useless if we couldn't positively identify the men. The D.A. knew all that. He was going ahead with the case for the publicity it would get him, and he would have allowed them to turn you into a poster girl for his cause. It was a big case, a big *hopeless* case, but he would have looked like a hero for trying to get the privileged perverts who hurt little girls."

She really didn't know what to say. She'd had no idea. Silent, she finished cleaning the wound on his head and applied a bandage. Then she wiped down his shoulders, arms and back. Scalp wounds bled furiously, and his was a mess, but other than bruises, she didn't see any significant wounds.

"Maybe you should wash your own chest," she suggested. "If there are broken ribs, I might hurt you."

She left the cloth and towel with him on the chair and crossed the room to look at a Georgia O'Keeffe print on the wall. An idea had come to her, and she needed a little distance to process it. She didn't really question his story. What would he have to gain from lying about it now? It was hard to believe anyone would go to such extremes to keep a street kid from being exploited, but she hadn't lived his life. And that life did kill kids. She'd seen it herself. She and Dar were very lucky not to have been statistics.

"What are you doing?"

His question was edgy and impatient. Possibly from the pain, she told herself. "Thinking." She turned to him. "I was thinking about us. I want us to make an alliance, you and me. Someone is after both of us, and there may be a connection. We should work together."

He shook his head slowly, disbelieving.

She went over to him. "I need your help."

"Why should I help you?"

"Why did you help me before?" She stared into his eyes and waited for an answer. He didn't look like one of the good guys, even knowing what he'd done for her, but with his investigative background, he was her best choice—and possibly her only choice.

He seemed to be considering her question, and she wanted an answer. What had he seen in her worth saving, worth sacrificing for? What had he seen?

Finally, he spoke. "I'll provide you with the alibi you need for the morning Black was killed. That's what you're after, isn't it?"

She sighed. "The alibi is only part of it. I need to find out who's attacking my clients and who tried to frame me. There's something evil at work here, and don't give me that look," she said as his expression turned skeptical. "You're one of their targets, too."

"You need to get some rest." He heaved himself up and out of the chair, grimacing. "And so do I. This target is going to take a nap. I'd suggest you do the same—at *your own place.*"

She watched him limp across the living room, a hand pressed to his ribs. "You're turning me down? You don't want my help? You're crazy," she said angrily. "Look at you. You can hardly walk."

He disappeared into the hallway, and she got to his bedroom just in time to watch him sprawl on the bed, groaning in pain. He was asleep as soon as his head hit the pillow. She thought about waking him but decided against it. He'd lost blood, and he needed some rest.

Lane made an instant decision. Quick fixes were required in her line of work. She would sort through the debris and look for clues to the identity of the intruders. There was no point in trying not to disturb the crime scene. Rick had already made it clear the cops weren't going to be involved, so he was getting her help whether he needed it or not.

A half hour later, she'd gone through the living room, cleaned up all the blood, aware that she was probably eliminating fingerprints, but it couldn't be helped. She put everything back in its place, and went through the rest of the house, which had been ransacked and searched, as well. Rick hadn't admitted it, but she was now reasonably certain the intruders had been looking for the hunting-lodge evidence. She wondered if it was actually here, and if they'd found it. Probably only Rick could tell her that.

She went from room to room, searching for anything that might reveal who'd been there. She also racked her brain, trying to remember the men she'd encountered during her stay at the lodge, but too many of them had come and gone over the years. If she'd seen the evidence pictures, she might have been able to identify some of them.

She'd always wondered if the man who tried to molest her was in that group of pictures. She wouldn't quickly forget his face. He'd slipped into her bedroom at night and once he'd found her hiding in the closet. He'd spoken in whispers, tempting her with promises of jewelry, clothes, makeup, even drugs—anything a budding adolescent might want—and coaxing her with suggestions that were veiled attempts at seduction. He'd never actually touched her in a sexual way, but she'd known it was inevitable, and later, when the police questioned her, she'd described him in as much detail as she could. She had wanted him caught and punished, him and Hank Fontana.

The search of Rick's house turned up nothing, except some bloody fingerprints on a sofa pillow that were probably Rick's, but she stashed the pillow in a plastic bag in case there was an opportunity to follow up. She ended her search in Rick's bedroom, and once she'd quietly and carefully gone through that room, she turned to the sleeping man on the bed. He'd found a reason to help her once before. He'd thought her worth saving. Now she could help him, except that he wouldn't let her. Either he didn't believe that *he* was worth the effort, or he assumed she would be a liability to his mission and get in his way. It was an error in judgment men always made about women. They had no idea how ruthless a female could be when it came to protecting what was important to her.

She sat down on the bed to look at his head wound. The bandage seemed to be holding up, so she wouldn't have to disturb him. She'd already decided to stay all night, if that's what it took to convince him she was right about teaming up. She had a gut feeling she wouldn't get through this without Rick Bayless. But more than that, he needed her, and Lane had never been able to resist that pull. She still believed she could have saved her father if she'd been there. And she would have risked anything to help Darwin. Call it a savior complex, call it delusional, but she might even be able to fix Rick Bayless, if only he would give her a chance.

She touched his close-cropped hair, brushing her fingers over the dark gold surface and remembering how it had felt when she'd touched it before. Much softer than she'd expected. More like a sable brush than the wiry stubble she'd prepared herself for. She touched his eyebrow, still wondering. And then she found herself tracing the lines of his face, his jaw.

His hand flashed up and grabbed hers. Without opening his eyes, he said, "If you really want to help me, don't stop doing that."

34

Maybe he was trying to scare her. Rick wasn't thinking too clearly, except that he was incredibly frustrated. He'd heard her going through his house, and now she was playing with his hair and his face, as if she had a right to be touching him and making over him that way. Like a woman who had some claim on his heart. Or his body, if that's all she happened to be interested in. But no one had that right anymore. No one had a claim.

Still, he'd told her not to stop. And he had a death grip on her wrist.

"Rick," she said, her voice a soft mess of confusion, "what are you asking me to do?"

"God, if I only knew." They were in an awkward position. He was on his side with his back to her and if he had any brains he would stay that way. He didn't know much, but he knew once they were face-to-face, all bets would be off.

But there were powerful forces militating against his better judgment. He couldn't remember anything feeling better than her fingers in his hair, at least not since the morning she kissed him. Male hormones were flowing, making him ache in every fiber to be closer to her. She was assaulting him with her softness and her body heat and most of all, her concern. Her voice was a balm. It promised all the sex and succor he'd written about in his case notes.

He grimaced as he rolled over and looked up at her, sitting curled up and expectant. It felt as if his ribs were stabbing him, but he wasn't sure anything could have stopped him. Whatever his glands were pumping out, it was powerful stuff. He could feel the pain, but it barely registered.

"You shouldn't be here," he said. "We both know that."

"You want me to go?"

"Yes, but I'm hoping you won't listen to me. Wouldn't be the first time."

What was he doing? God, what?

She lay down on the bed, her head on the adjacent pillow, facing him. Her eyes were full of apprehension and wonder and something else that made his heart pound.

With her gaze fastened on his mouth, she tapped the cut on his lip. "Would it hurt you if I kissed you here?"

"Yes, but do it anyway."

His throat tightened as she came close. She hovered over him, staring into his eyes, melding with him as if they were lovers and did this all the time. Maybe they did. He was groggy, drunk with the notion of getting to know her and feeling as if he'd known her forever.

"Why is it always violent with you and me?" he asked.

Her breath rushed out, warm and startled. "I don't know. Let's make this one nonviolent."

Such a soft mouth, he thought as she proceeded to do everything but kiss him with it. Tickling and teasing, whispering her secrets. She murmured over the split on his lip, christening it as if with holy water. It was very near the scar that she herself had given him. He must look like quite the thug.

Rick swallowed a groan. This was nothing like their first kiss. There was no clash of titans in this featherlight coupling. It was all breathless desire. It made him ache for something deeper, harder.

He gripped the nape of her neck, his thumb sinking into her cheek. "Now, really kiss me," he said.

Their mouths met, held, crushed. He felt the sting, and then nothing but joy. She was buzzing over him like a bee. It was so strange lying flat on his back, unable to pull her into his arms and roll her over. He imagined himself helpless to stop her as her hands roamed his body, raking the hair on his chest. They dropped lower, grazing the zipper of his jeans, sliding between his legs. God, that was incredible. She was taking liberties.

"Tell me if I'm hurting you," she said.

He wanted to laugh. Hurting him? She was destroying him. She touched him and he was hard, full. It was a roaring, surging feeling. Like water crashing on rocks. No man in his right mind would want her to stop now, and he didn't. He definitely didn't, except for one thing. He couldn't breathe.

Maybe it was the ribs. No, it was her.

February 23, 1993: She walks free today, her eighteenth birthday. God help the weak of will and the feeble of mind, especially if they're male.

She was lethal, and he was nearing the point where stopping would be like turning back a stampede of horses. He'd worried about her pitying him, but there was no pity in this woman. It was something else driving her, curiosity maybe, but no matter what her motivation it wouldn't make sex with her any less a head-on collision. When he arrested her on the streets, he'd forbidden himself to have feelings for her, a teenager. It wasn't any different now, except for the reason.

He didn't want to feel what she could arouse in him. He couldn't even imagine how painful that would be, getting a taste of the real thing, feeling the hunger and knowing it was going to be ripped away. Better not to feel anything than to go through that.

He caught her by the wrist, holding her back.

"What's wrong?" she asked him.

"Where are we going with this? What's the point?"

"Does there have to be a point? How about because we want to, because—"

"It feels good?" he finished cynically. "Nothing matters but right now, this moment, the hell with later? Lane, I haven't *got* later."

Emotion burned in her eyes. "You have *now*. Are you going to throw that away because you don't have later? That leaves you with nothing."

"You don't get it, do you? The better it is between us the more we have to lose when it's over. So, why do this? Why make it more painful than it has to be?"

"The better it is the worse it is?" She shook her head, laughing, the sound almost radiant. "It's painful anyway, isn't it? Losing someone you care about is always painful, no matter how it happens. But I would rather have you now than not at all. And that's the alternative, Rick. We have now or nothing."

"Nothing doesn't hurt as much."

"Nothing is a big black empty void! Don't you want to feel alive while you *are* alive?" She urged him softly, "Let's take now."

Rick had never felt more out of control, and it was fair to say that he despised the feeling. He really didn't understand her willingness to get involved when he was so deeply reluctant. And he didn't trust it. But she had not wavered for a second. And he could see something in her expression that told him this had nothing to do with an act of charity. It wasn't about her suggestion that they join forces, either. She actually wanted to be here, with him. Maybe she needed to be here as much as he did, but for an entirely different reason. She still had something to prove.

The fires burned low in her eyes, and they were beautiful. If he'd had to guess, he would have said that this was about longing, crazy and impulsive, to be with a man she feared almost as much as she desired. But it was also about the cop who'd bullied her, even though he thought he was protecting her. Rick and Lane were back to the clash of the titans—and Rick was flat on his back.

"Well?" she said, sliding off the bed.

She began to unbutton her blouse. It was a black silky thing that rolled off her white shoulders with almost no encouragement from her. Her bra was black, too, and when her slacks dropped, he saw that she was one of those women who wore matching underwear. Frilly stuff. Sheer lacy pieces that barely veiled a woman's secrets— and begged a man to take them off her.

She unhooked her bra and let it fall. Her breasts were blue-veined and nearly translucent. The tips were steamy pink.

"Now?" she said.

He nodded. He would have mangled the word.

She came back to the bed, seeming a little embarrassed at her naked display. So, she was shy, too. Not quite the seductress she pretended. For some reason, that inflamed him more. Her hand came to rest on his chest and then slowly began to move downward until her fingertips brushed over the crotch of his jeans. His poor deranged dick throbbed against the denim material, and she fumbled a bit as she tried to unzip him, probably because he'd already taken up all the available space. As she pulled his jeans down and tossed them to the floor, the aching member rose.

Now, that was embarrassing.

He wanted to take control of the situation—and the woman—but mostly he wanted to take control of himself. But that wasn't going to happen, and not just because of his ribs. This really was about fifteen years ago when she had been forced to surrender all control. She was taking it back now.

She brought his hand to her belly and her thighs, closing her eyes as she guided him to exactly the places she wanted to be touched. The only thing softer than her flesh was the fleece between her legs. Her panties gave way to his coaxing. As his fingers trailed along the curls, Rick remembered trying to catch wisps of dandelion fluff, floating on the breeze. Damn. It wasn't right for anything to feel this good.

What are you asking me to do?

He groaned. The heat coming off her was intense and matched the flame leaping inside him. He began to stroke her, and her head fell back. Her jaw went slack. He touched her again and felt the well of sweet water between her legs.

"If you want to help me, don't stop now," she whispered.

He thought of rainstorms on coastal highways, with steam coming off the streets as the rain hit. He was that highway, and she was the rain.

She rolled up on him, her body shivering as she mounted him.

"Wait." He gripped her hips, stopping her. "Give me a minute." He'd never felt anything so warm and soft and enveloping. He couldn't explain it without sounding incredibly foolish, but he wanted to sustain the feeling. He needed to remember this. He was within seconds of being inside her, the one thing that could make him regret his death.

Sadness and sweetness and every other emotion he'd ever known choked him. He couldn't even identify the feelings. They welled in his throat and brought him reeling back to life, to some dazed notion of his existence. It was crazy, but he couldn't catch his breath. His body shook with feelings and needs. Heat pooled in his groin, aching and electrical.

"Now," he said. He released her hips and she tightened around him, swaying forward as she dropped and then rose again. The motion startled a groan out of him. She was wild, beautiful. Her flying hair covered her face, reminding him of the defiant young girl who had scorched him with her turquoise eyes. Thank God she was a woman now. Thank God she'd come back.

She bent to kiss him and touch his face, still murmuring over the cut on his lip. He felt a sharp sensation and thought it was his ribs. Ah, God! She'd bitten him, he realized. Her hands and nails were pressing into his biceps and she was sweetly assaulting his nipples.

He had to stop her. He grabbed her hips, his thumbs digging into her flesh. But all he could do was buck and roll, rocking himself deeper and deeper into her, and listening to her cry with pleasure. She rose up and her head fell back. A gasp came out of her, as if she couldn't get enough air.

"Now," she whispered.

She squeezed him so tightly he groaned. A shudder racked her body, and it was hard not to come as he watched her tremble and quake. And then without warning, he joined her. Light pooled in his groin and burst into his clenched thighs. It unlocked his spine and streamed upward, a torrent.

He could feel her pulsating, but he had no idea if she'd actually climaxed until she collapsed on top of him. His own body continued to surge with pleasure, as if he was still releasing. He couldn't seem to stop.

"Let's take now," she whispered, still shuddering, laughing. Or was she crying? Were those her tears wetting his face? For all he knew, they could have been his. When it was over, they were in a heap. A sweating, breathless heap of flesh.

Lane lay beside him, still awake and listening to the rhythm of his breathing. She couldn't sleep. She was still humming with sensations. He rolled over, groaning softly. The sound was more pleasure than pain. It filled her with happiness.

He studied her face in the moonlight, his hand sliding into her hair.

"Again?" She touched his mouth, aware of the notch that was her mark, her claim on this man, and she felt the deep flooding thrill of sexual need. Amazing. Perfection in the midst of such loss and desolation.

He moved over her, and she opened her legs to receive him.

"I hope we didn't crack any more ribs," she said.

"If we'd cracked them all, it would have been worth it."

"That may be the most romantic thing any man has ever said to me."

Lane smiled in the darkness. She was curved toward Rick, her hand resting on his thigh. She was afraid to get closer after the rather strenuous sex. She wasn't sure how he'd managed it.

He found her hand and held it. "I can't believe men aren't constantly plying you with hearts and flowers."

"Well, there was one when I was in college, an older man desperately in need of my organizational skills. That was my big romance." She sighed. "Not exactly the life of sin that you predicted for me."

"Thank God for that."

"Okay, promise me you won't laugh?" She wanted to talk to him, she realized. She wanted to tell him things about herself, the way she'd done with almost no one in her life, except her father and Darwin. "I thought I was frigid for the longest time. And it does make some sense, considering what I was exposed to at the lodge."

"You're not frigid," he said, bringing her hand to his lips. "I would swear on the Bible and take an oath before God."

"Thank you, but that won't be necessary. I'll take your word for it." Her voice lost strength as he kissed her fingertips. "I even got a little slutty, making out with boys in college and trying to light the spark. But making out was as far as it went, and it did nothing for me. My first real liaison was a professor who hired me to help him organize his life. Nice, but not exactly fireworks."

"Is that why you listen to heartbreak music?"

She let out a soft gasp. "You know about that?"

"You were listening to 'Everybody Hurts' by REM the night I came to your office. I figured it was because of some guy."

"It was because there was no guy," she said. "And

probably because I shut down emotionally after my dad died. The music touches me. It reminds me what I should be feeling."

"Your father had a heart condition, right?"

She didn't know how he'd learned that, unless it had been during her juvenile case. "He passed away shortly after I went to live with my sister, and I still feel badly that I wasn't there. He'd known he was dying for a long time, and so had I. To help me deal with it, he used to read me a poem called 'Hold On.'"

She thought back, trying to remember the words. "'Hold on to what is good, even if it's a handful of earth. Hold on to what you believe, even if it's a tree that stands alone. Hold on to what you must do, even if it's a long way from here. Hold on to your life, even if it's easier to let go. Hold on to my hand, even if someday I'll be gone away from you.'"

She could hear Rick's breathing. Finally, he said, "Ned came and asked for my help the night before he died. I sent him away."

She wanted to exhort him, *You could be there this time, for me. For yourself. You have the chance. We both do.* But it felt too intrusive. Whatever bond they had was a thread that would snap with any pressure. So, instead, she asked him questions about his family. She knew nothing about his personal life, despite Dar's background check.

"My mom and dad were older when they had me," he told her. "They're in their eighties now, and I didn't want to worry them, so I haven't said anything about my condition. They'll know soon enough."

"There's just your mom and dad?"

"I have a sister who's twenty years older. She's married, no children, and lives in the Valley, near my parents. She'd already left the house when I came along, so we never really got close."

Lane could understand wanting to avoid the very difficult conversation, but to surprise his family would be cruel. "They may already be aware of the condition since it runs in your family. And if they aren't aware of it, you have to tell them. What if your sister decided to have children?"

"There's a genetic component, but the syndrome is very rare. I'm not aware of anyone in my family who's had it."

"Still, they need to be ready for what's coming, Rick. And you—are you ready?"

"How do you get ready for that? Do *you* know?"

He sounded defensive, even angry. That told her he wasn't ready, not even to talk about such things. Some people never were.

"No, I just— Have you thought about it at all, talking to them? There might be things you'll regret not having said."

"I'm regretting this conversation."

She felt despair, realizing that she might never get through to him, never find the connection she was seeking, whatever it was. What did she want from Rick Bayless? Why couldn't she let him be? She was afraid of loss, too. She didn't want to love him and lose him, and he was giving her a way out, a free pass. She didn't have to engage with him, that's what he was telling her. He didn't even want her to.

"What if it's you," she said, feeling horribly awkward.

"What's me?"

"What if you're the guy in those heartbreak songs?"

"The guy who breaks hearts?"

"No, the one the girl waits for."

"You being the girl?"

She said nothing, trying to steel herself, but nothing could have prepared her for his outburst.

He swore under his breath. "You don't get it, do you? All this crap about living while you're alive—it's just a way to avoid the cold hard fact that I'm going to be human fertilizer. Bug food. That's the void, Lane. That's the big black empty void you're talking about."

"I know all about the void," she snapped. "I lived there after my dad died. You don't have to die to be dead, Rick. I *was*. And look at you. You're already a ghost."

It hit her hard that this was inevitable. Some things couldn't be fixed. Maybe she *was* in avoidance—or trying somehow to make up for not being there with her dad. But there was one incontrovertible truth. Rick was going to die and she couldn't change that. The thought ripped at her. It made her want to rage at the unfairness—and hell, yes, she wanted to run away, too. No one welcomed that kind of pain. She would have done anything to protect herself, except push him away.

They should be clinging to each other and packing as much feeling as they could into every moment. Not just living, but opening their hearts and soaring. But he wouldn't allow that, she knew. He really did want no attachments, nothing to lose. She curled her fingers into her palm, aware that her hand had slipped out of his.

35

Simon Shan crept soundlessly down the unlit hallway, his feet bare, his movements slow enough to keep his silk pajama bottoms from rustling. It was Sunday night and late, after midnight. He had a meeting with his defense team on Tuesday, but he was too distracted to prepare for it. He was still grappling with the meaning of the text messages he'd found on her SIMmate. He didn't know whether to confront Jai or wait until he had irrefutable evidence that she was JGK.

She'd come back hours ago from picking up the supplies he'd asked for, but he could see from the light under the doorway of her room that she was still up. He wondered when bodyguards slept. This one never seemed to. As far as he could tell, she didn't do any of the normal things like eat, sleep or go to the bathroom, unless she waited until he was asleep. He was beginning to wonder if she was human. She was highly trained and capable of anything, including deadly force. But who the hell was she when she wasn't guarding bodies?

He listened at the door, surprised to hear signs of life inside. It sounded like someone murmuring, but it was so faint he couldn't tell if it was her voice or discern anything that was being said. He hadn't known her to use the television or the clock radio. She could have been talking to herself or on the phone. Or was someone in there with her?

There was no way he could have bugged her room or installed a surveillance camera. She would have found it. But this time he had no intention of politely knocking on the door. He wanted to surprise her. He'd left the door unlocked just for this purpose.

He opened the door enough to see in. She wasn't sitting at the desk, but she wasn't facing him, either. She was pacing, talking softly on her cell phone, and the conversation was about him.

"I can handle Simon Shan. Please believe me. It's not a problem."

A moment later she said, "Yes, yes, I *will* do it. Count on me to resolve this exactly the way you want, but this isn't the time. He doesn't trust me yet. I need him off guard and totally vulnerable."

Didn't trust her? She had no idea. He should have aimed for her jugular when he'd thrown the dagger at her. Time to put an end to this sham. If he'd had any doubts about her being the enemy, this had put them to rest.

Simon came up behind her and took the phone from her hand. "Who is this?" he said, speaking into the mouthpiece. He heard silence at the other end, and then a click. He hadn't actually expected a response. He just wanted her and whoever had hired her to know the game was over. And he wanted the other party's number from her incoming-call queue.

"My phone, if you don't mind."

Jai reached for the phone and Simon knocked her hand away, fully expecting her to retaliate. She had Israeli martial arts training, but he still had seventy-five pounds on her.

"Who sent you here?" he asked her. "Was it someone from TPC? Who's trying to ruin me?"

She didn't respond, and he moved in on her, aggressively backing her to the bed, and constantly expecting an aggressive reaction. She did nothing but look into his eyes, her strange amber gaze fastened to his. She might be trying to use hypnosis, but he wasn't going to give her time for that.

He pushed her onto the bed, and she sat down, offering no resistance.

"Who hired you to take me out?" he asked her.

She glanced around him, as if there was someone behind him, but he wasn't going to fall for that ploy. She wanted him to turn and look.

"I asked who hired you."

"It's not what you think," she said.

He laughed harshly. "No, Christ! It never is."

Her hand flashed out, but he couldn't see what she was reaching for. A weapon? It all happened so fast he couldn't get to her. He gasped and arched his back. Something had pierced his spine. It felt sharp, like a needle.

Before the burning, stinging pain had stopped, he began to get warm and sweaty. "Wh-what the f-fuck?" Wooziness rushed through his brain, making him slur his words. His balance was off as he tried to turn. *There was no one behind him.*

He turned back to Jai. "What did you do?"

She was still sitting on the bed, her gaze clinging to his. Suddenly she was a double image, triple. Was he losing his mind? It looked as if she was waving to him. *"Zai jian,"* she said in her barely discernible voice. The word was familiar, but his brain wouldn't process it. It seemed to take him forever to grasp that *zai jian* was goodbye in Chinese.

By that time, he'd already crashed to the floor.

* * *

Pris stood on the tiny fifth-floor balcony, wrapped in the hotel's terry robe and smoking a mentholated cigarette as she stared out at the ocean. The beach was deserted on this chilly Sunday night, but the moon was high and the waves iridescent. This was what she'd imagined the good life would be like when she'd dreamed of fame and fortune as a kid. The cigarette had seemed glamorous then. Now it was a rude, nasty habit that she couldn't seem to kick for any length of time, but she was allowing herself some indulgences tonight. It had been one royally fucked-up day.

She'd escaped the paparazzi by paying the gardener a huge sum of money to hide in the back of his van when he'd left her house. She'd packed an overnight bag and asked him to drive her down to Loew's, a swanky hotel on the beach that boasted fabulous oceanfront suites. There'd been no problem registering under another name, paying in cash and ordering room service whenever she felt like it, a Caesar salad, lobster bisque, filet, whatever she wanted.

She also hadn't turned on the television.

Pris had discovered something about herself in all of the recent insanity. She didn't like bad news. It had been impossible to cut herself off from the media at her home with those psycho stalkers right outside her gate and the helicopters flying overhead. She'd just wanted to get away from all of it, her jangling phone, her imploding career, and obsessing over what else could go wrong. She'd had to escape for a while, especially being Priscilla Brandt.

She stubbed out the cigarette on the railing, flicked the butt over the side and went back inside, shivering. The hotel bed was still littered with trays of food, most of it uneaten, and she'd barely touched the Cristal champagne in the ice bucket. Maybe she would have a midnight snack and watch some TV after all. It should be too late for things like celebrity news.

The room had a large flat-screen TV, which she clicked on with the remote once she was curled up on the bed, cushioned by pillows. A pay-per-view movie would keep the news at bay, but first she took a quick surf of the channels. You had to do some surfing when you were at the beach.

Pleased with her little joke, she stopped when she heard a familiar name.

"Mr. McGinnis, are you going to sue Priscilla Brandt for calling you all those names?"

It was a cable-news channel, and Skip McGinnis was surrounded by reporters as he came out of a restaurant. Pris should have kept going, but she was stunned at the sight of her nemesis on the screen. It couldn't be coincidence that this clip was the first thing she'd hit. The station must have been playing it in heavy rotation.

She fully expected McGinnis to refuse comment and push through the crush, but he didn't do that. He stopped and spoke to them.

"Ms. Brandt has bigger problems than a slander suit," he said, enunciating for the mikes that were thrust into his face. "A well-known Beverly Hills hairstylist has accused her of plagiarism. She swears Priscilla stole ninety percent of the material for her manners book—and the word is out that Brandt's publisher intends to start pulling books off the shelves of bookstores across the country."

He shrugged and walked away, ignoring all other questions.

Pris stared at the huge screen, the remote clutched in

her hand. She was in shock. Dazed and speechless. Her brain was on spin cycle. Normally she would have exploded and flung the remote at the screen by now. But this was too big, too monstrous, even for her.

Skip McGinnis had publicly accused her of plagiarism. Somehow he'd found out about that hairstylist's ridiculous plan to self-publish an e-book on sex and dating etiquette, and now he was accusing Pris of stealing it. *Wrong.* Pris had perfected it. She'd taken the woman's lump of anthracite and turned it into a diamond. Into a national bestseller!

She clicked off the television, pulled the champagne bottle out of the ice bucket and went back out to the balcony. Just moments ago, the rolling waves had soothed her. Now the breaking foam looked like dirty laundry suds. McGinnis had vowed to ruin her, and he'd done it. He had actually done it. She was finished. It was all over.

"Not fair," she whispered, a sob rising in her throat. "Not fucking fair."

Maybe she should climb up on the railing and jump, go out in a blaze of glory. If she couldn't be immortalized in life, then she would be immortalized in death. Her untimely demise would be broadcast around the world. People would mourn her and shed tears for the young wonder woman caught so tragically in the harsh and unforgiving glare of the media spotlight.

Fuck that, she thought, taking a swig of the champagne. If anyone was going to splatter it would be Skip McGinnis. And along with him, a few other rude people of Priscilla Brandt's acquaintance. Was there anyone in this pathetic city who didn't need to be taught some manners? Pris had found her calling, and no one was going to sully that, certainly not because of some pathetic plagiarism charges. What did it matter if she'd borrowed a few etiquette tips from a snippy hairstylist? Pris was the only one with the guts and the vision to bring a message of this importance to the masses. She was one of them. She understood them. It was her mandate, and it was unfortunate that miscreants like Skip McGinnis didn't see it that way. But he would, she vowed. Oh, he would.

36

Lane shivered and drew the sheet up to cover herself, but it had more to do with feeling awkward at waking up naked in bed with a stranger than with the chill in the house. She'd slept fitfully, trying to reconcile the motives of the man she'd given herself to last night and the man who'd pushed her away afterward. She understood that he was trying to protect himself, and she had to respect that, but after the closeness they'd shared, it was hard.

She thought she'd reached him in some way. They had little in common, except the isolation and loneliness that should have been their bond. But she didn't dare reach out to him now. She'd already triggered a backlash that made her question who she was dealing with. She'd even flashed back on the cop who arrested her, and oddly that man seemed more approachable than this one. He'd cared, at least.

She bundled the covers around her and sat up. Their clothes still lay on the floor from last night.

She shivered again, wondering where he'd gone. She could hear noises coming from the kitchen. Maybe she should use this opportunity to get dressed and go. He might even be hoping she would. Regardless, it would be awkward once he came back. This was like a very bad blind date, only worse. Blind dates didn't have a star-crossed past—or a doomed future.

"Hot coffee? Girl Scout cookies?" Rick walked into the bedroom carrying a tray with two mugs of coffee and a plate of what may have once been cookies. Maybe the intruders got to them, too.

It startled Lane that he was speaking, much less almost amiable. It also made her just a bit wary, wondering what he was up to. He was wearing a T-shirt and jeans, which disappointed her, she realized. The bare-chested look must have grown on her. She blushed at the thought of him laid out on the bed, naked and very much at her mercy.

"I have peanut butter, the real thing, broken into a million delicious bite-size pieces. Can I tempt you?" He winced as he set the tray on the bed.

"Your ribs?" she asked him.

"Yeah, they're killing me this morning."

No big surprise there, everything considered. She pretended to be looking over the broken cookies and making her choices. "In that case, I may forgive you."

He actually seemed to know what she meant. "I shouldn't have said what I did," he admitted. "I don't have the right to take my moods out on you. No one does, no matter what they're going through."

She looked up and he had his hands in the pockets of his jeans and his shoulders hunched. His expression said he meant it, he was sincere, and her breath caught as she realized what a huge admission that was for someone like him. "Okay, you get a pass."

"Thanks." He studied her bundled body. "Are you okay?"

"A little chilly. Some of that hot coffee might help."

He sat down on the bed and pushed the tray toward her. "Take anything in it? I hope not." He laughed, still apologetic. "I don't have anything."

"Black is fine," she said, a small fib in the interests of their truce.

"I've been thinking about your suggestion that we partner up and check some things out. But I'd like to start with someone you know."

She had a cookie piece halfway to her mouth. "Yeah, who?"

"I need to talk to your sister, Sandra. Actually, I'd like you there, too. Can you set that up?"

"Sure, but why?" She could hardly believe he was suggesting it.

He handed her one of the coffees, and she took it gladly, her frozen fingers warming against the heat of the large mug.

"It's possible that whoever ransacked this place believes I have the evidence, which could mean it's a member of the lodge, and someone your sister might have known. I need to ask her some questions."

"What kind of questions?"

He shrugged. "I'm still formulating them."

He didn't seem to want to say, and Lane was uneasy that he wouldn't take her into his confidence, but she wanted to know what her sister was up to, as well.

"I'll call her and set something up," she said, still hesitant.

"Good, but first, there's something else. I should have told you last night, but it's taken me a while to get it straight in my head. You were right."

He drew in a breath, as if not quite sure how to convey

what he needed to, and finally with a shrug that was intended to be offhand, he said, "I don't want to be a ghost."

She was so startled she set down her coffee and nearly missed the tray. She really didn't know what to say, but he wasn't finished.

He reached over and took hold of her hand. "Your dad was a smart man," he told her. "He knew you wanted to be there with him. He knew."

Sandra answered Lane's call on the first ring, as if she'd been sitting by the phone. "Are you all right?" she asked Lane. "I've barely heard from you since your trip to Dallas."

"I know, and I'm sorry." Lane was quick to apologize, even though she had called Sandra since the trip and been brushed off. "I've been crazy busy. Listen, I'm on my way into work and running behind, so I don't have a lot of time. Could you meet me for a late breakfast today, say, at ten?"

"You want to meet today, this morning?"

"Sure, just to talk, catch up. We haven't seen each other, and I thought we could discuss that job you mentioned."

Lane glanced in the rearview mirror, hoping she didn't look too disheveled. She wasn't dressed for a Monday morning at work. She'd splashed some cold water on her face, done what she could with her hair and then thrown on the same clothes she'd been wearing yesterday, the black silk blouse and slacks. She didn't want to take the time to go home, and she did have a pantsuit at the office she could slip into.

"Lane, what do you want? Is something wrong?"

Sandra's bluntness startled her. "No, of course not. I'm

late, and I can't talk now. Just meet me, okay? I want us to spend some time together. It's important."

Sandra said yes, but reluctantly. They agreed on the restaurant and the time, but Lane wasn't at all sure her sister would show up. Lane's next call was to Rick, but he didn't pick up, so she left a message with the details about when and where.

"I'll meet you and Sandra at the restaurant," she told him, "but don't approach her until I get there. She's not expecting you." Lane wasn't going to let him have his meeting with Sandra without her.

Lane heard a call-waiting beep in her ear as she hung up. She ignored it, just as she'd been ignoring the beep that told her she had messages. She still had to call Mary at TPC. Lane was rarely late, and she wanted Mary to alert everyone that she was on her way. The only thing scheduled for that morning was the usual Monday-morning staff meeting, this one with Val *and* Dar, which Lane was praying would go smoothly after yesterday's confrontation. She didn't want to bring in a computer-forensics expert, but it might be necessary—and wise to have backup, especially if there was any chance they'd be facing a lawsuit from Priscilla.

For the first time that Lane could remember, she had time on her hands, which she planned to use to call clients and do whatever damage control she could. Normally she would have had several calls from potential clients, high-profile types inquiring about a Premiere membership, but there had been zero inquiries since she became a person of interest in the Seth Black murder. Bad news traveled fast. It was very possible she was already a pariah in this town, especially after Pris's most recent public tirade and the gossip Web site frenzy. Lane hadn't checked any of the gossip sites, but she imagined they must be having a field day with the woman suspected of killing one of their own.

She began changing lanes as the traffic slowed down on the 405 Freeway. She was aware of the churning sensation in her stomach. It seemed nearly constant now. She lived in a state of turmoil. She really should contact the service's attorney about the voice-mail leak. He might also be able to advise her on retaining a criminal-defense lawyer. It seemed premature, but better to be prepared. At the meeting this morning, she was going to insist on bringing together the entire headquarters staff as soon as possible. It might be the only way to take back some control over what was happening to her company.

Mary also answered on the first ring. "Oh, Lane, thank God, I was just going to call you. It's Dar—"

"What's wrong?" Lane cut in. Mary sounded frantic.

"He needs to talk to you," she said. "I'm sorry, that's really all I should say. Please just get here as soon as you can."

Mary hung up, leaving Lane stunned. She tossed her phone on the passenger seat without remembering to turn it off, and hit the gas.

Sandra threw the last of her things into her open suitcase and shut the lid. Her shaking fingers fumbled the latch repeatedly before she got it locked. She glanced around the hotel room, looking for anything she might have missed in her rush. Damn, if only there had been time to go through the room again and pull the bed apart, check the drawers. She couldn't afford to leave anything behind that might lead someone to her.

Regret prickled like needles. Once again she was

sneaking out the back door and checking over her shoulder, trying not to feel like the evil sister. Was it always one sibling's fate to compare badly to the other, to be the loser? Sandra had felt like that for as long as she could remember.

Her room-service tray was still sitting on the bed where she'd had breakfast. Longingly she considered the fine china and fresh flowers. This was the nicest place she'd ever stayed in, and damn, it was fun while it lasted. Too bad she had to leave it looking like a tornado had rolled through. But she had to get out while she still could—and she wasn't stopping to check out of this fine establishment, either.

It had never been her intention to throw her sister under the bus, but Sandra was in far worse trouble than Lane. A semi was coming Sandra's way, and her only option now was to disappear. She grabbed the suitcase and headed for the door, wobbling on her high heels before she caught her balance. She'd tucked her cell phone in the pocket of her jacket. There was just one last thing she had to do before she went into hiding, one last act of subterfuge. Once she was on the road she would toss the phone out the window.

Mary's ashen face said it all. Something was terribly wrong. "He's in there, waiting for you," she told Lane, gesturing toward the hallway that led to Dar's cave.

"Thanks." Lane hurried past the reception desk without trying to coax more information out of Mary, although probably she should have.

Dar's door was shut but unlocked. Lane opened it to find him at his desk, emptying the open drawers and stuffing things into a packing box.

"What are you doing?" she asked him.

He didn't look up or stop packing. The top of his desk was bare, and she saw several other boxes in the room, already packed with his books, magazines and other paraphernalia.

Panic set in as Lane strode to his desk. She took the stapler out of his hand. "Dar, what's going on?"

He peered at her from under the lid of the Dodgers cap he'd pulled down steeply, covering his eyes. His lean face was a mask of guilt and sadness. He didn't seem able to find the words, so he picked up a thin sheaf of papers and handed them to her.

"Read this," he said, adding "please," as though he was begging her not to make him explain.

Lane took the papers and skimmed them. It was the transcript of Priscilla Brandt's voice-mail messages. Halfway through, she glanced up at Dar. "Why did you give me this?"

"Because it's my fault. I *can* tap our clients' conversations and their voice mail, and I have in the past when there were problems of harassment and every exchange needed to be documented. It was always in the interest of protecting our clients. The problem is, I didn't always have their permission, and Priscilla Brandt is one of those cases."

"You were wiretapping her? But you didn't leak her voice mails. I don't believe that."

His voice was strained and raspy. "Not intentionally. I've been capturing all her cell-phone activity for the last several days. As far as I can tell, someone hacked into my system and got to it, but it's my fault they were able to access the infrastructure. There should have been a whole system of security protocols in place, but it's tedious and time-consuming, and I kept putting it off. Whoever broke into the system did so through the portal I created."

Lane held up the papers. "Where did this transcript come from?"

"Val found it in my printer tray."

"Could Val have done this?"

"Anyone who could hack into an insufficiently protected computer system could do it." He shook his head, still unable to look at her. "Lane, it was negligence, and nobody's fault but my own. I didn't protect our clients, I made them vulnerable."

Lane's voice went shrill. "Where is Val?" she said. "I want him in here. If he's accusing you of something, I want to hear it from him."

"You're hearing it from me. I'm confessing. There's no need for Val to be here, and if I saw his face again, I'd probably kill him."

"Are you letting Val force you to leave? What's really going on?" It saddened Lane terribly that Dar and Val's feud had come to this, that one could be accusing the other of such a heinous thing. But she needed to hear it from Val, too. If he had anything to do with this, which she actually hoped was the case, she would have his head.

"No one is forcing me to go," he said. "This is my choice. Val knows nothing about it."

"Dar," she breathed. "You're not leaving. You can't leave."

"I have to, Lane. I'm responsible. Val was right. He's been right all along about me. I've been negligent, even reckless."

She shook her head, unable to believe it, even though everything he said made sense. He was a magician with their cell-phone system, capable of creating things out of thin air, but he'd never been careful about security, which was ironic since he'd called his prototype phone an electronic bodyguard. Still, something was missing here. She couldn't accept what he was telling her, and not because she didn't understand the technical aspects. She didn't understand the moral ones. It sounded as if Dar was spying on their clients. Would he have ever gone that far?

"I may never understand how you did any of this, Dar, but I do need to understand *why* you did it, especially when there was so much at stake for all of us."

He shook his head. "I can't explain it any better than I already have."

"You have to, Dar, because you're not leaving like this."

"Lane, trust me, it's time to hire those computer-forensics experts you talked about. I can't fix this problem because I caused it. It would be suicide for TPC. Once this gets out, and it will, no one's ever going to trust me again, especially our clients—and why should they?"

Lane felt as if someone had kicked her in the gut, but she knew he was right. "Will you talk to the experts at least? Tell them what you did?"

"I'll do whatever you want, except stay here." He began dumping things in the box, obviously in a hurry to get away. Lane had never seen him like this before. His only concern seemed to be the business, and she understood the reason. He was riddled with guilt and shame. He blamed himself entirely. But she couldn't get beyond what this would mean for their relationship. He was her only family. She loved him.

"I'm sorry" was all he seemed to be able to manage.

Lane didn't respond. She couldn't even manage a

nod. Watching him put his treasured books and manuals
in a cardboard box and prepare to leave in disgrace was
breaking her heart.

Rick was being followed, and the guy was an amateur.
He'd been close enough that Rick could see some of the
details of his face in the rearview mirror—and his license-
plate number. Rick didn't recognize the man's square-
jawed face and pug features, but he doubted this was a
coincidence. It had something to do with the recent attacks
on him, and Rick had decided that he and this tail needed
to have a talk, even if that meant Rick was late for the
breakfast meeting Lane had set up with Sandra.

Rick was on a main thoroughfare, heading for the
freeway that would take him into L.A., but he turned onto
a less-traveled road. The lighter the traffic the better, given
the maneuver he had in mind. The tail was right behind
him, another sign of inexperience.

Rick had taped his ribs that morning and taken some
pain medication. Now he was glad he had. He slowed
down, using the gears to make it look as if his car was fal-
tering. He came to a stop on the shoulder. As he expected,
the tail stopped, too. Anyone experienced in surveillance
would have passed by and kept going. The tail's car was
probably stolen or a rental, in which case the license-
plate number wouldn't be of much help.

Rick sat tight, waiting for the tail to get out, come to
the car and offer help, pretending to be a concerned
motorist. It was a tired old ploy. If he didn't approach,
Rick had another way to get his attention.

Rick gave him a few minutes to get out of the car, and
then he started the Jeep. He wedged the piece of foam he'd
brought between his ribs and the steering wheel, where it

could act as a shock absorber. Once he'd made sure there was no traffic, he hit the gas and sped forward on the shoulder. The tail gunned it, too, trying to catch him, but Rick had something else in mind. He hit the brakes hard.

Rick was prepared for the impact, even with his cracked ribs. But the tail wasn't. They weren't going fast enough to deploy air bags, but Rick's Jeep hadn't stopped vibrating before he was out and sprinting back to the other car. The plan was to get the jump on the guy, catch him before he could recover, but suddenly the other car roared straight at Rick.

A warning lit Rick's mind like a highway flare. Maybe this guy wasn't just a tail. Maybe he had another mission, like killing him.

Rick leaped free of the car's grinding tires, but he hit the gravel with a bone-crushing thud. Shit, there went all the rest of his ribs. Pain ripped through his body, enraging him to the point where all he wanted to do was kill the slimy little bastard. The hell with talking to him.

He rolled to his side and drew a 9 mm semiautomatic from his hip holster. As the other car pulled way, he took aim at the squealing tires and shot out the two back ones. He then pumped several shots into the rear windshield and the car came to a shuddering stop.

Adrenaline got Rick off the ground and over to the car. The driver was slumped against the steering wheel, alive but terrified. "I'm sorry," he said. "I didn't mean to—"

"I don't care what you meant. Who hired you to kill me?"

"No, not kill you!"

Rick pulled back the hammer, shutting him up. "Who hired you? Tell me or I'll be more than happy to put my last bullet in your brain."

"No, please!" the driver squealed. "It was a woman. I don't know her name and I didn't see her face. It was dark. She gave me a thousand dollars and told me to scare you, just scare you."

A woman. Interesting. That simply added to Rick's suspicions and confirmed that he was on the right track.

Lane sat in a booth with a view of the restaurant's door. She'd already been there twenty minutes and neither Rick nor Sandra had showed. She'd tried both on their cell phones, and left them multiple messages. Rick's rang several times before it went to voice mail, which meant it was probably turned on but he wasn't answering. Sandra's went to voice mail immediately, which usually meant the phone was off.

Both situations worried her. It made her think that Rick couldn't answer, and Sandra wouldn't.

She glanced at her watch again, wondering how long she should stay. She'd picked a restaurant she knew wouldn't be busy, where they could talk undisturbed, but the waitress could only pour so much coffee. And Lane had the weight of the world pressing on her heart. It felt as if she was losing everything, her business, her best friend, the sister she'd never had, and even Rick, a man whose situation she could barely comprehend, but who had made a deep and profound impression on her world.

She was getting up to go when her cell rang, startling her. She hit the Talk button and heard Rick's voice saying her name. He told her there'd been an accident, but no one was hurt. It frightened her terribly when he told her the rest of the story, that the other man in the accident had been tailing him and had admitted that a woman had hired him to scare Rick.

"A woman," Lane echoed. "That couldn't be someone from the hunting-lodge incident. There were only men involved."

"The DNA evidence was pictures and condoms with male semen, but there was a woman involved," Rick said. "Sandra."

"What do you mean?"

"She worked at the lodge and her thug boyfriend was the manager. She must have known about every illicit, illegal thing that was going on, including the prostitution. I'm sorry to have to say this, Lane, but if I'm right, your sister didn't meet you at the restaurant because she's on the run. I think she's the woman who set up the attacks on me."

"Sandra? Why?"

"Because she's the one who hid the DNA evidence in your stuffed animal fifteen years ago. She had some plan to use it, maybe to blackmail the lodge's clients. You ruined her plans by running away and taking the stuffed animal with you, but now she's figured out who took the backpack from the evidence room all those years ago, and she's decided late is better than never."

Lane shook her head in denial, aware that he couldn't see her. It wasn't so much that she needed to defend her sister. She and Sandra had no fierce familial bond. And what Rick was saying might be true. Certainly Lane had not hidden the evidence in the stuffed animal. But how could she know if Sandra was the culprit?

Lane had taken too many blows today. She might have been able to deal with being blindsided by news about her sister if she hadn't already been blindsided by Darwin's leaving, and by all the rest of it. Her sister?

"Lane, you have to help me find Sandra," Rick said.

"Not today, not now. I need—" She hung up the phone, unable to finish the sentence. She had no idea what she needed, except to get out of that restaurant. As she left some money on the table and went out the door, she was overcome with an exhaustion so profound she wasn't sure she could drive. She could barely walk…and she had no idea where she was going.

37

Rick took elaborate precautions, checking the courtyard and the French doors, making sure they were still locked before he let himself into his own house. He entered through the front door because he could see directly down the hallway that led to the kitchen. Less chance of ambush, he reasoned.

He checked the dining room to his right and then entered the living room through the arch to his left, but by the time he got down the west hall to the master bath and retrieved some ibuprofen from the cabinet, he didn't really give a shit whether he was alone in the house or not. He was tired. He hurt like hell. And he had no idea what his next move would be. Without Lane's cooperation it was going to be difficult to track down her sister. He couldn't even be certain that Sandra's last name was Cox, although that was where he would start.

Finally he had the bridge between past and present, and it was Lane's sister. He hadn't known her sister was in town until he'd gone over to Lane's last Saturday morning. Lane had said she was expecting Sandra, but the significance of that hadn't registered then. He was there to accuse Lane of lying about Ned being a member of her service, and then one thing led to another, and they'd ended up kissing and breaking pottery. But Sandra had come into his mind several times since then, and he'd finally realized she was the link.

His stomach rumbled so loudly the sound echoed in the tiled room. He'd picked up some fast food, a couple of burgers from a drive-in and two large bags of fries, thinking he would need enough to share with the rodent. It really was the pits having a roommate who mooched your food *and* paid no rent.

He swallowed three of the five-hundred-milligram gel caps and then washed up, carefully scrubbing his hands and splashing his face with icy-cold water, which felt good against the fresh cuts and bruises from that morning's skate across the roadside gravel. He got out of his torn shirt and dropped it in the laundry hamper, noting that his bandages seemed to have held up fairly well. He was too hungry to take the time to change them.

He picked a denim shirt with buttons up the front from his closet on the theory that it would be easier to deal with than a pullover. But nothing was easy when your body ached in every muscle fiber. His ribs throbbed when he breathed, and he was exhausted, he realized, so tired it was getting hard to hold up his head. All he wanted was to lie down and sleep, restore himself. But there was that damn mouse, probably sitting at the dining room table with a bib on, waiting for its dinner.

He left the shirt unbuttoned, grabbed the bag of fast food from the dresser where he'd left it and headed for the kitchen. The first thing he saw as he walked into the room was the garbage strewn all over the kitchen floor.

The wicker trash basket next to the refrigerator had been overturned. That stopped him cold. Maybe the house had been hit again. He hadn't checked the kitchen on the way in. The only thing on his mind had been pain meds. But something told him this wasn't intruders.

He took a roll of paper towels from the countertop and knelt down next to the overturned basket, wincing at the pressure on his ribs. That morning's coffee grounds were everywhere, along with the pills he'd thrown away the other day. There wouldn't have been much else to sort through, except that he'd been tossing the newspapers in the basket, too.

He started with the papers, most of which were soaked with coffee grounds. When he lifted the sports page, he saw the mouse. As he stared at the limp, unresponsive body, his knee give way, dumping him onto the floor. He hit hard enough to fracture something, but he felt nothing, no pain. His body was numb, cold. Ice-cold.

Oh, no.

It didn't look as if the mouse was breathing, but something seemed to be caught in its paws. He bent forward, moving in slow motion, even though he was aware of the urgency. There wasn't any pain, he just couldn't fucking do anything. *But he had to move.* Maybe it wasn't dead yet.

The mouse had a red plastic capsule hooked on one of its claws. An open capsule of Rick's medicine. There was no food in the house, and the poor thing must have been hungry enough to break open one of the pills and eat the contents. Rick began to sort through the garbage, searching for the rest of the medication. He found one capsule after another, intact, and just the tiniest glimmer of hope made him keep searching, ripping through wet, smelly newsprint. If the mouse had only eaten one pill, maybe there was a chance…

"I'm sorry, this is a cat clinic. We don't treat mice."

Rick had just walked through the veterinary clinic's

doors. He'd wrapped the mouse in a kitchen towel and was carrying it in his hands. He'd been driving around looking for a different vet, based on a listing he'd found in the phone book. But he'd seen the sign and pulled in.

"What do you mean you don't treat mice?" Rick stared at the unyielding young woman behind the counter as if she was crazy. She *was* crazy. "You've got a vet here somewhere, right? Someone who treats animals? Well, this is an animal. He got some of my medication, and he's dying. *Look.*"

Rick fished the pills out of his pocket and set them on the counter. He then opened the towel so she could see the mouse's unresponsive body. "Do something, for Christ's sake. Help him."

"We only treat cats here, sir. I'm sorry. If this is an emergency, there's a clinic in the next city—"

"Does it *look* like an emergency to you? Do something! Are you licensed to treat animals? I'll have them take your license!"

She blinked at him, clearly alarmed, but she moved closer to look at the mouse. She touched its neck, feeling for a pulse. She began to shake her head.

"I'm sorry. I'm really sorry, but this mouse is dead."

"No—" Rick's voice dropped low, searingly harsh. "No, it's not dead. That mouse is too stupid and stubborn to die. You hear me? That mouse can't be dead."

He turned and walked to the door, enraged, ready to break something, ready to rip the fucking world a new asshole. Just as swiftly he stopped and swung around. The woman ducked under the counter, clearly terrified. He had done that, terrified her. Not what he wanted. Not what he wanted at all.

Rick's gaze settled on the lifeless animal, and he gave

out a low groan of pain. The woman reappeared, peeking at him.

"Please," Rick said, "please, do what you can."

Only one of us is supposed to die, and it's not him.

Lane couldn't sleep. She'd come home from the restaurant and her aborted meeting with Rick unable to concentrate on anything, even the phone calls to clients that she so desperately needed to make. She knew there was no point in resorting to chocolate or mood music, her usual consolations. They wouldn't touch this mood.

She'd gone out to her condo's roof garden and sat under the arbor until the sun went down, listening to the soft rush of fountain water, but finally it got too chilly. She had her phone with her, but it hadn't rung all evening. That in itself was strange. She would have thought the phone wasn't working, but she'd used it several times to try to call Sandra. Each time, she got her sister's voice mail. And finally, Lane had given up and gone to bed.

Now she lay in darkness, wondering if she should have called Rick back and told him what happened, that she needed some time. She wasn't sure she would ever be able to help him. He was after her sister. He'd implied that Sandra was a blackmailer. He hadn't accused her of having anything to do with Ned's death, but he would have if she'd let him.

Lane pulled the comforter around her, shivering. She'd stayed outside too long. She was chilled to the bone and would never get warm. Suddenly she flung off the covers, sat up and turned on the lamp. The hotel. She would call Sandra's hotel, have them put her through to the room.

She used 411 to get the number, but when she asked for her sister's room the clerk told her that Sandra Cox had checked out that morning. Lane hung up the phone, trying to absorb what she'd just heard. Sandra was gone. That seemed to confirm what Rick had been trying to tell her. But how was she supposed to help him find someone who'd disappeared?

38

Two men in gray suits were waiting in the reception area when Val got to work Tuesday morning bright and early. It was 7:00 a.m., and even Mary hadn't yet arrived at TPC corporate headquarters, which officially opened its doors at nine. Val was always the first one there. Until this morning.

"How did you get in here?" he asked the men. Their close-cropped hair and unblinking eyes were so similar that Val wouldn't have been able to distinguish between them if one hadn't been several inches taller. Val had a bad feeling they were law enforcement, and the badge the shorter one flashed confirmed that.

"The security guard was happy to let us in," the man said, moving closer to let Val look at his credentials. "FBI. We'd like to ask you some questions."

Jesus, FBI? Val began to sweat profusely. Thank God it was only wet palms, and didn't show. Sweat would have ruined his Brioni two-button sports jacket, but that was the least of his problems. To refuse the FBI was to invite suspicion, but he was fairly certain he didn't have to volunteer any information unless they had some legal means to compel him. At the very least he should ask why they were here. Not to would be suspicious, too.

"Do you have a client named Priscilla Brandt?" the shorter man asked, ending Val's dilemma. He seemed by far the more aggressive of the two, even hostile. Val wondered if this was going to be a good cop, bad cop routine.

"I'm so sorry," Val said, wincing to convey the deep regret he felt, "but I can't give out client information. We have a strict confidentiality policy. Is Priscilla in some difficulty?" When was Priscilla not?

"No, but you are, Mr. Drummond. It is Mr. Drummond, isn't it? *You* may be in some difficulty and your company may be in a lot. Ms. Brandt has accused this concierge service of illegal wiretapping, eavesdropping and data mining."

The sweat pooled in Val's palms, soaked the back of his neck and filled his armpits. Kiss the Brioni jacket goodbye. Nip this inquiry in the bud, he told himself. Amputate it before it becomes gangrenous and destroys everything you've worked for.

"I can explain," he said. "TPC goes to great lengths, extraordinary lengths, to protect its clients. Security and privacy are the cornerstones of our service. They are how we've made our name, and we're very proud of our record—"

"Mr. Drummond, we're not looking to join. We're here because—"

"I know why you're here," Val said quickly. "I know everything, and I've already taken steps to deal with it. The person you want is Darwin LeMaster, our chief technology officer. He was the creator of our Darwin phone system and it was because of him that our security measures were breached and Ms. Brandt's voice mail was leaked. He's been fired, of course, but I can tell you where to find him."

Val went to the reception desk to get one of Dar's cards. All the principals and local concierges had cards available in small lead-crystal holders, and Dar's had not yet been removed. Val jotted down Dar's home address and landline number.

The shorter man took the card. "We've already been to Mr. LeMaster's house. He isn't there, and the neighbors said they hadn't seen him in days."

"That's because he was here over the weekend, pretending to fix the problem he caused. But he was fired yesterday. He must have gone home. What about his girlfriend, Janet? Have you talked to her? They may be together, probably are."

"Janet Bonofiglio? We paid a visit to her apartment this morning, but she wasn't there, and she's not answering either phone, her landline or her cell."

Val decided to say no more. Clearly the FBI knew more than he did. He wondered just how much they did know. Had Dar and Janet skipped the country? Val was drenched to the skin, which must be very obvious to his visitors. He would have to burn the jacket. What a stench. Leave it to the boy genius to screw up the greatest opportunity of Val's life—and after all Val's meticulous planning. He'd had the patience of Job, not rushing anything and letting everyone play themselves out. They'd dug their own holes, as he'd known they would, but somehow those holes were now a gaping excavation, big enough for a mass burial and waiting for the bodies to fall, including his.

She knew where Sandra was!

Lane woke up on the living room couch with that one

thought in her head. She'd wandered the house last night in her bathrobe, preferring that to lying on her bed, frozen. She'd always walked to clear her head, the forward motion helping her blaze a mental path, but it hadn't worked that way this time. She wasn't going forward. She was going in circles.

Eventually she'd landed on the living room couch and dropped off to sleep, slumped over on her side. She hadn't even removed her slippers or freed the arm that was caught beneath her body. She'd slept hard, until a realization woke her.

She knew where Sandra was.

Her cell was right there on the coffee table, but she wasn't sure she could trust it after what Dar had told her about the portal he'd created. She grabbed the landline and called Rick, hoping she wasn't too late.

This had to be a first. The video camera purred softly, in stark contrast to the shocking violence JGK witnessed through its viewfinder lens. Jack struggled to hold the camera steady enough to keep the targets in range. Priscilla Brandt was trying to run down a television talk-show producer with her Range Rover. Jack didn't know what Skip McGinnis looked like, but this was his home, based on Jack's research, and McGinnis was the guy she'd maligned in her voice mails. Right now the producer's quick reflexes were the only thing keeping him alive.

Pris would have nailed McGinnis in his own driveway if he hadn't leaped out of the way. He'd stormed out of his house about five minutes earlier, apparently to see who was shouting and honking the horn, and she'd made certain he was directly in her path before she hit the gas and rocketed straight at him. The man was quick. Now she was backing up to go across the lawn after him.

Jack opened the van's back door, risking being seen in order to catch Pris tearing up the luxury estate's privet hedges and grinding up the perfectly manicured lawn. McGinnis was yelling at someone in the house to call the police, but no one responded. And it wouldn't have made any difference anyway. Pris might as well have been a suicide bomber. The way she was going, the man would be lawn fertilizer long before the cops showed up.

Jack gasped as McGinnis tripped on a sprinkler head and sprawled on his face. He was down, and it didn't look like he was getting up. Pris gunned the engine, maneuvered the car across the front walk and through another row of privet hedges. She hit the gas again and rolled over the fallen man's body as if he were a speed bump.

Jack could only hope the wet, soggy grass had cushioned him from being crushed. Holy shit, talk about witnessing an attempted murder. The poor guy hadn't moved. He was exactly where she'd laid him out flat, and now she had the car in Reverse. She was going over him again.

Jack threw the camera in the van and grabbed a cell phone to call 911—and get the hell out of there. All the while Priscilla rolled the car back and forth over the prone body. No hit-and-run driver, this one. It looked as if the world would have one less television producer—and Pris Brandt would be checking into the gray-bar hotel, maybe forever.

The 911 dispatcher came on the line, but Jack didn't get a chance to tell her anything. Footsteps sounded from behind, and Jack's head snapped forward and back. The world went bloodred. A massive blow to the base of the skull forced a shriek of agony. The next blow brought thundering silence.

Jack sprawled facedown in the back of the van, as helpless as Pris's victim. The blows continued, but as consciousness seeped away, one searing moment of clarity broke through. Jack's assailant could be Priscilla Brandt herself. If she'd realized she was under surveillance she would have to get rid of the eyewitness to her crime.

The freeway traffic lightened up as soon as Rick and Lane hit the Foothill Freeway on their way to the San Gabriel Mountains. Rick was driving, and going well past the speed limit. Lane braced herself with her feet and held the handgrip, knowing a blowout could be fatal at this speed. Still, she felt the same sense of urgency that he did. She just hoped the premonition she'd had about Sandra was right.

Rick had sounded groggy when she'd called him at dawn. She'd had a feeling he hadn't slept well, either. He'd mumbled something about the mouse she'd seen at his place, but she'd cut him off, saying she might know where her sister was. He'd said he would come right over.

The Shadow Hills Hunting Lodge was nestled in the San Gabriel foothills on a multiacre estate that had been the last vestige of the area's horse culture until it was turned into a rustic luxury resort, catering to the last vestige of gentlemen hunters. Lane hadn't seen the place since she ran away. But she remembered her first impression of the area as a wooded wilderness with a fairy-tale castle made of imposing stone towers, graceful arches and multipaned windows. The castle had turned out to be a three-story lodge, as impressive inside as out. But the place was no Disneyland. The all-male membership had an air of entitlement that had made her feel unsafe and on guard from the moment she set foot in the place.

Young Lucy Cox had never gotten used to the boisterous habits of the men who lounged in the leather chairs, sipped the fifty-year-old single-malt scotch and smoked the illegal Cuban cigars as if it was their birthright to enjoy all the luxuries such a place could provide. But it hadn't taken her long to figure out that this was a certain breed of man, self-made and successful, who had earned whatever his money could buy him—and had learned that it could buy him almost anything.

Not unlike some of her TPC clients, she realized.

But now, as Rick sped up the driveway and the lodge came into view, Lane was startled at how badly the baronial estate had deteriorated. Abandoned after the scandal, the property had gone into receivership and was still owned by the bank. There were several No Trespassing signs, but the evidence of vandalism was everywhere. Windows were broken out and the stone walls had been hit by spray-paint graffiti artists.

Sandra had been driving a rental car, but Lane didn't know what make. She didn't see any cars at all, but Sandra may have hidden hers, not wanting to be found. Perhaps Rick had the same thought. Neither said a word as Rick parked and they got out of his Jeep. Lane led the way in. She was familiar with the layout, but it took her a moment to get her bearings. The place was thick with cobwebs and dust. Even the grand staircase, leading upstairs, looked different, less sweeping and formidable. At ten, she used to think she would never make it to the top. Now, sadly, it looked like the creaky set piece of an old-fashioned horror movie.

She moved quickly up the steps, beckoning for Rick to follow.

Lane found her sister in the upstairs reading room.

Sandra had a small fire going and was huddled in front of it, a black cardigan draped over her shoulders. This had always been Sandra's favorite room because it was off-limits to the male clients.

Lane walked over to her sister and knelt beside her, but Sandra wouldn't even look at her. She turned her back in a show of defiance, but her profile revealed tortured emotions. Guilt was Lane's first thought.

"If you know anything about who attacked Rick you have to tell us," Lane said softly. "My life is at stake, Sandra, my future. So is Rick's."

"Did you hide the evidence that your boyfriend collected on the lodge members?" Rick asked. "Were you going to blackmail those men?"

Sandra mumbled something Lane couldn't hear. Rick signaled Lane to move away, and he knelt behind Sandra, speaking in a low, compelling tone. "You know how it goes, don't you, Sandra? This can be hard or it can be easy. Don't make it hard on yourself."

He pressed his knuckles into her back and she flinched, clearly thinking it was a weapon.

"Were you going to blackmail those men?" he asked her.

"No," she said angrily, "it was nothing like that. I wanted some way to protect Lane and myself from my boyfriend. He'd set up closed-circuit cameras in the bedrooms and he'd collected used condoms from the trash cans, probably in case he ever needed leverage against any of the members."

"And you stole it from him," Lane said, realizing what Sandra had done.

She nodded. "I had still copies made from the videos, and I replaced the condoms with new ones that looked used, thanks to a little liquid starch. It wasn't that difficult. I just had to be sure he didn't find out what I'd done. My plan was to threaten him with exposure if he ever tried to hurt you or me."

Sandra had kept all of this to herself. Lane wondered what else she'd been hiding—and whether she could believe anything her sister was saying. "Is it just a coincidence that you came looking for me now, when someone is trying to harm me and my business?"

Sandra pulled her legs up and buried her head in her knees. "No, it's not a coincidence," she admitted at last. "But I came here to protect you, not to harm you."

"Protect me from whom?" Lane asked.

"I can't tell you." Sandra shook her head, still tucked into herself. "I've already said too much. I'm as good as dead now."

39

Janet Bonofiglio woke to a strange, hot-pink haze and a piercing headache. The reddish light seemed to pulse from somewhere inside her eyes, possibly from the source of the needlelike pain. Someone could have been blowing a police whistle in short bursts, trying to warn her. But scary as that was, she was aware of a much more disturbing sensation. A deep throb came from the base of her skull, and she was lying in a pool of something warm and sticky. It felt as if her brains were seeping out the back of her head.

No, impossible. She wouldn't be conscious. She wouldn't be able to think, feel. Think, Janet. Think.

She had no idea where she was or how she got there. The last thing she could remember was watching Priscilla Brandt run down her producer and roll over him repeatedly with her car. What kind of a bizarre dream was that?

Janet tried to move, but nothing worked. She was lying on her side on what looked like the stage of a small movie theater that seemed to be under construction. The rows of seats had been ripped up and stacked against a side wall and the old-fashioned balcony section was propped up with steel support beams. The place appeared to be empty, but then how did she get here?

She tried again to get up, but her arms were caught

awkwardly behind her and her legs were numb. Her first terrified thought was paralysis. She would rather be dead, rather have her brains fall out. Frantic, she kept trying to move. At last, a prickly rush of sensation in the tips of her fingers brought some feeling back. Shit. She was tied up, not paralyzed. She could feel the ropes now. Her wrists were bound behind her. Was that good news or bad?

The rubbery squeak of footsteps caught her attention. "Who is it?" she called out.

No one answered, but a dark figure in black sneakers came from the wings of the stage and stopped near her feet, looming over her and casting a shadow that seemed to engulf the auditorium. With great difficulty, she turned her throbbing head enough to see him—and a gasp slipped from her lips. She could have been staring at Jack the Giant Killer. He was wearing a black ski mask, a hooded sweatshirt and jeans, the same outfit that the infamous paparazzo wore.

But that was impossible. *She* was JGK. She'd been wearing a black hooded sweatshirt and jeans before someone took them off her. Now she had on nothing but her underwear, thong panties and a bra. But she *had* seen Priscilla mauling a man with her car. Janet had been videotaping it before someone clobbered her with what felt like a baseball bat. She'd thought it was Priscilla who'd sneaked up on her, but this was clearly a guy, just from the height and the shoulders. Unless he looked taller because she was on the floor.

"Darwin?" she said. "Darwin, is that you? Take off that silly mask, would you? It's scaring me."

Silent, he stood over her and peered down at her through eyeholes cut out of the black knit material.

"I know it's you," she said, wincing at the stabbing pain

in her eye socket. "And I know you're angry at me for spying on all those TPC clients. You probably figured out it was me, right?"

His unblinking scrutiny made her heart thud. "I'm sorry you got the blame for what happened to Priscilla Brandt's voice mail," she rattled on, "but you were the one who showed me how to do it. Not that I really needed help. I have a genius IQ, and I'm majoring in computer science. Oh, did I forget to tell you that?"

"Genius?" Laughter hissed in his throat. "You're a fucking idiot. What do you think this is, a joke? I don't know whether to lop off that stupid head of yours or start with your fingers and amputate from there, until there's nothing left of you but bloody pieces."

Janet wasn't so sure it was Darwin anymore—or that she could cajole her way out of this mess. He didn't sound like Darwin at all, even in a rage, although she'd never actually heard Darwin in a rage. She struggled to think who else it could be, but she was dizzy and sick and he was swimming in red. Everything was swimming in red.

"Bayless?" Janet seized on the private eye as her next suspect. Maybe he'd figured out she was the one who'd set up the attacks on him. "Are you R-Rick?" She swallowed back sudden icy fear. "I'm really sorry."

Still, no response. His silent stare confounded her. She didn't know who would want to do this to her. Except that it wasn't her, of course, it was JGK they wanted to hurt, and that opened the field. There was Val Drummond from TPC. He loathed the paparazzi. Or Burton Carr, the senator she videotaped after his son blew him off. She'd caught Carr's meltdown on camera from beginning to end.

Or was this man the police? She'd breached the

security of Darwin's computer and violated Priscilla Brandt's privacy. She'd broken laws.

Her captor grabbed hold of her bare feet and spun her around. Apparently he wanted to direct her attention to the wings on the other side of the stage. When he got to the curtain, he turned with a flourish, a magician about to dazzle the crowd with his big reveal. He drew back the curtain and a body fell out. It crashed to the floor with a thud that shook the stage.

It was Darwin, Janet realized. He was bound and gagged. She couldn't tell if he was dead or just unconscious, but there was no movement there, no life. Heartsick, she said only, "Why him?"

"Just because you like him," her captor said softly, and then he pulled off the ski mask, revealing his identity.

"Oh, God, no," Janet whispered, but it was despair more than surprise. This was so much worse than she'd feared. She'd put her faith in a crusader who had turned into a monster. She had begun to suspect that her coconspirator was less interested in truth and justice than in greed and personal gain. Obviously, she'd greatly underestimated that interest—and now she was going to die for her error.

Terror vibrated deep in the marrow of Janet's bones. A whimper set fire to her throat. She was balanced on her tiptoes on a wobbly three-legged stool with a hangman's noose around her neck. If the stool tipped, she would hang. Worse, she would release a torch that had been rigged above Darwin's body.

He'd been doused with gasoline by the monster who created this torture chamber and then took off, leaving Janet trapped in the noose. That was at least a half hour ago. She was shaking, twitching, exhausted. Blood from her head wound clumped in her lashes and filmed her eyes. But if she moved, his body would go up in flames. And she would see it all happen just before her own life was snuffed out.

She felt the stool wobble beneath her. Panic unhinged her, and she let out a cry. The noose jerked her head up, making it difficult to breathe. But somehow it also stabilized her enough to bring the stool back. Relief washed over her, blessed, drowning relief, but she couldn't give in to the weakness again.

God help her, she was exhausted, dead on her feet.

A tiny hysterical sound slipped out. Dead on her feet? Had she thought that? Her eyes drifted shut and she forced them open again. Every time she teetered, it shocked her, electrifying her senses. The adrenaline flowing through her might be the only thing keeping her on her feet, and alive. But how long before it burned out like a matchstick?

Lane drove Rick's Jeep while Rick sat in the backseat with Sandra, in part to keep her from jumping out of the SUV. Sandra had finally revealed the name of the person who so terrified her, but Lane still could not believe what she'd heard.

Jerry Blair? Lane was still reeling from the shock. Jerry was her friend, her silent partner and financial angel. Why would he mount a brutal vendetta against a company he'd helped to build? She'd ruled him out as a suspect long ago. Even if he had some kind of secret grudge against her, why would he do this? Self-interest alone should have stopped him.

Sandra also accused him of something much more heinous, something Lane simply could not fathom. It had made her so nauseous she'd had to fight not to wretch, and she'd come that close to calling Sandra a liar to her face. Lane had already lost one dear friend to this mess, several clients and possibly her business. She wasn't going let anyone else she cared about be destroyed.

But Rick had convinced Lane they didn't have time to fight. If there was any chance that Sandra was telling the truth about Jerry, they had to act now, before Jerry found out that his cover had been blown.

"He's in Brentwood," Rick said. He was using the GPS system on Lane's cell to track down Blair and pinpoint his location. Lane's phone had been modified to locate anyone with a TPC cell phone, courtesy of Darwin.

"Take the 405 Freeway to the Sunset Boulevard exit," he directed.

"I know how to get there," Lane snapped. She'd been to Jerry's Brentwood home many times, but never for anything like this. He was one of two people in the world she trusted with things deeply important to her. It made no sense that he would try to bring her down, and Sandra had no real proof of it, only suspicions. But she had told them in detail what she knew of Jerry's past, and that was damning enough, especially with regard to Ned Talbert.

"Any idea why Blair would be home on a Tuesday morning?" Rick asked.

"Maybe he's ill, or maybe his daughter's ill, and he stayed home to be with her. We can't forget that he has a sixteen-year-old child."

A half hour later, Lane pulled up to the guard gate of Blair's elegant Mediterranean mansion and was instantly recognized by the security staff. They waved her through, and she parked in the circular driveway, her heart pounding. The staff may have notified Jerry of her arrival, but that shouldn't have set off any warning signals, except possibly that she hadn't called first.

Rick spoke quietly to Lane and Sandra before they got out of the SUV, going over their hasty plan to deal with Blair. Quick and dirty, Lane had called it, assuring Rick that she knew how to use the camera in her cell phone and could handle her part of it. She also reminded him she was the obvious one to get them inside the house.

"True," he said, "but once we're in there, please let me take the lead." To Sandra, he said, "You stick with me. I'm armed, and I know how to use a weapon. I don't think it will come to that, but if it does, drop to the floor and stay down."

Lane agreed without question, mostly to get Sandra to go along. Rick complimented them on their teamwork with just a touch of irony in his voice—and then he told them to sit tight for a few more minutes while he went back to the guard gate and had a word with the boys.

A word with the boys? What the hell did that mean? Lane had little choice but to agree again, although his cloak-and-dagger tactics were getting on her nerves. She was used to running things. If information had to be concealed, she was the one to make that decision. This guy operated unilaterally, telling her what to do, what came next.

He was damn bossy for a dying man. And he had damn well better know what he was doing, she thought, but said nothing. Maybe Sandra was buying his routine. If she wasn't, they were all screwed. Sandra's story was the only thing they had against Blair. Lane wasn't sure Sandra could have made it up, even though she wanted to believe that more than she wanted to believe her own sister. Jerry was a dear friend and a good man, as far as Lane knew, the only real angel in her life. For Lane, it all came down to Jerry's reaction when they confronted him—and she was praying she could read him right.

Not ten minutes later, Lane rang the mansion's doorbell. Just behind her, Rick had Sandra by the arm. She'd promised to cooperate, but she was clearly so terrified of Blair that she couldn't be trusted.

40

Blair's housekeeper offered to go and get him, but Lane wouldn't hear of it. "No need, Luisa," she said, pretending a familiarity she didn't actually have with the woman. "I want to surprise Jerry with some old friends. Did you say he was out by the pool? I know the way, thanks."

Lane tugged at the rubber band on her wrist, hoping she didn't break it. Jerry's being out by the pool was better luck than she'd dared to hope for—and she'd also asked about his daughter. Felicity was away at school, gone for the day, thank God. Lane didn't want her exposed to any of this.

She stepped around Luisa and headed for the atrium at the back of the enormous house, followed closely by Rick and Sandra. The entry flowed into a hallway featuring Jerry's showy modern-art collection and some distinctly erotic statuary. Lane shouldn't have been surprised at the conspicuous consumption. She'd helped Jerry buy several of the pieces, but she hadn't seen it all on display like this, and he'd obviously added the erotic art on his own. Somehow, that didn't bode well with a sixteen-year-old in the house.

They found Jerry in the Jacuzzi with two women who looked as if they'd been referred by an escort service from the wrong end of Wilshire. Their poufy hair, makeup and overflowing bikini bras were unmistakable. Lane had seen the look at the lodge in her younger days and had come to the conclusion that in the sex-for-sale business, trashy was mandatory. It never seemed to change no matter what the current fashion, because God forbid anyone should miss the point.

Maybe Lane shouldn't have been shocked at Jerry's pool party, but she was, mostly at the possibility that her sister might have been telling the truth about Jerry. This could explain why he was at home on a Tuesday morning. He saved his extracurricular activities for school days when Felicity would be gone.

Lane fished her cell from the pocket of her jacket and got two quick shots of the festivities. She hadn't expected to be taking pictures this soon, or this obviously, but neither had she expected to find Jerry in the Jacuzzi with two adult female blow-up dolls.

"Lane? What the hell are you doing?" Jerry nearly drenched his guests as he jumped up and climbed out of the spa. Lane continued taking pictures as he turned his back and hustled over to the nearest lounge chair. With his thick brown hair and full beard, he reminded Lane of a bear after a dip in the pool, except that he didn't shake himself.

"Why didn't Luisa tell me you were here?" Jerry demanded, grabbing a bathrobe to wrap around his dripping frame. "And what are you doing with that cell-phone camera?"

When he saw Rick and Sandra his face changed shape and color. Sunglasses masked his eyes, but the muscles around them flattened, and his always amiable smile became a sneer. "What the fuck are you doing here?"

Lane's stomach turned over. She could hear it in his voice and see it in his expression. Jerry Blair had come face-to-face with his demons. Not Rick or Sandra, his own personal demons. They were merely the messengers, like the kid who dared to tell the emperor he was naked when everyone else was raving about his magnificent new clothes. She wondered if Blair could be forced to face his own ugliness and depravity, or was he blinded by corruption, like the emperor? Lane still didn't want to let herself believe it, but she had personally experienced some of that depravity.

Sandra had told the truth about him. Lane knew that now, in her gut.

She rushed over to Sandra, who looked ready to bolt. Lane was shaking and weak on her feet. She wanted to run, too—run screaming—but they had to see this through. "You must mean my sister," she said. "I thought you two had met."

Jerry turned to address the women in the pool. "Time to go," he told them. "And on your way out tell my housekeeper she can go, too. I'm giving her the rest of the day off."

The women were gone within moments, leaving little puddles of spa water behind them. Rick suggested they all sit down and talk, but Jerry lumbered over to confront him.

"Sit and talk about what?" he spat. "Get the hell out of my house, or I'll call security and have you thrown out."

"Sit down and talk about Ned Talbert," Rick said in a low voice.

"Conversation's over!" Jerry shoved Rick, and Rick shoulder-butted him, dumping the heavier man into the nearest lounge chair. "Don't bother calling security," Rick told him. "Your boys are taking a long break."

Jerry still didn't seem to realize what he was dealing with, probably because people so rarely said no to him. He swung his beefy legs off the chair and started to get up. He stopped only as he saw the gun.

A Colt .357 Python. Trained at his fat head.

"Are we going to talk?" Rick said. "Or shall I send you on a long break, too? Maybe floating at the bottom of your Jacuzzi?"

Jerry dropped back, his arms falling to his sides. He shot Sandra a murderous glare, but remained silent while she haltingly confessed everything she knew about him. Clinging to Lane, she revealed that Jerry's real name was Peter Kell, and that he was one of the lodge members the district attorney had intended to prosecute.

She explained that none of the men had ever been charged, but some of them had left the area, perhaps hoping to avoid association with the scandal. Kell had actually fled to Costa Rica and dropped totally out of sight. When he'd come back a year later it was with an added forty pounds to his lean six-foot-plus frame, a full beard and glasses—darkly tinted to ease his migraines, he'd said. His new identity included a wife and a two-year-old child, plus credentials impressive enough to get him a top-tier executive position with TopCo, the company he now ran.

Jerry scoffed at her. "You can't prove any of this."

Sandra raised her quaking voice to him. "Maybe not, but every word of it came from you."

"And why would I tell you anything?" He seemed to be anticipating her answer, which made Lane wonder if he was challenging her or egging her on.

"Because you had something on me that you knew would keep me quiet."

Jerry nodded slowly. "That's right, Sandra—and I still do."

Sandra averted her eyes, refusing to look at him. It was some kind of standoff, Lane realized, but she couldn't allow that. Sandra was the only weapon they had against him.

Lane quickly checked her cell phone before she slipped it back in her pocket. The message button had been flashing all morning, but she'd thought it was Val, trying to find out why she hadn't come to work. She clicked through to a text message marked urgent and realized it was Val. He was telling her that Darwin had disappeared and the FBI was looking for him.

She froze, not sure what to do. Sandra was convinced that Dar had been conspiring with Blair to target TPC's clients and sabotage the company. Why either Darwin or Blair would want to do that, Sandra couldn't explain, but she swore she'd found an e-mail with an attachment to Blair on Darwin's computer. She'd also admitted to screwing up the phone system herself, hoping someone would investigate and see what Darwin was up to.

Lane had to break the impasse between her sister and Jerry. "Sandra, what is he talking about? Please, this is not the time to hold anything back."

"Maybe she's holding back because of you, Lane." Jerry shrugged. "Amazing how cooperative your sister became when I told her what you did to her boyfriend."

The cell slipped from Lane's hand and hit the stone tiles. She registered Jerry's smug expression, but she didn't ask him what he was talking about. She knew. Lane needed to pick up her cell phone. The pictures she'd taken of Jerry were crucial to any case they might have against him, even if he didn't realize that yet. But she didn't move.

"We aren't here to talk about me," Lane said emphatically. Sandra still wouldn't look at her, but Rick hadn't taken his eyes off her. He was observing this new confrontation with narrow-eyed interest.

"Maybe we should be," Jerry countered. "You're so much more interesting than I am. Not a week after you got out of juvenile hall, *someone* set up poor Hank Fontana for a fatal car accident. That person tampered with a road sign warning of a dangerous curve, and Fontana turned his Ferrari into the wall of a cliff at eighty miles an hour."

"Hank drove like a maniac," Lane said. "He was going to kill himself or someone else eventually."

"Interesting defense," Blair allowed.

"What if no defense is needed? What if the sign was in the wrong place and whoever moved it put it back where it belonged? A Good Samaritan."

"Nice try, but it's on videotape, Lane. The sign was exactly where it belonged until *you* moved it. And by the way, murder has no statute of limitations."

Lane couldn't believe it. This should have been Jerry Blair's day of reckoning, and yet it felt like hers. Everything she'd been trying to do all these years now promised to be her *un*doing, even when she'd been acting with the best of intentions. When they let her out of juvie, she'd gone straight back to Shadow Hills, lying in wait just long enough to verify that Hank still liked to push his cars to the limit on a certain unlit deserted canyon road. Turned out he was even more reckless with the shiny black Ferrari, which could reach top speeds approaching two hundred miles an hour.

If Lane hadn't done it, her sister would still be under the control of a sick bastard who'd turned her into a den mother for his hookers, and worse, an abuse victim. Lane had figured out that Hank had beaten and terrorized Sandra so badly she'd ended up in the hospital, unable to testify for Lane at her trial. Lane had spent most of her time in juvenile hall trying to figure out how to free her sister. Now it looked as if she'd made Sandra a hostage to a monster like Jerry Blair.

41

"You made a deal with Peter Kell?" Lane asked Sandra.

"It was an agreement. I didn't blow his cover, and he didn't turn you in to the cops. He's been keeping track of you since you left juvenile hall."

Lane could imagine that she'd been a huge threat to Peter Kell, in more than one way, but the truth was she'd never seen the evidence hidden in her stuffed animal. It had been confiscated when Rick arrested her, and she hadn't been shown the pictures, even under the intense questioning she endured, perhaps because she was underage. Nor had she recognized her star client and silent partner, Jerry Blair, as Peter Kell from the hunting lodge. Kell was tall and thin to the point of emaciation. His angular face had always been free of facial hair and he'd spoken in whispers, not Jerry's friendly baritone.

Kell, she remembered vividly, down to the flattened eyes and the smile that turned into a sneer when he was angry. The exact sneer that had just transformed Jerry Blair's face. Kell was the man who'd repeatedly tried to molest her.

Blair was sneering now. "I'm right here and you're talking about me in the third person. That's rude." He laughed explosively. "Good luck blowing my cover,

Sandra. What are you going to use for proof? The missing evidence from the hunting-lodge case? Even Rick Bayless, the cop who stole it, can't put his hands on it, am I right, Rick? Or have you got the package stashed somewhere?"

Rick's eyes glinted. "So, now we're on a first-name basis? I guess you saw right through the real-estate-developer imitation when I came to your office. You're a much better actor than I am."

Jerry hesitated, as if he'd forgotten he wasn't supposed to know who Rick Bayless was. Rick ignored him and plunged straight on. "But you're right, Jerry." Rick tipped his head to him, as if he'd said something brilliant. "You sure are. I have no idea what happened to the evidence."

"Not that it matters." Jerry was suddenly cocky again. "There's a ten-year statute of limitations on sex crimes, and less when minors are involved. We're well beyond it now. That was fifteen years ago."

Lane was too furious to keep her mouth shut. "You're forgetting the court of public opinion, Jerry, or Peter, or whatever your name is. That's the most bloodthirsty tribunal there is. Not to mention hungry. These days even the mainstream media is happy to boost their ratings with all the nasty stuff on the Internet gossip sites."

Jerry's nonchalant shrug infuriated her. She had no proof that he'd tried to sabotage her company, and she still didn't understand why, but Sandra's theory was getting easier to believe by the minute, even that Jerry might have been working with Darwin.

Her throat dried up. "I don't know how you got to Darwin LeMaster," she said, forcing out the words, "but he was my brother, closer to me than anyone in this life—and you turned him against me."

"What are you talking about?"

"I'm talking about taking you down, Jerry. I'm talking about not resting until I destroy you and everything you stand for."

"You're going to take me down? With *what?* Those silly pictures you took when you walked out here? Who cares about a couple bimbos in my Jacuzzi. They're getting well paid."

"You and the bimbos are just window dressing. No one would care if that was all we had. Would you like to see the picture I got of you walking to the chaise to get your robe? It captures every detail of that port-wine birthmark on your left shoulder. The one that looks like a spider. You should have had it removed, Jerry."

"So I have a birthmark. So what?"

"Peter Kell has the identical birthmark on his shoulder. What are the odds of that? And Kell's birthmark is documented in the evidence pictures. His face can't be seen, but the mark is very prominent."

"The evidence pictures that are *missing?*" Blair rolled his eyes.

"Not all of them." Sandra spoke up. "In my rush to get everything sewn into Lucy's giraffe, I noticed that I had a duplicate of one photograph, a shot that had cropped off the man's head. His face couldn't be seen, but the scar on his shoulder could. I kept the duplicate, not realizing it was anyone other than Peter Kell until years later when a friend told me about a package she found. She'd been doing some snooping at her boyfriend's place, and from the way she described the pictures and the condoms that were in the package, I knew she'd found the missing evidence."

Sandra drew a breath. "She recognized one of the men

by his birthmark. But she didn't know him from the hunting lodge. She waitressed for me at the restaurant I managed after the lodge shut down. She was putting herself through massage school at that time. This guy was a new massage client of hers and fabulously wealthy. She used to go to his house. She said his name was Jerry Blair."

She faced Blair. "My girlfriend was Holly Miller—and she made the fatal mistake of trying to blackmail you. That's how you found out the evidence had been given to Ned Talbert by Rick Bayless. You made Holly believe you would set her up for life if she gave you the evidence, but she couldn't because when she went back to get the package it had disappeared again. You assumed Ned got suspicious and found another hiding place for it. That's when you decided to get rid of both of them, Holly *and* Ned, but not until after you tried to torture Ned into telling you what he'd done with it."

If Blair was pale at that news, he was chalk-dust white by the time Rick finished telling him his theory of how Blair had coerced Ned into committing suicide to save Holly.

Rick's voice was soft and steady as he cocked the gun aimed directly at Blair's head. "If you have a talent for anything," he told the other man, "it's reading people. You bet everything on your hunch that Ned would sacrifice himself to stop you from killing Holly by slow suffocation, and you won. He's dead. They're both dead. And so will you be when I pull this trigger."

Rick closed the distance between himself and Jerry Blair in a few steps. "Be grateful I'm more merciful than you are. This will be fast." He pressed the barrel of the revolver to Blair's temple.

"Don't be a fool! You'll go to jail, death row."

Rick laughed. He nearly fell over laughing. "Threaten me with something that matters. I have less than two months to live."

Blair began to sweat. It poured off him. "I want my attorney. I'm allowed one call to my attorney."

"I'm not a cop, man. You don't hear me reading you your Miranda rights, do you? I don't give a shit what happens to you, now or ever. I just want the truth out of your ugly mouth. Did you get what you wanted from Ned? Did he tell you where the evidence was?"

"I don't know what you're talking about."

Rick removed the bullets from his gun, reloaded one chamber, and gave the cylinder a spin. He pressed the barrel to Jerry's head and fired. Jerry fell forward in a heap and Lane screamed. She ran over to him, expecting to see blood gushing from a bullet wound, but he was moaning and gasping for breath. He hadn't been hit. He'd fainted from fear.

"Tell him the truth," she begged Jerry. "He'll kill you. I swear he will. He doesn't care what happens to him."

Jerry heaved himself up and shoved Lane away. He was snarling at Rick, who'd backed away, but still had him at gunpoint. "You'll go to prison, you stupid fuck! They'll execute you for this."

Rick couldn't seem to stop laughing. He looked and sounded crazy. "I wish to hell they would," he said. "Lethal injection has to be better than losing control of every bodily function."

Rick took aim, targeting Jerry right between the eyes, and squeezed the trigger again. A dry click. Another empty chamber.

Jerry squealed like a pig. "Stop! For the love of God, *stop!*"

"Maybe you should press your thumbs together over your heart, Blair. Get those three heartbeats going while you still can."

Jerry sprang from the lounge, howling. He wanted to make a run at the insane ex-cop playing Russian roulette, but fear wouldn't let him.

Click. Chamber number three.

CLICK. Chamber number four.

"You're not dying!" Blair screamed at Rick. "You don't have a terminal illness. It's the medication you're taking that's making you sick."

Rick's eyes narrowed. His whole body registered disbelief. He stared at Jerry, apparently trying to process the information. Lane couldn't take it in, either. Rick wasn't dying?

Jerry sniffed at Sandra, as if disparaging her sleuthing abilities. "I hired a private detective years ago to find out what happened to the evidence. That's how I know who killed Hank Fontana. The detective had Hank under surveillance the night Lane engineered his crash. But as it turned out, neither Hank nor Sandra had the goods."

He sneered at Rick. "The detective strongly suspected you after all the fuss with the D.A. and your leaving the force so abruptly, and I've been watching you ever since, ready to deal with you if I needed to."

"Maybe you shouldn't have waited," Rick said.

"Let sleeping dogs lie—and if they wake up, shoot them." Jerry laughed. "As long as you didn't bother me, I decided not to bother you. However, Holly's ridiculous attempt to blackmail me told me that all three of you had to be shot like strays. Except that you're an enforcer, a professional, and I would have had to hire a pro to bring you down and make it look like an accident. But that wouldn't have been any fun, would it?"

Jerry pulled at the lapel of his robe, as if was too warm. "You get your medical care through one of those for-profit HMOs where you see a different doctor every visit. I did some background checking and found a doctor mired in gambling debts. It wasn't difficult to convince him to find some distressing symptoms during your annual exam. He wrote you up for a battery of tests, and it was just a matter of having the lab results altered. The second opinion you requested could have been a problem, except that I know how health coverage works these days. To save money, specialists use the same lab results. New tests are ordered only if they disagree with the diagnosis or suspect a false result. Fortunately, the specialist you were referred to suspected nothing."

Lane didn't understand. "What was the point?"

"I needed your friend Rick disabled, but at the same time, I needed him alive long enough to do my work for me, which was to help frame you. That's why I left your card at the crime scene *after* I had Ned write the word *extortion* on the back. And then there was the missing evidence."

Blair shrugged as if to say no big deal, but Lane pounced on it. "And you desperately wanted that package. Holly had already ID'd you from the pictures. If you didn't have them in your possession, you would have spent the rest of your life looking over your shoulder and wondering who else you might have to kill."

"So you thought *I* had the package?" Rick asked Blair. "And you were going to do what? Kill me after I led you to it?"

"Only if you didn't kill yourself. If I do anything well,

it's read people, remember? I can usually predict what they'll do when certain pressures are brought to bear. Ned was a Boy Scout, rescuing puppies, children—and tawdry women from themselves. You fancy yourself an enforcer. That's exactly the sort of man who ends it quickly and neatly, rather than face a long, disfiguring death. Look at what you did today. You have a death wish."

Lane was pretty good at reading people, too, and she'd already realized that Jerry was dangerously delusional, thinking not only that he could control people's lives, but that he had a right to. What kind of complex was that?

Jerry inclined his head toward Rick. "You can stop acting like an idiot now. You're not terminal."

Rick dry-fired again. He was down to his last bullet. This was the one that would kill the bastard. Rick's revolver had a notched cylinder, and he'd known all along which chambers were empty. Lane had discovered that when he'd dry-fired the gun on her in the taxi.

"You never answered my question," Rick growled. "What did Ned tell you about the package? Did he say I had it?"

"No, he didn't say anything. That's why he's dead."

"He wouldn't be dead if he'd told you?"

"Of course he would. Do you think I'm crazy?"

"How did you get Darwin to go in on this with you?" Rick was shouting at Blair, and Lane feared any moment the man would be dead, no matter what he said. "How did you get him to sabotage Lane's clients?"

Blair dropped to his knees, babbling about the good he'd done for TopCo, the role model he'd been for other CEOs, how he was going to testify before Congress about CEO compensation and corporate ethics.

Watching him, Lane was gripped by a premonition.

Sheer horror made her push Rick aside, gun and all, and confront Blair. She crouched in front of him and forced him to look up, her fingers digging into the flesh of his checks.

"Where is Darwin?" she asked him. "Where is he?"

A strange light burned in the tears oozing from Jerry's eyes, a sad and crazy energy that triggered emotions in Lane much worse than the horror that had just frozen her solid. Helplessness. Despair. Lane felt despair unlike anything she'd felt since her father died.

"It's too late," Jerry whispered. "Darwin is already dead, and so is his girlfriend. They're both dead."

42

Pris's rage had vanished even before she'd piled out of the SUV and seen the irrefutable proof of what she'd done. She'd begun to shake and twitch as the adrenaline drained from her system. Like runoff through a storm drain, it had roared out of her and vaporized. She hadn't been able to walk or control her legs and by the time she'd reached the fallen man, she was on her knees and crawling.

"Don't be dead," she'd told him. "Don't do that to me."

She'd bent over him, looking for signs of life. There were tire tracks and dirty grass stains on his clothing, but other than that, she hadn't seen anything that said death by vehicular homicide. But then she'd made the mistake of turning him over.

"Oh, shit." She'd rocked back on her haunches, gaping at his face. "Oh, *shit.*"

Now she was lying on the ground, too, with her back to the man's body, as if that could block the image from her mind. She could hear the screaming, the shrieking, the pleading for help, but they were her own screams. Her mom had worked nights and couldn't afford a sitter, so she'd left her four-year-old daughter in the care of her twelve-year-old brother, who was the favorite, the scholar, the perfect child. And secretly, a sadist.

He'd once lashed Pris to the garage door and thrown knives at her, telling her he was going to give her to the traveling-carnival people, and this was what it would be like. Every night it was some new horror, and there was no one there to stop him. No one to believe the golden boy would do such things. Pris had shown her mother the cuts on her arms and legs—and been accused of cutting herself. He'd convinced their mother that she was self-mutilating.

Pris had never understood why he wanted to torment her, or how he could have taken such sick delight in her cries. She had never done anything to hurt him. She was a child, an innocent. And so was this man who lay behind her. He was an innocent bystander. Why had it been so utterly necessary to hurt him? Who had hurt her brother? Why did people hurt each other for no known reason?

She heard the sirens coming, but there was nothing she could do about it. She was in pieces, the shrapnel from an exploded bomb. Nothing was left but abject horror. She didn't know the man she'd run over. Literally didn't know him. She'd never seen him before. In her blind rage she'd spied a man coming out of the house, and she'd wanted him to be Skip McGinnis so she could kill him. She would have killed anyone, anything, at that point. She just needed to destroy something. God, that was lunacy.

They put lunatics away, didn't they? Somewhere where they could never hurt anyone again.

"Ma'am, what happened to this man?"

She opened her eyes and saw the shiny black shoes of a policeman not two feet from her. He must have asked that very stupid question. "Can't you tell?" Pris said, surprised at the even tone of her voice. "Someone ran over him with the car and killed him."

"Ma'am, did *you* run over him?"

Pris thought about that. "Yes, I did."

"Why did you do that, ma'am?"

"I don't know." She really didn't know. None of it made sense. It was all gone now, the urgency to be rich and famous, to have a say in things, to matter in the world. The need to be golden like her brother. She couldn't imagine why that had been so important to her. It seemed sort of pointless now, and so did her rage at Skip McGinnis. He'd held her fate in his hands and carelessly tossed it all away without a second thought, like blowing his nose and tossing away the tissue. She was mucus, snot. That was how it had felt. But all he'd really done was yank the brass ring out of her hand. A brass ring. Big fucking deal.

"Ma'am, we need you to come with us."

"All right." Pris nodded, aware that one of the officers, a man, was reading her rights while a woman gripped her by the shoulders and helped her to her feet. Pris put her hands behind her back with very little prompting. She felt the tug on her shoulder joints and her elbows, felt the strain of having them pulled the wrong way. Muscles and tendons protested, aching. She felt the cuffs snap shut around her wrists, and then the pressure was gone.

Good. It was all over.

When Janet closed her eyes, she saw a fire, a roaring fire. She felt no fear, only warmth and the beautiful crackling energy of the elements. It had a sound, that energy. Like music, it lulled her to sleep.

Her head dropped down, and the noose snapped it back up. Her feet lost contact with the stool, and suddenly she was falling, flailing. The rope clenched tight. Her mouth flew open and her entire body convulsed in a scream. But nothing came out except a dry, burning rasp.

As she lost consciousness, the torch that hung over Darwin's body fell.

"It's gone. It burned to the ground, and they're both dead."

"Shut up!" Lane screamed from the wheel of Rick's Jeep. She was driving because she knew exactly what theater Jerry was babbling about. She'd picked the location for his daughter's sweet-sixteen party. Jerry was in the back, being held at gunpoint by Rick, and was driving Lane crazy with his predictions of doom, especially since they didn't know what he'd done. He was either too distraught to explain, or pretending to be, and there wasn't time to force the truth out of him. But that hadn't stopped his dire warnings. It was almost as if he couldn't imagine that any of his twisted plans had gone awry. Failure wasn't part of his mind-set.

Lane held in her mind an image of the old theater as it was when she'd taken Jerry to see it. She couldn't even bring herself to pray that it was still standing because that would allow for the possibility that it wasn't. She just had to keep going, driving.

Sandra sat in front with Lane, silent and hanging on to the handgrip. Neither woman had said a word, not even about Hank's death, which Lane knew must have come as a shock to Sandra when Blair told her. It didn't feel safe to talk. They were in suspended animation. Lane sped down several more blocks and rounded a corner onto the street where the theater was located. She was shocked to see the building intact. There was no smoke, no flames.

She pulled into the theater's parking lot, screaming,

"What fire, Jerry? Huh, what fire, you stupid ass!" She couldn't help herself. Everything she'd ever felt for the man had reversed itself. Love was hatred. Respect was contempt. Why would he make something like that up? But then, why not? His whole life was a lie.

"Lane!" Rick shouted at her to wait, but she didn't listen. Darwin was inside the theater, unless Jerry was lying about that, too. She dived out of the car and ran to the double doors at the front of the building. When she pulled them open, a blast of heat and billowing black smoke knocked her backward. Inside, a fire was raging.

Rick got to her before she'd caught her balance. He picked her up and heaved her away from the entrance. "Watch Jerry," he told her. "I'll go inside."

Lane had a horrible moment of wondering if this was a trap, if all along Jerry's intention had been for them to run into a burning building. But Rick had already disappeared inside. Lane turned back to the lot and saw that Rick had given the gun to Sandra. A mistake, she knew instantly.

Jerry batted the gun from Sandra's hand before Lane could get there. He plowed into Sandra, a closed fist to her jaw, and she went down. Lane leaped on his back and he whirled like a dervish, throwing her off. The Jeep stopped her fall, but she hit the hood so hard it knocked the wind out of her.

She slid to the ground and stayed there, pretending to be unconscious. Through half-closed lids she saw Jerry aim the gun at her head. Somehow she kept herself from screaming.

"One fucking bullet left," he said. "I can't waste that on you."

Lane forced herself to get up as Jerry disappeared into

the theater. She went to the Jeep and found the closest thing she could to a weapon, a wrench that Rick kept in a toolbox in the back, and then she started in after Jerry, hesitating long enough to take out her contact lenses and throw them away. She was afraid they might melt from the heat. The last thing she did was pull off her sweater and tie it around her mouth and nose.

The heat and the stench inside the building were suffocating. Red embers swirled like snow and burning debris dropped all around her. She could just make out Rick, dragging Janet's limp body toward a side exit door that was open. Darwin was nowhere to be seen, and Lane was horrified at the thought that he could be lost in the flames.

Smoke poured from Lane's clothing. She ducked to avoid a falling beam, but the showering sparks ignited her hair. As Rick bent to pick Janet up in his arms, Jerry Blair roared out of the flames. He aimed the gun at Rick's back and fired.

Lane's shrieks were drowned out by the inferno's roar. She ran at Blair, swinging the wrench at his head. It slammed up against his temple and dropped him to his knees. He came around to fire at her, but the gun only had one bullet and he'd just used it on Rick. She kicked him as hard as she could, catching him under the chin with the toe of her shoe and snapping his head backward.

Down he went, flat out on his back, eyes open. He looked unconscious, but there was no time to check. Rick was down, too. Lane knelt next to Rick's prone body. He wasn't a foot from the door. She couldn't see well enough to tell where he'd been shot, but the gun had been trained on his back, and she was afraid to move him.

Dear God, what should she do? The fire was about to

engulf both of them, and she couldn't see Janet anymore. Tears streamed down Lane's face, and the smoke scorched her lungs. She closed her burning eyes. It was too late. She was on fire, inside and out. There was no way to save Rick, and she was too weak to do anything else but lie down beside him. The thunder of the collapsing building drowned out every other sound, but as she threw herself against Rick's body, deciding finally to try to move him, she thought she heard the wail of sirens.

43

Simon Shan's first awareness was of fine vibrations rippling up and down his spine and the soft purring of an engine in his ears. His head was too heavy to lift, but he wasn't lying down. He was sitting, cushioned by what felt like soft, supple leather. He did manage to open his eyes, only to see a pair of intense dark orbs staring into his.

"Stay still," Jai said. "You've been sleeping a long time."

"Sleeping?" Simon struggled to sit up, but his hands were tied. He was in the back of a stretch limo with windows so darkly tinted he couldn't see out, and his wrists and ankles were intricately wrapped, looped and knotted with rope that was as smooth as satin, but stronger than cable or chains. He could not move. "You knocked me out with some kind of injection in my spine."

"It was a tranquilizing dart," she explained, her voice almost eager, "launched from a remote-controlled pneumatic air gun on the dresser behind you. If you'd seen the gun, you would have thought it was a piece of Oriental art."

She took great pride in her cunning and stealth. And what a brilliant spy she was, he had to admit. Anger burned away the bitter disappointment he felt. She'd dazzled him with that business about locking herself in her room until he could bring himself to trust her. Obviously, he'd wanted to believe she was as devoted to him as she'd claimed. *Obviously,* he was a very stupid man.

"I had no choice," she said, her voice hushed and urgent. She seemed to want him to understand. "The dart contains a time-release sleeping agent that's perfectly safe. What else could I do when it became clear that you weren't going to cooperate? I had to put you to sleep until it was time to catch our flight."

"Flight? What are you talking about?" He glanced at his wrist, but of course his watch was gone. "I have a hearing on Tuesday—"

"This is Tuesday. The hearing is this afternoon, but you can't go. You won't get a fair trial in the American courts. I'm taking you back to China. That's the plan."

"Plan?" He stared at her, bewildered. He'd assumed she was working for whoever framed him, but why set him up and then smuggle him out of the country to avoid prosecution? "Who's behind this? Who do you work for?"

"Your parents."

"My parents framed me for smuggling in opium?"

"No, of course not. I have no idea who framed you or why. Your father, for all his pride and talk of family honor, is afraid for you. He sent me to protect you, and now he wants you home."

Simon continued to stare in disbelief at the deceptively delicate creature who had made his world so incredibly complicated. "You're not a bodyguard from TPC? But they sent you to my home."

"I've had you under surveillance since the day the drugs were discovered in your car. A background check revealed that you'd used bodyguards in the past, so I joined the local security service that TPC uses, and when you requested protection, I altered TPC's faxed orders to make it look as if you'd made a personal request for me. My credentials are quite impressive. No one questioned them or your request."

"Are your credentials authentic?"

"My experience is much more extensive than my credentials suggest. I didn't want to frighten anyone."

So, he was dealing with an agent, a double agent, an assassin? What? "You've been lying to me all along, and apparently that's what you do for a living. Lie? Spy? Why should I believe you now?"

"I brought something from your parents. Here, let me show you." She took a velvet drawstring pouch from an inner pocket of her leather jacket, opened the pouch and shook the contents into her palm. What dropped out was a bone-white mah-jongg tile inscribed with the word *xi*.

Simon recognized it immediately as a Wind tile from the rare ivory mah-jongg set that belonged to his parents. The tiles were named for the four directions of the wind— east, west, north and south. *Xi* meant west.

"If my father gave you this, then you must know that the set is a family heirloom," Shan said, testing her, "but one tile is missing."

"Yes, the tile that represents east, *dong*. Your father gave it to you when he sent you away to boarding school in London. He wanted to be sure you would never forget your home. He told you it would bring you safely back one day, and until then the set would be incomplete."

Simon couldn't respond for a moment. She had quoted his father almost word for word. Simon had carried the tile with him since his boarding school days. Now it was in his home safe, and treasured above all his many material possessions, but he hadn't been able to bring himself to look at it since his father disowned him. He'd even thought that he should send it back so the set would be complete, even though their family never would be.

The limo made a sudden turn, and Simon realized they might be nearing the airport. "Is the driver of this car working with you, too?"

"No, I work alone." She touched his thigh, almost absently, her fingers drifting, lifting. "But I paid him well, and he will do whatever I ask."

Simon felt a flash of something hot. Anger, jealousy? "You paid him well? With what? Seduction, sex?"

Her exotic eyes narrowed. She looked startled that he could have suggested such a thing. "I paid him with the money your parents provided," she said. "I could only have sex with another man if it was necessary to protect you."

"You don't need to protect me *that* well." Simon relaxed a little on both counts. She hadn't seduced the driver with anything but money. A man who could be bought would always go with the highest bidder, which gave Simon a fighting chance in this situation, but only if he convinced her to let him go.

"You can return the tile to its case," he told her. "I believe you. I'm convinced that it's authentic."

She did as he asked, surprising him as she tucked the pouch in his jacket pocket rather than her own. When it was done, she bowed her head in a show of respect and deference.

"And now you can untie me," he said.

"Oh, no, I can't release you until you trust me. Completely. You must place yourself in my hands. Otherwise, I will have failed in my mission."

He thought about it for a moment. "I do trust you."

"Enough to come back to China with me?"

He returned her soft, piercing gaze and felt his chest tighten. She didn't need weapons with those eyes. She could suck the air right out of your lungs. With a slight inclination of his head, he agreed to her terms.

Her fingers darted over the intricate loops that bound his wrists. With one tug on an exposed end of the rope, he was free. All the knots and spirals unraveled like magic, and the silky chains fell away. He'd heard about Asian bondage, but had never experienced it firsthand. He could only imagine what other exotic surprises a woman like this would have in store. No, actually, he couldn't.

"No sudden moves," she warned him. "You'll be weak and unsteady after so much time immobilized."

"And drugged out of my mind." He gave her an accusatory look as he reached over and felt the pockets of her jacket. Ignoring her obvious surprise, he began to pat her down, feeling for weapons through her clothing. The breast pocket was a nice touch.

"What are you doing? I thought you trusted me."

"I do trust you. I just don't want to come into contact with another one of those death darts, even accidentally."

He slid his hand inside the collar of her leather jacket, aware of the rapid tick of her pulse beneath his fingers. She moaned softly as he delved into the heat of her armpit and revisited her breast. Her breathing changed. It was fast and shallow, like a panting kitten. Irresistible. Suddenly he was kissing her.

Move like a thundering wave. When still, be like a mountain.

She vaulted the space between them and dropped into his lap. Their kiss turned sweetly frantic. She'd surprised him. She was *always* surprising him. Male energy surged into his groin. At least one part of him wasn't immobilized. Not so weak after all, he thought.

"Now, my dear Jai, you must trust me," he said. "Trust means nothing unless it's mutual."

She gazed at him with such intensity he felt as if he were melting inside, but she seemed to understand that he wasn't referring to a trip to China. This was about the two of them, and whatever it was that had ensnared and entangled them like the ropes, like Asian bondage. With his help, she slipped out of her jacket and left it on the seat, as if to show him that she was hiding nothing.

"I place myself in your hands," she said.

Her hair fell forward as she bowed her head. He caressed the silky black tresses, and was overcome with tender lust. Determined to control himself, he secured her wrists with the same rope she'd used on him, and then he kissed her willing lips, knowing she had the skill to escape if she chose to, and knowing she wouldn't. She had given her word, as had he.

"No one is going back to China," he told her. "At least not today."

Burt Carr was damn grateful to be awake. He'd collapsed from exhaustion and landed facedown on his desk blotter, where he'd dreamed wild dreams, one of them about an intruder who was stalking him with a switchblade knife. It was the clicking sound that had roused him. *Click click click.* The blade zinging in and out with a tap of the switch.

Terrifying dream, he thought as he rolled his aching neck, trying to stretch out the kinks. He'd come to in a cold sweat. Thank God it was just a dream.

Both the hands of his desk clock were on twelve. It had to be noon because it was light outside, but he wasn't quite sure what day it was. Enough of this craziness. He needed a shower, some food and time to clear his head.

The house fell ominously quiet as he turned off the computer and the television. Both had probably been playing for days. He'd lost track of everything. He rose from the chair, hesitating where he stood, listening. He'd heard something, and it had sounded like the switchblade in his dream.

Click. Click click click.

Sweat began to pour off him again. Was someone in the house with him? The lights had been on for days and they were still blazing. He had no weapons in the house and nowhere to hide, but he did not want to be taken by surprise. He dropped down behind his desk, his thoughts darting chaotically. They had come for him. They were going to get rid of him. Not the boys themselves. Whoever they'd hired to do their dirty work.

The clicking stopped, and Burt heard footsteps. Someone was in the house, and they were walking this way, toward the den. Huddled behind his own desk, Burton Carr had a realization. He couldn't go out like this, cowering in fear. He had to go down fighting, no matter who they'd sent to take him out.

The footsteps stopped at his office door. Burt opened the desk drawer next to him, searching for something to throw. He'd crouched right next to a power surge suppressor. He ripped the plugs out of the heavy plastic casing, gripped it like a small bat and sprang up.

"Dad?"

It was his namesake standing in the doorway, his teenage son, Burt Jr. But Burt Sr. hardly recognized him.

The auburn hair had been sheared off, leaving a brushy red buzz cut and exposing a high, intelligent forehead. His eyes were a startlingly deep blue, and he looked taller, older. It didn't seem possible he could have changed so much in just a few days.

"What's that in your hand, Dad?" he asked. "I'm sorry I scared you. I had some trouble getting the front door open. The key stuck."

Burt set down the surge suppressor, feeling foolish. "I thought you were someone else. Never mind." He was relieved to see his boy, but his gut told him this must be more bad news. He hadn't had anything but bad news in so long. "Is everyone all right? Your mother, is she all right?"

"Yeah, she's okay. I mean, she's not sick or anything." Burt Jr. hesitated, the tentative kid again. "But this has been hard on her."

"I know, and I'm so sorry. The charges are false, son, please believe me. I've become a threat to some very powerful men, and they're trying to ruin me with these heinous—"

"Dad! Mom didn't leave you because of the child-porn charges. She knew that wasn't true. We all knew that."

Burt didn't understand. "Why didn't she tell me? Why wouldn't she talk to me?"

"Dad, she's been telling you for years. You wouldn't listen. You wouldn't listen to anybody…so she stopped talking."

Burt shook his head, confused. "Listen to her about what?"

"About having to raise her kids alone, about her husband missing the birth of every one of his children because there was always something more important, about forgetting their birthdays like they didn't *exist,* his own kids. Did you know she'd started calling herself a widow?"

His voice broke with emotion. "Dad, I know how much you want to make things better for people. I know what's in your heart. You're a good man, the best there is, but your priorities suck. Is it worth it to fix the whole world and destroy your family?"

Burt felt very old at that moment—and very humbled by his son's wisdom. He could feel himself swaying and he wanted desperately to sit down, but something kept him on his feet. Fix the world? Had he really accomplished anything of importance? He felt like an abject failure.

"You have to make a choice, Dad," his son said. "If you want to save the world—"

"No, I don't, son, that's not what I want—"

"Listen to me," Burt Jr. said firmly. "If you want to save the world, then make us part of your team. We're ready to help."

Burt nodded, but he found it difficult to grasp what his son was saying. He was still caught up in trying to understand what had happened. He had always loved his family, but he had never needed them, and therefore had never valued them. He'd been oblivious to their true strength, their character. Their individuality. Now he understood what it felt like to have nowhere else to turn, and he saw everything, saw it clearly. His life was in shambles, and the only ones standing by him were his family.

"Mom's out in the car," Burt Jr. said. "So are Beth and Andy. We read your blog and came over to see how you're doing."

Tears burned Burt's eyes. "Better now that you're here," he said. "I'm doing much better."

"Maybe we should go outside and talk, all of us?"

Burt nodded. "You guys can talk. I'll listen."

Burt Jr. offered his hand and Burt Sr. took it, wondering how the man had turned into a child and the child into a man. He thought his son was offering steadiness and support, even a helping hand to get outside, if his father wanted it. But it was Burt Jr.'s intention to shake his father's hand. Grip it firmly and shake it.

Together the two of them walked side by side through the open front door and out to the car, where the rest of Burton Carr's family waited.

44

Lane was a mess of tubing, clips and needle sticks. The emergency-room staff had her hooked up to monitors that beeped, an inflatable blood-pressure device that whooshed like a bellows and a funnel-nosed contraption that blew hot medicinal vapor in her face, which she was supposed to be inhaling. Things were clipped to her fingers and a cannula was hooked to her nose for oxygen. She'd been forbidden to speak because of smoke damage to her throat and vocal cords, and she was desperately queasy, but dared not throw up.

She was alive, but not well.

Sandra had been hovering at her bedside in the E.R. when Lane woke up a half hour ago. Sandra was the only one who'd survived the fire without requiring medical care, and once she knew Lane was okay, she'd rushed off to check on the status of the others, who were in more serious condition and had been admitted to the hospital. Rick, Darwin and Janet had all been rescued from the fire, mostly because of Sandra's heroism.

Sandra had regained consciousness in the parking lot and called 911, but before the engines got there she'd managed to drag Janet and Lane out of the burning theater through the side door, and she'd found a water hose to keep the flames away from Rick until help arrived.

Darwin had already been rescued. Rick had carried him out first and gone back in for Janet when Jerry Blair shot him. Sandra never saw Jerry Blair—and Lane hoped he had roasted like a pig on a spit. But she was deeply worried about the others, and Rick most of all. He'd been shot in the back and there was no word on his condition.

"Here, let me help you!" Sandra came back into the room while Lane was trying to negotiate a drink of water from a plastic pitcher. Her sister took the pitcher away and poured a glass, but Lane refused the water.

"How are they?" she asked, mouthing the words. She wanted to ask about Rick specifically, but her voice was gone—and a part of her was afraid of the answer.

"Dar and Janet are being treated for second- and third-degree burns," Sandra told her. "They're going to need bronchotomies, which are minor surgical procedures to determine the damage to their lungs. They may also need hyperbaric-oxygen therapy for carbon-monoxide poisoning, but they're both going to recover. They'll be okay, Lane."

"Thank God," Lane rasped. "And Rick?"

"They're taking him to surgery right now. The bullet grazed his spine and he's—" She shook her head, unable to get the rest of it out.

Watching her sister fight tears, Lane went ice-cold inside. "He's what? Paralyzed?"

Sandra nodded. "From the waist down, but it may only be temporary. We just need to think positive, Lane. He's strong. He'll be all right."

"What floor is he on?" Lane was already pulling the blood-pressure monitor off her arm as she asked the question.

"Six, the surgical unit. Lane, what are you doing?"

"I'm going up there." Lane unclipped the blood-oxygen indicator from her finger, pulled the cannula from her nose, unhooked herself from the various monitors and swung around to slide off the high bed. She gasped as she hit the floor. Clearly she had some burns, too. The back of her legs stung as if she'd been sitting in a patch of nettles.

"Lane, you can't do this. You're not well enough." Sandra moved in, gingerly trying to restrain her. "I'm going to call an E.R. nurse. *Nurse!*"

Lane clapped a hand over her sister's mouth, but found herself clinging to Sandra, trying to stop the room from spinning. God, she was dizzy, dizzy and sick. "Please." Her throat caught fire as she pleaded with her sister. "Don't rat me out, Sandra. I have to go see him."

Sandra gripped Lane's arms, clearly struggling with what to do. Her eyes were swimming with tears and anguish, and Lane realized she must have been under terrible stress for days on end, but especially today.

"Please," Lane croaked. "Sandra, *please.*"

Sandra let her hands fall away and stepped back. "Do what you have to," she said. "If anyone shows up, I'll try to ward them off. I'll tell them you're in the bathroom or something, but I can't promise they won't come looking for you."

Moments later, Lane stepped out of the elevator onto the sixth floor, wobbly on her feet and reading the directional signs. The area around the nurses' station buzzed with activity, but no one said a word to the crazy barefoot woman holding the back of her hospital gown together. They would have had a fight on their hands if they had.

She turned the corner to the surgical unit and saw a

gurney being wheeled down the hall by attendants in blue scrubs. As she ran to catch up with it, she got a glimpse of him.

"Wait, R-Rick!" she called, squeaking out his name.

The attendants slowed down long enough to let Lane speak to him. "I'll be here, waiting for you," she said, mouthing the words and praying he could understand her. He was clearly groggy, probably from something he'd been given to relax. "No matter what happens," she said, "I'll be here."

He gripped her hand briefly before they whisked him away again.

Lane stood there, heartsick, and struggling to close the panels of her gown behind her.

"Hold on," she heard Rick shout. "Let me talk to her."

She saw him beckoning to her. The gurney continued to roll toward the surgical unit as she scurried to catch up with it, short of breath, her lungs burning. What did he need to tell her? Was he afraid he was going to die and had some last words? A last request? She wasn't sure she could deal with that. She imagined everything from a declaration of love to an admission that he couldn't live without her. God, what would she do? She was barely functioning herself. She didn't want to break down in front of him. *She didn't want to lose him.*

"Lane, you and I, we—" Whatever Rick intended to say got twisted up in his throat, and the gurney began to roll again. Lane ran along beside him, giving up on her gown and letting if fly.

"Lane," he said, "I just wanted—"

"What? Say it!" she urged him. "They're taking you into surgery."

The bay doors opened, and one of the surgical team

came out. "Mr. Bayless, we don't have time," an attendant said. Another one grabbed Lane and held her back. "Ma'am, you can't go in there."

"Check on the mouse for me," Rick called out. "He got sick, and I took him to the vet."

They rolled him through the doors and Lane stood there, staring after him blankly. The mouse? He'd called her back for *that?*

"Sick m-m-mouse?" Lane couldn't make herself understood by croaking and gesturing with her hands, so she wrote the question on a piece of paper and handed it to the eager young veterinary technician, whose badge said her name was Sheri.

Sheri read the note aloud. "'I think my friend left a sick mouse here.'" She seemed perplexed. "Are you sure, ma'am? We only treat cats here."

Lane nodded. "I'm sure," she croaked. She'd checked every other vet in the vicinity of Rick's Manhattan Beach house, but none had treated a mouse. It had to be this one, even though the sign did say it was a cat clinic.

Sheri smiled, seeming a bit wary of the woman who'd rushed into her clinic wearing stinky, scorched clothing and a scarf that didn't quite cover her burned hair. Lane hadn't realized how frightening she looked until she'd made the decision to get dressed and go find the mouse. When she'd gone into the E.R. bathroom to clean up, she'd seen her wild, singed hair, bloodshot eyes and reddened, sunburned skin. No wonder Rick had been unable to speak. He'd been terrified at the sight of her.

Sheri was looking through the clinic's appointment book. "Do you know when your friend brought the mouse in?"

Lane was certain Rick hadn't had an appointment. She shook her head, mouthing the words "Two or three days ago."

Lane had thought about asking Sandra to track down the mouse. Sandra was definitely in better condition, and that would have been the smartest way to handle it. But something had told Lane she needed to do it. If the mouse had met an untimely fate, she needed to be the one to hear the bad news, and somehow impart it to Rick. She couldn't quite fathom what the beady-eyed little creature meant to him, but clearly this was important, and he'd entrusted Lane with the mission.

Lane had made her escape from the emergency room after convincing Sandra to take a break and go to the cafeteria for something to eat. Fortunately this E.R. was nothing like the ones on television. All but the urgent patients were left in their tiny curtained-off sections for hours on end until someone could get to them, which gave Lane plenty of time. She'd left Sandra a note promising to be back shortly, and in a locker by her bed she found her purse, her clothing, a spare pair of contact lenses and even the green rubber band. She carefully got herself dressed, taking care not to disturb the first- and second-degree burns on her legs and arms. According to Sandra, they'd been treated with some kind of antiseptic mist that had taken most of the sting away and was supposed to provide a protective seal, while still allowing the air to penetrate.

Lane had called for a taxi, requesting a driver familiar with the Manhattan Beach area, Rick's neighborhood—and to her eternal gratitude the very patient man had taken her to one vet after another. He was waiting outside for her now.

This had to be the right clinic and the mouse had to have survived. Lane was running out of strength and was in considerable pain. Her throat was raw meat and her clothing chafed and irritated her burned skin. She wanted to be back by the time Rick got out of surgery. But most of all, she wanted good news. On all fronts. Good news, *please.*

"Oh, wait," Sheri said, "*that* man? The one who threatened to shut down the clinic? I heard about him. He was *really* upset. He left the mouse here with a sample of the medication that poisoned it. His name was Bayless, right?"

Lane nodded, but her heart sank. The mouse had eaten the same medication that had made Rick so violently ill? Lane wanted to ask if the mouse was okay, but Sheri's eager expression had changed. It was shaded with concern.

Lane steadied herself against the counter. This wasn't going to be good news.

"Ma'am, are you all right?" Sheri reached out to touch Lane's hand. "Would you like to sit down while I go back and get our veterinarian? He'll talk to you about Mr. Bayless's mouse."

Lane shook her head. She didn't want to sit down. She just wanted everything to be all right. She didn't want anyone to die today, even a mouse. She was still shaking her head as Sheri left, and she could feel a salty tear rolling down her cheek, burning a slow path over her tender skin.

"You're a bigger mess than I am, Bayless." Lane stood at Rick's bedside, gazing down at the cuts, bruises and burns marring his handsome features, and whispering insults as if he were conscious. They'd removed the bullet from his back, but delicate nerves along his spinal cord had been damaged, and they might not know for weeks whether he would walk again. It was too much for Lane to bear.

She leaned close, whispering in his ear, "The mouse is fine, you bonehead."

Her tears spilled all over his battered face. She couldn't stop them, and didn't even try. "They pumped his stomach or something and got all that garbage out of him," she explained. "He's weak, like you, and he'll have to stay at the vet's for a while. Apparently they created mouse rehab just for him. Who knew? But he's fine. He's good.

"Now, you get better, dammit," she warned, her voice reduced to squeaks and hisses, "because I don't want to spend the rest of my days with only Mickey for companionship."

This man had truly been through hell. Now he was paralyzed, possibly for life, and all Lane could manage to do was swear at him and threaten him. Her heart felt as if it was ripping in two, slowly, fiber by fiber. She had been helpless to change her father's fate, and she did not want to lose this man, not this way.

45

Lane poured herself a glass of room-temperature water. The ice had melted and the limes were missing because no one was expecting her to come in to work today, the day after she'd been in the emergency room, and she probably shouldn't have. The searing heat of her burns actually gave her gooseflesh, but she couldn't stay home. Her pristine condo seemed austere and forbidding, and the silence haunted her. So, she'd decided to come in and do what damage control she could, given that the Jerry Blair and JGK stories were all over the airwaves.

The murdering CEO and his gossipmonger accomplice were now the object of nationwide gossip. But so was TCP. There was speculation about what role the concierge service had played in Blair's scheme to take down his enemies, and Lane had no idea what effect it would have on her clientele, her business or her life, but given her nature, it was easier to be here, dealing with the fallout than sitting at home, thinking about the pain she was in—or how Rick was doing. She'd already been to the hospital this morning, but he wasn't awake and the nurses had reported no change in his condition.

She drank deeply, but felt none of the water's soothing effects. The magic potion was gone, and it had nothing to do with ice or limes. Even her office had lost the hush of a sanctuary. Whatever illusions she'd had that she was protected and safe were gone. Nothing was safe. The things you loved could be torn away at any time. She was grateful Darwin would recover fully, but as much as she tried to hold on to that feeling, her heart was heavy and unresponsive.

She'd also begun to question the meaning of what she did for a living. What was the deeper significance of making privileged people feel even more pampered? It disturbed her to think that her services might have contributed to Priscilla Brandt's grandiosity or to Peter Kell's lethal sense of entitlement. Kell was on a criminal path long before he joined her service, and Priscilla seemed destined for trouble, as well, but Lane was unsettled. Maybe when things calmed down, if that ever happened, she could make some sense of it. But right now, she had an obligation to her clients and her employees, which gave her a sense of purpose, if nothing else.

"Lane, can I come in?"

The raspy male voice startled her. She turned to see Val in the doorway, but she wasn't prepared for the wrinkled clothes and the bloodshot eyes. It was as close to disheveled as she'd ever seen him, and his drawn features made her think he'd been crying. This wasn't the Val she knew, but she resisted a motherly impulse to ask if he was okay.

Val had created havoc around here, laying traps for Darwin and trying to undercut him when he, Val, should have shown some leadership. He was the second in command at TPC. As it turned out, he was right to be concerned about the lax security, but he'd made it personal, a vendetta. He wanted to bring Darwin down so badly he lost sight of how he might be damaging the service. Lane wasn't sure she could ever trust his judgment again.

She set the water glass down. "Come in."

"I didn't know you were here." He marched to her desk and stiff-armed her a letter-size envelope. "I was going to leave this for you."

"What is it?"

"My letter of resignation."

She didn't like the sound of that. If this was another grandstand play by Val, she was going to escort him out of the building herself. Without a word, she opened it and frowned at the blank page. "There's nothing here."

"I know. Everything I wrote sounded stupid, considering what a total shit I've been. I don't know how it happened, but I let my worst impulses take over. Ten-year-old schoolyard bullies show more maturity than I did, and there's no excuse for that behavior. I can't even explain it. Maybe you should fire me, Lane. Maybe I don't deserve the chance to resign."

"Don't push your luck," she warned him. "I'm not sure I can express how deep my disappointment runs, Val. I relied on you to run things for me. The welfare of this service was in your hands, and you didn't honor that responsibility. You took advantage of it."

His face contorted. Now he was fighting tears. "Jesus, I feel so bad. I mean, you could have died. Dar nearly did—and I couldn't even make myself go to the hospital. I knew he wouldn't want me there. *I* wouldn't want me there if I were him."

He took a breath, trying to shore himself up. "Look, I understand how you must feel. You think I'm a colossal schmuck, or if you don't, you should. Dar's a brilliant guy, but he's also reality challenged, and I exploited that instead of trying to protect the service by insisting on extra security measures. That was unethical. It was immoral. If you don't fire me, I will quit."

Lane sighed. "Not so long ago I heard a similar speech from Dar."

"And that was my fault, too."

"Not entirely, Val. Dar screwed up, too, badly. He exercised bad judgment. You both did. You put your self-seeking personal needs ahead of the service."

"Guilty as charged." He shrugged, defeated. "Do whatever you have to, with my blessings, for whatever they're worth."

Lane went silent, wondering if she should let him go. She didn't doubt his sincerity, but he was so demoralized he might not be able to function on the job. Besides, everyone needed some time to heal. Finally, she spoke. "Let me think about all of this, Val."

"Sure, take all the time you need. I'll be at my place. You can get me on the cell." He stepped back as if to leave. "Lane, you don't have to do this. You don't owe me anything, if that's what you're thinking."

That wasn't entirely true. He'd been the steady one—the glue—from the beginning. And he'd had to hold things together through all of this. She wasn't sure how he'd done it. Also, she appreciated his obvious remorse. It made her think he might have learned something valuable about humility and honor, and what else was life about if not on-the-job experience.

He turned to go, his shirttail hanging out.

Lane found herself smiling. "Val, while I'm thinking," she said, "stick around, okay? We need each and every body we've got around here."

He took a breath. It may have been his first.

"Yeah, sure," he said. "Absolutely."

Three weeks later

Ned Talbert's palatial home looked forlorn and deserted in the painfully bright November sunlight. Rick walked haltingly up the stone path that led to the front door, refusing to use the three-pronged cane that his physical therapists had been foisting on him since he started rehab. What good was a cane that hogged all the room and tried to trip you? Fortunately, he wasn't in much pain anymore. It was all about coordination and control and retraining motor nerves, but he'd been working doggedly, and he was improving. His therapists had told him he would be walking without the cane by Christmas.

He loved it when people underestimated him. He would be down on the floor and dancing like a Cossack by Christmas.

He let himself into the house, feeling the oddness of being there as he took in the soaring cathedral ceilings and two-story windows. Not because it was Ned's place and his friend was gone. This had never felt like Ned's home to him, which made it all the more difficult to believe that Ned would have left it to him in his will. Other than a few generous bequests to charities, Rick had been given everything, the house and all its furnishings, Ned's stock portfolio and his personal effects.

Ned's net worth was in the tens of millions, and he had no one else to leave it to. Rick was still trying to get used to the idea. He'd thought about a foundation or a scholarship program for young athletes, something that would honor his friend's memory, but he had serious doubts about keeping the house. He had an appointment today with a real-estate agent to talk about listing it.

"Ned, buddy, why did you leave me this mausoleum?"

Rick's voice echoed in the house's rotundalike foyer. "You must have thought you were doing a good thing, but what am I going to do with it?"

The bell rang behind him. "Come in," Rick called out, thinking it was the real-estate agent. Instead, Ned's tiny housekeeper struggled to get in the door, carrying a box that was almost as big as she was.

Rick labored to get over to her and help, but she'd muscled her way inside before he could get there. Tiny, but tough. He liked that in a woman.

"These are some of Ned's trophies," she said, huffing and puffing. "One of them was broken, and I wanted to surprise him. I got it fixed, and I took a couple of the other older ones to have them polished—and then Ned died, and I forgot all about them. I'm sorry."

"No need, Jenny. Here, let me help you with that." Rick took the box and set it on the foyer table.

"Here, look at this one. I think you're on it, too!" She ripped open the box and pulled out a large, cumbersome resin trophy with many flourishes, including a baseball and bat, and proudly displayed it. "It was stuck together with Scotch tape and when I pulled off the tape, a package fell out. I saved that, too, in case it was something important, although Ned has no need of any of this now, does he?"

She gazed at the trophy, her smile sad. "Can you believe how beautiful they made it look? Maybe you would like to have it?"

Rick felt a wave of sadness, too. The trophy was from their middle school days. Their team had won the league championship, and each of their names had been engraved in the brass plate, including Rick's. Many years later their coach had given it to Ned because he'd been MVP.

But something else Jenny said had struck Rick. "Did I hear you right, Jenny? A package fell out of this trophy?"

She took a padded envelope from the box. It was badly crushed, but Rick could see that it was sealed shut, and he could even detect some of the original cracked and yellowing tape he'd used. He knew exactly what was inside. The hunting-lodge evidence. Ned must have hidden it in the hollow base of the trophy, probably after he suspected Holly of tampering with the package.

Rick took the package from Jenny, wondering how things might have been different if Holly had found this evidence and given it to Jerry Blair, who was really Peter Kell. Ned might still be alive, but that was unlikely. Kell wouldn't have taken chances with anyone who'd seen the evidence or might have copies of the pictures. Holly and Ned would probably have died, but not so gruesomely. And Kell would have targeted Rick, too, for the same reasons.

But Kell's trial was coming up, and this evidence was crucial. It would prove he had a motive to kill Ned and Holly, and to make an attempt on Rick's life. The fire had partially blinded him and he'd required several skin grafts, but his doctors had said he would be ready to stand trial soon, and a court date had been set. In addition to two counts of premeditated and one count of attempted murder, he'd been charged with framing Simon Shan and Burton Carr with crimes they didn't commit. And he was also under suspicion of having killed Seth Black and framing Lane for Black's murder.

LAPD's Robbery Homicide Division was in charge of the investigation against Kell, and they'd been assisted by Darwin LeMaster, who'd admitted to assuming the blame for the voice-mail leaks and withholding evidence in order to protect his girlfriend when he began to suspect her of being Jack the Giant Killer. Darwin had used his technical expertise and his phone system to track down one of Kell's accomplices, an ex-cop who was paid by Kell to plant drugs in Shan's car and child porn on Carr's computer.

Sandra was also scheduled to testify against Kell, and Janet Bonofiglio would provide the rest of the nails for Peter Kell's coffin. She'd made a deal with the D.A. It wasn't clear how deeply Janet, the infamous JGK, had been involved in Kell's schemes. But apparently she knew enough that the prosecution was willing to offer her the plum in the pudding, immunity.

Jenny set the baseball trophy on the table. "You take this when you go," she told Rick. "Ned loved you and he would want you to have it."

Rick gave the diminutive woman a hug and thanked her. No need to tell her that Ned had already given him the trophy, along with everything else. She seemed to know that this one keepsake would mean more than all the rest of it. And Rick knew that Ned had loved her, too, and would have found a way to provide for her if he'd foreseen his life ending so abruptly.

"Ned would have been a total mess without you, Jenny," Rick said, walking her to the door. "Literally, a mess. He appreciated everything you did for him, but he never got a chance to tell you, not in the way he would have wanted to. So, don't be nervous when you get a call from his lawyer. It will be good news."

After Jenny left, Rick walked over to the trophy and realized he had the makings of a grin on his face, the shitty kind where you knew you had your best friend— and toughest competitor—over a barrel. "I hope I'm doing right by your money, buddy. I don't doubt you'll find a way to let me know if I'm not."

His watch told him the real-estate agent was already a half hour late, and Rick decided not to wait any longer. There would be plenty of time to talk about listing the house. He picked up the trophy, tucked it under his arm, and left, locking the door behind him.

Odd, the things that came to his mind as he walked to his car. Seeing the trophy come out of that box had taken him back, and it was almost as if he had his friend right there with him, shambling along beside him the way they always had when they were kids.

"Strange how it turned out, huh, buddy?" he said, murmuring to himself. "I figured it would be me buying the farm and you trying to figure out what to do with my little place at the beach. No doubt you would have turned my private sanctuary into a party house by now."

His grin faded, subdued by an entirely different concern. "What about this girl, Ned? What do you make of her? She's taken over my life, man. She's smothering me. She reminds me about my rehab appointments and she's appointed herself my home-exercise partner. She comes over every damn day after work, bringing supplements and books for me to read. It's like I'm pregnant and she's my labor coach."

He looked up and realized he'd walked past his own car. Or rather, limped. You really couldn't call it walking. Frustrated, he said, "But here's the really weird part. I *like* having her around. I know, it makes no sense. I hate people hanging around, pestering me. You know me, the original mountain-man recluse."

He sighed heavily. "I keep waiting for the other shoe to drop. I know I'm going to disappoint her in some way. She's going to walk out."

Feeling foolish, he glanced around to see if anyone was listening, but the street appeared deserted, and he continued his trek to the car. "When things got tough, remember what we always said? Lead, follow or get the hell out of the way. Or was it Patton who always said that? Shit."

Another profoundly heavy sigh. "Maybe it's time for me to get the hell out of my own way."

He unlocked the car and laboriously lifted himself into the driver's seat, relying mostly on upper-body strength. "I know exactly what *you'd* say, man, something supremely stupid, like follow my heart. Even knowing how much I hate platitudes, you would say that, wouldn't you? Jerk. But you know I'd make her miserable. You know that."

Once in the seat, he just sat there, the key in his hand, not quite sure what to do with it. "The thing is, when she thought I was dying, she asked me about regrets, and I don't want her to be one of them."

He put the key in the ignition and turned it. "The *other* thing is she's taken my mouse hostage."

46

"Peter Kell sent a series of anonymous e-mails to my alter ego, Jack the Giant Killer, imploring Jack to expose certain tyrants who were abusing their power and victimizing people. Of course, I had to do it. That's what a giant killer does, kill giants. Ruthless, abusive, unconscionable giants."

Janet Bonofiglio sat tall in the witness stand, pale and humbled yet still proud, as she described how Kell, posing as Jerry Blair, first approached JGK through Gotcha.com, determined to persuade her alter ego that only JGK could bring down pedophiles like Burton Carr and drug smugglers like Simon Shan. Apparently Janet had gone after Priscilla Brandt on her own because Pris had "borrowed" most of the material for her book from a Hollywood hairstylist who was Janet's good friend, because Pris's ambition knew no bounds, and because she was mean and nasty purely for the sake of being mean and nasty.

Lane didn't disagree with any of that, but she'd visited Pris in a women's institution in Riverside County, where she was serving time for attempted vehicular manslaughter, and she'd sensed deep remorse in Pris. Unlike Peter Kell, who'd pleaded innocent to two counts of first-degree murder and one of attempted murder and then plea-bargained all the other charges, Pris had taken responsibility for her actions and pleaded guilty to all counts. She was just lucky that the male house sitter she'd repeatedly run over didn't die. He'd sunk into the wet grass and been cushioned by its spongy softness, sustaining only minor injuries. Pris would probably be out in a couple years with good behavior, and Lane felt certain if she put her boundless drive to good purpose she could be a successful human being.

Lane glanced at Darwin, who sat next to her in the courtroom gallery. He hadn't seen or spoken to Janet Bonofiglio since the fire in the theater, where he could so easily have died. But he had decided to brave the proceedings today, knowing she would be testifying. He'd told Lane he was looking for closure. He wanted to hear what Janet had to say for herself and try to understand.

"You okay?" Lane whispered to him.

He nodded. "She looks exactly like Jezebel Truly."

"Is that good or bad?"

"Good," Dar said, fixated on the bleached-blond woman on the stand.

Lane used her best, calm voice. "Dar, she lied to you and betrayed you. When women betray you that's not good."

Dar frowned. "Yes, but she was doing bad things for a good reason, like Jezebel did. Do you get it? Jezebel. Truly. Bad-good."

Lane got it, but she didn't like it. She wanted the perfect woman for her dearest friend, and Janet was…what? Delusional? A loony comic-book heroine who moonlighted as a caped crusader for victims' rights? Dar needed someone to balance his flights of fancy, not encourage them. He still bore the burn scars on his body from his attempt to save Janet's life. He'd regained consciousness in the theater and actually crawled to where Janet hung so he could balance her feet on his body. He might have been able to save himself, but he hadn't tried. That was how Rick had found the two of them, both unconscious from smoke inhalation, Darwin lying beneath Janet, propping her up with his body so she didn't strangle. Rick had had to cut Janet down before he could get either one of them out of the building.

"Did you ever meet Peter Kell in person?" the prosecutor asked Janet.

"I did," she said. "To protect my identity, I often had to act on anonymous tips, but I couldn't do that with accusations this grave. I insisted on meeting with the tipper and seeing proof that the crimes had been committed by Shan and Carr."

"And where did you meet the anonymous e-mail tipper?"

"The first time was a dark bar on the west side. I was disguised as JGK, and Jerry Blair, as he introduced himself to me, had plenty of proof, since he'd orchestrated the crimes. I asked him why he didn't turn Shan and Carr in himself. He said he wanted to stay out of the limelight. Given his visibility, if the focus was on him it would disrupt the important work he was trying to do. I didn't become suspicious of his real motives until Seth Black was murdered. That's when I began to follow Blair, and when I became a threat to him."

"Objection!" the defense lawyer exclaimed. "Mr. Kell is not on trial for Seth Black's murder."

The judge sustained the objection, forcing the prosecutor to try another line of questioning. But Lane had already heard the rumors through Rick and his law enforcement contacts that Seth had been having JGK followed, trying to discover the identity of the paparazzo, and Blair had been caught on video meeting secretly with JGK. Shortly afterward, Black was dead. The identity—and the fate—of the videographer were not known.

"And do you see the person who called himself Jerry Blair in this courtroom? Please answer for the record and point to that person."

"Yes." Janet pointed to Peter Kell.

This came as no surprise since Kell had already plea-bargained his way out of multiple felony charges for framing Simon Shan and Burton Carr and admitted that he'd used Lane's service to spy on them both. It seemed Shan had rejected Blair's offer to launch Shan's products in favor of a rival, slightly more upscale chain, the Goldstar Collection. Blair had retaliated by ruining Shan just prior to the launch, knowing that Goldstar had a substantial financial stake and would take a huge hit, too.

Burton Carr had anointed Jerry Blair one of the rare good-guy CEOs and subpoenaed him to testify before his congressional committee, but Blair feared scrutiny of that kind, even though favorable, could unmask him. He had to run Carr's plan off the rails. With Janet's help, he'd used the Darwin cell-phone system to track both of his targets.

Lane now wondered how many other rivals "Jerry Blair" had recommended to the service with the plan of setting them up for public exposure and ruin. He'd been using her company to keep close tabs on his targets and when it became necessary, he'd begun to implicate Lane in the crimes, first as a way to detract attention from himself, but later, he'd thrown her to the wolves by planting her pen in Seth Black's apartment. At least that was Lane's theory. Kell hadn't been charged with Black's murder. There wasn't enough evidence. Yet.

The people who may have suffered most from Kell's master plan were his make-believe wife and daughter. Lane had read a newspaper account that said Kell had stolen the real Jerry Blair's identity when Blair, a thriving retailer, doing business in Costa Rica, died in a small plane crash. Blair and Kell had just brokered some kind of deal when Blair's Cessna crashed in the jungle. Neither Blair or the plane were ever found, and it was believed that Kell took advantage of Blair's widow's grief. He seduced her with consolation and highly addictive prescription medication, and ultimately convinced her that her husband's vast experience and glowing résumé could be put to good use in the States.

It wasn't likely anyone would ever know the details of Kell's identity theft unless he chose to reveal them because the wife he stole from a dead man was now dead herself of a drug overdose, and the daughter couldn't fill in the blanks because Felicity Blair was two years old when it happened, and had no memory of any father but Peter Kell. But Felicity had recently been quoted in the media as saying that she'd always held the man she thought was her father responsible for her mother's fatal drug addiction. She also revealed that he'd started making inappropriate remarks about her physical appearance when she turned fourteen, and she'd become angry and defensive to keep him at bay.

It was a little easier to understand Felicity's acting out now.

The judge announced a half-hour midmorning

recess, which gave Lane a chance to do a little more motherly snooping around in Dar's love life. "What do think of the new office manager we hired?" she asked him as they left the courtroom. "Mary said you took her out to lunch."

"She's okay," Dar said. "Highly efficient. We talked about online billing systems."

"Efficient?" Lane couldn't believe it. The woman was a flame-haired vixen in horn-rimmed glasses, and exactly Dar's age. "Don't ever tell her. It doesn't get much more depressing than that."

Dar shrugged. "Lane, I'm sorry to disappoint you, but there's just this one little problem."

She cocked her head, waiting for the answer. With a sigh of resignation, he said, "You can't tell your heart who to love."

The trial was big news and the crowds in the hall were large and curious. Dar dragged Lane over to a quiet corner where they could continue talking. "I've been waiting for the right time to tell you," he said, "but it never seems to come. I'm giving serious thought to opening my own business, or maybe I should say my own lab. It won't be much of a business until I discover something."

"Dar, are you sure? You were never charged with anything, and I would want you at TPC, regardless. You're the company spark plug and my moral support. You're what makes us cutting edge."

"Yeah…" He grinned. "Maybe too cutting edge. I may look like a tech geek, but I'm an inventor at heart. I took the Darwin-phone concept too far because I was bored and needed to explore new things. I think we'll all be safer if I'm in my own lab, but I do have one condition. I want Command and Control Center 1 kept exactly as it is."

"You mean, a dark, cavernous room with the windows boarded up?"

He grinned. "Sure, you know, sort of immortalized like a shrine, if for no other reason than to keep Val on his toes."

Lane laughed. "Val is already on point. I kept him on at TPC on the condition that he accept Sandra as his full-time right-hand person, and the woman is yin to his yang, highly organized but chaotic at the same time. With her around, he has to play at the top of his game."

"Sounds like the odd couple to me," Dar said. "And speaking of couples, where's lover boy?"

Lane assumed he meant Rick. "He's at home with the mouse."

Lane had been babysitting Rick's mouse since the day she'd sneaked out of the hospital and picked him up at the vet's. Rick had been in recovery mode for several weeks and couldn't take care of the little squeaker, so Lane had volunteered, and she'd become rather fond of Mickey. Today, however, she'd told Rick he could do the honors while she came here to watch the prosecution hammer home their case against Peter Kell, and to hold Darwin's hand.

Darwin's teasing smile had made Lane realize how much she wanted to go home to the man and the mouse. It was quite a step for her. Rick was completely self-suffi-cient now, and normally that would have been enough to scare her away. Apparently caring for wounded warriors gave her the illusion of control. If the man in her life needed her more than she needed him, maybe he wouldn't leave her? Something like that? But Rick was strong, healthy, virile, and a man who loved mice. He was every-thing *she* needed.

Her stomach did a somersault. Talk about the illusion of control. Hell, there was none. Even Blair with all his power and crazy machinations could not control his own life. And Lane Chandler wasn't frightened. She was terrified, but in a good way.

Dar's phone buzzed, signaling a text message. His face lit up as he saw who the texter was. Lane craned her neck, snooping. The coded message was signed "Jezebel." So, it was mutual. Janet was still carrying a torch for Dar, too. Lane felt like a mother who had lost her child to the temptations of the big cruel world. But what Dar had said was true. We couldn't tell our hearts who to love. And maybe Janet *was* the perfect woman for a dreamer like Dar. Time would tell.

Dar went off to respond to his message, and Lane turned to see Simon Shan coming out of the courtroom with a striking Asian woman at his side. The trial had been going on for a month, and Lane had seen him at the proceedings before, but there hadn't been an opportunity to speak. She went over and greeted him warmly. He seemed just as pleased to see her.

"And of course, you know Jai Long, my former bodyguard," he said, proudly presenting the lithe creature on his arm.

Lane was baffled. "This was your bodyguard? I remember the paperwork and the picture, but the woman was—"

"Not so bold or beautiful?" His smile was mysterious, and Lane knew there was more to the story of Simon Shan's bodyguard…but now was not the time to pursue it.

"I heard that Goldstar is wooing you again," Lane said. "They must be desperate to get you back." She was pleased that he was recovering so rapidly from the career damage Peter Kell had inflicted. The media was all over Simon and Burton Carr, and it looked as if both could easily soar to the heights with whatever they chose to do. She'd heard that Burton Carr planned to leave Congress after his current term to write, lecture and continue his political activism on his own terms. He also wanted to hang out with his family.

"Goldstar has been in touch," Simon conceded, "but I don't do business with fair-weather friends, which is why you can count on my concierge business, Lane. I'm renewing my contract with TPC—and recommending you to friends."

She thanked him, thrilled. Even TPC seemed to be benefiting from the Jerry Blair effect. Lane, Sandra and Rick had been recognized for their bravery in bringing Peter Kell to justice, and Lane was no longer under any suspicion in the Seth Black case. Even Kell's threat to implicate Lane in Hank Fontana's fatal car accident had turned out to be an empty one. The videotaped evidence was dark, murky and virtually unusable. And the detective Kell had hired was in jail on bribery and extortion charges.

"Do you have any immediate plans?" Lane asked Simon. She'd meant business, but he described a trip to China that he and Jai were taking to see his parents. He showed Lane an ivory mah-jongg tile that had been in his family for generations and said he needed to return it, something about completing the set. Lane wasn't quite sure of the significance, but it didn't matter, she realized. She could see how happy he was. At that very moment, she decided not to go back into the courtroom after recess. She wanted to go home.

* * *

Lane had a horrifying accident as she struggled to get two large bags of groceries out of the passenger seat of her car. She broke the rubber band on her wrist. It caught on the door handle, stretched out like a slingshot and snapped from her arm with enough force to propel it across the condo's parking lot.

She couldn't move for a moment. It was the thing holding her life together, that rubber band. The groceries hit the deck as she dumped them and dashed after her keepsake. Thank God it was green. She might be able to see it against the sea of gray concrete. Her father had given her the rubber band when it was clear he probably wouldn't be around to see her grow up. He'd wanted her to know that she would be okay on her own. He'd told her to pluck the band when she felt overwhelmed or afraid. It would remind her how strong and resilient she was.

For some reason, Lane had told no one how she came to have the keepsake, not even Dar or Rick. And now she'd lost it. A sigh burned through her as she spotted the green string lying near the tire of a neighbor's car. She knelt to pick it up, knowing it couldn't be salvaged. As she stared at the limp and useless talisman in her palm, a realization slowly took hold. The keepsake may have served its purpose. She was on her own now, and she was fine. Maybe this was her father's way of reminding her.

She tucked it in her jacket pocket for safekeeping. She had crossed so many bridges to get to where she was today. Her past had put her to the test repeatedly. She'd passed some and failed some, but she was still here, stronger for the ordeals, maybe even a little wiser.

A short time later, the grocery bags recovered, she opened the condo's front door to mood music—and another mess. Her living room looked like the morning after an all-night poker party. Rick was stretched out on her pristine white couch, dead asleep with a can of beer in his hand and wearing nothing but military-drab boxer shorts, which actually looked better on him than she cared to admit at the moment. Worse, his free hand had stolen just under the waistband of the shorts in the way that men's hands so often did, and for mysterious purposes only they could explain.

She refused to be distracted by the tension in her stomach. Apparently he'd had a picnic lunch of pizza and beer on her chestnut Portman coffee table, although she couldn't imagine why. The flat-screen TV and comfy recliner were in the great room down the hall.

She set the grocery bags on the coffee table. As she checked the couch for stains, she saw Rick's coconspirator. The mouse was having a picnic of his own on an Egyptian-cotton blanket that had been spread on the living room rug. Mickey was sitting on his haunches, munching on a large piece of peanut-butter Girl Scout cookie. Apparently Rick had gotten the creature addicted to those things.

Wide-eyed, Mickey set the contraband down and blinked at Lane, watchful. Who was going to get their whiskers trimmed this time? he seemed to be saying.

Lane shook her head in disbelief. Rick was now feeding the mouse in her living room? They'd already taken over the rest of the house, the two of them, making messes wherever they went. Couldn't they confine their picnics and naps to the great room?

Rick's eyes blinked open, as if he'd heard her. "You back? Hey, how'd it go?"

"Peter Kell took a beating, but he fared better than this place."

"Oh, sorry, I'll clean it up."

Lane rolled her eyes. "This from the man who puts dirty dishes on the kitchen floor for the mouse to clean?"

He grinned.

"You bonehead," she whispered.

He held out his arms, looking for a hug—and forgiveness—but Lane never wavered from her stern expression. "You're a slob and a bad example for the mouse," she said. Inside, however, she was smiling. She'd just learned something important. Messiness was not terminal. And decor didn't make a house a home. Love did.

Another bridge crossed.

An enthralling new legal thriller by

JOSEPH TELLER

Criminal defense attorney Harrison J. Walker, aka Jaywalker,
has just been suspended for receiving "gratitude" in the
courtroom stairwell from a client charged with prostitution.
Convincing the judge that his other clients are counting on
him, Jaywalker is allowed to complete ten cases. But it's the
last case that truly tests his abilities....

Samara Moss stabbed her husband. Or so everyone believes.
Having married the billionaire when she was an 18-year-old
prostitute, Samara appears to be a gold digger. But Jaywalker
knows all too well that appearances can be deceiving.
Has Samara been framed? Or is Jaywalker just driven by
his need to win his clients' cases?

THE
TENTH
CASE

*Available the first week of October 2008
wherever paperbacks are sold!*

MIRA®

MJT2605

REQUEST YOUR FREE BOOKS!

2 FREE NOVELS FROM THE ROMANCE/SUSPENSE COLLECTION PLUS 2 FREE GIFTS!

YES! Please send me 2 FREE novels from the Romance/Suspense Collection and my 2 FREE gifts (gifts are worth about $10). After receiving them, if I don't wish to receive any more books, I can return the shipping statement marked "cancel." If I don't cancel, I will receive 4 brand-new novels every month and be billed just $5.49 per book in the U.S. or $5.99 per book in Canada, plus 25¢ shipping and handling per book plus applicable taxes, if any*. That's a savings of at least 20% off the cover price! I understand that accepting the 2 free books and gifts places me under no obligation to buy anything. I can always return a shipment and cancel at any time. Even if I never buy another book from the Reader Service, the two free books and gifts are mine to keep forever.

185 MDN EF5Y   385 MDN EF6C

Name _____ (PLEASE PRINT) _____

Address _____ Apt. # _____

City _____ State/Prov. _____ Zip/Postal Code _____

Signature (if under 18, a parent or guardian must sign)

Mail to **The Reader Service:**
IN U.S.A.: P.O. Box 1867, Buffalo, NY 14240-1867
IN CANADA: P.O. Box 609, Fort Erie, Ontario L2A 5X3

Not valid to current subscribers to the Romance Collection,
the Suspense Collection or the Romance/Suspense Collection.

Want to try two free books from another line?
Call 1-800-873-8635 or visit www.morefreebooks.com.

* Terms and prices subject to change without notice. N.Y. residents add applicable sales tax. Canadian residents will be charged applicable provincial taxes and GST. Offer not valid in Quebec. This offer is limited to one order per household. All orders subject to approval. Credit or debit balances in a customer's account(s) may be offset by any other outstanding balance owed by or to the customer. Please allow 4 to 6 weeks for delivery. Offer available while quantities last.

Your Privacy: Harlequin is committed to protecting your privacy. Our Privacy Policy is available online at www.eHarlequin.com or upon request from the Reader Service. From time to time we make our lists of customers available to reputable third parties who may have a product or service of interest to you. If you would prefer we not share your name and address, please check here. ☐

BOB08R

SUZANNE FORSTER

32426 THE ARRANGEMENT ___ $6.99 U.S. ___ $8.50 CAN.

(limited quantities available)

TOTAL AMOUNT	$ _____
POSTAGE & HANDLING	$ _____
($1.00 FOR 1 BOOK, 50¢ for each additional)	
APPLICABLE TAXES*	$ _____
TOTAL PAYABLE	$ _____

(check or money order—please do not send cash)

To order, complete this form and send it, along with a check or money order for the total above, payable to MIRA Books, to: **In the U.S.:** 3010 Walden Avenue, P.O. Box 9077, Buffalo, NY 14269-9077; **In Canada:** P.O. Box 636, Fort Erie, Ontario, L2A 5X3.

Name: _____
Address: _____ City: _____
State/Prov.: _____ Zip/Postal Code: _____
Account Number (if applicable): _____

075 CSAS

*New York residents remit applicable sales taxes.
*Canadian residents remit applicable GST and provincial taxes.

MIRA®

www.MIRABooks.com   MSF1008BL